ARISTEIA

Book One

REVOLUTIONARY RIGHT

BY WAYNE BASTA

grey gecko press

Published by Grey Gecko Press, Katy, Texas.

www.greygeckopress.com

Printed in the United States of America

Design by Grey Gecko Press

Illustration / cover art by Oliver Wetter / Fantasio Fine Arts — http://fantasio.info

Library of Congress Cataloging-in-Publication Data

Basta, Wayne

Aristeia: revolutionary right / Wayne Basta

Library of Congress Control Number: 2011944727

ISBN 978-0-9836185-6-0

10 9 8 7 6 5 4 3 2 1

First Edition

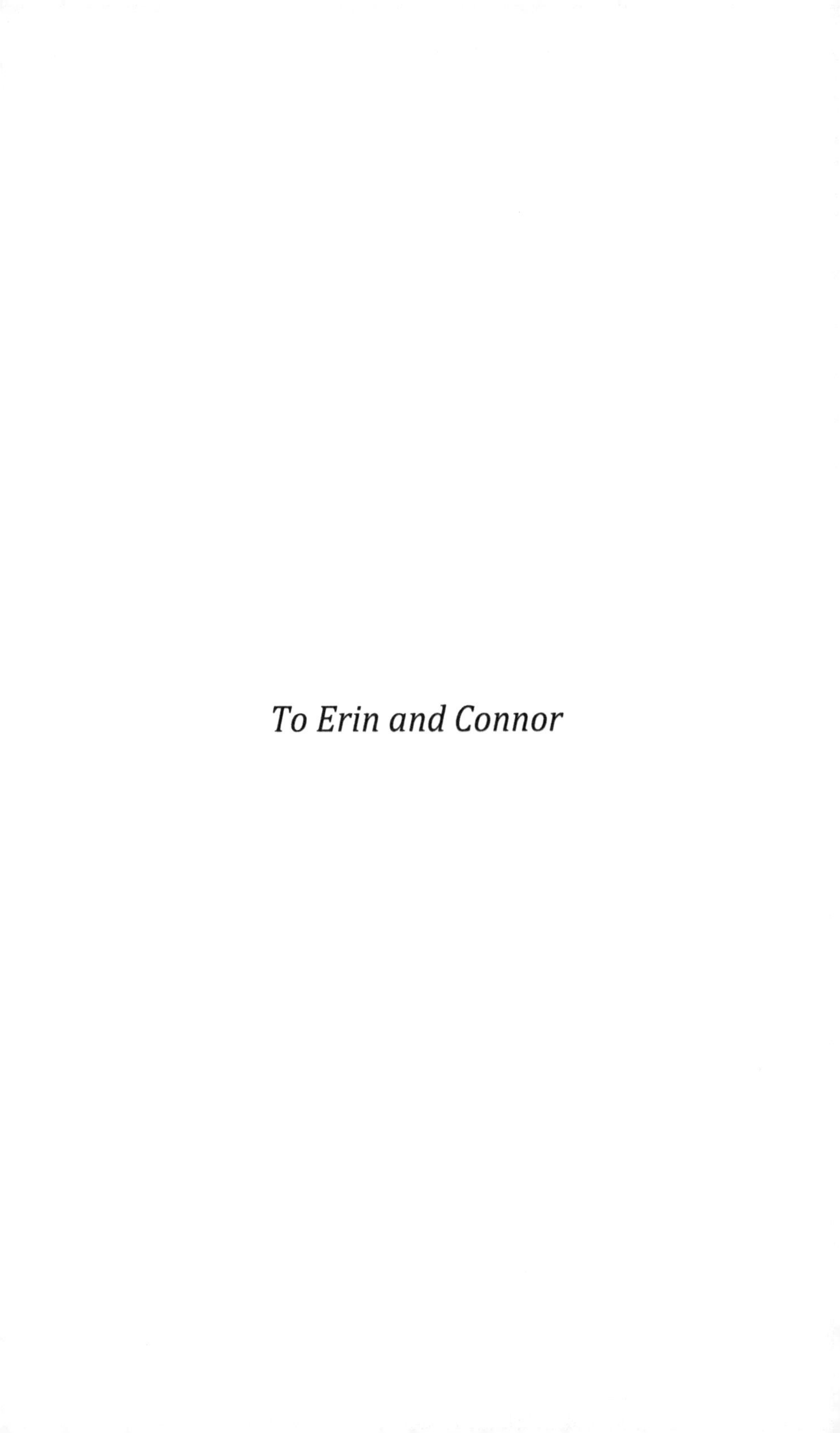

To Erin and Connor

"This country, with its institutions, belongs to the people who inhabit it. Whenever they shall grow weary of the existing government, they can exercise their constitutional right of amending it, or their revolutionary right to dismember or overthrow it."

--Abraham Lincoln

CHAPTER ONE

Maarkean Ocaitchi felt an unsettling sense of nostalgia wash over him as he moved down the corridor. Despite the passage of more than a decade, he still vividly recalled his time serving the Alliance Navy onboard ships like this one. The dull grey walls were like those he had seen many times before, and he could almost imagine that he was back in the old days. When the door he was approaching opened, however, the illusion was broken.

Though it still had the name 'Ready Room,' it bore only a few similarities to its original purpose. The dimly lit, crowded room was filled with a varied collection of beings; the many smells from the different species hit Maarkean's nose, and nausea replaced the feelings of nostalgia. He was on an Alliance military carrier, but it no longer served as such.

Adjusting to the dimmer light of the room, Maarkean surveyed the people and located a dark-haired Terran male. He carefully worked his way through the crowd and managed to reach the man without disturbing any of the other clientele.

The Terran at the table looked up at Maarkean, a sly smile on his face. The man surely knew how much meeting here annoyed Maarkean.

"Joss," Maarkean said, refusing to let his feelings show as he took a seat across from the other man.

Josserand continued to smile. "Always good to see you, Maark. How's your sister?"

"Still not interested in you," Maarkean said.

"Pity. Despite the horns, and the fact she's related to you, she is a fine-looking woman."

"You Terrans, always focusing on the differences between species."

Josserand smiled suggestively. "Oh, trust me, I truly appreciate the aspects of your sister that are similar to Terrans."

Trying not to let the man get to him, Maarkean tried to change the subject. "I hear you have a job for me."

Surveying the room, Josserand said in a noncommittal tone, "I may have a job. Whether or not it's for you remains to be seen."

Maarkean took a breath and tried to keep desperation and annoyance from creeping into his voice. He had worked for Josserand several times before and had always performed better than any of his other contractors. Times had been tough recently, and he needed to get this job if he was going to keep flying.

"Of course it's for me. You want it to get where it needs to go and not into the hands of an Alliance official."

Josserand gave him another sly smile. "That is true. You do know how to be slippery when it comes to the Alliance. It's almost as if you know how they think."

Ignoring the barb, Maarkean remained silent, waiting for Josserand to accept that he wasn't going to be baited this time. Josserand had succeeded many times in the past. The man enjoyed getting Maarkean to react, giving his bodyguards an opportunity to show how intimidating they could look. Every time he had succeeded in getting Maarkean to do or say something in anger, he had still been willing to hire him – at half the going rate. Maarkean hated working for the man and avoided it when he could.

"You must be in a bit of a financial bind to come back to me looking for work," Josserand said with a slight smile.

How the man knew the predicament Maarkean and his sister faced, he didn't know. They had arrived on the *Black Market* several days before and had not yet found any jobs. Ever since the smuggling ring they had worked with had run afoul of some pirates, they had been experiencing a dry spell in job opportunities. Josserand was his last hope.

"What makes you think that? Maybe I just missed working for you?" Maarkean said, trying to sound relaxed.

Josserand let out a chuckle. "There's no need to lie. We don't like each other. But you do have a fast ship. I'll tell you what: to help you out, I'll take her off your hands. I'll give you a great price on her and even drop you off on any planet you want to go to."

This was not the first time Josserand had tried to buy Maarkean's ship. The *Cutty Sark* was old, but the Swift class was no longer produced, which made her a classic. Plus, few made it this far from the homeworlds, which made them rare.

Maarkean had no doubt Josserand would indeed give him a good price, but selling the *Cutty Sark* was not an option he would ever seriously consider. She was his home and his livelihood.

Josserand finally dropped his smile and pushed a data pad across the table. "I see you've turned down my offer yet again. If you weren't so good at what you did, I might take it personally. Very well, twenty thousand, if you can make the rendezvous. Nothing if you're late. And you owe me if you get caught."

"Five thousand up front, and if the cargo's not waiting at my ship when I get there, I get to keep the advance, even if I'm late."

Josserand's eyes narrowed.

Maarkean was pushing hard. Desperation was making him take a risk in demanding the advance, but he had never missed a delivery. He could only assume that was why

Josserand kept hiring him, despite the animosity between them.

A tense moment dragged on, and Maarkean began to think he had pushed too far, before Josserand said, "I like the new you. Confident, calm. Very well. Five thousand in advance. The cargo will be onboard your ship before you get there."

Relief washed over Maarkean; he struggled to keep it from showing. He simply stood up and nodded his head to Josserand. "A pleasure doing business with you, as always."

As Maarkean entered the main hangar deck, sound immediately bombarded his senses. The maintenance deck of any carrier was always a cacophony of noise as ships were moved, machinery was used to make repairs and people went about their business. On this ship, these sounds were magnified by the wide range of species, personalities and types of docked ships.

Making his way across the deck proved difficult. While the hangar would have been cavernous if it were empty, every available spot was packed with ships and cargo. Massive freighters that had never been designed to land in a hangar bay were crammed next to small courier ships, with cargo filling all the spaces in between. Load-lifting robots laden with crates moved between the ships at surprising speeds.

The ship he was on was a Victory-class command carrier and had once seen service in the Alliance Navy. Rumors ran rampant as to how it had come under the private control of a shadowy crime lord known only as the Fox. The stories ranged: some said the Fox stormed aboard with a commando team and stole it from a dry-dock; others said he bought it as it was about to be decommissioned; other stories covered everything in between.

The Alliance denied that one of its carriers was in civilian hands. This merely added fuel to the rumors. Each story said it was a different ship that had been taken. That left Maarkean not knowing what ship this had once been, or if he had ever served aboard her. She was known now simply as the *Black Market,* which gave no hint to her past.

These days, the place was crowded with groups of people with short tempers and quick trigger fingers. If you were to take any two of these people and stick them this close together in any other place, there was a better than average chance the result would be bloodshed, but the Fox, kept everyone in check. The *Black Market* was a potential gold mine for thugs, criminals, smugglers, and semi-reputable businessmen. This prospect of profit kept most of the visitors on their best behavior, and, more importantly, violence onboard resulted in banishment from the ship – sometimes without a space suit.

Knowing this didn't ease Maarkean's mind much. Violence still happened occasionally. The people who came here to do business came expressly because they held little regard for the normal rules of society.

Maarkean moved through the bay, following a group of tough-looking Dotran. The Dotrans' scales were a shiny bronze color, which meant they were of the type that would likely take the touch of an inferior species as a grave insult. As a pilot for the Alliance, he had not had much face-to-face contact with Dotran, but his time on the fringe had taught him to avoid the bronze and gold ones.

Treading lightly, Maarkean made his way past them without incident, and finally caught sight of his destination: his *Cutty Sark.* Despite the faded paint, worn hull, and other signs that the ship had seen better days, he was always pleased with the sight of her. She was *home.*

As he got closer to the ship, he saw his much younger sister, Saracasi, standing at the bottom of the ship's cargo ramp. Her ponytail of red hair at the back of her otherwise bald head was always instantly recognizable. From the back, when clothed, Braz and Terrans looked similar. It wasn't until they turned around that you got a good look at the small circle of cranial bone ridges on their foreheads, referred to as horns by most non-Braz, and the markings on their faces.

The violet screfa clan tattoo on Saracasi's left cheek matched the color of her eyes, which were fixed on the robots moving the crates up the ramp. The screfa matched the one on Maarkean's face; it marked them as members of the Ocait clan. As she was his younger sister, they were also both members of the Chi family.

Maarkean had the same color eyes, and the pattern and shape of the cranial horns was similar enough to suggest a relation. Those were all common traits for family members. Unlike his sister, Maarkean was completely bald, as were almost all Braz males. He stood head and shoulders taller than Saracasi and was much bulkier, though less of that bulk was muscle than it had once been. Compared with her pale skin color, his was much darker. This gave her a sharp contrast between her skin and screfa, which was considered an attractive feature among Braz. Pale skin, red hair, and violet screfa and eyes – she made a compelling picture.

The sight of the cargo being loaded was a mixed blessing for Maarkean. It meant that he wouldn't get to keep the advance if the delivery was late or didn't happen. He had been hoping to get that, as the advance would keep them flying at least long enough to find their next job. However, there would be no delays in their departure.

After a moment, Saracasi noticed him approaching and smiled. The sight of his sister caused his stress about their financial situation to ease. Years ago, when their parents and his wife had died in a tragic vehicle accident, she had become his responsibility to raise. Because of their age difference, twelve standard years, they had previously not been close. The tragedy had brought them together, and now he was more of a father than a brother to her. When she'd gotten herself in trouble years later, even though she was fully grown and on her own at a university, he had responded as a father would and did what was necessary to protect her. That was why he was here living at the edge of destitution on the fringes of society. But it was all worth it.

"I see you managed to get Joss to give us a job," Saracasi said by way of greeting.

"I finally agreed to sell you to him. Shipping this cargo was his price for taking you off my hands."

Turning away from her to examine the next crate due to go onto the ship, he barely glimpsed the tongue she stuck out at him. The cargo crates were nondescript rectangles of heavy black plastic, giving no clue about what was contained inside. Maarkean preferred it that way. Ignorance was bliss, as the saying went. As long as the cargo wasn't inherently dangerous, he was just fine with not knowing.

On the other hand, not knowing drove Saracasi crazy, because she worried about whether the cargo might potentially be harmful to someone. But she accepted the arrangement logically as the way business was conducted. Maarkean thought she had a disconnect between rationality and emotion. She liked to have all the information, but then her response would be hasty and based more on emotion than facts.

They also held opposite opinions about their criminal activity. While Saracasi worried about the moral implications of the cargo, she was unconcerned that their smuggling broke the law. She saw the trade restrictions that made them smugglers as unjust and, therefore, not worth obeying. But Maarkean had spent his youth defending the Alliance and all it stood for, so breaking Alliance law bothered him as much as not knowing what they were carrying bothered her.

The last crate was placed onboard the *Cutty Sark*, and the loading robots rolled down the ramp. They disappeared into the sea of other robots and people without any paperwork for them to fill out. That, at least, was one thing that did appeal to him about a life of crime: no paperwork. Paperwork was evidence that led to arrests. If the goods were not delivered on time, Josserand wouldn't need a signature to track him down.

The two of them started up the ramp into the ship as soon as the robots rolled off. Without a word, they started the task of securing the cargo and sealing up the ship. The robots had done a good job of placing the crates and strapping them in went quickly. Within thirty minutes, they moved up to the flight deck and brought the ship to life.

Saracasi activated the communication system and said, "*Black Market* control, this is *Cutty Sark* requesting clearance to depart."

"*Cutty Sark*, stand by. You are third in line for departure," came the reply.

Leaning back in her chair, Saracasi turned to Maarkean. "Well, looks like we've got a bit of a wait."

Maarkean grunted in reply as he finished the ship's start up sequence. The crew of the *Black Market* was very efficient in cramming in as many ships as possible. This came at the expense of speed in departure. With so many inside, there was little room left for taxiing to the elevator that would take them up to the launch deck. All ship movement inside was done by tractor beam emplacements, which were kept running non-stop.

"You going to tell me where we're going?" Saracasi asked impatiently.

"As soon as I know, I'll tell you," Maarkean replied, which got a sigh from Saracasi.

"You're still insisting on not knowing where we're going? Last time, we nearly missed our drop because of the time we wasted on your false course."

"Late's better than dead," Maarkean replied.

Before departing for any illicit delivery, he always plotted a random hyperspace jump. He would never look at the real destination until they were safely in hyperspace and away from any watching sensors. He didn't want that knowledge to affect his false course. The biggest business on the *Black Market* was information, and knowing where someone was headed with a potentially valuable cargo was always worth something.

Their last random jump had, by pure bad luck, taken them in the opposite direction of where they needed to go, nearly doubling the overall length of the trip. They had made their delivery by a narrow margin, only after pushing the engines beyond the recommended limits.

"There are very few ships out there that are faster than the *Cutty Sark*, and most are military craft. Even if someone knew where we were going, they couldn't get there first," Saracasi argued. This was an argument they had had several times before.

"As proven by the *Black Market*, not all military craft remain in military hands. A packet ship could beat us easily."

"Who would ever think we're worth the cost of sending a packet ship?"

Comm systems that made long-distance communication possible only moved at the speed of light, causing delays even within a single solar system, and decades-long delays between solar systems. Travel across light-years of space took days, weeks, months or even years for most space craft. This necessitated the development of packet ships: specially designed craft that were essentially just powerful hyperdrives. They were expensive to operate and had no room for cargo or luxuries, but they could get across the expanse of space in half the time of any other ship.

"Probably no one," Maarkean conceded. "But, regardless, if anyone does try to beat us to our destination, letting them know where our cargo goes can be a danger to our clients, the recipient, or even us."

This point was ultimately the only reason Saracasi ever agreed to the plan. The desire not to put anyone in danger overcame her misgivings. She did not object to the delay or disagree that the plan made logical sense. The truth was that she did not trust their clients to have set enough time for them to make the delivery and did not understand how this did not worry Maarkean. Their clients would stab them in the back for a credit. She could not fathom how he took it on faith that they wouldn't try to screw them out of their fee by giving them less time than was necessary.

After another twenty minutes, the communications panel chirped to life. Saracasi reopened the link to the docking master, who said, "*Cutty Sark*, stand by for tractoring."

The warning was immediately followed by a vibration through the ship as a tractor beam locked on. The *Cutty Sark* lifted up off the hangar deck and was slowly guided to one of the few open areas. Coming in behind them, another ship was lowered into the spot they had been occupying.

After they were suspended in the open space for a few moments, another tractor beam activated above them. The first one shut off, and they were pulled upwards into a large airlock. The door below them sealed, and then the exterior door above opened. The tractor beam pulled them up through the opening and onto the launch deck, which was currently open to space.

Using maneuvering thrusters, Maarkean lifted the *Cutty Sark* off of the launch deck. With short bursts, he flew through the opening and out into deep space. When they were clear, Maarkean powered up the main sublight engines and left the *Black Market* behind.

With a rush of escaping air, the concealed door panel on the cargo crate cracked open. Carefully, Zeric Dustlighter eased the door open and examined the room. His view was partially obstructed by other cargo crates, but there was no one he could see. Slowly, he squeezed just far enough out of the crate to get a better view.

The cargo bay contained little other than crates similar to the one he was crawling out of. Compared to the total darkness Zeric had experienced inside the container, the dim lighting of the cargo bay proved more than adequate. The cavernous space was only partially filled, leaving him little to survey.

After pausing for several moments to listen, Zeric felt reassured no one had seen or heard him coming out of the cargo container. He reached back inside and pulled his pack out. Opening the bag, he pulled his gun and holster, strapping them around his waist. He then drew out the ball cap he always wore. It was emblazoned with the logo of the Ba'aar Razors, his favorite hockey team. He placed the cap on his head, covering his close-cropped reddish-brown hair.

Zeric then turned his attention to examining the other containers. It took him a few minutes to find the ones with the telltale mark. The first one was easy to get open, revealing a tan-skinned Liw'kel male, Gu'od Dos'redna, who crawled out and took his own survey of the room without saying a word.

Externally, the Liw'kel were similar to Braz and Terrans, aside from a set of antennae that they used for limited communication with one another, no body hair, and a few other minor differences. The biggest difference was that they had a wider range of skin colors, from tan to purple to red. While those colors were a dull shade, not bright like the scales of a Dotran, they did stand out next to the limited range of tans and browns of Terrans and almost universally pale cream of Braz.

Gu'od himself was well muscled and slightly taller than Zeric. His strong jaw and powerful arms were similar to what you'd see on any male in an advertisement. Zeric considered himself quite attractive, but always felt inadequate if anyone were to compare the two of them side by side. He was more of an everyday type, unlike Gu'od, with his powerful, athletic look.

Together they found the final container, but when they did, Zeric let out a curse. The container was packed in tightly next to another container. The way they were aligned prevented the secret hatch from opening. More containers were packed on top, which made moving them slow and difficult.

"What do you want to do?" Zeric asked.

With a determined expression, Gu'od turned away from the container. "We stick to the plan."

"But Gamaly..."

"Would tell us to stick to the plan. We'll get her out later."

Zeric shrugged and drew the AY-19 pistol on his hip. "All right, she's your wife."

With a final look back at the container, Gu'od turned to follow his friend toward the set of stairs at the back of the cargo bay. Zeric trained his pistol up the stairs while Gu'od began moving up them with slow, quiet steps.

While Gu'od climbed, Zeric shifted his weight nervously. He tried to keep his pistol steady and aimed up the ramp. This part was what always made him nervous. The insertion with the cargo, the long wait in the dark, the constant chance of discovery -- none of that fazed him. Anything that went wrong then was outside his control. But in this moment, it all came down to him. The confrontation with the ship's crew could go many different ways. Despite their planning, many things could go wrong. There could be more crew than they knew about, or the crew could be better armed than they expected. Anything could result in their deaths or the deaths of the crew. While he had no problem with killing when necessary, and had killed before, he didn't like doing it.

Zeric had seen combat most of his adult life. He had joined the Alliance Marines as a teenager during the last few years of the Colonial War against the Dotran Confederacy. They said some of the battles he had been in had been some of the worst the galaxy had experienced since the Kravic Invasion. Since there was no one in the known galaxy who had been alive when the Kravic had been in control, much less during the initial invasion, Zeric assumed that was hyperbole.

Even still, the battles had been intense. For a long while after that, he thought he could face anything without fear. Since the war, he had not been involved in anything that deadly, but he had still seen his share of firefights. The realization had eventually come to him that a fight was a fight. A major battle and a one-on-one shoot-out both usually resulted in the same problem: someone dead.

The difference was in scale. In a major battle, thousands, or even hundreds of thousands, could die. Those fights usually involved thousands or millions fighting on either side, though casualty rates rarely went above 30%. But in a one-on-one fight, you were almost guaranteed a 50% casualty rate. Zeric had grown much more cautious when going into combat in the fourteen years that had passed since his Marine days.

Once at the top of the stairs, Gu'od looked down at Zeric, who tightened the grip on his pistol and nodded, trying to keep the nervousness from showing. He envied Gu'od's composed and calm demeanor. Not for the first time, he wished he could learn that trick.

At Zeric's nod, Gu'od triggered the door controls. As the door slid open, a slight mechanical noise rang like an entire symphony orchestra to Zeric's ears. As soon as the door started to open, Gu'od poked his head inside the room and then back out again. He then held his hand up and gestured forward with it. Before the door was completely open, Zeric charged up the stairs.

Reaching the top in a matter of seconds, Zeric dashed into the room above. The doorway led into a cramped living area with several dilapidated couches and chairs set around a table built into the floor. Sweeping his pistol to his right,

Zeric turned to scan the rest of the room. A small counter and kitchen area were to the right of the door he'd come through. There was a pot billowing steam from the stove top.

Zeric took all of this in and dismissed it just as quickly when he saw no people. He continued his turn to the right as he entered the room, which brought him to a view down the central corridor of the ship. There, he came face to face with a tall male Braz, a look of surprise covering his face.

For a second, they stood staring at each other. Zeric recovered a split second after the Braz and lifted his pistol up to get better aim. By the time he had steadied his pistol and commanded the Braz to get down on the ground, Zeric found himself also staring down the barrel of a gun. The Braz had drawn an SK-9 from his hip holster, and now Zeric found himself in a standoff.

Internally, Zeric cursed himself for hesitating. This was the kind of situation he always feared he'd find himself in. He considered his position. Gu'od was still behind him, but Zeric's position in the room blocked his ally from being able to help. Fortunately, it also prevented the Braz from seeing Gu'od.

"What are you doing on my ship?" the Braz asked. His voice was level, and he held his pistol steady, which was far more than Zeric thought he would be able to manage if their roles were reversed.

"This is my ship now. Lower your weapon, and no one has to get hurt."

"Funny, I was about to say the same thing to you," replied the Braz.

"Good, now that we've got that out of the way, how about we both lower our weapons, so no one gets hurt unnecessarily."

The Braz smirked at that. "Sounds good. You go first so your buddy doesn't get any bright ideas."

So much for that plan, Zeric thought. He considered just shooting and hoping the stun effect took the Braz down before he could return the shot, but he dismissed it as probably resulting in his death. Taking a second to move his eyes away from the Braz's, he tried to see if the SK-9 was also set to stun. Taking a stun blast wasn't fun, but he would feel a lot better about attempting to shoot if he knew failure wouldn't result in his immediate death. Unfortunately, at this angle, he was unable to tell the setting of the pistol.

Zeric returned to locking eyes with the Braz. They resumed their standoff for what felt like the second year. Time was on the Braz's side. The longer they stood here staring at each other, the sooner the other crew members could come to help. They had been told there were only two, but that information had been wrong before.

"Maark, what's going on?"

The voice broke Zeric's concentration and his eyes shifted. His eyes drifted off the Braz for a split second, and he saw a figure down the corridor. He only took a quick look, enough to see that it was probably a female and that she was not brandishing a weapon. He immediately shifted his gaze back to the Braz, but with a suddenness that surprised Zeric, the Braz leaped into motion and dropped to Zeric's left. Zeric pulled his trigger and saw the blast flash through the space where the Braz had been a moment before. His shot flew down the corridor, hitting the female. Then Zeric felt the sensation of his neurons misfiring, and the world went black.

For a moment, Maarkean stared at the limp form of the man he had just stunned. His body wanted to stay right where he was, but his mind knew the man wouldn't have been alone. He had no idea how anyone had gotten aboard while the ship was in hyperspace, but he couldn't think about that now.

Easing up carefully, Maarkean moved to the edge of the kitchen counter in a squat. Moving slowly, he tried to peer around the corner to see the door that led to the cargo bay. The moment he did so, pain shot through him. Thrown backward from the force of the blow to his head, Maarkean dropped his pistol as he fell. The last thing he saw was the blurry image of a figure towering over him.

CHAPTER TWO

When Zeric woke up, he expected to either have Gu'od tending to him or find himself restrained and a captive. What he did not expect to see was an Alliance Internal Security officer standing over him while he rested comfortably in a hospital bed. He had to double-check his wrists to make sure they were unbound.

"Ah, Mr. Franklin, good, you're awake," the AIS officer said as Zeric turned his eyes from his wrists to the officer.

It took Zeric a moment to realize the officer was using the name of the fake ID he had been carrying. Fortunately, the officer didn't notice his hesitation to respond.

"Uh, yes?" Zeric finally managed to get out.

"You are in an Alliance hospital in Ciread, Sulas. Do you remember what happened?"

Zeric paused to consider his answer. It was a good sign that he wasn't restrained and that the officer was using his fake name. He decided that ignorance was the best approach.

"No, how did I get here?"

The officer nodded as if he had expected that. "Stun blasts can mess with your short-term memory sometimes. Your ship was boarded by pirates. You were knocked out."

"Pirates?" Zeric asked, trying to sound confused and scared. It did not prove that difficult to convey.

"Yes, a pair of nasty Bobbles. They hid in your cargo containers."

Zeric struggled to keep the frown from creeping onto his face. 'Bobbles' was a derogatory slur some Terrans and Braz used to describe Liw'kel; the word described the constant movement of their antennae.

"How did you stop them?" Zeric asked, trying to redirect some of his disgust. He hated bigots, but under the circumstances, he decided it was best to play along.

The officer smiled, seemingly pleased at the chance to explain his heroics.

"It seems the pair was bright enough to sneak aboard your ship but then too stupid to know how to operate the ship. They pulled out of hyperspace too close to the planet in a zone being patrolled by one of our ships. We detained them and boarded the ship. That's when we found you, your captain and the rest of your crew unconscious."

Zeric cursed their luck. It appeared Gu'od had succeeded in taking the ship and getting Gamaly out of the cargo container, only to have been snapped up because of sheer bad luck. Why the officer thought he was one of the crew, Zeric still did not know, but as long as it kept him out of prison, he would roll with it.

"The captain?" Zeric asked. He was disappointed that the officer didn't think he was the captain. He supposed he couldn't have everything.

"Yes, Captain Maaron Ocaitvik," the officer said, indicating a bed beside Zeric's.

Lying in the bed, still unconscious, was the Braz Zeric had had the standoff with. Now able to get a good look at the man, Zeric figured him to be at least couple years older than himself, probably in his late thirties or early forties. The screfa was one of the lower-key kinds, only covering a small part of his face.

The officer continued, "He appears to have taken quite a beating trying to fight off the pirates. He still hasn't regained consciousness. There was also another crew member, a Sarca Ocaitric. What can you tell me about her?"

Zeric tried to think of something noncommittal. "Um, not much. I didn't get to know her very well."

"As I suspected," the officer said as he wrote notes in his data pad. "I guessed she hadn't been with you long. Probably played on your captain's sense of clan obligation to get the job."

Zeric just shrugged, and the officer continued to write as he spoke. "Turns out her real name is Saracasi Ocaitchi, a wanted criminal back on Braz. Looks like there was some benefit to this after all, Mr. Franklin. You got a criminal off your ship, and those slimy Bobbles are in custody as well."

The officer looked at his watch. "I think that's all I need from you. Let your captain know that his ship is at docking bay 4A. We had to impound the cargo as evidence, but you're free to return to your ship once the doctors clear you. Oh, and don't leave the planet. We'll need your official testimony."

With that, the officer turned and left the room without another word. A nurse moved over beside Zeric and began checking his vitals. Zeric pondered what had just happened. He had been shot during a hijacking attempt and was now being let go by the police. To top that off, he had been told exactly where to find the ship he had been trying to steal – and that it was unprotected.

When the nurse finished, Zeric asked where he could find his clothes.

The trip over to the starport from the hospital was uneventful for Zeric. The public transit car he rode in was relatively empty, giving him plenty of time to consider his options.

Gu'od and Gamaly being in prison left him in a tight spot. If he moved quickly, he could take the ship and get off-world before the police realized their mistake. But leaving now would mean abandoning Gu'od and Gamaly to the Alliance criminal justice system.

On the other hand, prison was not a place he wished to end up, which was the exact reason he thought he shouldn't stay. Finding them a good lawyer would only cause the AIS to take another look at him and breaking them out of jail was not within his means. It wasn't like he was abandoning them to die alone on some remote world or leaving them in the hands of a bloodthirsty crime lord – both of which he had faced before.

With this reasoning firmly in mind, Zeric suppressed his conscience and resolved to get off the planet at his first opportunity.

When he finally arrived at the spaceport, it took him longer than he would have liked to navigate the facility. The building was massive, with long stretches of expansive corridors that ran between docking bays. The bays themselves were nothing more than open-air spaces of reinforced blast-proof landing pads separated from one another by a chain-link fence.

As Zeric walked, he noted many holes in the starport security. Briefly, he considered stealing another ship and leaving the *Cutty Sark* where she was. It would be easy enough to slip aboard any of the commercial delivery or passenger transports and get away before anyone caught on. After a few minutes, he dismissed this idea as being too risky. Without doing proper surveillance beforehand, it was unlikely that he could find a ship that was fueled, had a good hyperdrive, and was either fast enough to evade capture or well enough armed to fight, should the authorities catch on. He doubted more than a handful of the craft here had any defenses beyond a light shield. This was, after all, a civilized Alliance planet, free of pirates and smugglers that would have necessitated civilians arming themselves.

Continuing to the *Cutty Sark* may have made him predictable, but Zeric decided that this was worth the risk. The ship was the perfect candidate for him. She was based on a courier design, which meant she was fast both in and out of hyperspace, and Zeric had noticed decent shielding and at least one weapon.

He had no desire to get into a situation where he might have to test the ship's defenses, but he knew the shield and weapon would get him a better price.

When he finally reached the docking bay with the *Cutty Sark*, he found the ship sitting unattended with the cargo bay ramp down. Seeing the empty bay reminded Zeric that the Alliance officer had said they had confiscated the cargo as evidence. That included the cargo container he had snuck aboard in. Once their forensic teams began their work, they would quickly find his DNA all over the third stowaway crate and realize that Zeric hadn't been a member of the crew. Realizing this redoubled Zeric's determination to leave, and he immediately headed for the ship's flight deck.

There, he found one of the more cramped spaces on the ship. There were three stations: the helm, the system operations console, and a weapons console. Zeric considered himself a fair pilot and knew ships such as these could be operated, with some difficulty, by one person. If he encountered any technical issues, he might be in some trouble. At first glance, though, the ship looked to be in relatively good condition.

Zeric moved between the operations and pilot stations as he began the startup sequence. The ship came to life with little protest, though he noticed with some dismay that the fuel gauge was only at forty percent. Like most civilian craft, the ship ran its fusion reactor off deuterium. The hydrogen isotope was reasonably cheap, but he doubted he could refill the ship's tanks without setting off some alarm bells. He wasn't supposed to leave the planet, after all, and the fuel he had would run the ship in dock for months.

As Zeric tried to calculate how far he could get on forty percent fuel, he suddenly froze at the sound of a voice.

"Going somewhere?"

Zeric's first thought was that the police had figured out their mistake already. He decided to play innocent. "Um, no, officer, just checking the ship's— "

As he turned around, he cursed his mistake. Instinctively, he reached down to his hip where he normally kept his pistol. That was when he remembered that he hadn't gotten it back. He contented himself with raising his hands above his head.

Facing Zeric was the Braz he had shot earlier and who the Alliance officer had identified as the ship's owner. What made the Braz instantly recognizable, besides his violet screfa and eyes, was the barrel of his SK-9 pistol once again pointing at Zeric's head. This time, the Braz didn't look surprised so much as angry. In Zeric's mind, angry and armed were not two things that should go together.

"Looking for this?" the Braz asked, nodding toward Zeric's weapon in his other hand. "Had you waited a few more moments at the hospital, they would have returned it to you. Since you are, after all, a law-abiding member of my crew."

Zeric closed his eyes. "Go ahead, shoot me. Or turn me in. Let's just get this over with."

He sincerely hoped that the Braz did not take him up on the first offer. With reasonable confidence, he thought that if he got into the narrow corridors of the ship, he had a fair chance of overpowering the Braz. Zeric was not nearly as good at hand-to-hand combat as Gu'od, but he doubted the other man had any training. Though, given the way the Braz had drawn his pistol and taken Zeric out with a quick shot in their first meeting, he questioned how much of a chance he had at turning this confrontation into a hand-to-hand fight.

"I'm not going to shoot you. I did that already," the Braz said, surprising Zeric. "You are going to tell me what happened to your friend and my sister."

Sister? Zeric thought. So the Braz had been deliberately hiding a wanted criminal. Not many arrest warrants made it all the way out to this sector from the homeworld.

If the Braz's real name hadn't been identified, but the girl's had, it meant he was either hiding her or had not gotten caught doing whatever it was she had done.

Either way, Zeric again rethought attempting to disarm the Braz.

"So your name isn't Maaron Ocaitvik?"

"And your name isn't James Franklin. Now that we've gotten the obvious out of the way, let's go back to my question."

Zeric considered the situation and decided that the truth wouldn't harm him. The Braz already knew he had slipped aboard and tried to steal his ship. Admitting it to him wouldn't make a difference.

He relayed what the Alliance officer had told him and what he knew about the girl and his friends, which was not all that much.

When he heard that the girl had been identified and arrested, the Braz's face changed from anger to hopelessness, his horns shifting as he furrowed his forehead. The guns dropped slightly, and Zeric considered seizing the opportunity. But the chance lasted only a moment before the Braz spoke again.

"What's your plan for breaking your friends out?"

This question took Zeric completely by surprise. "Um, what?"

"Your plan to rescue your friends. I assume you were getting ready to go break them out."

"Why should I tell you?" Zeric retorted, not sure how to respond.

The Braz's face shifted again to a look of icy determination, his violet eyes burning into his own. "Because you're also going to break my sister out."

If Maarkean thought the Terran had looked surprised when he burst onto the flight deck, the look he gave when Maarkean told him about breaking his sister out topped that. Terrans were always so expressive with their emotions. Yet, they were also wildly unpredictable.

Despite holding two weapons on the Terran, Maarkean felt uncomfortable. He was not a particularly good fighter. Until their meeting earlier, he had never shot anyone before, with a pistol at least. All his efforts in the military had been from the relative comfort of a ship's cockpit. He had received training, but it had been years since he had been to a firing range. He had, however, spent countless hours practicing a quick draw. That had been enough, in most conflicts, to get him out of needing to actually shoot anyone.

That was until this Terran and his compatriots had tried to hijack his ship. Maarkean felt no guilt about having shot the Terran in that situation, though he admitted to himself the lack of guilt was due, in no small part, to having had his weapon set on stun. But now he found himself in a similar spot.

Trying to suppress his nerves, Maarkean spoke again. "I'll ask again, how are you planning on breaking your friends out of prison?"

The Terran licked his lips before speaking. "I wasn't."

Maarkean considered him for a moment. "Of course. Now it makes more sense. When the Alliance caught you, you turned on them, played on Terran prejudices and got yourself released, leaving your friends to take the fall."

"That's not true!" the Terran blurted out. His face reddened under his Razors cap. "Those idiotic investigators played on their prejudices all by themselves. I woke up in the hospital next to you and just agreed with them when they assumed I was part of the crew instead of one of the criminals. So, yes, I let them think I was innocent, and I walked away, but I did not betray my friends!"

To Maarkean's surprise, he found that he believed the Terran. His voice betrayed a hint of guilt, and the story felt all too plausible. It was, after all, almost the same situation he was in. He was just as guilty of a crime as Saracasi, yet his false ID had worked, and hers had failed. He had walked out of the hospital and away from the authorities, while she was arrested.

Despite still seething at the Terran for attempting to steal his ship and for getting him into this situation to begin with, he was suddenly glad he had not shot the man as soon as he came onboard. He knew he would be foolish to trust this man, but he also knew that they shared a similar predicament. It was true the man had admitted he was going to flee and leave his friends behind. But were it not Saracasi in prison, Maarkean wasn't sure he would do any different.

Deciding a little gesture could go a long way, Maarkean lowered the pistols he was holding. His fingers never left the triggers, and he was confident he could bring a gun up faster than the Terran could cross the space between them, but it was still a risk. Conversations at gunpoint never went very well, though.

The Terran visibly relaxed. Maarkean spoke first. "Let's say I believe you. And let's say I'll overlook, for now, the fact that you've tried to steal my ship not once, but twice. We share a similar problem."

"And what might that similar problem be?"

"Both of us were released when we shouldn't have been, and both of us could find that error corrected at any moment. Your solution was to run before they figured it out. I can understand that; what is one man capable of doing?"

As Maarkean spoke, the Terran seemed to be listening. Maarkean was not foolish enough to think that he wasn't simultaneously looking for any chance to jump him, but he pressed on regardless. "By every right, I should shoot you, throw you off my ship and get out of here just like you were planning to do. But I don't have that option. I can't leave my sister behind. Which means I have to find some way of getting her free from prison."

Maarkean looked straight into the Terran's brown eyes. "Legal options are, unfortunately, not open to me. And just like you, I face the question, what chance does one man have?"

The next moment stretched on into what Maarkean felt had to have been eternity. The Terran never wavered from his gaze, but Maarkean had no notion of what was going through his head. In his hands, the pistols felt heavy, and the longer the silence continued, the more Maarkean feared he would have to use them.

Finally, the Terran said, "What chance do two men have?"

Despite the skepticism in the Terran's voice, Maarkean smiled. "I'd say the odds are about one hundred percent better."

Saracasi awoke from the stun blast and was quickly hauled out of the hospital bed. From there, she was deposited into a small room. Three walls were made of stark concrete and one was made of metal bars. There were three uncomfortable benches running the length of the room and a public toilet in one corner.

Filled with a handful of other Braz and a few Terrans, the cell held little free space. Across a walkway stood another, similar room, holding a wider variety of species. The other room contained about twice as many occupants as her cell did. Clearly, Braz and Terrans got better treatment around here.

After only a short time, a group of six armed AIS officers appeared and started directing some people from the other cell out, one at a time.

Once about two-thirds of the occupants had been removed, the officers turned toward her cell. One of the male Braz officers sneered at her as he ordered her to exit. She ignored him as they escorted her out of the cell and down a narrow corridor. They walked past the group that had been taken from the other cell. She watched as the officers loaded the group into the back of a small ground transport.

From there, Saracasi was led into a small courtroom. The room contained no jury box, just a high, benched seat for a judge. She waited in the courtroom for several minutes, surrounded by her guards. The four men did not appear talkative, and she dropped any ideas about trying to engage them in conversation.

The door at the rear of the room opened, and a female Terran wearing a formal court robe entered. She took a seat at the bench and then addressed Saracasi.

"Please enter your name for the court records."

For a moment, Saracasi considered how to answer that. The last thing she remembered was that she had been shot by a stun bolt and then had found herself in prison. She knew they would not tell her what charges she faced until she entered her name. If she told them the fake name she had been using, and they already knew her real identity, they could add perjury to the list of charges against her. Though, if they already knew her real name, perjury wouldn't make much difference.

"Sarca Ocaitric."

The judge barely acknowledged her. "Let the record show that the defendant entered a false name. Her true name is Saracasi Ocaitchi."

A cold sense of dread filled Saracasi. She had suspected that her identity had been found out, but to have it confirmed brought forth the fears she had been suppressing. Everything Maarkean had tried to save her from was coming true, and she had no idea what had even happened to her brother.

"You are being held under warrant for treason from the world of Braz. In addition, charges are being added which include attempting to enter a world under a false identity, obtaining work under a false identity, aiding and abetting pirates in the attempted theft of the courier transport *Cutty Sark*, evading law enforcement officials, and perjury in a court of law. How do you plead to these new charges?"

Saracasi blinked as the charges were read. Half of them did not make any sense to her, but she didn't have the presence of mind to truly consider them. "Not guilty."

"As the original charge of treason carries the gravest stance and is the original warrant, the defendant will be remanded to the Olan Detention Camp until transport can be arranged to deliver her back to Braz."

With that, the judge stood up and left the courtroom as quickly as she had entered. The entire proceeding had taken less than five minutes. Saracasi, feeling too stunned to process what was happening, found herself being whisked from the room and thrown into the back of the prison ground transport, which was already stuffed to overflowing with other prisoners.

The journey out to the prison felt like one of the longest in Saracasi's life. She was jammed in between the transport's door and an unwashed Kowwok. Every time they hit a bump, she faced a choice between banging into the metal wall or getting a face full of sweaty fur. When they started, she assumed the fur would be the better choice. Even if it smelled, it was soft. She soon realized that, with her hands shackled, she couldn't wipe off the fur and sweat that transferred to her face. In the end, she opted for the head trauma.

The darkened interior of the transport made it hard to see the other occupants. Braz had better darkvision than most species, except Ronids. Even still, she could only determine a few species, but not any facial details. The space contained a few other Kowwoks, two Liw'kel, a Ronid, a couple Dotran and a few Notha. It took a few moments to realize she was the only Braz in the group and that there were no Terrans.

As an Alliance-controlled world, Sulas' population was dominated by Terrans and Braz. However, compared with most heavily populated worlds in the Alliance, Sulas had a diverse population. Originally colonized by a variety of species over the course of a century, it had remained mostly independent. Each group had maintained loose ties to their homeworlds, but the planet had no had single governing body. Sixty years ago, that had changed when the Alliance assumed control during the colony grab. That conflict had eventually led to the Great Colonial War with the Dotran Confederacy.

After what seemed like hours of riding along fairly quietly, the transport stopped. Saracasi felt her anxiety increase along with the rest of the occupants. No one made a sound, as if they hoped the Alliance guards might just forget about them.

Several minutes passed, and the silence gave way to fidgeting. Finally, the rear doors opened. Light flooded the small interior of the transport.

The downside to having good darkvision was that the sudden light blinded Saracasi for far longer than it did anyone else. As she was hauled out of the transport and shoved forward, she couldn't see any of her surroundings. After she had taken a dozen or so steps, her eyes started adjusting and she saw where the AIS had brought her.

The transport unloaded the prisoners into the middle of an open concrete space. Fences surrounded the space on three sides, and a high wall with a door stood on the remaining side. The prisoners were being guided toward the door in a less-than-friendly fashion.

The wall, topped with razor wire, spotlights and guard towers, extended a long distance in either direction from the door. Saracasi had never been in a prison, but she had heard all the stories. She felt sure she was unprepared to face it. The *Black Market*, and some of the other places she and Maarkean had gotten work, had been rough. You always had to watch your back. But even in those places, she had been armed, or there had been harsh consequences for anyone causing trouble. From what she had heard of prison, the strong did what they wanted as long as it was only to other prisoners. The weak survived by submitting.

Saracasi had never considered herself weak. But she wasn't sure she was capable of doing what it might take to not be the one to submit. This had been the fate Maarkean had warned her about before any of the trouble had started. The things he had done to keep her from this had shown what he was capable of doing. She knew she didn't want to find out what *she* was capable of doing.

Moved along by the guards, the group passed through the door and lined up along the inside of the outer wall. Guards immediately began shouting at them to remove their clothes. Other guards began moving down the line, putting their clothing into bags.

Some of the people began stripping as if they weren't surrounded by dozens of strangers. The Kowwoks in particular had no issues with nudity; they only wore clothes to conform to other species, or when the cold was too much for even their fur to handle. The Dotran, being cold blooded, were the most displeased. They all immediately started shivering in the cold room.

For her part, being surrounded by Terran and Braz guards, Saracasi felt self-conscious as she stripped.

Some of the guards wore impassive, professional faces regardless of the prisoner from which they were taking clothes. They accepted the clothes and moved on without another look. One of the Braz males, however, was particularly obvious with his expression. He looked at several of the species with disgust. But some of the females, Saracasi included, he looked at with a lust that made her feel even more powerless than she had been feeling before.

When the guard got to the only Liw'kel female in the group, he stopped for several moments. Liw'kel were considered by many to be the most sensual and beautiful species, and this blue-skinned female was no exception. Terran and Braz in particular found the females hard to resist, as the three species were similar in size and skin texture. Under different circumstances, Saracasi would have found it difficult not to stare at this one, with her light blue color and well-shaped body.

After several moments of leering, the guard said something Saracasi couldn't hear, and the Liw'kel unleashed a sharp blow with her fist to the guard's face.

The guard staggered back, put one hand to his face and raised his baton. Before he could bring it down, the tan-colored male Liw'kel next to the female became a blur. The movement was so fast that Saracasi wasn't sure what was happening. The guard was suddenly lying on the ground several meters away, cradling a broken nose that was gushing blood.

A moment later, the other guards swarmed the Liw'kel male and pinned him to the ground. Several started to beat him with their batons. Saracasi was horrified to see him just lay there and take the beating.

Screaming with fury, the female Liw'kel tried to pry the guards off the male. One of them knocked her in the face and she fell to the ground. Then the male started fighting back.

He twisted the arm of one of the guards until it broke, forcing him to drop his baton. He struck out at another, whose nose began gushing blood. Then one of the unengaged guards shot the Liw'kel with a stun pistol, and the struggle was over.

More guards swarmed into the room and surrounded the prisoners. The three injured guards were escorted out, but the two Liw'kel were left where they had fallen. The female was conscious but delirious from the blow to her head. Despite that, she looked upset at the bloody state her mate was in. She tried to move over to the male several times, but the guards beat her back.

After a few more moments, a semblance of calm reappeared in the room, though the tension remained high.

The whole fight had taken only a matter of seconds, and none of the other prisoners had moved; most appeared to be as scared as Saracasi. Saracasi had been shocked at the events, but when she thought about it later, she realized it would have been an excellent opportunity for an escape attempt. There had been more prisoners than guards, and only one door between them and the outside world.

A Terran entered the room, dressed in a business suit rather than a prison guard uniform. He surveyed the room and took in each prisoner. Unlike the guards, he did not look over any of their bodies. His face did display pure contempt as he, in turn, looked each of them in the eye. Most of the prisoners quickly averted their gaze as he turned to them.

Not wanting to call any more attention to herself than being the only Braz in the lineup already did, Saracasi looked down as soon as the man got to her. When he stood there and considered her for longer than the others, though, she could not help but glance up. She saw him giving her entire body a thorough look. It was not lust, like the guard, but contempt. It made her want to cover herself even more.

The man finally turned away and began pacing the room. "Welcome to Olan Detention Center. I am Warden O'Hare. I see you have already learned the first lesson: do not mess with the guards. Do as you are told, and your stay will be a relatively painless one. Make trouble, and you'll suffer the consequences. Make any attempt to escape, and the consequences will be swift and final.

"You will be cleaned and given your new favorite clothes. Then you will be shown to your cells. Once you have proven you can behave yourselves, you will be allowed time in the yard for exercise and maybe even a job within the center. I trust that all of you will be well behaved."

O'Hare turned to one of the guards as he walked out, saying, "Take them to the showers, Sergeant."

The ordeal of the showers proved to be less humiliating than Saracasi had predicted, at least when compared with the events in the initial room. The Liw'kel female had been dragged into the showers with the rest of the group, but the male had not rejoined them.

After the showers, they were all allowed to put on a yellow jumpsuit, and then a tracking device was secured to their ankles. From there, the group was directed into the prison barracks. Saracasi had expected to find stark, small cells just big enough for two or three people. What she found instead surprised her.

The group was herded out of the main facility through a set of fence gates. They moved toward a large, flimsy-looking structure that looked more like a military barracks than a prison cell. The building was adjacent to a central courtyard of concrete, along with three other similar buildings. In the courtyard were a few tables, a Terran basketball hoop and a Braz Terrac goal. Saracasi could see through the fence that there were several other buildings set up in the same formation.

Once in the courtyard, the group was split into three and moved into different buildings. Saracasi's group was the largest and included the Liw'kel female and the Kowwok she had been sitting next to on the transport. A pair of guards preceded them into the building, shouting for the occupants to stand clear.

Inside the building, the resemblance to a military barracks was even greater. The building was lined with rows of triple-high bunk beds. There was no other furniture in the large room, and the few windows all had bars covering them. A variety of people from every species Saracasi had ever heard about stood at the bunks. She noticed a few Terrans and Braz among the mix – the first she had seen who weren't guards.

When everyone had been moved inside, their escorts pushed through the group back toward the exit. The occupants of the building began moving toward the newcomers. Without a word, the guards exited and sealed the door with a loud clang.

As the swarm of people enveloped the newcomers, Saracasi recalled the stories she had heard about what happened to new people in prison. She started wondering if the Liw'kel male had been the lucky one. He would be spending his first night in a hospital bed, and the story of him fighting off several guards would surely spread. She wondered whether she should do something similar in an attempt to scare these people off. But she knew she'd just make herself a target, as there was no way she could fight off several people at once.

The crowd of people stopped and then parted as a Notha male made his way to the front. He stopped in front of the newcomers, his short tail twitching slightly as he studied them. There was an air of authority about him. Saracasi decided he must be the one in charge in this building. As she looked at him, she couldn't figure out why. He stood at average height for a Notha, which was short compared to most other species. The fur that covered his entire body was primarily black but streaked with grey, suggesting age. Despite the typical sharp teeth that protruded up from his lower jaw, he did not look intimidating.

"I am Faide Darkthorne. Welcome to Building 15. This will be your home for the foreseeable future. Let me explain the rules, and we should be able to make this experience as endurable as possible."

Saracasi dreaded what would come next. Her worst fears were coming to life. They would each be given to one of the other prisoners to be used as their personal plaything. They would all have to beg to be fed. Thousands of other possibilities raced through her head.

"First, it does not matter why you are here. Unless you are Terran or Braz, I am sure you were never presented with formal charges. Despite that, I am sure some of you have a good idea why you were sent here. I am also sure many of you really have no idea. No matter where you fall, it does not matter. Forget about the why for now.

"Second, if you think you know why you are here, and it is because you are not Terran or Braz, I point out that there are several Terrans and Braz here among you, one even among this new group. They were sent here rather than one of the Alliance-only prisons. They are here in the same conditions as you. So even if you want to blame the Alliance, blame the Terrans, blame the Braz, it was not *these* Terrans or *these* Braz who are to blame.

"Third, no fighting. We all have to live together here. We are thrown in together into tight spaces. Multiple species with different customs, sleeping habits, hygiene and dietary needs. We are locked in here with no way out and no one supervising us. There was an incident last year in one of the other buildings, and a full-scale riot broke out inside. The guards waited a full day before going in to tend to the wounded. While they were neglectful, they had not hurt anyone. Let us not do their dirty work for them."

Faide surveyed the group again, and when no one spoke, he turned back toward the original prisoners. "Please show them to open beds."

Several individuals moved forward into the group. Two Kowwoks approached Saracasi; one was short, with brown fur, and the other was taller, with white and tan fur. The short one smiled at her while the taller one maintained a passive expression.

"I am Chavatwor and this is Larin," the shorter one said. "What's your name?"

"Saracasi," she replied nervously.

Chavatwor led her down the rows of beds toward a stack in the middle of the room. "Welcome to Building 15. It's not much, but it keeps the rain out."

"Sometimes," Larin said with a half laugh, half grunt.

"Thank you... I think," Saracasi replied. None of these people were behaving the way she had expected. The atmosphere was more of a friendly community than she had imagined was possible in a prison. "This is not what I expected."

Chavatwor nodded. "We do what we can. None of us want to be here. So we're all in it together. Things used to be ugly, but Faide turned things around when he was transferred to this building. He was one of the first non-Confederates put in here."

"First non-Confederate? This used to be a POW camp?"

The Kowwok nodded. "Yes. During the war. Once the war ended, the POW's were released. After that, it was turned into a prison for everyone."

"Wait, after the war? That was sixteen years ago!"

Chavatwor nodded. "Yep, Faide's been here ever since."

CHAPTER THREE

Maarkean felt uneasy sitting across from Zeric. Facing the Terran without a pistol in his hand felt wrong somehow. For the thousandth time, he questioned his sanity. It had not been easy to decide to trust the person who had twice tried to steal his ship. Still, every time he questioned himself, he kept coming back to the inevitable truth: there were no other alternatives, nothing he could do alone.

They had left the ship in favor of a public café and were now seated at tables right off a public park in the middle of the city. There were lots of people smiling and moving about their lives. It was a pleasant, sunny day with a light breeze coming in from the south. The setting and the weather did not match the situation at all.

Maarkean was not sure how comfortable he felt having given Zeric his gun back, but holding on to it would not have built the trust they were going to need to work together. That was the main reason he had suggested leaving the ship. Being in public, where they had both been forced to leave their weapons behind to avoid scrutiny, was a safer bet than being alone on the ship.

Maarkean had tried to question Zeric about how he had managed to sneak aboard the *Cutty Sark*. The man's answer had not been particularly informative. He admitted to slipping in as part of the cargo, but didn't know why Maarkean's ship had been their target. It seemed one of his associates, Gamaly, had been given the details by a contact on the *Black Market*, a man called Renard.

The possibility occurred to Maarkean that Renard and Josserand may have been in league, which would explain the ease of Zeric's insertion. This was one case where Maarkean wished there were better records kept. With no paperwork to clarify how many cargo containers Josserand had intended to ship, there was no way to know if he was just as much of a victim as Maarkean.

Regardless of Josserand's involvement, Maarkean knew he couldn't go back to the *Black Market* when this was over. He had lost Josserand's cargo and failed in making the delivery. It had been pure luck that the cargo had not been anything illegal and that the AIS hadn't looked into the paperwork very closely. That had kept him from joining his sister in prison.

Getting her free overrode any of his other concerns, including Zeric's trustworthiness.

"So what's your plan?" Zeric asked.

That was the last question Maarkean wanted Zeric to ask. He had no answer to give. Despite spending several years in the Alliance military, which had included advanced tactics and war theory classes, he had never been trained in how to break someone out of an Alliance prison. Years of smuggling had only taught him how to avoid Alliance prisons; the general consensus was that if you got caught, you were screwed.

"First, we need to find out where they're being held."

"My friends will be in Olan Detention Center," Zeric said. "Your sister, what did you say she did again?"

"I didn't. But she'll be charged with treason."

To him, the charge of treason his sister faced was unreasonably harsh. The Alliance did a lot of good things and stood for a lot of principles he believed in, but it took acts of sedition seriously. Even though he didn't agree with his sister's long-standing activism, he didn't consider it treasonous. Yes, she'd been there, actively participating, when a rally had turned into a riot back on Braz, but she had not personally attacked anyone. But he couldn't afford to let a lawyer argue that her involvement, while illegal, wasn't treasonous. Victory would result in life in prison, but failure would carry the death penalty.

Zeric gave him a considering look, but nodded. "Then she'll most likely end up there, too. It's where they send all the 'undesirables.'"

"Undesirables?" Maarkean asked, confused.

"Yeah, all non-Terrans or Braz or any Terran or Braz who appear to like consorting with aliens. I would guess a treasonous Braz fits that bill."

Maarkean gave Zeric a questioning look. "You sound like my sister. The Alliance may have some issues, but there are strong antidiscrimination laws. They don't have separate prisons."

Zeric shook his head at Maarkean. "For a smuggler, you're pretty blind. Maybe on Braz or Terra they don't, where there's one alien for every ten thousand natives. But out here, the war ended with the Confederacy, but it didn't with the locals. There are some pretty strict laws for non-natural Alliance citizens. You're a smuggler, you know about the trade laws."

"Sure – trade laws say everyone must trade with the core worlds, and that's why there's so much smuggling business. But that has nothing to do with alien oppression. It's to avoid trading with the Confederacy."

Zeric shrugged. "I don't really care. I'm a ship thief and not interested in polit....'

Zeric's voiced trailed off as his gaze drifted. He became fixated on something in the distance. Maarkean turned around in his seat to find out what Zeric was staring at. In the window of the café was a video screen running a news story. The screen showed a Terran female news anchor and the news ticker at the bottom.

With the video too far away for them to hear any of the sound, Maarkean assumed Zeric was focused on the ticker. The headline didn't tell him much, but the ticker did talk about the recent capture of a criminal wanted for several crimes, including murder, treason, terrorism and intention to incite riots. Maarkean became concerned that they were talking about his sister. The charges were similar, if exaggerated. After a while, the ticker said that the suspect was part of a multi-planet terrorist group called the Kreogh Sector Congress, and Maarkean breathed a sigh of relief. He knew his sister was not involved in anything like that.

"Someone you know?" Maarkean asked, no longer interested in the story.

"Huh?" Zeric said after a moment. "Yes... uh, no, sort of."

Zeric broke his gaze from the video. "That story was about Lei-mey Darshawn, a supposed radical terrorist leader who was recently apprehended."

"Old girlfriend?" Maarkean asked as a joke.

"Close. I did have a short relationship with her sister, Ceta. I never met Lei-mey, but Ceta always talked about how her little sister was some wonderful political activist who was championing the rights of freedom or some other nonsense."

Confused, Maarkean grew impatient. "So you dated the sister of a terrorist who has been caught. What does that have to do with us?"

Zeric replied, "Where do you think they put terrorists?"

"Prison?" Maarkean asked, confused.

Exasperated, Zeric said, "And in which prison do they put dangerous undesirables, such as terrorists?"

"Olan Detention Center," Maarkean said, starting to see where Zeric's mind was going.

"Exactly," Zeric said. "I bet a person like that has all kinds of friends who are eager to see her get out of jail."

"You want us to break a terrorist out of prison?" Maarkean asked, shocked.

"I highly doubt Lei-mey is any more of a terrorist than my friends, or your sister. Criminal, probably. Terrorist, doubtful," Zeric replied. "You said your odds of succeeding doubled if I agreed to help. We should go look up Ceta and see if we can increase those odds some more."

Reluctantly, Maarkean nodded his head in agreement, and wondered how far he was going to have to go to save his sister this time.

Zeric smiled as he watched the Braz female who twirled around the pole and then leaned over in his direction. He had never been too fond of the cranial horns Braz had. Unlike their three-toed feet, their heads looked similar to Terrans', so much so that the horns looked out of place. But between the knees and the neck, you couldn't tell the difference at all. And he was definitely not looking at this Braz girl's head.

The woman moved across the stage in another direction and Zeric turned to give an appreciative nod to Maarkean. He had always thought that there was no better way to bond with another guy than prowling for women or watching them dance naked. This place would provide an excellent opportunity to test that theory, as there was quite a gulf to bridge with the man.

When he saw Maarkean's face, he began to rethink his theory. The Braz did not appear at all amused. Neither did he merely look bored and uninterested in women. His violet eyes flashed with annoyance and impatience

Zeric hastened to say, "The manager said he'd send Ceta out after she finished a private dance. Might as well enjoy ourselves while we wait."

Maarkean's look thawed slightly. Zeric took this as proof that his theory wasn't wrong, it just required more time with some people. He thought about trying to get that Braz dancer's attention. If anyone could use a lap dance from someone like her, it was Maarkean.

Contenting himself with looking as they waited, Zeric considered what he would say to Ceta. They hadn't exactly parted on great terms. In his defense, it wasn't like they had been in a serious long-term relationship. Granted, it had been one of his longest: over a week. But it had all been about the sex, and he was sure she knew that.

The music stopped and the Braz female left the stage, replaced by a pair of Terran twins. The crowd became more excited, and Zeric began to think even Maarkean would be interested. What male could resist naked, dancing twins? That was when he felt the tap on his shoulder.

Turning around, he saw a beautiful brunette Terran standing behind him. He immediately recognized Ceta Darshawn glowering at him while standing there wearing what, in any other place, would be called scandalously little clothing. *Perfect timing*, he thought bitterly as he reluctantly turned away from the stage. Standing up, he put his arms out and smiled at Ceta.

The sting of the slap on his cheek registered before his eyes saw the hand. Zeric worked his jaw for a second to make sure it still opened and closed, and then he said, "I suppose I deserve that."

Privately, Zeric disagreed, but he had learned a long time ago that telling a girl that wanted to slap you that you didn't deserve it just made things worse. Especially when you needed the girl's help. He decided to act like the slap had hurt more than it did, in hopes she wouldn't do it again.

The reaction from Maarkean showed that the Braz had some ability to be amused. "I think I like her already, Zeric."

"Ceta, meet Maarkean," Zeric said, still rubbing his cheek.

Ceta turned her angry glare away from Zeric and instantly switched to a warm, friendly smile. "Maarkean, nice to meet you. Welcome to the Tyren Dancer. Though, I have to question your company."

Maarkean rubbed the insult in with a smile. "Beggars can't be choosers. Is there some place we can talk?"

With a coy smile, Ceta replied, "So you just want to 'talk'?"

The serious expression returned to Maarkean's face, and Zeric interjected, "It's about Lei-mey, Ceta."

The girl's playful smile instantly evaporated. A look of panic came to her blue eyes as she looked around nervously. She grabbed Zeric and Maarkean by the arm, dragging them toward the exit, shoving people out of the way as she went. Once outside, she rounded on Zeric and slapped him again.

"You have a lot of nerve talking about that. I might have forgiven you for leaving like you did. But if you've come here to try to 'comfort' me because my sister's been arrested, you can just go back under whatever rock you live under."

Defensively, Zeric put his arms up to shield himself from several more blows. He was only willing to take so much. The onslaught went on for several moments before Maarkean stepped in and gently grabbed Ceta's wrists, pulling her off Zeric. He then calmly spoke.

"Ceta, we're interested in helping her. I promise you that Zeric's intentions, at least in this, are entirely honorable."

Standing outside in the dark in her skimpy outfit, Ceta began shivering now that she had stopped pounding on Zeric. She looked back and forth between Zeric and Maarkean. Her expression was a mix of relief and confusion.

After a moment, she said, "Why would you want to help my sister? She's at Olan. There's nothing you can help her with. Neither of you look like lawyers, and anyway, I doubt there will ever be a real trial."

Zeric risked moving back into range of Ceta's arms. "Maarkean's sister is in there, too. When we saw that Lei-mey had been taken, we thought we might be able to work with her friends to get them both out. The news mentioned a terrorist cell. We were hoping you could direct us to them."

A laugh escaped from Ceta, surprising Zeric. "Terrorist cell? My sister? She's not part of a terrorist cell."

It was Zeric's turn to be surprised. "All right, not terrorist cell. But I assume they're some kind of resistance group. You always talked about her being a big political activist. You mentioned followers and a goal of kicking the Alliance off Sulas."

Ceta nodded. "Sure, she led a political movement. They were opposed to the unelected governor the Alliance has in place, along with the unwarranted imprisonments in places like Olan. But they only stage peaceful protests and petitions. They are entirely peaceful. She has a lot of support, which is why the legislature chose her as the leader of the delegation to the Kreogh Sector Congress. That's why she was arrested."

The look of relief on Maarkean's face was clearly visible. Zeric, however, grumbled to himself. He knew this group wasn't a bunch of suicide-bombing nut jobs, but if they were entirely peaceful, that did not bode well for their plans.

He didn't know what this Kreogh Sector Congress was, but he had been counting on something more than a political party. With a name like that, he hoped they would have resources and connections coming from all seven worlds in the sector.

"Whatever they are," Maarkean said, "they have to want to get her free as much as we do. Even if they aren't terrorists, at least some of her friends have to be more than just politicians. We'd like to meet them."

Ceta pursed her lips into a frown as she considered Maarkean. Suspicion was clear on her face, but after a moment, a feeble look of hope appeared in her eyes. Maarkean looked at her sympathetically. Zeric was sure the man could understand her position. He would probably be overjoyed if someone showed up and offered to get his sister out.

In the end, Ceta nodded, some enthusiasm breaking through her suspicion. "Very well. If there is even a chance that you can get Lei-mey out, it's worth it."

During the trip out to meet the supposed terrorist group, Maarkean pondered what he was doing. Despite all that he had done in recent years, he still considered himself a *mostly* law-abiding citizen. He had gotten Saracasi off Braz before the arrest warrant was issued, so technically he had not aided a fugitive in escaping. Smuggling had been a necessity, but that he considered only a morally grey area.

Now, he followed a pirate and a stripper to meet a so-called terrorist group so he could break criminals out of jail. If the situation hadn't been so dire, he would have considered that to be the set-up for some kind of joke. He wasn't positive that the whole thing *wasn't* some kind of cosmic prank on him.

When Ceta had laughed at the idea that the people they were going to meet were dangerous, it had surprised him. Based on the news articles he had read while waiting for Ceta's shift to end, this group of Lei-mey's followers had sounded like they were bloodthirsty rebels out to destroy civilization. During the trip, he reconsidered what he had read. The group Saracasi had belonged to had been described in similar ways, and Saracasi certainly wasn't a bloodthirsty killer.

The house they pulled up to was like any of the others in the neighborhood. It was a much nicer area than the strip club had been in, which was another surprise for Maarkean. Upon further reflection, it started to make sense. The news articles had described the group as low-life alien lovers. Maybe living in a middle-class district populated primarily by Braz and Terrans helped them lie low.

Opening the door to the house was a tall brown-haired Terran male, about Zeric's height but a few years younger.

He took one look at Ceta and then pulled the three of them inside. Slamming the door shut, the man rounded on Ceta angrily.

"What are you doing here? If the authorities see you talking to us, they could figure out who we are," he growled, narrowing his black eyes.

"Relax," Zeric said. "If the AIS even suspected Ceta, she would be in Olan with her sister."

The man turned to face Zeric, pale skin flushed with anger. "Who the hell are you?"

Ceta fumbled her words as she tried to speak. "They want to help Lei-mey."

"And you brought them here?!" the man said heatedly.

"Pasha, they wanted to find people who might be willing to help them," Ceta said trying to calm him. "I know Zeric from a while back. His friend, Maarkean, has a sister who's locked up too. When they saw that Lei-mey had been captured, they sought me out hoping to team up with you to break them both out."

The man, Pasha, appeared to relax slightly, and then he said, "Well, he's right. If AIS even suspected us, they would be here already. But let's go someplace more private to talk."

Pasha led them through the house to a set of stairs. He led them down into the basement, which held three people sitting around a table. Once it became obvious that Pasha wasn't alone, the group all stood up, tense and ready for action. The Ronid and the Terran male held weapons, but the Kowwok remained unarmed.

Maarkean leaned over to whisper to Ceta, "I thought you said they were peaceful."

The blond Terran male with the gun spoke first. "Pasha, who are these people?"

Pasha stopped at the bottom of the stairs and turned to face the guests. "You all know Ceta, Lei-mey's sister. And these are her friends Maarkean and Zeric. They apparently are here to help Lei-mey."

Seizing the opportunity, Maarkean decided to speak. He did not draw a weapon, and he didn't trust Zeric not to make things worse. Unfortunately, Zeric apparently thought the same thing and was able to speak first. "That's right. We heard that Lei-mey had been arrested and we wanted to get her out."

The Ronid in the group had a dark green carapace with a light green underside. He clacked his mandibles and puckered his long mouth in a skeptical way, his voice with that characteristic Ronid high-pitched hissing undertone making his words sound even more ominous. "Really? You just decided out of the blue to come hunt down Lei-mey's associates, right after she is arrested, in order to help us. A couple of complete strangers who know nothing about us, but offer help in breaking into a secure detention facility. I smell a set-up."

The Kowwok looked contemplative for a moment, but then nodded. "Very well. Stun them to be safe."

As the Terran and the Ronid took aim, Maarkean looked at Zeric. "You idiot."

Waking up from his second stunning in as many days, Zeric tried to recall where he was. It was much less comfortable than the last time. Instead of lying in a soft hospital bed, Zeric found himself tied to a chair. He appeared to still be in the basement, but there was a bright light shining down on him and the rest of the room was in darkness.

Swiveling his head as best he could, Zeric saw that Maarkean was strapped to a chair behind him. Movement in the darkness beyond the light caught his attention. Zeric started to reconsider how dangerous this group might be.

Zeric struggled against his bonds and realized that they were ordinary rope. Some types of cuffs could be picked, and zip cords were easy to cut if you could find something sharp, but rope was child's play. As subtly as he could, he began shifting his wrists, trying to loosen the knots.

In an attempt to distract attention from anyone who might be watching in the dark, he said, "Maark, you awake?"

"I was beginning to wonder if you'd ever wake up," came Maarkean's hoarse reply.

"You know us Terrans, we like to sleep."

"You still think this was a good idea?"

"Of course," quipped Zeric, a wry grin on his thin lips.

"You're still an idiot."

"Silence!" a voice from the darkness called out.

Zeric thought he recognized the voice as that of the Kowwok who had ordered them to be stunned. There were other whispers from the darkness and the sounds of people shifting around. For a moment, it looked like someone was about to step into the light, but then the figure backed away.

"So," the voice said, "You wanted us to help you break people out of Olan Detention Center."

"Yes."

"What agency do you work for?"

"What?" Zeric asked, surprised.

Maarkean let out a small laugh. "They think we're Alliance agents trying to set them up. You do know that if we were AIS agents we couldn't arrest you for planning to break into the prison after we suggested it. That's entrapment."

The first voice called out from the darkness, "You seem to be well versed in AIS policy."

"You mean Alliance law?" Maarkean asked. "Yeah, I've been an Alliance citizen for thirty-nine years. I've picked up a few things."

"We ask again, why are you here?"

Maarkean let out a loud sigh. "Well, it's obvious you aren't going to believe us when we tell the truth. So what's your plan? Shout at us from the dark until we agree with your silly theory? And what's the point of the light, anyway? We've already seen your faces."

Internally, Zeric groaned. Pointing out to an enemy group that you've seen their faces did not strike him as the best strategy. He would have preferred the 'we haven't seen or heard anything' approach. But, he admitted, Maarkean was proving to be a good distraction. He also realized that every time the Braz shifted to make an agitated point, the ropes that bound them moved in a beneficial way for Zeric.

"You're just going to have to kill us," Maarkean said.

There were loud whispers coming from the darkness. Zeric heard a female voice say something that sounded like 'we can't kill them' and then several voices started arguing. Zeric began working the ropes furiously. He thought he understood Maarkean's tactic. No one who had been in the basement had the look of hardened criminals. Everything they had done was the mark of amateurs. Even amateurs could kill, though, and Zeric was not sold on the idea of encouraging that line of thinking.

"If you don't cooperate, we may have to," the Kowwok's deep rumbling voice said, though without conviction. It continued with more determination. "Tell us why you are here, and you may yet live."

A little over dramatic, Zeric thought, but he kept that opinion to himself.

"Look, we're all on the same side here," Zeric said, trying to sound friendly.

A frustrated growl came from the darkness. "Fine, if none of you will do what's necessary to get them to tell us the truth, I will."

A female's voice cried, "Jairyd, no!"

"Are you just about done?" Maarkean asked, a note of urgency in his voice.

The question struck Zeric as odd until he realized it was directed at him. Turning his head, he saw the blond-haired Terran striding toward them from the darkness, a determined look in his eyes. With a few final slips of his wrists, Zeric replied, "Yeah, just about."

As soon as the ropes became loose, Zeric bolted upright, and Maarkean did the same, but moving in the opposite direction, both away from the Terran. Zeric charged into the darkness, making it several paces before stun bolts flashed out of the darkness. The first several missed and he managed to grab someone just on the edge of the light. Then one of the bolts connected.

The now-familiar feel of the stun bolt cascaded over his body. When Zeric realized he wasn't unconscious, he was confused. The stun pulse surged through him and then down his arms into the person he had just grabbed. The thin, wiry Terran female he had been grappling with dropped to the ground with a thud.

Two more stun bolts hit him and then surged down his body into the ground. Zeric found the entire experience unsettling, but he wasted no time. Moving quickly, he dashed toward the place where the stun bolts had originated and found the Ronid.

Zeric charged, and the Ronid threw down his apparently useless pistol and charged as well. The pair met in the middle. Zeric managed to twist aside and let the Ronid go past. He had not picked up many of Gu'od's fighting techniques, but he still remembered some tricks from his childhood. Hockey was his preferred sport, but he'd been good at avoiding tackles, too.

Slipping past the Ronid, Zeric dove for the ground where the pistol had fallen. Picking it up, he twirled around and shot the Ronid, who was just turning to come back for him.

Surveying the room, Zeric saw that the female he'd grabbed was still down on the other side of the room.

Maarkean was grappling with the Kowwok. Zeric considered shooting at them and seeing if Maarkean was as immune to stun bolts as he was, but he knew that at least one of the Terrans was still unaccounted for.

Fumbling around in the darkness, Zeric tried to find the others, or at least a light switch. With no darkvision, he tripped over a few things, banging his shin painfully, before stumbling into a lamp. As he fumbled to switch it on, a blast ripped through the room. A full-power blaster bolt emerged from a gun at the top of the stairs and destroyed an ottoman near Maarkean and the Kowwok.

Maarkean and the Kowwok froze. The Kowwok looked torn between resuming his fight and staring with disbelief at the dark, glowering man identified as Jairyd. Silence filled the room for a moment before Jairyd spoke.

"I know that stunning you won't do any good, at least for the next few hours, but as you saw, I'm no longer set to stun."

The idea clicked in Zeric's head, and he remembered the down side to low-power stun shots. While most normal stun shots put a person out for several hours, low-power shots, especially from commercial home defense weapons, only knocked a person out for one to two hours.

When a person was stunned, their body became slightly charged from the shot; the charge would not dissipate for about six hours. Shooting someone again before that charge dissipated would have no effect, meaning they were effectively immune.

Deciding to test his luck, Zeric raised his weapon toward Jairyd. "Good, I'm not set to stun, either. Makes this a good, old-fashioned standoff."

Jairyd eyed Zeric out of the corner of his eye while keeping his gun pointed at Maarkean. "Lower your weapon, or I'll kill your friend."

Zeric smiled, trying to put as much of a sinister look into his expression as possible. "We're not that close. But shoot him, and you'll be dead before you can hope to target me. Then your friends will be defenseless."

Edging away, Maarkean tried to put some distance between himself and the Kowwok he had been fighting.

At first, the Kowwok let him go, but then he seemed to change his mind. He put himself between Maarkean and Jairyd.

Clearly, not everyone in this group agreed with Jairyd's plan. There had to be some way he could use that to his advantage.

While Zeric considered his options, the Kowwok said, "Let's everyone lower our weapons. No one needs to die tonight."

"Sounds reasonable to me," Zeric replied, keeping his eyes on Jairyd.

When still nobody moved, Zeric decided someone needed to act first. Hoping he wasn't sealing his own death sentence, he lowered his weapon slightly. Since Jairyd was not aiming at him, he felt confident enough to give that much ground, but it was still a risk.

Everyone's eyes shifted toward Jairyd, who now held the only readied weapon. The scrutiny did its trick. After a pause, and with a shake of his blond-haired head, Jairyd lowered his weapon, too.

CHAPTER FOUR

A shake of her shoulder brought Saracasi awake. Barely any sunlight came through the room's small windows, casting the prison barracks in an eerie shadow. Struggling to open her eyes, she saw Chavatwor hovering above her. The shaggy grey and brown Kowwok smiled down at her, his blue lips barely visible through his facial hair.

"Breakfast time."

Nodding groggily, Saracasi pulled herself out of bed. The other residents of Building 15 were all lining up in the central aisle. She followed Chavatwor and Larin into the line, feeling out of place next to the furry Kowwoks. There were no guards visible, and she was surprised at how orderly and rhythmically everything happened. Her stomach rumbled, reminding her that she had not eaten in some time. She fought down the urge to push forward.

Once everyone lined up, the doors to the outside world opened. Guards outside directed them through the courtyard and past the fences into the main building, where she had initially been processed. The line shuffled along at a moderate pace, and after only a few minutes, Saracasi smelled food.

The moderate pace of the line then slowed to an agonizing crawl. Inching forward, they moved closer to a set of double doors where the food smells were coming from. After an eternity, Saracasi moved into the room and found a cafeteria-style set-up. As the line progressed, each person grabbed a tray and then moved to where a worker handed them a plate of food. Despite the different dietary needs, everyone received the same watery concoction.

After she was handed hers, Saracasi followed Chavatwor into a large room filled with tables. She was surprised at the number of people in the room; she realized there were far more people than had come out of Building 15. Once she thought about it, it made sense. With at least fifteen buildings full of prisoners, the guards couldn't bring them in one building at a time, or they'd never get done.

Chavatwor led them to a table in the left corner of the room. Saracasi recognized the blue-skinned Liw'kel woman who had arrived with her, seated with a purple-toned Liw'kel woman and Faide Darkthorne. Chavatwor smiled at the group and took a seat beside Faide. Saracasi followed his lead and sat down at the only open spot, next to the new Liw'kel woman.

Not waiting on ceremony, Saracasi dug into her food. She had heard that prison food was the worst slop ever created, hardly worthy of the name "food." However, at this moment, it tasted like the best thing she had ever eaten.

Several minutes later, when she had consumed most of what was on her plate, she looked at the group seated around her. None of them ate with the vigor she had displayed. Chavatwor sat in silence with his eyes closed, though his lips moved as if speaking under his breath. After a moment, he placed his hand to his forehead and took a small, hesitant bite of his food. Faide talked quietly to the blue Liw'kel, who had not touched her food. The new purple-skinned Liw'kel caught Saracasi's eye.

The woman picked at her food slowly while watching Faide and the other Liw'kel. She was perhaps the most beautiful woman Saracasi had ever seen. Her skin was nice shade of purple and her face had soft feminine features. The look of compassion she wore for the other woman gave her face a sense of warmth and her antennae flowed in a comforting dance. When she noticed Saracasi, she smiled. Saracasi felt herself getting lost in the other woman's jade green eyes.

"Hi," she said in a melodious voice, breaking Saracasi from her reverie. "I'm Asirzi Z'ren."

Stumbling over her words, Saracasi managed to get her name out.

Asirzi's smile broadened. "You were part of the new group who arrived yesterday?"

Saracasi nodded, and Asirzi continued, "So was Gamaly. She's taking it harder than you, unfortunately. I've only been able to get her name."

Looking back across the table at Gamaly, Saracasi saw the saddened and vacant look in the Liw'kel's eyes. She recognized that Faide and Asirzi had been trying to talk to the woman all this time, but she hadn't responded. Remembering what had happened when they first arrived at the prison, Saracasi felt for her.

"A friend of hers tried to protect her when we arrived. He was beaten and taken away," Saracasi explained to the others.

Asirzi gave Gamaly another look of compassion, and Faide nodded as if he finally understood something. He patted Gamaly's delicate long-boned hand with his hairy paw and tried to smile. The Notha's sharp teeth gave the expression an unfortunate, dangerous tinge.

"They will have taken him to isolation, then. Once he's been in there for a short time he'll be returned to the regular prison population." His consoling smile faded as he continued, "Unfortunately, there is no guarantee he will end up in our building. But, on the bright side, to prevent us from making regular contact with other buildings, the guards rotate the groups we eat with. In time, we'll see him in here for meals, no matter which building he ends up in."

Gamaly seemed to brighten slightly at that news and finally spoke. "That is, if they ever let him out. I doubt he'll stop fighting until he finds me again. Gu'od is incredibly stubborn about some things."

Asirzi and Faide brightened when Gamaly spoke, and Saracasi decided to seize the opportunity to keep her talking. "He was quite amazing. It took several guards to bring him down. Where did he learn to fight like that?"

Gamaly looked up at her. "Gu'od was once a Ni'jar. He left the order when we met, but he still practices the arts."

Saracasi nodded in appreciation. A secluded group of monks that originated on the Liw'kel homeworld, the Ni'jar were renowned throughout the galaxy for their martial arts skills. Common belief said that no one could a match a Ni'jar master in a one-on-one fight. They were renowned as much for their isolation as for their fighting skills. Few ever left a Ni'jar conclave after they joined, and the Ni'jar refused to involve themselves in galactic affairs.

"He must love you very much," Faide said consolingly.

Gamaly nodded. "He does. Which is why I worry so much. If they put him into another building, he'll just try to escape and find me. Then they might kill him."

Faide put a comforting hand on Gamaly's shoulder. "I wouldn't worry about that. I've been here a long time, and despite lots of neglect and some abuse, I've never seen, or even heard rumor of, the guards killing anybody. Even unruly prisoners."

Even though the message was directed to Gamaly, it made Saracasi feel better. She had known abuses like this prison occurred on some worlds in the Alliance. That had been part of why she'd gotten herself involved in the protest group on Braz. But it was comforting to know that things had not decayed to such an extent that helpless prisoners were being slaughtered.

Or at least it wasn't to a point where they were killing prisoners *and* it was common knowledge, her cynical mind thought. Lots of terrible things were done in secret. These prisons were a good example: they were not common knowledge on most worlds in the Alliance. Killing prisoners was not outside the realm of possibility.

But if anyone would know about it, at least in this prison, it would be someone who had been here as long as Faide.

"Now eat up," Faide said, picking up his own spoon. "According to our young Braz friend, the food here is excellent."

Saracasi smiled sheepishly as she realized she had already started eating again while she was thinking.

Maarkean watched as Zeric shifted for what must have been the tenth time in the last few minutes. They had been sitting at this table for the last fifteen minutes, staring across at Jairyd and their former captors. No one had said much since the standoff had ended. Names had been exchanged, and then Maarkean and Zeric had been left alone while the stunned people had recovered. Now Jairyd was glaring at Maarkean and Zeric, and the rest of his group seemed unsure how to proceed.

The introductions had been brief, but Maarkean learned that the white Kowwok was known as Lahkaba, the Ronid as Lohcja Cargon, and the slim, petite dark-haired Terran female as Meyka. The Terran male, Pasha Nolan, who had shown them inside, had returned to the upper part of the house.

Looking over the four of them, Maarkean tried to get a sense of them. They appeared to be younger than him, though he wasn't sure about Lahkaba. It was notoriously hard to determine Kowwok ages without being a Kowwok. Only very old Kowwoks displayed their age in the form of grey fur. And with white fur predominating, Lahkaba could have had many grey hairs among them and Maarkean would never know.

Occasionally, Jairyd would tap his finger on the hilt of his holstered gun. This behavior appeared to distress Meyka, who sat next to him. She had been doing most of the talking, telling Jairyd that he wasn't a killer and that murder was against everything they stood for. He seemed to be ignoring her, but Maarkean judged her to be successful, since they were still alive.

In contrast, Lahkaba and Lohcja seemed more relaxed. They sat beside each other, occasionally making quiet comments that only the other could hear. It was difficult to be sure, but Lohcja occasionally made noises that might have even been laughter.

The two undoubtedly had more of a reason to take issue with the Alliance than the two Terrans. Despite many worlds in the Kreogh sector having significant populations of non-Alliance species, they would not have any voting rights in Alliance elections. They might in local government elections, but not for Alliance representatives or governors.

Reading the intents and emotions of others had always been a talent of his, but it was harder the further from Braz a species was. Ronids, with their compound eyes, antennae and exoskeletal carapace were one of the most alien species in the known galaxy. None of the physical signs that you could normally use to gauge someone's mood existed in a species that did not see, blink, or sweat the same way.

Despite those limitations, Maarkean got the impression that the pair of them, at least, didn't want to kill him and Zeric outright, especially since Lahkaba had convinced Jairyd to lower his weapon earlier.

Shifting again, Zeric spoke out of impatience. "All right, we've been staring at each other for a while now. Is someone going to speak?"

"An excellent idea," Meyka replied. Her voice was calm, and she appeared relieved that someone had broken the stalemate.

Silence threatened to retake its hold, as no one was sure who should begin. Zeric beat it back when he continued, "All right, well, I'll go. We came here looking for some help. We know you have a friend in Olan that you might want to get out. So do we."

With a sneer, Jairyd said, "Yes, we've been over this. You want us to break people out of a heavily guarded Alliance prison facility. You come to us out of nowhere and try to get us to agree to a major crime that would likely get us all killed."

"They didn't come out of nowhere," Meyka chided Jairyd. "Ceta brought them."

Jairyd snorted. "Even worse. Lei-mey's prostitute sister brings them here. For all we know, she made a deal with the cops: us for her sister's release."

"Lei-mey would never allow something like that," Lahkaba said loudly, speaking to the group for the first time.

Eyeing the Kowwok suspiciously, Jairyd retorted, "Maybe not, but that doesn't mean Ceta didn't do it on her own."

"Hey!" Zeric said, getting angry. "Ceta did not betray you. We had to convince her to take us here. She only wants to help her sister. What happened to her, anyway?"

"She's upstairs, probably giving Pasha a freebie," Jairyd said, and then leaned forward in his chair. "Of course she wants to help her sister. But what about you? I suppose you just want to do it out of the goodness of your heart."

"We told you before; we want to get people out as well," Zeric countered, leaning forward and his voice rising.

"My sister," Maarkean said quietly. "We want to get my sister and some of Zeric's friends out. We have the same motivation that Ceta does."

Everyone turned to look at Maarkean. They had to strain to hear him compared to the others.

Maarkean took the attention as an opportunity to continue. "I don't know anything about your group. I don't know your politics, or why your friend is in prison. But I suspect that if it's for the same reason my sister is in there, she doesn't deserve to be. I can understand why you don't trust us. I don't trust you, either."

Maarkean paused for a moment, but continued before anyone else could speak. "But I do trust Ceta. I don't know her any better than the rest of you, but I do understand her motivations. She wants to get her sister out, just like I do. She said you all could help me get them both out. So I'm willing to put aside my distrust and work with you. Even after you tied us up and threatened to kill us. The only real question is – are you willing to do the same?"

Silence filled the air. Their four captors considered his words. Even Jairyd appeared to be taking them at face value. Meyka had a small smile on her delicately-shaped face and a look of sympathy directed toward Maarkean.

Zeric spoke next. "Two days ago, I tried to steal Maarkean's ship. We were only moderately successful, and the Alliance captured my friends and Maarkean's sister. Instead of killing me for that, Maarkean convinced me that we needed to work together. If we can get along, there is no reason we can't work with the rest of you, despite our rough introduction."

Maarkean inwardly groaned, but to his surprise, Zeric's admission of being a ship thief did not immediately destroy the headway he thought he had made. Lahkaba and Lohcja shared a look where they appeared to consider the news. After a moment, they nodded in the affirmative to each other. Meyka scrunched up her face in disapproval, but dour-faced Jairyd relaxed slightly.

"All right, let's talk," Jairyd said and leaned back in his chair. "We'll assume for the sake of conversation that we might all be willing to work together. But how?"

It was progress, Maarkean decided. Jairyd's statement wasn't exactly an endorsement of friendship, but it wasn't a threat, either. Unfortunately, he didn't have an answer to the question. He and Zeric had been making everything up as they went along. Finding people who might be willing to work with them had been as far as they had gotten.

Despite being glad that they were not terrorists, Maarkean had held out hope that they already had a plan to break Lei-mey out, and could just be convinced to break Saracasi out at the same time. So far, they'd viewed the idea of a prison break as just a way of framing them for an arrest. That didn't bode well for them having any such plan.

"No one has ever been released from Olan, despite many court cases," Meyka said. "Attempts have been made by the planetary legislature to release people, but they have all been vetoed by Governor Howell. Lei-mey is a member of the legislature."

That news left Maarkean dumbstruck for a second. They had alluded to Lei-mey being more legitimate than the news articles claimed, but that she was an elected official had not occurred to him.

In the end, it didn't affect anything. Had he thought that he had even a remote chance of using legal means to save Saracasi, he never would have fled Braz all those years ago.

He tried not to sound impatient. "As I'm sure will surprise none of you, a court case isn't going to achieve our results. As we said when we arrived, we want your help to break them out."

The group considered him. Meyka was clearly still bothered by this recurring suggestion, though there was less resistance this time from the others.

Lahkaba leaned forward. "Perhaps you don't know what you're suggesting. Olan is a fortress. It's in the middle of nowhere and under tight AIS control. Most prisons are contracted out, but Olan is staffed by full-time Alliance personnel."

"Nothing is impenetrable," Maarkean said determinedly, "but you're right, I don't know anything about Olan, as I have spent almost no time on Sulas. That's where we need to start. I would like to see the place for myself."

Lohcja spread his pincers in what looked like a grin. "If you want to see it, just go up to any AIS officer and tell them what we've been talking about. You'll get to see a whole lot of it."

Despite the seriousness of their situation, the Ronid's joke made Maarkean smile. "I had a different, less permanent, idea than that."

"This is crazy," Zeric said for the thousandth time.

Sitting in the back of a cab, Zeric watched as the walls of the prison got closer. He had spent much of his adult life trying to avoid going to prison, and now he was expected to sit calmly while he was driven straight toward one. Out of habit, he felt for the gun he knew wouldn't be there.

Beside him on the seat, Maarkean ignored him, his violet eyes staring fixedly ahead. He had stopped reacting to Zeric's antics half an hour ago, when they had left the city proper. He had been sitting quietly with his eyes closed for most of the journey. Zeric doubted the Braz was as calm as he tried to pretend. Zeric did not normally consider himself a nervous person, but he couldn't control his nerves now.

The plan had made sense the night before. It was simple, straightforward and logical. Zeric liked simple plans. Less could go wrong. But that had been before, when he was relatively safe, in the basement of a group of people who were only sort of dangerous. Now, he sat in a cab driving toward a prison with a man who, at least on some level, probably wanted to kill him.

The cab came slowly to a stop at the outer fence of the prison. The walls of the building still lay about five hundred meters away across an open field. Lohcja, who had unexpectedly revealed that he was employed as a cab driver, leaned out of the window and spoke to the Terran manning the guard booth. They conversed for a moment, and then the guard directed Lohcja to move the vehicle to a parking area outside the fence.

Once they started moving again, Lohcja spoke to them. "He said no vehicles are allowed in. I'm to let you off here and wait while he shows you inside."

"As we assumed," Maarkean said. "Hopefully we'll be back soon."

"I'll be here when you get out. Just try to make it within my lifetime; the meter's not running," Lohcja said with a widening of his mandibles that Zeric hoped was meant as a smile.

Zeric would have felt better if they had gotten the vehicle all the way to the front door, where they could have used it to get away more quickly. Climbing out of the cab, Zeric followed Maarkean back toward the guard's booth. Still feeling jittery, he hoped Maarkean was prepared to do all the talking.

Once they stepped up to the window, the guard leaned down and said, "Nature of your visit?"

"We're here to see some prisoners," Maarkean answered, much more calmly than Zeric thought he could have.

"Names," the guard said with a bored tone.

"Ours or theirs?" Maarkean asked.

"Both."

"Maaron Ocaitvik and James Franklin," Maarkean answered. "We're here to see Saracasi Ocaitchi, Gu'od Dos'redna, and Gamaly Dos'redna."

The guard typed all of this into his computer and then asked for their ID cards. Maarkean and Zeric handed them over. This was a risk, as Zeric would eventually be identified. Lahkaba apparently had some connections and had confirmed that no warrants had, as yet, been issued for either of them. The guard swiped the IDs and continued typing. "Nature of your relationship with the prisoners?"

Now came the tricky part.

"They tried to pirate our ship. We want to confront them."

The guard looked at them appraisingly. "Understandable. If anyone did that to me, I'd love the opportunity to see them behind bars."

Zeric realized he had been holding his breath, and released it.

The guard handed them two visitor badges and even smiled. "Follow the path to the building. Jimmy will meet you there and show you inside. Enjoy seeing justice in action."

Zeric nodded to the guard as he took his badge. He tried to appear excited, but was sure he just looked sick. He hoped the guard took his nervousness as being about facing his attackers, and not about the fact that he was walking into a prison while being wanted for numerous crimes and hoping that his cheap fake ID was good enough to get him out again.

Once they were out of earshot of the guard, Maarkean said quietly, "You look as nervous as I feel."

That got a laugh out of Zeric. The Braz appeared almost as calm as Gu'od usually did. Zeric knew that Braz simply were not as expressive as Terrans, but there was more to it than that. Maarkean was definitely someone he wanted on his side in a tense situation. The events of the previous evening had proven that.

Shrugging aside his nerves as best he could, Zeric began examining the prison structure. The wall was made of concrete and extended out for several hundred meters in either direction. It must have been several meters thick, since pairs of guards patrolled along the top. Evenly spaced along the wall were tower structures that housed more guards.

Attached to each of the towers were a giant spotlight and several pieces of equipment that he assumed was an array of sensors and cameras. Each guard along the wall and in the towers carried a stun baton and a rifle slung on his back. Zeric took a count of the guards that he could see, assumed a similar number on the three walls he couldn't see, and added that to the number he had seen in the guardhouse at the front gate. That made at least twenty guards just on the prison's perimeter.

When they reached the wall, a door opened, allowing a guard to step out. He smiled at them and gestured for them to come inside. Zeric took a deep breath as he followed, the sound of the door closing behind him ringing loud in his head. Up until now, there had been nothing stopping him from turning around and walking away, and only a flimsy chain-link fence and several guards between him and freedom. Once he was inside, though, he felt the weight of the walls and the heavy door blocking his way.

"I'm Jimmy," the guard said. "We don't get a lot of visitors here. Who wants to talk to an alien in a prison? But you guys got a great opportunity here."

Zeric knew that the guard wasn't being entirely truthful. According to Meyka, the families of those imprisoned here came all the time to try to see their loved ones, but were turned away. Braz and Terrans were permitted to enter, but few Braz and Terrans would admit to being friends of an alien imprisoned here. If everyone here was a serious criminal, he wondered why the guards weren't curious as to why more victims didn't come to face the prisoners.

"We're thankful for it," Maarkean said. "Glad we can see justice served to those scum."

Internally, Zeric squirmed. Maarkean's voice had been a little too honest when he said that. He supposed he couldn't blame him too much. Gu'od and Gamaly had attacked him, and they were now in prison for it. Justice had been done there.

"We also want to see the Braz who lied to us and impersonated a member of our crew," Zeric added.

"Of course," the guard agreed. "Did they tell you what she did? I couldn't imagine living with someone on a small ship and then learning what kind of traitor she was."

Zeric almost said that they had not been told what she had done, which was true. He was quite curious what sort of crime would get a warrant sent out here all the way from the core worlds. A look at Maarkean's face made him decide to say nothing. The man's normally stoic expression had been replaced by a look of regret, and if Zeric was correct, guilt.

They walked the rest of the way in silence. The guard showed them to a room with a clear wall across the middle of it. They were left alone for a few minutes, and then a door on the other side was opened and two females were shown in.

Zeric was relieved to see Gamaly in relatively good condition, and he recognized the other as the woman he had shot on the ship, which must make her Maarkean's sister. His momentary relief at seeing Gamaly was immediately replaced by fear. This was where things could go horribly, horribly wrong.

When Saracasi came in and saw Maarkean, her face showed her joy, even through the trademark Braz calm. It must have been a monumental effort for Maarkean's face to remain cold and impassive. For the first time, he appeared to not know what to say. Zeric decided he'd better intervene before the wrong thing was said.

"It's good to see you, Sarca. After all that time on the ship pretending to be someone you aren't. Maaron and I were disappointed to learn the truth about you."

Saracasi looked at him blankly. He realized that she didn't know who he was, but he hoped that emphasizing their fake identities might clue her in. Maarkean was pretty perceptive, and he hoped it ran in the family.

Gamaly took the whole thing in stride. Considering that Zeric was not in there with her, she knew he had some trick.

She remained quiet and merely looked at him, waiting to find out what her part was.

"Where is the other one you betrayed us to? We were told there were two."

Gamaly's face drooped slightly at his question, but she picked up on where he was going. "They took him away to solitary confinement."

"Good, he deserves to suffer," Zeric said, trying to keep up the act. Inside, he cursed. Gu'od being in solitary made their job harder.

"I hope they are treating the rest of you traitors equally harshly. Guards patrolling and beating you regularly," Maarkean finally said. He was trying to make his words as harsh as his expression, and was almost managing it.

"You'll be saddened to know that they don't beat us. We're left pretty much alone in Building 15 on the west side. Just us and several dozen other low-life aliens," Gamaly said, continuing the act. "We only deal with the few guards at meals and the ones on the walls. I should be able to slip past them when I decide to come after you. Just as soon as my partner is released from solitary."

Good girl, Zeric thought. He had known Gu'od would have a complete floor plan memorized and an escape attempt planned, but he had been unsure about Gamaly. Her skills lay in negotiating good deals for their stolen goods and talking her way past problems. She was okay in a fight, but had always had Gu'od at her side. She appeared to have kept her wits about her enough to notice how well they were guarded. And her news was good – things were easier without a lot of guards on the inside.

For a Braz, Saracasi still looked confused and worried. She'd started fidgeting with her prison jumper. The worried expression ruined any attraction her relatively plain features would have held for him. In contrast, Zeric thought Gamaly looked as amazing as always, standing there defiantly and trying her best to look intimidating. Saracasi was clearly the wild card in this encounter, and that made Zeric nervous. If she was unsure what was really going on, she could give the whole thing away.

The door behind them opened, and Jimmy poked his head in. "Sorry, gentlemen, but that's all the time we can give you."

Zeric looked at Gamaly and gave her a small nod of support before saying, "I hope you all suffer in here for a long time."

He turned toward the exit. He was surprised when Saracasi dropped to her knees and said, "Please, I was your shipmate. I didn't do anything. They confused me with someone else and are now going to ship me back to Braz for execution."

Maarkean stopped to speak on his way out, hiding the pain he must feel. "Good, I'm glad to hear that. As a traitor to the clan, you deserve what's coming to you."

Once outside the room, Jimmy led them back the way they had come in. Zeric tried to take the opportunity to learn more. "Is it true that they are not guarded all the time?"

Jimmy laughed. "No, we have eyes on all the prisoners at all times. But there are so many of them that we have to focus our attention on only those moving about for meals. I assure you the compound is quite secure. There is no chance they can get out of this building."

When they stepped outside, Jimmy gestured across the field. "Even if they somehow got out of their cells, we call this stretch to the fence our kill zone. Nothing can move across that without us seeing it and getting it. We have sensors of all kinds, and the ground is even lined with mines. You're perfectly safe with them inside... just stay on the path."

Zeric nodded, trying to sound impressed. "That's good to hear. No one can escape from here and live to tell the tale."

"Absolutely. Hope you boys got what you came for." Jimmy then nodded to them and closed the door to the prison.

Walking quietly away, Zeric considered what they had learned. He had been incredibly nervous going into the prison, even though it had merely been a reconnaissance mission. Now that he knew what they were up against, he wasn't sure he felt any better.

Inside, the prisoners were mostly left alone. That was a major plus. Once they could get inside, the opposition would be light. But getting to the prison was going to be a problem.

They would be seen well before getting to the outer fence. And, if Jimmy was right, even if they could sneak up at night, they would have a whole array of sensors and guards with guns to get past. As they walked, Zeric looked over at Maarkean and was surprised to see him smiling. "What are you so happy about?"

"I know how we can get them out."

During the walk back to Building 15, Saracasi thought about the meeting that had just occurred. It had been wonderful to see Maarkean again, but she did not quite understand what had happened. She was able to piece together that Maarkean was checking on her and that the Terran male knew Gamaly. Why he pretended that he had been part of her crew, she had no idea. Maybe it had been the only way to get him into the prison with Maarkean. It could also explain some of the charges against her.

She could not figure out what connection Gamaly had. Gamaly had played along with the whole thing as if it were natural and had revealed information about where they were located. Maarkean couldn't possibly be planning to rescue her with the help of that Terran, could he?

She dismissed that thought. She knew her brother loved her; by taking her off Braz, he had set aside his life to save hers. But that had been a simple matter of taking her off the planet before the arrest warrant had even been issued. It pained her to admit it, but she wasn't so sure he would have done it had the AIS already been coming for her.

When they were back in the barracks, Faide came up to them. He looked relieved when he saw them. "When they came and took the two of you, I was worried. What did they want?"

Startled out of her musing, Saracasi looked at the Notha's anxious, furry face. "Worried? I thought you said they treated the inmates pretty reasonably as long as we behaved. What did you think they were going to do to us?"

Faide looked a little ashamed. "It is true that most of us are left alone. But, in the past, sometimes attractive females were taken away for... special interrogation sessions with the old commandant. We have been hoping that the new commandant is different."

The admission shocked Saracasi enough that she momentarily forgot about what had just transpired. She had just begun to feel safe here.

"What?" This came out of Gamaly, and it startled Saracasi, since she had been about to say the same thing.

Nodding slowly, Faide said, "It is something we do not talk about. It didn't happen very often, and we tried to forget about it."

"You tell us this now? *After* we're taken?" Gamaly said angrily, her antennae waving around wildly with her fury.

Faide looked apologetic. "We did not want to alarm you. I apologize for that."

Not saying another word to Faide, Gamaly stormed off toward the small restroom in the back of the barracks. The Notha made no effort to stop her and turned his apologetic look to Saracasi, but she quickly followed Gamaly.

"That's ridiculous," Gamaly fumed, "*hoping* the guards weren't taking us to be raped instead of *warning* us."

"It wouldn't have made a difference, though, would it?" Saracasi said. "I was worried enough about where we were going without that thought hanging over my head."

Gamaly sighed and looked at the younger woman. "You're probably right."

"What I'm most concerned with is what really happened in that meeting with my brother," Saracasi mused.

"That was your brother?" Gamaly asked, to which Saracasi gave a nod. A look of regret crossed Gamaly's face. "We should talk about that. But not here."

When the two entered the restroom, Gamaly leaned against the door so that no one else could enter. Saracasi turned to face her and was surprised at how apprehensive Gamaly looked. She had assumed the other woman was just as confused by what had happened as she had been, but now she had her doubts.

"All right, what was that whole meeting about?"

Gamaly shrugged. "I wish I knew exactly. I can only figure that Zeric and your brother are planning something. He must have been mistaken for someone else."

She paused and took a deep breath. "After Faide's speech when we first got here, I was hoping I wouldn't have to share this, but now I think I probably should. Unlike most people, I'm not in here for the simple crime of not being Braz or Terran. I was a ship thief, along with my husband and our partner, Zeric, the Terran we just met. He must have been mistaken for part of the ship's crew when the Alliance seized us."

The information slammed into place in Saracasi's head. Gamaly was a ship thief and Maarkean was with her partner; that could not be a coincidence. Questions began spinning around in her head like a vortex. Was Maarkean forced by this Zeric to be there, or were they working together? What was Gamaly going to do to her now? Then another thought struck her. Gamaly did not appear to know whose ship she had attacked.

Saracasi said, "That was our ship you tried to steal."

Gamaly's antennae twitched and her eyes grew about as big as Saracasi was sure hers had been just a moment ago. The two women stared at each other as the true nature of their connection sank in. Suddenly, Saracasi felt nervous about being alone with Gamaly in this tiny room.

The silence between them stretched out uncomfortably. Saracasi wondered if Gamaly was just as worried about being alone in here with her. Then she dismissed that thought; she knew she was in no way a threat. Plus, Gamaly was married to a Ni'jar master; she surely knew some fighting skills.

"Well, now what?" Saracasi asked.

CHAPTER FIVE

When Saracasi and Gamaly finally left the restroom, there was a small line of impatient residents waiting to get inside. Saracasi smiled sheepishly and apologized quickly before making her way past them to her bunk. She was relieved to not find Chavatwor or Larin there, and she climbed quietly into her bed.

The day had been quite a wild ride. She was not sure what to make of it all.

When she and Gamaly had been called out of the building, she had not been sure what to expect. In hindsight, she was glad Faide had not mentioned the 'special interrogations' the former commandant had done. Had she known that, the entire journey to the meeting would have been pure terror.

Seeing Maarkean again had been comforting. She had wondered what had happened to him, and it was a relief to know for sure he was alive and free. But now she knew she was stuck in a prison with the two people who had tried to steal her ship and were the reason she got caught. What Maarkean was doing with their other partner, she still had no idea, but at least she had been able to let Maark know that she wouldn't be here long. She just hoped he wasn't foolish enough to follow her when she was shipped back to Braz. His fake ID might work out here on the fringe planets, but it wouldn't work on the homeworld.

Gamaly seemed convinced Zeric and Maarkean were working together on some sort of plan to get them all out, and that scared her. So far, he had just helped his sister escape being arrested. He would face prison for that, but it would only be a light sentence. If he were to do anything stupid, like attempt a rescue, they would both be executed.

Lost in her thoughts, Saracasi did not notice when Asirzi moved to stand beside her bed. The Liw'kel coughed quietly, breaking Saracasi's train of thought. She turned her head and was surprised to see Asirzi. She would have expected Faide to come back to continue the questioning.

"It's been an interesting morning," Asirzi began nervously.

Sitting up on the side of her bunk, Saracasi considered the Liw'kel. When they had first met, she had been captivated by the other woman's beauty. Liw'kel attracted her more than most species, she knew, but there was something particularly appealing about this one. They had not talked much since that first meal, though she had caught herself watching Asirzi at various times.

"You could say that," Saracasi answered.

She tried to keep her wits about her. Despite being enamored, she knew she had to stay focused. She didn't know what she wanted to reveal to the rest of the inmates yet about what had happened. In spite of learning that Gamaly had been responsible for her imprisonment, she found that she quite liked the woman, though not in the same way she found herself attracted to Asirzi. She remembered the torment Gamaly had gone through over seeing her husband beaten before her eyes, and it made a difference in how Saracasi viewed her. It was difficult to cross back over the line to seeing her as a cold-hearted thief. Yet those feelings were there, too.

"You and Gamaly must have had a lot to talk about," Asirzi said.

Her tone betrayed a curiosity that made Saracasi suspect she had learned something. Until she decided how she was going to deal with Gamaly, she would keep the woman's secret. This meant she had to limit what she said about what had happened.

Saracasi answered, "We had to face some people from her past who upset her. We did not get a chance to talk about it until we got back here." She felt that was not exactly a lie, without actually revealing anything.

Asirzi considered it and nodded. To Saracasi's surprise, she sounded relieved. "Even though it upset Gamaly, I am glad that you were taken for that reason. At least you did not have to face the commandant."

The way Asirzi said the last part made Saracasi wonder. She decided to follow her hunch. "I don't know what I would do in a situation like that. I don't even like men, and to find one forcing himself on me...."

Asirzi appeared to shrink into herself when Saracasi spoke. The way her face became sad and her eyes grew distant made Saracasi regret saying anything. Her hunch had probably been correct, but she wished fervently it had not been.

"When do you think we'll get some time outside?" Saracasi said, trying to change the subject. "During the brief periods I was out there, it was very nice weather."

Asirzi didn't respond, so Saracasi continued to ramble on about the weather and then about how she had spent most of the last few years living aboard a starship. When she mentioned life aboard ship, Asirzi's face brightened. Saracasi continued to describe the ship and life aboard until Asirzi spoke. "Have you been to many different planets?"

Saracasi nodded. "Several. We've probably visited most of the planets in Kreogh sector. And a couple in the Trepon and Loisa sectors as well."

"What were they like?" Asirzi asked, clearly interested. "I've never left Sulas."

Smiling, Saracasi described everything she could remember about the worlds she had visited. From there, the conversation took many turns, and Saracasi found herself happily forgetting where she was for a time.

"All right," Zeric said eagerly. "You've been quiet the entire ride back from the prison. Now we're back. Out with it."

Maarkean considered the Terran. He had been glad the man had taken the lead during the meeting with Saracasi. The sight of his sister in the prison jumper had frozen his tongue and made him afraid to say anything for fear of giving something away. That appreciation had dimmed somewhat during the return journey as Zeric and Lohcja had both pestered him to reveal his plan.

When they had arrived at the prison, Maarkean had been surprised by how light the security was. The sensor equipment guarding the approach to the building was of low quality, and the guards left significant gaps in their coverage. Once they had gotten inside, there were no checkpoints.

Despite Zeric's pestering, he had decided to wait until they got back to the group before saying any more. He was always chastising Saracasi for wanting to act hastily, so he took his own advice and gave himself the duration of the ride to think his idea through several times. During that period, he had imagined several additional ways his plan could go horribly wrong. But even with those realizations, he kept coming to the conclusion that his plan was better than any of the alternatives.

As they had approached the house, Lohcja had called ahead, and everyone from the previous night had assembled. Walking into the basement, they had been confronted by a variety of expressions. Jairyd was as sour as ever, Meyka looked worried, Ceta was anxious and Lahkaba seemed curious. Pasha tried to maintain a blank expression.

"I think we can get them out," Maarkean began. "Security inside the facility is pretty light. Once we're inside, it will be no problem getting to the prisoners."

"I concur. My concern is with the approach to the prison," Zeric said to Maarkean. "It's a wide open field. I noticed gaps in their coverage, but maneuvering a group through those gaps will be difficult. Plus, even if things go easily once we're inside, getting back out will be difficult. Most of the defenses are designed to keep people in, after all. Plus, we'll have to comb the whole prison looking for the right cell. Gamaly revealed her and your sister's general location, but we don't know where Gu'od or Lei-mey are being kept."

Jairyd sneered at Maarkean. "Looks like even your friend disagrees with you. We're not going on any suicide mission just to get your sister out. If we can't find Lei-mey, we aren't going in at all."

Maarkean tried to suppress his response. The man was seriously starting to get on his nerves. If he didn't need the man's cooperation, he would have hit him a long time ago. He still wasn't sure it wouldn't come to that.

"That's why we're not going to sneak in. It would take too long, since we don't know where everyone is held. Once stealth was lost, we'd be done for."

"You're not thinking of some kind of frontal assault, are you?" Lohcja asked nervously. He had been to the prison, too, and had seen what they would be up against. "Their defenses were spread thin, but with only seven of us, we would still get cut down."

Despite claiming that he didn't want to go on a suicide mission, Jairyd brightened, for the first time, at the idea of a frontal assault. That disturbed Maarkean more than anything the man had done so far. People excited by the idea of dying in a futile charge at the enemy had been in Maarkean's military units before; they had not returned from many missions.

"Make that *six* of you," Meyka said, more defiantly than you would expect from a small Terran woman. "I will not participate in any foolish violence that gets us and a lot of others killed."

Maarkean held up his hands to forestall any more arguments. "I'm not thinking of any foolish frontal assault or any near-impossible covert infiltration. There is one line of attack that the prison is completely vulnerable to."

Lohcja and Zeric looked curious and were obviously mentally reviewing what they had seen to try to find what they had missed. The rest were just waiting.

"Air assault," Maarkean said. "The prison has no defenses against an air raid. No anti-aircraft weapons, no shield generators. We fly in and take out their guard towers from the air, then we land and get everyone out. And I mean everyone, not just our people."

The room was silent, everyone in disbelief. Maarkean had known that his idea was a little ambitious, but he had not expected this reaction.

Finally, Zeric spoke. "How exactly do we take out their defenses from the air? Your ship isn't a fighter craft. And even if your one turret gun is enough, it's certainly not big enough to get everyone in the prison out."

Maarkean said, "My ship will be enough to take out the defenses. But you're right, it's not big enough to carry everyone. That's where you come in. You're a ship thief. Prove how good you are. Steal us a bigger ship that can hold everyone."

Zeric considered this and then smiled. "I can probably find something."

"If you fly in and start attacking the prison from the air, the military is going to get involved," Lahkaba said. "Even if you can take out the prison defenses, we'll have fighters all over us."

Maarkean smiled. "I was a fighter pilot in the Alliance Navy. I doubt there are any fighters more advanced than AF-43's here on Sulas, and my ship is more than a match for them. We'll take out the communications tower first, which should buy us a little time. If we're quick, and Zeric can find us a ship that can take a few hits, we should be able to take off from the prison and escape into hyperspace before any big ships can respond."

The room was silent once more. Maarkean knew his idea was unorthodox, which was the very reason he thought it would work. The prison was defended against escape attempts from the inside and ground assaults from the outside. But no one had considered an air attack. There was no reason to. Who would attack a prison full of undesirable aliens from the air?

Without the others' help, there was no way that he and Zeric could pull this plan off. If both of them went on the *Cutty Sark*, there would be no one to provide cover while they infiltrated the prison. If Zeric took his own ship, he'd have to deal with the prison guards alone until he was able to reach the first group of prisoners. Everything rested on the consent of some wannabe revolutionaries, most of whom didn't appear to have any combat experience.

"So," Jairyd finally said. Maarkean feared what rant the man would give against the idea. He thought he had sold Zeric on it. It looked like Meyka was out for any idea that involved violence. Reading Lahkaba or Lohcja was still tough, but his gut told him they would be in for anything. Pasha and Jairyd were the wild cards.

"You want to steal a craft large enough for hundreds of prisoners. Attack an Alliance prison with a transport ship. Then land a large, stolen ship *inside* the prison, storm it with six people..."

"Five," Meyka said. "I won't participate in direct violence."

"Four, actually," Maarkean interrupted. "I'll need someone on my ship manning the turret."

"All right, storm a prison with four people. Those four have to deal with the guards and get hundreds of unaware *prisoners* onboard this ship as quickly as possible. Then escape from Alliance fighter craft with only the protection of a single, lightly-armed transport."

"That about sums it up," Maarkean said, trying to put as much confidence in his voice as he could.

"It's crazy," Jairyd said, but then he smiled. "I like it."

'You're a ship thief, just steal us a ship,' Zeric thought sarcastically. 'Sure, no problem.' 'But wait, Zeric, no one can know it's been stolen. And it has to be big enough to carry hundreds of people. And land without a docking facility. And it has to be tough enough to withstand a few hits, just in case.'

Zeric shivered and tried again to pull his dark green combat jacket tighter around himself. The night air was cold, and he was standing out in it for the second night in a row. He had scoured the planet's starports and starship dealers, trying to find an unguarded ship that met the specifications. The previous night, he had thought he had found a good candidate, and this was his second trip here to see if security was just as lax.

The Alliance impound storage facility was located on the outskirts of Ba'aar, a moderate city on the main continent's west coast. The capital of Ciread had been ruled out immediately, despite the locals' insistence that there would be more ships to choose from. They had not understood that if you wished to avoid detection, you didn't steal from a place with the best tracking stations and military presence. The Razors also played in Ba'aar, and his cap gave him perfect cover, letting him blend in like a local.

Not for the first time, he thought about stealing something smaller and just leaving the planet. It would be smarter. No prisons. No guards. No chance of sudden death. But then he would be leaving Gu'od and Gamaly to a life in prison.

Up until he had met them, he had followed the old thief code, "every man for himself." Even when he had worked for mercenary companies, he had stuck to that code. It had worked well, keeping him from jail and death on numerous occasions, though it might have worked against him sometimes. But his time with the two Liw'kel had reminded him what it was like to work with a team. A bond had developed that he had not felt since his time as a Marine.

While his service in the Marines had been brief – just four years as a front-line grunt when he had basically still been a child – he remembered the camaraderie that he had felt with the members of his unit. He certainly hadn't liked everyone he served with, and had even hated a few of them, but there was still a connection with each of them. He hated to admit it, even to himself, but leaving the Alliance Marines hadn't been his choice. The drawdown after the war had sent many Marines home for good. After he had been discharged, he had felt cut off and without direction. After the war, spending his life in college or working in an office had sounded like a fate worse than death.

Shaking off the reminiscing, Zeric refocused on the job at hand. The war had ended, and he'd had no prospects. Mercenary work had kept him fed, and watching out for his own back had kept him alive.

Looking down at his watch, he saw that it was just a few minutes before 2:00 a.m. local. Deciding that was close enough, he pulled the wire cutters out of his bag and starting cutting a hole in the chain-link fence. With a few clips, he made a hole big enough to slip through, and he was inside.

When he had found this place, he had been suspicious of the complete lack of security. An entire field was covered with ships that Alliance forces had confiscated for various reasons. Many of the ships looked like they had been here for far too long. Zeric wondered what it said about the Alliance that they left these ships unguarded: that they were over-confident, or that they were neglectful of their property?

That last thought had helped him decide on this place. Since this was an impound lot, everything here was technically Alliance property. Using Alliance property to break prisoners out of an Alliance jail gave him a small sense of pleasure.

Creeping through the compound in the dark was harder than he had anticipated. He had counted on the darkness to help him stay concealed, but it was close to impeding his progress. As he was debating turning on his flashlight, he stumbled around the edge of a ship and saw his destination.

Towering above him was the dark shape of a YM-82 mining freighter. Extending in either direction from him for several hundred meters was the central cargo pod that the ship rested on. He had been told to find something that was big and sturdy and that no one would miss. A YM-82, designed to mine asteroids, was sturdy enough to withstand several hits from asteroid debris and large enough to fit a couple hundred people in the cargo pods, assuming they were empty.

Zeric slowly edged up to the ship, searching for an access hatch. The ship's hull was cold and hard, but it did not take him long to find a control panel. Opening the outer covering, Zeric looked over the panel in the dim light. He considered how best to proceed in hacking open the door, then decided to just try the door release key first. To his surprise, the panel lit up green and the ship beside him started rumbling.

He was amazed by his luck. The cargo door began lowering, revealing the cavernous interior of the ship. Zeric stepped into the center of three cargo pods. He discovered that this central chamber was isolated from the other two. The massive room extended across to an identical door on the other side of the ship, but was sealed off from either of the other two cargo bays. The walls were a dark reddish brown, which gave them the impression of rust -- at least, Zeric hoped it was just an illusion.

When the door opened, dim yellow lights in the ceiling of the pod came on. Zeric immediately began looking for the interior controls for the door. Not wanting to press his luck, he closed the door behind him and hoped the lights coming from inside had not caught anyone's attention.

On either side of the room were doors that appeared to be airlocks to the other two cargo pods. The doors made Zeric feel confident that the bays could be pressurized. That had been his main concern with this ship. Cargo pods designed to pick up space rocks might have been incapable of holding an atmosphere. If there were airlocks, then at least this pod must be capable of keeping people alive.

Beside the aft airlock was another door that Zeric discovered was an elevator. Stepping inside, he rode up to the crew decks of the ship. The elevator opened into a narrow corridor that ran along the spine of the ship. Trying to keep his orientation, Zeric turned left toward where he assumed the bridge would be located.

Zeric followed the corridor until he came to an intersection. To his left and right were more corridors. Picturing the ship in his head, he assumed those led to the port and starboard extensions that held the ship's mining lasers and tractor emplacements. Continuing forward, he passed several unmarked rooms until he came to a stairwell that led up and down.

Zeric thought that whoever had designed this ship had been terrible with labels. Assuming the bridge would be on the top deck, he climbed the stairs and was rewarded by emerging into a spacious control room. The stairs led up into the middle of the room so Zeric had to spin completely around to see the whole room.

Lining the aft walls were several control stations and holographic display tables. Zeric assumed those were for monitoring mining activities. He realized the ship must have a decent sensor array to track hundreds of asteroid pieces.

That might come in handy if they were pursued by Alliance craft.

Walking around the safety railing encompassing the stairwell, Zeric headed toward the control stations at the bow of the ship. There were three of them and one display terminal. When he examined the stations, he finally found some labels and was able to identify the one that controlled the ship's systems.

Hoping his luck held, he attempted to bring the ship's reactor back online. With only a little protest, the fusion reaction started up and his display came fully to life. The terminal started an automatic diagnosis and, after a minute, gave him a basic status report.

The ship's fuel reserves were at twenty-five percent, which worried him, but the hull appeared to be completely intact. There were no indications of any breaches, which meant the ship was spaceworthy. Life support was coming online and the stale air of the bridge was being replaced. The log indicated the ship had been here for quite some time, which suggested no one would come looking for it, but would also be problematic, as it meant all the navigation data was far out of date.

Once the diagnosis finished, the ship reported that all primary systems were online. A prompt came up asking if he wanted to run a check on secondary systems. Zeric looked at the estimated time to run and decided that that was not necessary. The longer he sat here, the greater the chance he would be discovered. They wouldn't be using any of the secondary systems, anyway. Getting up from the terminal, he moved over to the helm controls and spent a few minutes familiarizing himself with the layout.

Zeric did not consider himself an excellent pilot, but out of necessity, he had learned to handle most craft. *At least in basic operations*, he thought.

If he had to handle this ship in any tricky maneuvers, it might be difficult. But, for now, all he had to do was lift off and get out of the compound.

With slow and deliberate steps, Zeric powered up the engines.

The ground starting to shake was the first indication that something was coming. The rest of the group appeared nervous, but Maarkean knew that it meant there was a large ship approaching, and he tried to steady himself. It would not do to start showing signs of weakness to this bunch now that they were so close to their objective. He only hoped it was Zeric and not someone else.

Suddenly, the air started to blow furiously, and lights appeared from the sky. Above them stretched out a massive ship. They had laid out a set of flares to mark out a landing zone, but when they saw the ship, Maarkean realized that it wasn't going to be large enough. He started waving everyone back until he realized it was unnecessary, since they were all practically fleeing.

As the big ship dropped from the sky, Maarkean hoped the field itself would be big enough. When he had told Zeric to find a large enough ship, he had been doubtful the man would be able to. He had been expecting something like a mid-range passenger shuttle.

Maarkean was surprised that the sight of Zeric returning made him feel more secure. He did not trust the group of revolutionaries they had hooked up with. Glancing over at the motley group, he thought about how idealistic and inexperienced they were. Some of them actually thought that, in breaking prisoners out of jail, they were doing something noble, when, in truth, they were just rebellious criminals. Maarkean shook his head, knowing he deserved to rot in prison for what he was doing now. While, *if* it were true, he could sympathize with the injustice of innocent people being imprisoned, there were legal ways to address that. Attacking a government institution was the act of a traitor.

What surprised Maarkean was not that he didn't trust them but that he trusted Zeric more. The man had tried, not only once, but twice, to steal Maarkean's ship, and he was trying to break his criminal friends out of prison. Yet Maarkean understood those motives. Zeric did this out of loyalty to his friends. The others did it out of some idealistic bullshit and commitment to a rabble-rousing terrorist.

He reminded himself that this group claimed to have not actually done anything illegal until he had come along. By every indication he got from them, it appeared to be true. They were far too optimistic to have been participating in dozens of terrorist plots before. But their leader must have done *something* to have ended up in prison. He didn't buy the story that she was just a protester and a delegate to some congress.

With another sharp vibration of the ground, the large ship touched down. A cloud of choking dust filled the air, obscuring their view and irritating Maarkean's throat. After a minute, the dust settled, and he was able to see again. When Maarkean got a good look at the ship, his opinion of Zeric's abilities improved slightly. It was exactly what they would need, if a bit larger than he had expected.

The noise of the engines receded and Maarkean could hear again. The silence was conspicuous by its sharp contrast to the noise the engines had made. It was a good thing they had set their rendezvous so far out in the middle of nowhere.

The welcome silence was broken by the whirring mechanical sounds of a door on the side of the ship beginning to open. Maarkean started toward it and the others followed, carrying a tool chest for removing tracking anklets and a few crates of civilian clothes they had gathered for the prisoners to change into. The door opened up into a cavernous space. By the time the group climbed inside, Zeric emerged from a door along one wall.

The Terran smiled at the group, looking distinctly proud of himself. "Well, what do you think?"

Before Maarkean could speak, Lohcja said incredulously, "This is a hunk of junk. It's too big. It's a bloody freighter. We can't escape from Alliance patrols in this. And how will we land in the prison without crushing the whole place?"

"That's exactly the plan," Zeric said with a cocksure grin. "We crush the perimeter wall with this thing. Makes it easier to get inside."

That idea had not occurred to Maarkean, but it dealt with a hole in the plan he had not yet worked out. The weapons on the *Cutty Sark* would be adequate to take out the guard towers, but it would take some concentrated fire from them to break a hole in the prison's perimeter walls. This huge ship might do what Zeric was suggesting.

"He's right," Maarkean said. "This is perfect. Mining freighter, right?"

Zeric nodded and then pushed his ball cap up off his eyes as he patted the hull of the freighter. "Yep. Reinforced hull. This baby will be able to withstand quite a bit of punishment."

"I like it," Pasha said. This was surprising, given that the man had hardly said much since Maarkean had met him. If Pasha liked it, he was sure Jairyd would.

"She is a beast to fly," Zeric confessed, turning to Maarkean. "These cargo bays are big enough that the *Cutty Sark* could fit inside. Maybe you should be the one to fly her to the prison. You could take off from there."

Maarkean considered the idea, but he dismissed it quickly. "No, I'll need to be in the air running interference before you guys land. And the landing will be the trickiest part. Besides, those bays weren't designed as hangars. It would be an incredibly tight fit, and it would not be an easy launch and docking process. Certainly not something I'd want to do in combat."

Looking over the group, Maarkean wondered again about the stupidity of what they were about to attempt. If Saracasi's life wasn't on the line, he would just walk away right now.

"All right, we all know the plan. It's early evening at the prison, so it will be full dark by the time we arrive," Maarkean said, trying to sound confident. Then, in a rush of bravado, he said, "Let's go be heroes!"

With the exception of Zeric, who just raised a curious eyebrow, the platitude energized the others. Jairyd and Pasha gave a grunt of approval, grabbed their gear and headed toward the elevator door. More hesitantly, Ceta and Meyka followed. Lohcja nodded to Lahkaba, and then the Ronid turned to follow the rest. That left Maarkean and the Kowwok, Lahkaba, who would serve as Maarkean's gunner, alone in the cargo bay.

"You really think this will work?" Lahkaba asked, his voice betraying hesitation.

"It better," was all Maarkean could reply.

CHAPTER SIX

Saracasi smiled as she listened to Chavatwor. The Kowwok was well into the tenth minute of his speech – well, 'lecture' would be a more appropriate word. When he had started speaking, his normally timid nature had been replaced with an animated and excited flow.

When she had learned that Chavatwor had been a shipwright before coming to Olan, she had asked him about it. He had owned a starship repair shop where he made custom upgrades for ships. For wealthy clients, he had even had the chance to design a few custom ships from scratch.

Saracasi's undergraduate studies had been in starship engineering, and she had been considering an advanced degree in hyperspace theory. Despite having been close to graduation, she found that half of what Chavatwor said was over her head. The theories and formulas he had in his head, along with the specifications of countless ships and components, amazed her. She had learned more in the last ten minutes than she had in her entire last semester. Of course, then her attention had been on other things than school.

"Enough already!" Larin growled from the top bunk.

Chavatwor jumped visibly and Saracasi almost did the same. She had forgotten the other Kowwok had even been there. The occupants of the nearby beds were off in other parts of the small room. It had been oddly comforting to pretend for a brief time that it had just been her listening to Chavatwor with no one else around.

"Go jabber your techno-babble someplace else. Some of us are trying to get some sleep," Larin said angrily.

Chavatwor took Saracasi's arm and started to lead her down the aisle. "Don't worry about him. He gets like this sometimes when we haven't been allowed outside in a while. I can't really blame him. I feel it, too."

It had been three days since they had been let out of the barracks. Food had been brought to them in the form of boxed meals, so they had been denied even those brief sojourns outside. The others told her that the guards did this sometimes to mess with them. It was a way of preventing a routine and keeping the prisoners' spirits down.

Others took a different view. They declared that the fact that they were not being brought to the mess hall for food meant that the guards were short staffed and there were not enough personnel in the prison to adequately guard them all. Those who thought this suggested it would be an ideal time to attempt an escape. Luckily, not many were in this group, and it was made up mostly of relatively new arrivals.

Being trapped inside the building for three straight days was beginning to wear on even the calmest of the group. Most were snappish, like Larin, and a few scuffles had broken out. So far, Faide had managed to keep anything from escalating.

Gamaly appeared to be taking the situation the hardest. Her spirits had lifted somewhat when she had seen Zeric. She had been hoping to learn something about Gu'od from the other inmates during meals, but they had not been back to the mess hall since that first time. The lack of news had been wearing at the woman, and Saracasi wasn't sure how to help.

Part of her still wanted to be mad at Gamaly and blame her for the fact that she was in here. She had spent the first day avoiding the other woman. The second day, when it had become obvious that they were not going to get outside, Faide had organized some athletic games. The beds were pushed to the side. Everyone was broken up into teams, and Saracasi had ended up with Gamaly.

Competing together in what was ultimately a profoundly silly series of events had broken down any remaining resistance she had. Gamaly was just too likable, and the distress she felt about her husband made it impossible to view her as anything other than a person. She knew deep down that if they ever got out of here, they would have to deal with the past, but for the moment she put it aside.

She had spent most of the last few days getting to know the people of Building 15. Most were quiet people, and she could not hazard a guess as to why they had ended up in here. There were even a few families, which surprised Saracasi. Because of Gamaly, she had assumed most families were split up. One family of Ronids had been here for five years, and their son had spent almost all of his teenage years in prison.

When she was not meeting new people, Saracasi found herself spending a lot of her time with Asirzi. The young Liw'kel had been here for a couple years and was part of Faide's inner circle. She worked hard to help keep things calm and tempers down. Saracasi found herself more and more attracted to the woman, even beyond her initial impression of her beauty.

She tried to suppress these feelings. She had no idea how soon it would be before she was taken back to Braz, and she didn't want to become too close to anyone, emotionally or physically. Also, the building wasn't designed for privacy – although one of the bunks was pushed aside for a few hours each day and covered with blankets, and she had noticed a few of the couples slipping away to that bunk during those times. When she found herself wondering if it was first-come, first-served or if there was some kind of rotation in place, she decided to spend some time away from Asirzi.

To avoid those thoughts, she found herself with Chavatwor talking about starships. This was a topic that she found fascinating, and despite Larin's disapproval, she thought this would keep her occupied for a while. She and

Chavatwor made a few laps of the building and, while discussing hull design, found themselves near the building's entrance.

That was when the alarm sounded.

The old familiar anticipation before combat filled Maarkean. It had been sixteen years since he had last felt it. A cold sweat covered him as dread swirled around in his stomach. In the next few minutes, the fear would be wiped away, replaced by nothing but the focus required to stay alive. For now, though, his mind worked out every possible outcome that could occur, the majority of which involved his fiery death.

During the war with the Dotran, he had flown many sorties. The feelings had always been the same: dread before the battle, during the inevitable waiting period, and then sharp relief when adrenaline spiked, and utter calm once the battle began. Since the war, he had felt the sensations of combat before, such as when Zeric had attempted to steal the *Cutty Sark*. But all of those situations had been sudden and unexpected and had, consequently, spared him this period of anxiety. There was nothing like the build-up of emotions that came from intentionally planning to go into battle.

Looking over to his right, Maarkean considered his co-pilot. Lahkaba had engrossed himself in the ship's operations console. It was apparent that his shipboard experience was limited, though he was a quick learner. Operating the ship's systems was not why he was here, though.

"First time in combat?" Maarkean asked.

"No," Lahkaba said. "First time aboard a ship, though. I was in the Dotran infantry for a time."

"During the war?"

There was a pause before Lahkaba responded, "Yes."

In the war, Maarkean had flown against a number of adversaries, and he was sure at least some of them had been Kowwoks. It was a shock to realize that he was now sitting next to someone who had once been his enemy. And he was attacking representatives of his government with this former enemy.

Maarkean decided to meet the source of the tension head on. "Must be difficult fighting beside a former Alliance officer."

"No," Lahkaba replied. "I bear no grudge against the Alliance for the war. I only fought during the war because I was drafted. Despite what we are about to do, I prefer the Alliance over the Confederacy."

For the first time, Maarkean wondered how many of the Kowwoks he had fought in the war had been willing participants. The Kowwoks were technically members of the Dotran Confederacy, but unlike the Braz and Terrans, they were more like second-class citizens than equal members. They had been incorporated into the Confederacy centuries before, but had never really been assimilated into their society.

"If you'd rather live here than in the Confederacy," Maarkean asked, "then why fight the Alliance with your political group?"

"My home has always been Sulas. I fight the government's actions of imprisoning innocent people and treating them unfairly based on species. Up until now, our efforts have been peaceful. Our only consequences were harassment and brief arrests. I fight now to free people from unfair imprisonment. Like you do for your sister."

Maarkean had always been taught that the Alliance had its flaws but was better than any of the other governments out there. Despite his current associates, he still thought that those that came here to seek a better place and then complained when they arrived were ungrateful troublemakers. Saracasi had always argued with him that injustice was injustice, even if one injustice was not as bad as another. Now, that argument started to make some sense to him.

"I have the prison on my sensors," Lahkaba said, bringing Maarkean's attention back to the challenge at hand. He had almost forgotten his fears.

"Better get to the gun controls," Maarkean responded. "The fun's about to start."

Vibrations worked their way from the ship and up Zeric's body. The shaking was only one of many small distractions he was contending with. Ceta kept whimpering, and Lohcja kept unnecessarily calling out the distance to target every few seconds. He tried to tune all of those out and focus on the biggest distraction – the chillingly close ground.

The YM-82, while capable of sustained atmospheric flight, was not designed for it. Taking off and landing were about all you were supposed to do with something so massive. Flying at high speeds only a few hundred meters above the ground did not fit its design, but Maarkean had insisted on keeping the ships low to avoid orbital and planetary tracking stations.

Zeric understood that ground clutter would interfere with sensors, but he did not see why it mattered. No one would be tracking them until after they got to the prison; before then, they were just civilian transports. Only now they were civilian transports attempting to sneak around.

More importantly, he was all too aware of how easy it would be to go from confusing sensors by getting lost among ground clutter to becoming part of said ground clutter.

The first leg of the journey had been fairly easy. After departing their rendezvous location, they had flown to normal altitudes and headed east over the ocean. Although the prison was on the same continent, it was on the opposite side of it, and the continent was well populated. Going completely around the planet provided them the opportunity to approach from the coast.

The descent had been made over the ocean. Flying low had been easy over the smooth ocean surface. Once they had hit the east coast of the continent, the trouble had begun. Hills and trees provided abundant obstacles to be avoided. The freighter's controls were far from responsive. Zeric was sure that it would be easy to track them if anyone just followed the trail of decapitated trees.

"The *Cutty Sark* has reached the prison!" Lohcja called out from the operations station. "They have engaged the prison. One guard tower is in flames!"

The group around Zeric cheered. He attempted to ignore them as he struggled to gain altitude over a fast-approaching rise in the ground. Not for the first time, and he was sure not for the last time, he wished Maarkean had just killed him when they had first met.

"That's our cue," Jairyd said, his voice filled with excitement.

Lohcja stood up from the operations console and picked up his pistol, a cheap civilian stun weapon. Pasha inspected his weapon as he led the way down the stairs into the lower decks. Nervously, Ceta started to follow, but Jairyd stopped her.

"You don't have to go, you know," he said tenderly. Zeric was surprised at his tone, but he was forced to ignore it.

"Yes, I do," Ceta said defiantly. "You tried to keep me out of this from the start, but that is my sister down there."

Slowly, Jairyd stepped aside and let her descend the stairs. He gave a nod to Meyka, who had taken Lohcja's place, and then he looked in Zeric's direction. "We'll see you down there, then."

Trying to spare as little attention as possible, Zeric replied with a short, "Yep."

With Jairyd down the stairs, he was left alone on the bridge with Meyka. He did not understand the woman. She had refused to participate in violence, yet Lahkaba had managed to convince her to accompany them on this mission. Granted, she had refused to participate in the infiltration of the prison, but Zeric preferred having someone stay behind to keep the ship warm anyway. He just hoped her pacifism didn't extend to letting them get killed.

Suddenly the prison leapt into view as he cleared the trees and entered the open plain that contained it. It was lit like a beacon by bright white security lights and crackling, orange-red fires coming off the towers.

Lohcja's initial scan had indicated one of the towers had been hit. Zeric's visual scan showed more than that. Meyka confirmed it when she declared that four of the six towers had already been damaged. She said that the *Cutty Sark* was coming in for another pass on the east side of the prison.

"All right, then we're coming in on the west side." It had not been planned in advance, but Zeric assumed Maarkean had cleared the west side first and was now engaging the east so that Zeric would have a clear landing spot. West had been where Gamaly had indicated she and Saracasi were being held.

Covering the remaining distance to the prison quickly, Zeric slowed the freighter down as he went. Slowing down over a hundred thousand tons of freighter did not happen quickly. For the first time, Zeric was glad they were in an atmosphere, as the gravity and air friction were finally helping him do what he wanted to do.

Switching off the engines and going to thrusters and anti-grav fields, Zeric used the ship's remaining momentum to drift into position over the prison's west wall, which he fervently hoped had no one inside. Feeling that this situation required somewhat less care than he would normally take in a landing, Zeric let gravity do most of the work of pulling the ship's mass down onto the wall.

The shudder that ran through the ship, combined with the sound of cracking concrete and screeching metal, was greater than anything they had experienced during the flight. In hindsight, he considered whether the fall might cause some damage to the ship. He wondered how much faith he could place in the reinforced hull.

After another shudder and a slight shift to port, the ship came to a complete stop. The sound of tumbling debris continued for another few moments, and then silence fell. They were slanted to port a few degrees, but that was nothing that should interfere with movement. He hoped that the rubble would not prove a hindrance to exiting or entering the cargo bays.

Putting the engines into standby, Zeric removed himself from the helm and dashed to the stairs off the bridge. He gave a perfunctory word of encouragement to Meyka as he left. Taking the stairs two at a time, he turned the corner at the landing and propelled himself down the second set and into the corridor.

By the time he reached the elevator leading into the cargo bay, he welcomed the break.

The door to the elevator opened, and Zeric drew his pistol. As soon as he emerged, the high-pitched screams of weapon fire filled his ears. The night had an eerie glow of twilight, with buildings cast in darkness and backlit by fires. Building faces were briefly illuminated by the flashes from weapon blasts. The pungent smell of smoke filled the air, but it was not thick enough to interfere with the air quality.

Keeping low, he hugged the bulkhead of the cargo bay and headed for the open bay door. Peering out, he saw the remains of the prison wall littering the short distance from the ship to another building. The building itself had most of the facing wall collapsed. *Damn*, he thought. He hadn't meant to catch any other structures in his awkward landing.

He caught a quick glimpse of Pasha as he disappeared around the side of the building and considered his choices.

He could follow Pasha or head into the collapsed building. According to the map of the prison, it should be a prisoner barracks. He hoped not too many people had been hurt.

On the other hand, despite the claims that all of the prisoners were innocent political prisoners, Zeric was hesitant to go in alone. Gu'od and Gamaly were prisoners as well. While they were certainly dangerous in the right circumstances, they were not inherently violent. But they were criminals. He was sure there were more than a few real criminals who were far more violent inside this prison.

Hoping he wasn't going to regret this, Zeric headed for the building. Gamaly had said they were being kept on the west side, and he had come here for a purpose. Climbing over the rubble, Zeric peered into the hole in the side of the building. It was obscured by dust; the first things he perceived were sounds of coughing and a baby wailing.

"Everyone okay in there?" Zeric called.

"No," a voice replied. "There are many injured. I think some may be trapped under the rubble."

Zeric cursed the luck, but he knew he should have expected that when he saw the damage. "Get everyone who can walk up out of the building. There is a ship behind me where the wall used to be. Get everyone aboard."

"Who are you?"

"That doesn't matter. But I'm here to get you out; now move! Once everyone who can move is out, see if you can help anyone trapped under the rubble. But don't take too long. We can't risk sticking around, or no one's going to be getting out of here."

Zeric started scrambling back down the rubble again, knowing he couldn't afford to wait for a reply. He headed around the opposite side of the building that the others had taken. Ahead of him, he saw the remains of a fence and then another building similar to this one. People were already starting to stream out of it, so he assumed the others had gotten to them first.

Moving past the group of buildings, he headed toward another fenced-in area. These buildings were less affected by the damage, but the fence and one building wall were still down. Dashing between the twisted remains of the fence, he headed for the open courtyard in the middle of three buildings.

Once there, he surveyed the scene and was pleased to find no guards waiting for him. Moving fast, he went to the building that had lost part of its back wall and shot the door a few times. It swung open after the third blast, and he pushed it and went inside. The room was filled with dust, like the previous one, but this time he could clearly see the occupants. He quickly informed them about the freighter and then headed toward the next building.

He cleared the remaining two buildings off the courtyard in the same manner and headed toward the last set of buildings on this side of the prison. This trio was far enough away to have only been showered with debris. The building's walls and fence were all still intact.

Holstering his pistol, Zeric took the wire cutters out from his belt pouch and began cutting the chain links as quickly as he could. He took the time to cut a wide opening completely out, instead of just a sliver to slip through. This way, the prisoners could use the hole as a direct line toward the freighter. Once the fence piece fell free with a rattle, he headed toward the buildings.

Clearing the first two buildings went quickly, but on the third, he was stopped by a voice. "Zeric?"

Looking over the group in the building, he spotted the blue-skinned figure of Gamaly. Relief overtook him, and he fought through the fleeing group toward her. They embraced, and then he looked around for Gu'od. Not seeing him, he asked the obvious question.

Clearly upset, Gamaly replied, "I have no idea. I haven't seen him since my first day here."

Zeric cursed to himself again. "Well, we're freeing everyone. He must be with one of the other groups."

Zeric watched the crowd flow out and examined the few people who remained beside him and Gamaly. Recognizing Saracasi from their brief meeting, he was surprised that she seemed concerned for Gamaly. Beside her stood another Liw'kel female, an older Notha male, and a Kowwok male.

"Where's Maarkean?" Saracasi demanded, pushing past the others toward him.

"He's flying cover in the *Cutty Sark*, don't worry. This was his idea," Zeric hastily replied.

"It was what?" she replied more quietly. He didn't expect the look of shock that covered her face.

"We need to get all of you to the ship," Zeric said, trying to move things along.

"You are trying to clear the entire prison?" the Notha asked. "It is very big. Let us help you."

Zeric considered the elderly Notha. "We've got people already on that."

"We can help," the Notha insisted. "You can clear the way while we talk to the people."

Not wanting to waste any more time, Zeric nodded.

"Gamaly, you and Saracasi get to the ship. Gu is probably already there waiting for you."

She shook her head stubbornly. "I'm going with you."

"Me, too," Saracasi said determinedly. That took him aback. At their first meeting, he had taken Saracasi for someone without a lot of backbone. He should have known she would take after her brother.

"Fine," he said, rolling his eyes skyward. "But let's *move*."

Zeric led the small group out of the now empty building and toward the gate that opened into the central building of the prison. Not wasting any more time with the wire cutters, Zeric blasted the locked courtyard gate that led to the inner building and pushed it open. It took a few more shots to blast out the lock on the sturdier interior door.

"All right, since you're here, which way?" Zeric asked.

Upon entering the building, Faide took the lead in moving them through the building. Saracasi kept watch from the group's rear.

When they turned a corner and came face to face with a group of prison guards, Asirzi let out a fearful scream. Zeric didn't hesitate; he fired his pistol, taking them each out in quick succession. Picking up the guards' fallen weapons, Zeric handed one to Gamaly and attempted to hand one to Faide. The Notha refused the gun, and Zeric handed it to Chavatwor.

Saracasi laid a reassuring hand on Asirzi's arm; it seemed to calm her and she stopped hyperventilating. Faide nodded approvingly at her, and the group continued. Asirzi grasped Saracasi's hand and refused to let it go as they proceeded.

Several turns later, Saracasi was completely lost. She had only come into the building before for that one meal. With the power out, the building was lit only by the light coming in from the crackling fires outside. In the distance, there were the sounds of weapon fire and an occasional explosion. The whole experience had a surreal feeling.

Faide came to a halt in front of a set of heavy metal doors. He gestured to them. "You may find your friend in here. This is the isolation ward. If he was not released to the general population, he will have been kept here."

A glimmer of hope appeared on Gamaly's face as Zeric fired at the door. It took repeated blasts, but eventually the lock weakened, and they were able to pry the door open. Inside was a small cluster of cells along a short corridor. Zeric went down the row, blasting each cell's door. A handful of people stumbled out, but none of them were Liw'kel.

Gamaly appeared to be on the verge of despair, but Faide laid a gentle hand on her back. "This is a good sign. It means he was released before now. He must be with one of the other groups."

Nodding with grim determination, Gamaly turned and started leading the group deeper into the building. The group struggled to keep up. When they came across two more guards, Saracasi was startled and impressed by the speed with which Gamaly took both of them down.

Scooping up the guards' weapons, Zeric handed one to Saracasi and one to Asirzi. Saracasi was not particularly good with blasters, but she knew how to use them. She checked the safety and the weapon charge. She was unsurprised to see that the guards had not set it to stun. It took her a moment to decide, but she changed the setting.

Asirzi was clearly unfamiliar with weapons, so Saracasi pointed out the prominent features. The woman appeared relieved to learn of the stun and safety settings. Following as quickly as they could, they took turns watching the group's back.

They made their way out of the building before they encountered any more resistance. After exiting a door leading to another courtyard, shots started raining down at them from atop the east wall. Zeric rushed them all back inside the building. Saracasi peeked out the door and was dismayed at what she saw.

The courtyard had apparently already been reached by whoever had come with Zeric. She could see that the barrack doors were open. She also saw that the courtyard was filled with bodies. From up on the wall, the prison guards were shooting at anything that moved in the courtyard.

"We've got to take out those guards if those people are going to be able to get out," Faide said reluctantly. He sounded distressed at the inevitable violent outcome.

"Gamaly and I will head out there and break to the sides for cover against the buildings. The rest of you provide us with some covering fire. Stun won't work at this range, so you'll need to switch to full," Zeric said.

Saracasi had never considered herself a pacifist. She recognized that violence was necessary in certain situations. Despite that, the idea of keeping her weapon on stun had appealed to her. Switching the setting, she nodded to Zeric and took a position beside the door. Chavatwor moved to the opposite side, and Asirzi nervously took a position beside her.

Zeric looked to Gamaly, and the two shared a look. Saracasi had heard Maarkean talk about the bond that developed between people in combat. Now she thought she had an inkling of how much she had underestimated that connection. After a moment, they turned toward the door, and Zeric said they were ready.

Taking a deep breath, Saracasi stepped out from around the door and started firing. Her shots were wild, but they were aimed generally up at the wall. The shots from Asirzi, Faide and Chavatwor didn't appear to be any better aimed. Surprisingly, it appeared to be working, as the dim shapes of the guards on the wall dropped from view.

Charging out, Zeric and Gamaly ran through the fence gate and split toward opposite sides of the courtyard. Once they reached the protection of the walls, Saracasi stopped firing and moved back to safety. Chavatwor and Faide stopped a second later, but Asirzi continued firing, screaming wildly.

After several more seconds, her pistol stopping firing and made an artificial clicking noise, indicating that it was out of charge. Asirzi was looking down at the weapon, confused, when she suddenly fell backwards, letting out a howl of pain.

Desperately, Saracasi tried to reach out to her fallen friend, but the space between them filled with deadly shots. Chavatwor and Faide reached their guns around the door and fired wildly back up at the wall. The barrage slackened slightly, and Saracasi found enough courage to go out into it.

Lunging out from the safety of the wall, Saracasi grabbed Asirzi's arm and dragged the woman out from the open and to the side with her. The woman was covered in blood and shrapnel from the floor and wall. Panic swelled up inside Saracasi and threatened to overwhelm her.

From the look of Asirzi, Saracasi did not think she could still be alive. She had no idea how to treat blaster shots. Reverting back to instinct, Saracasi recalled the childhood Braz meditations her parents had taught her. She took in a deep breath and slowly let it out. She did it again and pushed her worry out with the air.

Recovering a modicum of self-awareness, she examined Asirzi. She recalled from biology classes that most bipedal species shared similar physiology, which included blood flow. Terrans and Braz were alike in that they both had a pulse at the neck and a heart in the chest, though not in precisely the same spots. She hoped Liw'kel were the same.

Fumbling around the woman's neck, Saracasi tried to find a pulse. Panic started to overcome her again when she found nothing but wet blood. Finally, after nearly giving up, she felt something. It wasn't a pulse, but there was air coming out of Asirzi's mouth. She was breathing.

Relief flooded her, and Saracasi went to what she thought should be the next step: stopping the blood flow. She looked over the body, finding several bleeding lacerations, but nothing serious. The blaster shot that must have brought her down had made a wound that had replaced what had been the woman's right breast. The blaster shot had cauterized the wound and very little blood was coming out.

The blood pool on the floor was still growing, so Saracasi continued her search. She found a deep cut across the inner side of Asirzi's right forearm. Blood was pumping out at an incredible pace. The wound was not burned at all, so it must have been caused by shrapnel as she lay under the barrage.

Saracasi tore off her jumpsuit's arm and feebly tried to use it as a tourniquet. The blood flow instantly soaked the fabric, but she kept trying. Engrossed as she was, she almost didn't notice Chavatwor's desperate shouts.

After getting the knot secured, she looked over to the Kowwok and saw him firing his blaster in her direction. Instinctively, she ducked her head and looked toward where he was firing. Two guards were trying to make their way down the corridor and returning fire at the Kowwok.

She looked around for where she had dropped her weapon and found it a meter away, against the wall. Just as she was about to lunge for it, the ground shook. The walls and ceiling rattled and dust spilled down on her from above. Coughing, she resumed her reach for the gun.

The guards had paused when the building started shaking, but now they were advancing again. She heard the distinctive click of Chavatwor's gun going dry, and she realized there was no longer anything stopping the guards. Flailing, she lunged for the gun.

Rolling over onto her back, she raised the weapon. As she prepared to fire, the guards suddenly collapsed. For a moment, she wondered if she had managed to fire without realizing it, but after a second, she saw another figure approach and stand over the guards.

As the dust settled, she recognized the Liw'kel from her first day at the prison. Gu'od looked more haggard than she remembered. His tan skin was taut around his face and bore bluish discoloration from bruising. She was amazed how different he looked after just the few days she had been here.

Moving quickly, he stepped over the downed figures of the guards and came to her side. He looked down at Asirzi and his face became visibly relieved – Saracasi could only guess he was glad it wasn't Gamaly. After a second, the relief was replaced with guilt and concern. "Is she all right?"

Shaking her head, Saracasi replied, "I don't know. I think I slowed the bleeding, but she's hurt pretty bad."

"Then we should get her to the ship that landed," he said. He bent over and gingerly picked her up.

"We've got to help those people get out of the barracks," Saracasi said. "Gamaly is pinned down by the guards on the wall."

With a sharp jerk of his head, Gu'od turned and looked toward the doorway. He started to rise and head out the door, but stopped at a sound from Chavatwor.

"Great One, protect us," Chavatwor gasped behind her. "The guards on the wall won't be a problem anymore." He was staring out of the open door with a dumbfounded expression. Saracasi stepped from behind her cover and followed his eyes. The top of the perimeter wall, where the guards had been firing from, was decimated.

Streaming in from the barracks was a swarm of people. Gu'od looked forlornly out at the stream, as if wanting to push past them and find his wife, but turned and picked up Asirzi. "She needs help and will get trampled by the crowd if we don't get her back to the ship."

Deciding Gu'od was right, Saracasi turned and led the way back through the building.

CHAPTER SEVEN

Watching the wall explode and the blast consume the prison guards did not fill Maarkean with remorse or sadness. He knew what he and Lahkaba were doing was terrible and many people were dying because of it. The remorse would come later. Right now, those people were the enemy, and it was his job to kill them.

Lahkaba's shooting had been impressive so far. The first few passes had resulted in more misses than hits, but when their goal was only to cause chaos in the prison, that didn't really matter. The white Kowwok had gotten better with each pass Maarkean took over the prison. Their last had taken out a collection of guards who were pinning down some prisoners from escaping their barracks.

"Nice shooting," Maarkean called back.

"Thanks," Lahkaba replied.

"I think that's most of the guards on the walls. From what I could see, the guards were either dead or injured, or have fled inside," Maarkean said as he did a slower fly-over of the prison. All of the fire that had been coming at them from the ground had stopped, and from the air he could only see a little movement in the darkness.

Lahkaba disengaged himself from the turret controls and moved back to the operations station. While both the pilot and gunners had some limited sensor controls, performing detailed scans required him to have access to the operation controls. The *Cutty Sark* was perfectly capable of being flown by one or two people, but for a true combat situation, she would be better served with a full crew of four: a pilot, a gunner, an operations crewman and an engineer to handle damage.

"Sky still looks clear," Lahkaba declared, after performing a sensor sweep. The ship's sensors were not top of the line. If anyone was approaching in the same manner that they had used, flying low over the ground, they probably wouldn't spot it. They were counting on any resistance to be obvious.

Maarkean activated the communication system and said, "Ground team, this is your air cover. What is your status?"

They had not decided on a call sign system before the operation, but Maarkean felt better not using anyone's name over an open frequency. If they were lucky, they would be able to keep all of their identities safe from the authorities. But that was unlikely, and he was already trying to figure out how to change the ship's transponder codes.

"Air cover, this is transport." The sound of Meyka's voice came nervously over the speaker. "No contact with the ground team yet."

Communication had been a hole in their plan. Maarkean had advocated for everyone to keep an open channel on their personal communicators. The others had declared it too risky, afraid it would allow them to be identified. While he agreed with the sentiment, their decision left them unable to communicate with the infiltration team.

"How are the passengers?" Lahkaba asked.

"We're filling up fast. This could prove taxing on the life support systems."

The life support systems aboard the freighter had been another potentially major flaw in their escape plan. Since no one knew exactly how many people they would be able to get out of the prison, they could only guess at how many people would have to breathe the freighter's air supply. While the cargo bays could be pressurized, they were not designed for passenger transport.

"Start running some calculations. Better find out now instead of halfway to the rendezvous point."

"Air, this is infiltration team." A new voice joined the conversation. Maarkean believed the voice to belong to Zeric.

"Good to hear you," Maarkean said. Zeric must have decided to risk using his communicator. Of all of the people involved, he was the only one who was already wanted under his real name.

"We've cleared the last barracks and are moving toward the ship. Sis and Mrs. G. secured. No word on Mr. G. or the leader. I've met up with P. and L. No word on J. or C. We'll be back at the ship within five minutes."

"Roger that, ground. Let us know when you're ready to depart."

Maarkean took the ship into a lazy circular orbit of the prison. There had been no new activity from the prison guards, but he doubted that most of them had been subdued. With a prison this full, the handful he had taken out from the air could only be a fraction of the total.

The operations panel began to emit an alarm sound. Lahkaba looked over it for a moment, trying to figure out the source of the alarm. When he did, he spoke with a worried voice. "We just picked up two incoming craft. Unidentified, but they are coming in fast and from the direction of the Ciread air station."

"How long?" Maarkean asked.

"Three minutes. They'll be here before the transport can launch."

Even though he had planned for it, this news worried him. If the fighters got too close, they would be able to disable the freighter before it could take off. Maarkean was faced with a choice. He could intercept the fighters and attempt to stop them, but that would leave those on the ground without cover if the prison guards made another push.

Keying the comm back to Zeric's frequency, Maarkean spoke. "Ground team, we've got incoming craft. We're moving to intercept. You'll be on your own for the final leg."

"Acknowledged. Good hunting."

Maarkean debated saying something to tell Saracasi in case he didn't survive the confrontation, but decided against it. There was nothing he could say that would matter, especially coming through a complete stranger. Instead, he closed the comm and turned the ship in the direction of the incoming fighters.

Until Maarkean had taken out the guards on the wall, Zeric had been sure he was done for. Getting out of the main building to a position behind one of the barracks had been a close enough call. When he saw the Liw'kel go down and the Kowwok run out of ammo, he knew their support was done. He and Gamaly, forced to switch their guns to the lethal setting for more range, had tried to fire some shots up at the wall, but neither of them had a very good angle.

The sounds of the *Cutty Sark* slashing through the air and her turret blasting the wall had been magical. Once the dust had cleared, he had wasted no time in getting the people out of the barracks. Needing no encouragement, the prisoners had swarmed out and headed into the main building. When he had gotten back inside, the Kowwok that had followed them had told them Saracasi had taken Asirzi – the Liw'kel, he assumed – back to the ship. With this set of buildings cleared, he had led their remaining group to the next set.

They had run into Lohcja and Pasha there and were pleased to learn that all of the buildings on this side of the complex were clear. Jairyd and Ceta had taken the rest on the other side, so the group had headed back across to look for him. That was when Maarkean informed him they had lost their air support. The guards must have been listening, or just lucky, because it was at that point that they became pinned down again.

Just after they exited a building, a group of guards came up behind them, from inside the building. They split to the outside of the doors, and Lohcja took a grazing shot to his arm; it was a small miracle that was the only injury. The guards were no longer using stun shots either.

The security fence hemmed them into a narrow alley directly in the path of the guards' field of fire through the door. They had nowhere to go.

"Looks like a standoff," Gamaly shouted. She, along with Lohcja, was caught on the opposite side of the doorway from Zeric and Pasha.

"Yeah," Zeric replied. "I'll cut through the fence and then toss the cutters to you."

"No good," Pasha growled. "Once we start running, the guards will swarm out from inside and shoot us in the back. Right now, if they come out, we've got them. If we move, they've got us."

Zeric considered his point. "Yeah, but there's nothing stopping them from coming around from another door and surrounding us. If we stay here, we're dead."

Pasha nodded. "Yeah, a standoff. But we're on the side with the disadvantage. Only thing to do is change the rules."

Without any further warning, Pasha stepped into the doorway and started firing wildly at the guards inside the building. There were surprised shouts from inside, a few screams of pain and then a barrage of return fire. Miraculously, the first barrage went all around Pasha, and he continued advancing. Then the next wave started.

Zeric noticed that the shots from the second barrage were fewer than there had been previously, and he decided to take the same chance. Just as the first shots began to strike Pasha, and he dropped to the ground, Zeric came out and started firing. Lohcja, despite his already injured arm, joined him, and so did Gamaly.

After the furious exchange of fire, there were no more guards standing inside the door. Zeric saw a few limp bodies, but he wasn't sure if any had escaped back around the nearest bend in the corridor. Not wanting to find out, he holstered his weapon and bent to pick up Pasha; amazingly, he was the only one who had taken any major wounds.

Hauling the unconscious man in a firefighter's carry, Zeric started moving as fast as he could back toward the ship. Limping behind him, Gamaly and Lohcja alternated between following and covering their retreat. Pasha proved heavier than he had expected, and it was a struggle for Zeric to keep moving. Luck proved to be with him because, as they got closer, some of the people aboard the ship saw them and rushed out to help.

With relief, Zeric handed Pasha over to two people and then drew his pistol again. Guards had appeared in the doorway again and were exchanging fire with Lohcja and Gamaly. He added his fire to the mix, but there was a fair distance between them and the guards. They were able to quickly get out of the guards' line of sight by moving next to the rear building, and from there they had a clear path toward the ship.

Reaching the ship's cargo bay, Zeric was shocked at the number of passengers they had taken on. The massive cargo bay was standing room only; it made him wish the other two bays could be pressurized to give them more space. Despite the crowd, one face stood out: Gu'od's. Gamaly squealed and ran ahead into his arms.

The sight of his friend filled Zeric with relief. During the entire operation, he had feared that Gu'od had been locked away somewhere they wouldn't find him. The idea of coming here, rescuing all of these people and not finding him was unsettling. He was sure that same idea had occurred to the rest of their band about their leader, Lei-mey. So far, there had been no sign of her.

Pulling out his comm unit, he called up to Meyka, "Any word from our other friends?"

"No. But our air support just met the fighters."

Maarkean's mind cleared itself of all thoughts. There was nothing he had to consciously do; his training had made it automatic. His focus zeroed in on the incoming fighter craft and how he was going to beat them. He had not been in fighter combat for sixteen years, but the training was well ingrained.

"How do we approach this?" Lahkaba asked nervously. He was still at the operations console, tracking the fighters until they got close enough for the gun's targeting sensors to take over.

"We come at them from below and hope they don't see us. Then we try hit-and-run tactics," Maarkean said, reviewing options in his head. "Those are AI-91's, at least 20 years old. Good fighters. But designed primarily for atmospheric flight. They are far more aerodynamic than we are and can fly circles around us. But their engines don't have the thrust capacity ours do."

Diving the ship as low as he dared, Maarkean accelerated. Not waiting for further explanation, Lahkaba got up and went to the weapons console. He reacquainted himself with the controls, and then he waited for the fighters to appear on his shorter range targeting sensors.

Despite steeling himself for the coming engagement, Maarkean felt a sliver of regret slice through his internal block. The sudden realization hit him that he was about to shoot down Alliance pilots. Despite the years that had gone by, he still considered himself one of them. Some of the older pilots in his squadron had had kids. Those kids could be old enough now to have followed in their parents' footsteps. For all he knew, he was about to shoot down the kid of one of his squadron buddies.

Guilt started to overcome him, and his focus slipped from the controls. The ship started bucking as it fought against gravity. Treetops were sacrificed as he dipped low enough to scrape them. Shooting at the prison guards had been bad enough. They at least had targeted the walls, just trying to remove their vantage points. He knew they had killed some, but they had all been indirect killings. Now he was about to go into direct combat with two Alliance fighters.

A further horror stuck him. Up until a few years ago, he had flown with the Reserves. These were the older craft typically used by the Reserves. He might even be about to engage people he knew and had flown with.

Taking in a deep breath, Maarkean focused on a Braz meditation technique. He tried to grab all of the thoughts of guilt and what ifs in his mind, bunch them together and expel them out with his next breath. It was a dangerous thing to attempt while flying perilously close to the ground, but if he didn't, there was no way he would be able to engage the fighters. And if the fighters got past them, the freighter was defenseless.

Releasing his breath and all of the stray thoughts, Maarkean felt calm return. Lahkaba called out a warning that the fighters were about to come into weapon range. Keeping the ship level with the ground, he waited for the fighters to appear in the sky.

"Lah," Maarkean said quietly, using the Kowwok's familiar name, "try to disable them if you can."

Knowing that was the only thing he could do for the two pilots, he pulled back on the controls and the *Cutty Sark* began rising at a steep angle. They were on course to fly directly between the two craft. As soon as their ascent began, he heard Lahkaba mumble something about the 'Great One' and then start firing the turret. Energy blasts streaked up ahead of them.

The improvement Lahkaba had gained with targeting the weapon at a stationary ground position was not translating over to shooting moving ships. Golden blaster shots were going all over the place around the fighters. By pure chance, one of the shots impacted the right fighter's engine mount and smoke began streaming out of the craft.

The *Cutty Sark* flashed rapidly between the two craft just as the right fighter started drifting out of formation. The smoke from the engine momentarily obscured Maarkean's view before they passed it. He let them continue for several seconds before beginning a sloping turn back toward the fighters.

"That didn't take much," Lahkaba said unexpectedly.

"They didn't have their shields up. We caught them by surprise," Maarkean said impassively. "The other one won't be as easy."

Directing the ship back the way they had come, Maarkean watched as the damaged fighter disengaged. Relief threatened to break through his calm shell as he saw that the pilot should make it back safely, or at least have enough time to eject. Focusing on the remaining fighter, he tried to anticipate its next move.

Putting himself in the other pilot's place, he tried to consider what he would do. Faced with a larger, faster but less maneuverable craft, and no wingman, how would he engage? Being designed for atmospheric combat, the AI-91 was best served keeping out of his line of fire. With a dorsal turret that gave him a 360-degree line of fire along one plane and 180 along another, Maarkean had only one line of attack: from below.

"Get ready," Maarkean said. "Just before we pass, he is going to pull back on his brakes so that he'll slow and end up beneath us with his nose pointed at us as we pass. Just as he does, I'm going to roll us so you have a shot."

"Okay," Lahkaba said skeptically.

Despite Lahkaba's doubts, Maarkean was confident in what was going to happen. At the last possible second, so as to not give any hint of his intentions to the other pilot, Maarkean rolled the ship. The ground on the horizon rotated, threatening to overcome his sense of direction, as the artificial gravity of the ship worked in the opposite direction from the planetary gravity. He remained firmly in his seat with the ground above his head.

Seated away from the front windshield, Lahkaba was oblivious to the change of direction, aside from the sensor data. As soon as the ship started rotating, Lahkaba began firing at the fighter, as the two craft twirled in a dance of death. Maarkean felt the impact shudder through the ship as the fighter's weapons found them.

Pulling back, Maarkean angled the nose of the ship down toward the planet so that the turret remained centered on the fighter. The shudders continued and then were replaced by much more massive shaking. The fighter exploded and buffeted the *Cutty Sark* with a shock wave that almost caused Maarkean to lose control.

Continuing the turn, Maarkean looped the ship around the explosion and then back up toward the sky. The whole encounter had taken a matter of seconds, but had felt like hours. Adrenaline surged through his system, and he felt more alive than he had in a long time.

Looking over his sensor board, he saw no further contacts, but his display was limited. "Get back over to ops. We need to know what kind of damage we took and how close the next wave is."

The shield indicator showed that their strength had been depleted, but that was a necessary side effect of absorbing weapon fire. There were no warning alarms or red lights, which led Maarkean to hope they had escaped any serious damage. Testing the controls as he flew back in the direction of the prison, he noticed there was a slight difficulty in turning to starboard.

Confirming his suspicion, Lahkaba said, "Shields down to 50% strength but regenerating. No major problems, but it looks like a port RCS cluster sustained some damage."

"We can live without that. Anything up in the air?"

"Not at the moment. I doubt that will last long," Lahkaba replied. "Wait, I am reading more signals."

"Comm the freighter and let them know they need to take off now."

A moment went by, and then Lahkaba cursed. "Looks like our transmitter is out, too. We can't communicate with the freighter."

A heavy decision weighed on Zeric. The flow of prisoners back to the ship had stopped. Maarkean was engaged with Alliance fighters. Several people were severely injured and close to death. But Jairyd and Ceta were not back yet.

What was more, no one had been able to find Lei-mey. Lohcja was the only one of their cell on his feet, and even he was injured. Lei-mey was known among the prisoners, and none of them had seen her. Some were from her barracks, and they reported having heard weapon fire behind them as they ran.

The old admonition, "never leave a man behind," conflicted with the logic of saving as many as possible. He was not actually sure the others would let him leave without Lei-mey; she had been the reason they had come along. But he knew that if they didn't leave soon, they wouldn't be leaving at all.

With Gu'od and Gamaly now here, he knew, if he had to, he could force the issue. Lohcja and Pasha were not in fighting shape, and Meyka would not fight. He didn't want it to come to that, because he really wasn't sure which side the crowd would come down on. As well known as Lei-mey was, he just hoped their desire for freedom was foremost on their minds.

As he was preparing himself to make the call to leave, a voice broke through the din of the crowd. He turned and saw a small group of people hobbling along from the north. He recognized Ceta's voice calling to him before he could make her out in the crowd.

Zeric turned and directed some of the prisoners who had managed to arm themselves, along with others who were in good shape, to go and assist the incoming group. Most of those approaching appeared to be injured. Ceta stumbled along, helping a Ronid woman walk. The group from the ship swarmed over them just as the sounds of weapon fire sounded behind them.

Deciding there was no more time for waiting, he spoke to Gamaly and Gu'od. "Get those people aboard. We're taking off as soon as they're inside."

Turning back to wade through the crowded hangar deck, he pulled out his comm device again. "Meyka, unlock the lift; I'm coming up."

As he reached the lift, he was stopped by a hand on his arm. He turned to see Saracasi, who said, "We have a lot of wounded. Is there some place on the ship we can take them? It's pretty crowded down here."

He considered the woman for a second. They had locked down the elevator to prevent the panicked prisoners from swarming the ship's interior. With so many people, they couldn't risk someone accidentally breaking something. But he knew Saracasi had a point. He had seen the condition Pasha was in, and the Liw'kel who had been with them couldn't be much better.

"All right," he conceded. "Take the seriously injured to the crew quarters on the main deck. Try to keep most people down here and everyone off of the bridge and out of the engine room. And try to find a doctor."

"We already have," Saracasi said, gesturing to a blue-carapaced Ronid, who was kneeling over Pasha. Zeric tried to consider himself open to all species, but the thought of the clammy hands of a Ronid tending to him when he was injured made him shiver.

Nodding to Saracasi, Zeric stepped aboard the elevator and rode up to the crew deck. Dashing down the spine of the ship, he climbed up to the bridge deck. He found Meyka sitting at one of the forward control stations. She had a headset on and looked nervous.

"Freighter to *Cutty Sark*. Maarkean, Lahkaba come in. Please."

"Watch the names!" Zeric shouted as soon as he realized what she was doing.

Meyka jumped and nearly came out of her seat. She let out a sigh of relief when she recognized him. She hit a control on the console and then moved the headset off one ear.

"They engaged the fighters a few minutes ago. I saw one ship break away and head back for Ciread. But then the remaining ships flew in real close, and one disappeared off the sensors. There's just one signal out there, and it's headed for us. I haven't been able to get a response, and I don't know how to tell one ship from another."

Moving up beside her, Zeric gave the console an inspection. The screen clearly showed the approaching craft. The distance was closing fast. Zeric ran the sequence to read the transponder. He was delighted when the query returned a civilian result.

"See this?" Zeric asked, pointing to the screen. "That's their transponder. It identifies who they are. Without a database, you won't know exactly what ship it is, but these letters here identify it as a light transport craft. Military craft have encoded transponders so you can't identify one ship from another, but they clearly reveal themselves as military with the ANS prefix. ANS is Alliance Naval Ship."

Zeric waited for Meyka to nod her understanding before moving to the helm controls. He hadn't really wanted to give a lesson in ship identification right at that moment, but he needed Meyka to be able to pick out threats from non-threats. It wouldn't do them much good if they ran from a civilian freighter and headed right into a destroyer.

"Open the ship's internal comm to the cargo bay," Zeric said as he powered up the engines from standby. Based on the rate they were warming up, he was glad he had left them in standby.

"I think I got it," Meyka said.

Zeric keyed the control for the speaker on his console and said, "We are preparing to lift off. Everyone stand clear of the doors. Lohcja, use the comm by the elevator to let me know we're clear."

Several tense moments went by. Zeric was eager to get the ship moving. He was sure that last group would have made it to the ship by now. They had to have. *What is taking Lohcja so long, then?* Zeric wondered.

"Umm... this is the cargo bay. You need to take off now," a voice said over the speakers.

"Who is this?" Meyka replied. "Where is Lohcja? Did Leimey and Jairyd make it onboard?"

"Uhh," the voice said again, "I don't know who those people are. Maybe they're fighting. There are guards everywhere. We need to take off now!"

"Good enough for me," Zeric said. He keyed the ignition sequence and the ship's thrusters and anti-grav field came to life. "Close the cargo bay doors. Controls should be somewhere in the mining operation controls in the back of the bridge."

"We can't leave yet!" Meyka shouted. "We don't know if we have everyone onboard!"

"I'm taking off. If you don't close those doors, people are going to start falling out."

Meyka stared at him in horrified shock. Zeric shouted at her again to move, and she finally ran back to the aft section. Returning his attention to the helm controls, he tried to lift off as gently as possible. But since they were not on a flat surface to start with, that was not easy.

"I can't find it!" Meyka yelled.

"Keep looking!" Zeric answered.

"Close the doors!" the unknown voice called over the comm.

Zeric got the ship all of the way off the ground and clear of the prison. He started moving slowly across the open field away from the prison. That should keep them all safe from the guards now, at least.

Then he kicked himself. He shouted into the comm, "There are controls for the cargo bay doors in the bay itself!"

"Oh," was the only reply he got. A moment later, the ship started to fight him. The doors were lifting back up into the ship, he realized, and they were changing the shape of the ship. As they closed, the lift they had generated as impromptu wings was lost, and he quickly tried to compensate with more vertical thrust.

The ship continued to fight him as the doors were closed unevenly. Finally, they sealed, and the ship steadied out. Now he only had to contend with gravity working on the ship's mass. With a sigh, he leaned back in his chair.

Then the warning alarm sounded.

"We've got four more fighters coming in," Lahkaba said nervously. "This time they are coming in faster. ETA, three minutes."

"You can bet this group won't have their shields down," Maarkean said. "How's it coming with communications?"

Lahkaba shook his head. "Not well. I'm not a mechanic or a computer expert. Nothing I try appears to do anything."

Maarkean had been afraid of that. Going into combat with people untrained in their respective roles had been an unfortunate necessity. Learning how to use the sensor console was a far cry from learning how to truly work ship systems. Anyone could read a data display.

"Don't worry about. It's likely the array is beyond repair from here. We'll need to physically get at it. Fortunately, if everything goes as planned, we won't need to talk to them."

Lahkaba let out a short laugh. "Yeah, things seem to be going to plan so far."

It had been meant as a joke, but Maarkean was surprised at how close to the truth that was. It had been a simple plan: attack the prison from the air, get everyone on board, and get to hyperspace. So far, they had accomplished two out of three steps. Granted, he had no idea how well things had gone on the ground, but he had seen lots of people get aboard the ship. And the freighter had finally taken off. Now they just had to make it to step three.

"You think you can figure out the shield controls? As in, how to adjust their settings across different directions?"

"I think so. The interface looks simple enough. At least when everything's working."

That brought a smile to Maarkean. "Nothing like a trial by fire. Go lock the turret to forward firing and transfer control to me. I'll need you tracking them and adjusting shields for me."

Lahkaba nodded and moved back to the weapons console. Fixing the weapon to forward firing gave Maarkean control, but also severely limited their angle of attack. The fighters were more maneuverable than they were, so the rotating turret had allowed them to even the odds in the last engagement.

Maarkean was hoping to trade weapon angle for diversity. One advantage multi-crew ships had over a single-seat fighter was the ability to do several things at once. A pilot could only focus his attention on a few things at a time. In a dogfight, that was almost always trying to avoid getting shot and trying to shoot the enemy. That did not leave a lot of attention for monitoring other enemies and fixing problems with the ship. Even though Lahkaba was inexperienced, Maarkean was betting that having him there would be the difference they needed.

"What's the freighter's altitude?"

"One hundred ten kilometers."

That brought a real smile to Maarkean's lips. "Best news I've heard all day."

"Why? They still have a long way to go before they can engage the hyperdrive."

"Yes, but they've cleared the densest part of the atmosphere. Those fighters will lose some of their maneuverability advantage. Very little air up there."

"I'll take what I can get," Lahkaba said. "One minute to intercept."

Maarkean continued to climb the ship. They were about twenty kilometers behind the freighter, but that would still put them well into the thermosphere by the time the fighters reached them. It was not the ideal place for a dogfight, though. All of the ionization in the upper atmosphere could interfere with shield strength. That could be beneficial if it affected the fighters' shields, but since they were the ones with the stronger shields, it had a greater chance of hurting them.

Everything balances out, Maarkean thought. *They lose some maneuverability, we lose some shield strength. We catch their first group off guard; they send twice as many ships.* Each side would have their strengths negated and their weaknesses shored up. It all came down to how you responded to the situation.

He had always been a believer in a cosmic balance in life. Some had called him pessimistic to think that every up would be followed by a down. It seemed to be simple logic to him. Things couldn't continually improve. When they did, he got nervous because he knew a major drop in fortune was going to happen sooner or later. The flip side to that, which no one else seemed to understand, was that no matter how low things got, they would always turn around.

"Here they come," Lahkaba said, trying to keep calm.

"Transfer shield strength to the forward array. Pull it from the aft array. Be prepared to shift it."

Maarkean looped the ship around from their ascent to point straight back at the incoming fighter group. Firing the engines at max thrust, he couldn't overcome their upward velocity, but it was enough to cause a rapid change in their speed relative to the fighters. The four fighters' blasts converged where the *Cutty Sark* had been, and only a few hit their reinforced shields. Before the group overshot them, Maarkean unleashed a torrent of fire from the turret at the lead fighter.

Once the fighters were past, Maarkean flipped the ship and fired the engines again for a longer burst. They started climbing, and he was able to fire a few long-range shots at the rearmost fighter. Most missed, but he was able to get a few in before they changed course out of the weapon arc.

"Fighter One took severe damage. Your shots penetrated the shields. No noticeable change to flight characteristics, though. Fighter Four's shields are weak aft, but there doesn't appear to be any penetration."

Maarkean was simultaneously impressed by Lahkaba's reading of the sensor data and regretful that he didn't have someone better trained reading them. An experienced operator would have been able to interpret the extent of the damage to the two fighters, possibly ruling Fighter One out as a threat if they had lost any major systems. Still, with the brief training he had had, Lahkaba was handling himself well.

"They are splitting up. Fighters One, Two and Three are coming around back toward us, Fighter Four is continuing on toward the freighter."

"Rookie mistake," Maarkean said as he fired the engines for another full-power blast. "Transfer shield power to the rear."

"But the fighters are still in front of us."

"Not for long."

Firing several shots at the fighters as they approached, Maarkean knew he was not going to hit anything, but he hoped it might interfere enough to prevent the fighters from getting good shots in on them. He felt a few shots hit them, and then they were past the group. Climbing toward the freighter, Maarkean tried to get a lock on Fighter Four.

As he got within weapon range, Maarkean was tempted to unload on the fighter in front of him, but they were close enough now that any missed shots would hit the massive freighter. The fighter was already firing its weapons into the freighter's engine section. Deciding he had little choice, Maarkean fired several short bursts from the turret. None would be strong enough to penetrate even the weakened shields of the fighter, but with luck, they would cause him to veer off his attack run.

The fighter continued climbing toward the freighter and firing. Almost all of its shots were hitting the freighter's aft engine section. The freighter's shields and hull should be able to withstand quite a few shots, but Maarkean had no idea what shape the shields were in. Taking careful aim, he stopped his suppressing fire and lined up a good shot. After several frustrating seconds, he managed to match Fighter Four's maneuvers and unleashed a long burst of fire.

Fighter Four exploded before them, and Maarkean pulled the ship up at a sharp angle to avoid the wreckage. It was only then that he noticed they had been taking fire from the rear. He cursed himself for his mistake. He had been so focused on his target that he had not noticed them coming in from behind. What he had viewed as a rookie mistake, going after a target alone and ignoring the rest of the battle, he had just committed himself.

"How we doing?" Maarkean asked, trying to sound confident.

"Aft shields at fifty percent. Most of the power was transferred from the fore shields, so they are at thirty percent," Lahkaba replied. "We took some hull damage, but it does not appear to be anything vital. One piece of good news: Fighter One is flying in formation but has not fired anything. I think we took out their weapons on that first pass."

"Good – one less thing shooting at us," Maarkean said.

The remorse he had felt earlier when they had engaged the first two fighters was no longer bothering him. When it had been a one-sided fight, he had had time to consider what he was doing. Now, the odds were against them and these fighters were trying to shoot down a defenseless transport: a transport that hopefully had his sister aboard. It was a subtle distinction, but Maarkean was now able to view these fighters solely as enemies.

"Now we finish this."

CHAPTER EIGHT

As Saracasi helped to put Asirzi down onto the makeshift bed, the ship suddenly rocked, and she nearly dropped her friend. Her first thought was that the inertial dampeners had failed, but she dismissed that idea immediately. Had those failed, she would be a puddle of goo on the aft wall, rather than struggling to stay upright. She concluded it must have been weapon fire. The inertial dampeners compensated for the ship's acceleration and movement, but they were not designed to counteract unexpected outside influences.

Stepping away from the bed, she looked to the Ronid doctor, Noti Istru. He took her place beside the bed and examined Asirzi. It had been fortunate that they had found at least one doctor amongst the group of prisoners.

It was even more fortunate that the doctor was Noti, as he had been put in the prison for running a clinic that treated all species. Alliance law forbade the treatment of any species except one's own. They claimed it was to prevent any tragedies from occurring because the doctor was not familiar with the biology of the patient. The truth was that many Terran and Braz doctors did not study the physiology of other species, while most other doctors did.

Noti began running a scanner over Asirzi. Their fortune had continued with the discovery of medical supplies. The ship did not include a real infirmary, but the crew common area did contain some medical supplies and was designed to be used as an emergency medical suite. Despite Zeric's order to take people only to the crew quarters, with that discovery they had diverted to the common area.

Lohcja was standing, holding his arm, on the other side of the room. Lying beside him, barely breathing, was Pasha. Several others who had been injured in the fighting were sitting around the room. There were a few more people moving about who had some medical experience or who had volunteered to help.

"I'll go see if I can help on the bridge," Saracasi said quickly. With one final look at Asirzi, she dashed out of the room toward the stairs.

Saracasi had to admit the truth to herself. Injuries and the sight of blood made her uncomfortable. Memories long suppressed threatened to come back to her. Once she was out of the room, she focused herself again and headed toward to the bridge.

While dashing up the stairs, the ship rocked several times, almost causing her to fall. Gripping the handrail, she climbed at a slower but steadier pace. When she emerged onto the cavernous bridge, it took her a moment to see anyone. She was led by the sound of shouting.

"How are we holding up?"

"I don't know! I think the one firing on us stopped."

She recognized Zeric at the fore of the bridge in the helm position and a Terran female at another console. The woman was almost hysterical. She could sympathize, as she was not quite sure how she had managed to keep herself together so far.

"Need any help?" she asked.

The woman almost jumped out of her seat, and Zeric spared a quick glance back at her. "I told you to keep everyone down below."

"We are," Saracasi said crossly. "I've flown with Maarkean for years and studied starship construction at university. Now do you want my help or not?"

"Thank the heavens," Zeric said. "Yes! I need to know if those shots we took did any major damage."

"Right," Saracasi said. She turned and examined the consoles in the rear bridge section. Most were controls for mining operations, but she found a set of engineering consoles next to environmental systems.

It took a moment to acquaint herself with the interface, but it was not long before she was able to bring up a diagnostic system. She ran a primary systems check and an analysis of the affected area. Fire had been concentrated on the after port engine section. While the diagnostic was running, she transferred shield power from other sections to shore up the depleted layer.

"It looks good. Primary systems appear to be undamaged. Looks like we took some hull damage, but it didn't penetrate the outer hull."

"Excellent," Zeric called back, sounding relieved. "You know how to plot a hyperspace jump?"

"Of course," Saracasi replied. She began moving back toward the front of the ship.

"Good. Meyka, go back and finish your calculations of our air usage. We need to know how long we have before we suffocate."

The Terran woman got up from the operations station, looking very relieved. It did not appear to bother her that she was being kicked off her station. Saracasi couldn't blame her. She would hate doing this if she didn't already know how.

Taking Meyka's place, she brought up the navigational computer. "Where are we going?"

"Kol," Zeric said.

"That makes sense," Saracasi replied as she began plotting a course. There was an abandoned outpost in one of the massive deserts of Kol that she and Maarkean had discovered. It had served as a safe haven on a few occasions. The planet was sparsely populated, especially the desert region, but the outpost had access to an underground water source. The previous occupants had also installed a greenhouse with that water, so it served as an oasis in the wastes.

As she started the calculation, she remembered Maarkean's insistence on setting a false course every time they left the *Black Market*. While it was impossible to track anything in hyperspace, if you knew the direction a ship was going when it entered, you could extrapolate its intended destination. She had always thought he was being paranoid. That had been before they had been hijacked and were being pursued by Alliance fighters. She began recalculating for another destination.

"I'm setting a course for the middle of nowhere so they can't track us to Kol," Saracasi told Zeric, and then called back to Meyka, "I need to know how long we'll last so I don't delay us too much."

Meyka acknowledged, and Saracasi shifted her attention to the sensor display. She saw the *Cutty Sark* engaged with three Alliance fighters. Wreckage from at least one other fighter was also evident. Despite herself, she was impressed. She had heard that Maarkean was a good pilot from some of his old squadron buddies, and she had seen him fly many times, but she had never seen him in combat.

"We're far enough away from the planet to engage the hyperdrive," Zeric said.

Meyka shook her head, indicating that the calculations weren't done.

"We'll just have to hope we can make it," Saracasi said.

Pressing the activation sequence for the hyperdrive, she prepared for the nausea that came when they first shifted out of real-space. Several seconds went by, and nothing happened. Trying the activation sequence again had the same result. She let out an uncharacteristic curse.

"Hyperdrive's not working."

"I thought you said we didn't take any damage?" Zeric asked.

"We didn't. It's just not working. Didn't show up on the diagnostics either. For some reason, it's marked as a secondary system," Saracasi said, getting back up from the operations station. She hesitated, then went back to the controls and opened the ship-wide comm.

"Chavatwor, grab anyone familiar with starship engineering and meet me in the ship's engineering compartment. Also, anyone familiar with starship operations, come up to the bridge."

She shut off the comm and then spoke to Zeric as she dashed back toward the stairs. "Don't argue. You need help up here. Just keep flying away, and we'll try to figure out what's wrong with the hyperdrive."

Not waiting for a response, Saracasi dashed down the stairs.

"Must take after her brother," Zeric thought again as Saracasi barked out orders and then left the bridge.

Zeric continued flying the ship away from the planet. The short-range sensor display he had access to showed the three fighters and the *Cutty Sark* slowly falling further behind them. All four ships had far better acceleration than the freighter did. They would all fall behind and then would attempt to make a dash toward the freighter. The *Cutty Sark* would reengage them, and the dogfight would resume. They were spending more time fighting each other than accelerating toward the freighter, so as long as that kept up, they remained out of weapon range.

Several minutes went by like that, while Zeric fervently wanted to know what else was out there. Finally deciding it was safe enough to leave the ship flying straight, he moved over to the operations station. What he saw made him curse. Another six fighters were on course toward them. And behind the fighters was a corvette.

By Zeric's calculation, at their speed, it would be some time before any of the new ships were able to catch up to them. But the six fighters would be on top of the *Cutty Sark* in a matter of minutes. When he told Meyka, she said what he was thinking: "That was the plan, wasn't it? If we got caught, they would hold the Alliance off?"

Zeric didn't think of himself as unusually perceptive, but he clearly heard the reluctance in her voice. Oddly, he felt that same reluctance. Maarkean and Lahkaba had been friends of convenience. It had been Maarkean's plan in the first place. If they continued on their course, he, and his friends, would get away.

The sounds of new voices interrupted his thinking. A Camari, a Kowwok, a Notha and a Terran were standing at the top of the stairs. They were looking around as if they weren't sure what they were supposed to do.

"What are you doing here?" Zeric asked, with more snap to his question than he intended.

"We heard you needed help up here from anyone with any experience," the Kowwok said. "We've all had some experience with starships."

At first he had been annoyed at Saracasi's call, but now he silently thanked her. "What kind of experience?"

The Kowwok answered by gesturing to the red rubbery-skinned Camari and then the brown-furred Notha. "Ceno here flew bulk transports, and Isaxo says he grew up around ships. My wife, Jasmaine," he said, gesturing to the Terran woman, "and I worked on mining freighters such as this. We never worked on the bridge, though."

Wife, Zeric thought. That explained why the Alliance had locked them up; they weren't partial to interspecies mating. He then dismissed it. "What did you do?"

"We operated the mining lasers."

Zeric eyes lit up as a sudden idea occurred to him. Despite it being the best chance for his health, he did not like the idea of running. A strange sense of guilt over it had been battling with the knowledge there wasn't anything he could do to change the situation. Now things might be different.

"All right, you, Ceno, was it? Take the helm and get us turned around. You, Isaxo, take ops and guide him toward a collection of Alliance fighters that are engaging a courier ship behind us. You, what was your name?"

"Chungum."

"You and your wife follow me," Zeric said, heading toward the bridge stairs.

As Zeric started to leave, the bulbous eyestalks of the Camari, Ceno, followed him and he reached out to Zeric with his clammy hand, "Wait, you want me to turn the ship around and head *toward* Alliance fighters?"

Zeric brushed past him, saying, "Yes. That ship they are fighting is about to get overwhelmed. The only reason you're not in that prison anymore is her pilot. We're going back to help."

Relief filled Maarkean as he watched the blast from his turret penetrate the shield of the Alliance fighter and a cloud of fast-freezing gas billow out. He wasn't sure if he hit the oxygen supply or deuterium canisters, but either way, it took the fighter out of the engagement. The pilot wouldn't be able to go far without air or fuel.

He didn't let himself enjoy the victory for long. Turning quickly, he barely got out of the way of a blast that might have done the same thing to him. Despite there only being one fighter with working weapons now, there were still two targets.

Maarkean took the ship into a corkscrew maneuver, and then he pulled the ship to face back up from where they had come, expecting to see the two fighters in pursuit. To his surprise, he saw nothing. Throwing the ship into an evasive maneuver, expecting an attack from anywhere, he called out to Lahkaba.

"Where did they go?"

"They're falling back, headed toward the planet," Lahkaba answered. "But I wouldn't celebrate yet. They've got friends. Six fighters coming in fast. They've got a different signature than the last set. There is also a larger ship a couple minutes behind them."

"Let me see."

Lahkaba transferred the data readings to Maarkean's display. Once he saw it, his short-lived celebration evaporated. "Those are SSF-19's. Space superiority fighters. They are designed for combat out here. Those other ships were probably low on fuel, which is why they're bugging out. I'm not positive, but based on the speed, that big ship looks like a corvette."

"Which should we be more worried about?"

"Both," Maarkean replied. "Corvettes are slower than we are, but not by much. They don't have many big guns, but they don't need them. They're designed as fast anti-fighter screens."

"Can we run?"

"We can try," Maarkean said, turning the ship away from the incoming fighters.

Gunning the engines for all they could manage, they shot away from the planet. The *Cutty Sark* had good acceleration for a transport ship, as it was designed to travel quickly to deliver small but necessary cargo, but the incoming fighters had already been traveling at a high speed. Checking the math, he knew right away the fighters would reach them before they could get their speed high enough.

"Better start the hyperspace calculation. We can't take on six ships, and they'll be on us soon."

Lahkaba nodded, and Maarkean asked a follow-up question. "What's the status of the freighter? Have they jumped yet?"

"No. They've actually turned around and are headed for us."

"What?" Maarkean exclaimed. The freighter had had more than enough time to activate their hyperdrive. As long as they were here, he couldn't risk jumping to hyperspace. Not for the first time, he regretted the loss of the comm.

"The freighter's sending out a message."

"I thought you said the comm was down."

"It is. We can't transmit, but it appears we can receive."

"Let's hear it."

Lahkaba activated the ship's speakers.

"Attention, Alliance fighters. This is the escaped prisoners from Olan Detention Center. Our hyperdrive is non-operational, and we are short on air. We are turning around and wish to surrender. Please hold your fire. The pursuing courier ship *Cutty Sark* has lost communication abilities. Hold your fire, and they will surrender as well."

Maarkean and Lahkaba both slumped back in their chairs. All of this had been for nothing. The entire operation was going to end in defeat. That one fighter that had been able to fire on the freighter had probably knocked out the hyperdrive. Despite all of the other successes and failures, that one failure was going to cost them everything.

"Hold your course, freighter, and prepare to be escorted back to the planet. *Cutty Sark*, power down your weapons and do the same. You will not get another warning."

Quietly, Lahkaba asked, "Should we do it? Or should we go down fighting?"

"What? No, of course not," Maarkean said, exasperated. "We're not going to go out in some foolish blaze of glory. If it would allow the freighter to get away, maybe. But you heard them. Their hyperdrive is out. There's no place for them to go. There are no other habitable planets in this system. If we die, they still get caught."

Lahkaba considered him for a moment. Maarkean really wished he had a better understanding of Kowwok expressions. *Contemplative* would have been his guess, but it could have just as easily have been *confusion*.

"Jairyd said we had to be prepared to give our lives for the cause if we were going to have any hope of succeeding. He warned us you might not be. I was told to take over if you weren't prepared to do what was necessary."

Despite himself, Maarkean laughed. He had no idea why. They were being pursued by Alliance fighters. The ship that was supposed to take his sister to safety was unable to escape. And he was a meter away from a Kowwok who just revealed he might be about to kill him.

"You're not going to kill me," Maarkean said, when he could get air.

"No, I'm not. Jairyd got pretty full of himself when Leimey was taken. I think he saw dying on this mission as a glorious way to further the cause."

"Better power down that turret, or we'll get to test that theory."

Getting up from the ops station, Lahkaba moved back to the turret controls. As he did so, alarms started shrieking. Maarkean recognized them immediately as a warning that they were in a target lock.

"Guess we waited too long. Keep that turret up. Get ready to shoot."

"Shoot what?" Lahkaba said hastily, strapping himself in.

"Missiles," Maarkean replied, and he took the ship into a fast series of maneuvers and course changes, trying to throw off the target lock. His sensor display showed two incoming missiles.

As the missiles drew closer, Lahkaba began laying down a stream of fire from the turret in their direction. Significantly smaller and faster than the fighters, the missiles proved a much harder target. Despite the fire, Maarkean knew they were done for as the missiles continued closer. It was a welcome shock when they suddenly exploded.

"I didn't hit them," Lahkaba said, dumbfounded.

"What did?"

Scrambling out of the gunner station, Lahkaba dropped down into the operations chair. He ran a more thorough scan of the area than the other station's short-range sensors allowed. Shock filled his voice when he spoke.

"The freighter."

"I thought that thing was unarmed?"

"They're using the mining lasers," Lahkaba said incredulously. "We just might win this thing!"

"Or they're going to get themselves killed."

Racing down the spine of the ship to the engineering section exhausted Saracasi. Exercise had never been her favorite activity, and spending the last few days trapped in a cramped building, and living aboard a transport ship before that, had not given her many opportunities. The heavy breathing that threatened to overcome her made her rethink her attitude toward it, though.

When she made it to the engineering room, she found Chavatwor and a female Notha waiting for her. Chavatwor introduced the Notha as La'ari Mahon; she had been a ship engineering student before being sent to Olan. She briefed them on the issue they were having with the hyperdrive.

The group spent the next several minutes familiarizing themselves with the room's layout before identifying the hyperdrive control panel. When they examined the display, Chavatwor mumbled several things in his native language which sounded to Saracasi like curses. She found herself glad she couldn't understand.

"This system is a complete mess," Chavatwor finally growled. "Hyperdrive as a secondary system? The way the systems are routed, I'm surprised it ever worked." He appeared to be completely captivated with his study of the system.

"Can we fix it?" Saracasi asked.

"Sure," Chavatwor said cheerfully, as if he were looking forward to the challenge. "Give me two months, a couple dozen workers and several new components, and I'll make it the most efficient system on this ship."

"Can we fix it before the Alliance blows us up?"

Chavatwor looked startled as he seemed to remember the crisis they were facing. "Um, sure. La'ari, go to the reactor control panel. I'm going to need you to make some adjustments. Saracasi, go back to the bridge; I'll need someone to make some changes from the controls there."

With a sigh, Saracasi headed back down the spine of the ship. She tried to run, but she could only manage a light jog for most of the way. The stairs at the end almost did her in, and she once again vowed to exercise more. She promised herself she would ensure there was a jogging path in the *Cutty Sark*'s cargo bay no matter what cargo they had onboard.

When she got up to the bridge, she headed straight for the engineering terminal. Once there, she sent a message to Chavatwor, but she only got a perfunctory response. While she waited for the Kowwok to tell her what she needed to do, she noticed that there were several new people on the bridge.

"Where's Zeric?" she asked.

The Terran woman she had seen up here before turned to her and looked startled. "He ordered us to turn around and then ran off."

Saracasi noticed two young men at the helm and operations stations. Both looked younger than she was, but you could never be certain with other species. The Notha introduced himself as Isaxo Mahon, and she recognized the family name as that of the Notha working with Chavatwor.

After several minutes, the bridge comm came alive, and she was surprised when it was Zeric and not Chavatwor who spoke. "All right, bridge, this is Zeric in the port laser control room. Get us in close to the Alliance ships; these lasers apparently don't have very good range before they lose power."

A sinking feeling came over Saracasi. "You're going to attack them? With mining equipment?"

"Who is this? Saracasi?" Zeric asked. "We're trying to help your brother. How's the hyperdrive coming?"

"Should have it working again in a few minutes," Saracasi said, though, in truth, she was only hoping that was true. Chavatwor had not given any estimates. "Those mining lasers can't be very powerful. You sure you can get through the shields on those fighters?"

There was a noticeable pause from Zeric's end, and when he replied, he sounded less confident. "Sure, we should be able to do it if we're close. Get us as close to the fighters as you can."

Deciding the best thing she could do was to get them all out of there, Saracasi went back to the engineering terminal. She noticed some of the changes Chavatwor and La'ari had made, and she thought she had an idea what they were attempting. While they worked, she spoke to the Terran woman, Meyka.

"Zeric said you were working on calculating how much air we had to breathe?"

Meyka nodded. "Yeah, turns out, not a lot. Our destination was supposed to be Kol, but I estimate that we'll be out of air before we get halfway there."

"I entered a set of coordinates for our first jump into deep space to throw off our pursuit. See if you can find a planet with a breathable atmosphere that we can reach from there."

Looking appreciative at having something productive to do, the woman went back to the environmental terminal she had been working from. Saracasi did not at all like the idea of running out of oxygen and suffocating. Rotting in an Alliance prison held more appeal. Maybe getting the hyperdrive working wasn't going to be the blessing it was supposed to be.

Alarms started sounding from terminals all over the bridge, and Saracasi realized that they were taking weapons fire. She ran a diagnostic and saw that nothing critical had been damaged. Remembering that the hyperdrive was not considered a primary system, she started a secondary diagnostic, wondering what other critical systems were listed as secondary.

The weapon fire against the ship continued for several minutes. Isaxo and the Camari flying the ship let out shouts of fear and excitement, and she heard someone yell, "We got one!" She spent her time adjusting the shield power to keep them protected as best she could.

"Bridge, what's going on up there?" Chavatwor called angrily. "I'm close to getting this thing working, but the power keeps fluctuating."

"I'm trying to keep the shields up," Saracasi yelled back.

"Stop for one minute, and I should be able to finish!"

Saracasi considered her choices. She could stop adjusting the shields, potentially letting them fail and having the ship be destroyed, or allowing them to escape to hyperspace. Or she could continue adjusting the shields, and keep them alive for a few more minutes – but they would eventually be destroyed anyway.

Reluctantly, she moved her hands from the controls. She brought up a status display for the hyperdrive and then called forward to Isaxo, "There should be a set of coordinates locked into the navigational computer. Bring them up, and then when I say to, engage the hyperdrive. Pilot, give us an appropriate heading so we can go as soon as I say."

The two acknowledged her, apparently relieved at the thought of getting away. Several tense moments went by as Saracasi watched the shield power decline and red warnings spring up about hull integrity and various systems taking damage. She fervently hoped she had made the right call in listening to Chavatwor.

When the status on the hyperdrive changed from offline to online she almost didn't believe it. It took Chavatwor screaming at her over the comm for her to accept it. She in turn shouted to Isaxo, "Go, Isaxo, go!"

The young Notha wasted no time, and the bridge windows were suddenly filled with the colors of hyperspace.

CHAPTER NINE

Zeric was greatly relieved when they jumped to hyperspace. There was no information about the status of the ship in the laser control section, but based on the number of hits they had taken, he was sure some things were broken.

Climbing down from the manual control station for the mining laser, he walked back to the central juncture of the ship. There, he nodded to Chungum, who had been operating the starboard laser. The Kowwok returned his nod and then dashed off toward the aft of the ship where his wife had been working a turret.

He shook his head as the Kowwok left. Zeric didn't consider himself prejudiced against any species, and he had no problem with interspecies relationships, but the thought of kissing, much less having sex with, something that hairy held no appeal for him. The next time a woman gave him a hard time about his goatee, he would have to tell her about that relationship.

When he reached the stairs that led up to the bridge, he found Lohcja coming up from the lower deck. He was wearing a sling on his injured arm, but he looked much better than when Zeric had last seen him. He said as much, and as best as Zeric could tell, the Ronid smiled. The lips were too long to make a proper smile, and the mandibles just gave it a creepy look.

"I saw that we made it to hyperspace. There are some people down there who wish to thank you. We managed to get Lei-mey with the last group," Lohcja said.

"Excellent," Zeric replied, trying to sound enthusiastic. He had never really cared if Lei-mey or anyone else made it out, beyond his friends. It certainly made things a lot nicer for him, though. Had they rescued his friends and not her, there might have been problems. And he certainly wasn't upset that she had been rescued. He just couldn't sum up the excitement Lohcja clearly felt.

"Lei-mey would like to thank you personally," Lohcja said.

A passing thought crossed Zeric's mind. Ceta was quite attractive. If that trait ran in the family, Lei-mey had been in prison for a while, and if she was grateful to him... He stopped that train of thought immediately. They weren't safe yet.

"Don't thank me yet," Zeric replied as he started up the stairs. "We haven't made it to safe ground."

Leaving Lohcja behind, Zeric climbed up to the bridge. He found Saracasi and Meyka conversing over the environmental station and Isaxo and Ceno talking excitedly to each other at the front of the bridge. Ignoring the young people, he went back to join the two women.

"Nice timing on that hyperdrive," Zeric said with a smile.

"Nice attempt at getting us all killed," Saracasi replied with an icy tone.

"Hey, now, I'll have you know our first two shots took out two missiles that were about to destroy your brother. The targeting systems on those lasers are quite nice," Zeric replied defensively. He had known it was a long shot, but he thought it worked out pretty well.

"First, thank you for that. Second, that was about the only thing you destroyed. Those lasers are designed to cut through rock with a sustained beam. They were not powerful enough to penetrate the shields on the fighters for the short bursts you were firing. Third, hell, those aren't even lasers – I don't know why people use that word." Saracasi said. She went from angry to grateful to frustrated in just a breath.

"Wait, they aren't lasers?" Zeric said, latching onto the least important thing Saracasi had said.

"No, they're a directed beam of energy, but a laser is a focused beam of light –"

Saracasi was cut off by a frustrated noise from Meyka, who said, "If you two are done, we have the matter of breathable air to deal with."

Zeric focused in on the woman's words. This had been a worry of his from the beginning. Suffocating in space was high on the list of ways he didn't want to die. It was a long list, and the top spot tended to change based on what the immediate danger was, but suffocation in any form was always pretty high.

"How long do we have?"

"That's kind of a mixed answer," Meyka replied. "This ship is designed to support a crew of forty for at least six months. Now, like most ships, the oxygen system uses recycled air most of the time, which, with the correct amount of crew, will keep the air flowing pretty much indefinitely. However, by my rough estimate, we have about seven hundred people onboard."

The number staggered Zeric. He had seen a lot of people, but had no idea it was that many. It gave him an uneasy feeling about their chances.

Meyka continued, "With that many people, we'll run out of oxygen reserves in a week."

Zeric brightened up. "A week should be enough time to reach Kol."

"I wasn't done," Meyka said, dashing Zeric's spirits. "We'll burn out the environmental system in three days and die from carbon dioxide poisoning inside of four."

Letting out a breath of air, Zeric tried to remain positive. "Okay, where can we reach in less than four days?"

This time, Saracasi spoke up. "I've been going over the possibilities and identified three worlds capable of supporting life."

She turned away from the environmental station and brought up a holographic display on one of the central tables. A galactic map appeared, showing Sulas and their approximate location not very far away from it. Kol was brought up on the opposite side of the table. Three of the stars lit up with a name beside them.

"We're about two days from Ailleroc. A well-colonized world, with heavy Alliance presence. Even if we can beat word of our escape, a packet ship from Sulas won't be too far behind us."

Saracasi pointed to the next world. "Mirthod, a lightly populated world, no major Alliance facilities but still a presence. The civilized areas aren't much more than trading posts."

Zeric shook his head. "Mirthod is lightly populated because it is so dangerous. Almost every native creature appears to be designed to kill you. Those trading posts' primary source of revenue is hunting trips. Lots of money to be made from some of those creatures, but lots of experienced people don't come back alive. With this many scared and hungry people, we'll be torn up."

By this time, Isaxo and Ceno had made their way to join the group by the holo display. Zeric didn't like the idea of their predicament spreading too far among the former prisoners, but there wasn't much he could do about it now. He just tried to give the two young people a look he hoped would get the message across not to share anything.

Saracasi continued with the last world. "That's it for established colonies. There are dozens of star systems in the sector that don't have any Alliance presence, but most have never been surveyed, so we have no idea what's in any of them. One that has, PX-1997, is the moon of a gas giant barely in the habitable zone for the system. It is undeveloped, so no Alliance presence, but also no place to refuel or resupply."

"Irod is not undeveloped," a new voice said. Zeric turned to see the Notha, Faide, his tail swishing behind him, coming onto the bridge. He was followed by Chavatwor and another Notha.

"According to the database, there was a survey of the moon about a hundred years ago, but no one has established a colony," Saracasi said.

"It won't appear in the database. The colony was set up seventeen years ago by a friend of mine, looking to get away from the war. His followers did not want to involve themselves in any more violence. I would have joined them, but I was arrested before I could leave."

Zeric considered Faide's words. There were lots of unidentified settlements on habitable worlds, so what he said was possible. But seventeen years was a long time. That many years in a prison was not something he wanted to consider.

"If your friend was setting up a colony that long ago and you've been in prison since then, how can you be sure it's still there? Most independent colony efforts fail."

Faide shrugged. "I can't be. But I do know the indigenous species are no more dangerous than you'd find on any world, unlike Mirthod, and there are no Alliance bases, unlike Ailleroc. But I leave the decision to you."

Not much of a choice when you put it like that, Zeric thought. He noticed the rest of the group looking at him expectantly. It took a moment, but he realized that, for some reason, everyone was leaving the final decision to him.

"Well, even if the colony isn't there anymore, there's a good chance they left some stuff behind. We can drop off most of the passengers and use the ship to get help from somewhere else if need be."

Saracasi nodded at him. "All right, I'll start calculating a new course. Should take us about three days to get there. It's going to get pretty stale in here, but we should live."

Saracasi never would have thought she would miss prison. Despite being denied her freedom and the threat of eventual execution hanging over her head, she had at least had a moderately comfortable bed. Here, she had to sleep on a cold metal deck surrounded by hundreds of people while she faced the painfully real possibility of suffocation. It made her wonder how the long-term prisoners felt.

All of the ship's beds had been given over to the injured. She had been both surprised and amazed by the number of wounded. During the brief time the breakout had occurred, dozens of people had been injured. There were also an unknown number of people who had been left behind. But it was also amazing how few people had been hurt, considering how many there were.

Their rescuers had brought along a collection of clothing, but it wasn't enough for everyone. Saracasi had elected to remain in her prison jumpsuit until they met up with Maarkean; all of her clothes were onboard *Cutty Sark*. She had been relieved to get the tracking bracelet removed, however. They dumped all of those into deep space when they had stopped to change course for Irod.

She left the engineering section, where all of the people experienced in ship maintenance were sleeping, and made her way down the ship's main corridor. This level was mostly empty. The corridors were too narrow for anyone to use to sleep and still allow anyone to walk down. Every room on the ship had been taken over by people looking to spread out from the cargo pod.

As Saracasi approached the stairs to the bridge, her attention was caught by a noise. Turning around, she recognized the noise as a giggle. She saw Zeric being led into a small storage room by a Terran female. The pair was barely able to keep their hands off each other.

At least someone was going to have some fun, she thought, assuming the storage room was not already occupied. It had been dubbed too small for anyone to sleep in, but she wouldn't put it past someone to have beaten Zeric to putting it to a different use. There wasn't a lot of private space on the ship.

Turning back around toward the stairs, Saracasi was startled to find herself face to face with a blue-carapaced Ronid female. The woman was staring past her at Zeric and the girl. Saracasi wasn't able to gauge any emotions from the Ronid's multi-faceted eyes, but the way the woman stared made her glad she wasn't the target.

After a moment, the woman turned her gaze off the pair and on to her. She smiled a comforting smile at Saracasi, which was unusual, as no other Ronid she had known had ever smiled without creeping her out, though she admitted she didn't know many. Doctor Istru had been the first one she had exchanged more than a few words with. This one lacked the dangerous-looking mandibles near the mouth that some Ronids had, which probably helped the effect. Saracasi returned the smile.

"You are Saracasi Ocaitchi, correct?" the Ronid said. Her voice was much clearer than that of most Ronids she'd met; it was mostly free from the usual heavy clacking sounds that most made as they spoke Galactic Standard.

Saracasi nodded, and the woman continued, "I am Leimey Darshawn. Do you have a few moments to talk?"

Curious, Saracasi replied, "Sure, I was headed to the bridge to run a systems check on the environmental systems. Care to join me?"

"Certainly."

Saracasi led the way up the stairs. She recognized Lei-mey's name. Meyka had told her that Lei-mey was the reason they had broken everyone out of the prison. She had been curious to meet the person who would inspire that kind of devotion.

"I understand it was your brother's idea to stage the jail break."

"So they tell me," Saracasi replied, shaking her head.

"You doubt your brother capable of this?" Lei-mey asked.

Saracasi considered the question. When Meyka had told her that it had been Maarkean's idea, it had surprised her. She had always known her brother as the loyal citizen and military officer. Taking her off Braz had been the only sign that he was more than a patriotic drone. She had been working on widening that first crack in his dogmatic belief in the infallibility of the Alliance, but she didn't think she had been very successful. Still, *capable* and *likely* were two different things.

To Lei-mey, she said, "No, not at all."

"I am curious what else he is capable of," Lei-mey continued.

"Was this the act of a desperate brother or of a champion of freedom?"

The question took Saracasi by surprise, and she was not sure how to respond. Saved from making an immediate answer by their arrival on the bridge, she made a noncommittal answer and began running her check of the environmental systems. While the diagnosis ran, she considered it.

Maarkean was many things, but a rebel against his government was not one of them. He had resigned himself to being a criminal, but she always knew that if he were caught, he would accept it as justice. Every argument she had made about the evils their government was committing, he had dismissed as either exaggerations or necessities.

The frustrating thing was that, deep down, he did believe in all of the same things that she did. He believed in the value of democracy over autocracy, universal freedoms regardless of species, and despite being a military man, he was not a fan of military actions that weren't primarily defensive. The problem, as she saw it, was that he had been brainwashed by their planet's media and traditions.

Dissent against the government's actions was not unheard of in the media. Even she wouldn't go so far as to say that the government controlled the media. They were just ingenious at manipulating it. Or rather, those in power were. Democracy was not dead in the Alliance; it was just not well utilized.

Most of the population was content living comfortable lives with stable jobs. They bought into the fantasy that everything was just as wonderful out in the colonies. Trust in government was instilled in everyone from an early age, and few challenged the government's actions. There were those who did so in the media, but that was little more than theater, in her mind. The opposition was always weak and never asked the important questions.

Those who did raise the questions were always cast either as rebellious youth who didn't quite understand things yet or as ungrateful aliens who should go back to their own planet if they didn't like how things were done.

The Alliance was trumpeted as a bastion of freedom, especially compared to every other galactic power, but few people ever looked at it closely. Places like Olan were clear examples that the Alliance did not practice what it preached, but she doubted many people even knew they existed.

Not sure how to answer Lei-mey, Saracasi instead asked, "Why were you in Olan?"

The woman replied, "Pardon?"

"You asked why my brother did what he did to get us all out. I'm just curious as to what kind of woman he broke out of prison."

"I'm not the terrorist the news channels claim, if that's what you're wondering." Lei-mey answered curtly. "I grew up with a Terran family. They were kind to me; they treated me like family. But outside of them, I was always an outsider, an alien.

"When I grew up and started to raise the issues we face to the public, my family turned away from me. They believed I was betraying their love by saying the government was responsible for all the prejudice I faced. All except my sister, but even she wouldn't stand up with me.

"Fortunately, there were others who would. It took a long time and some less-than-clean tactics, but we were eventually recognized by the Sulas legislature. When the Kreogh Sector Congress was called, I was one of the delegates selected to represent Sulas. Naturally, the Alliance viewed this as unacceptable, and all of us sent were declared traitors."

The story amazed Saracasi. Maarkean had never agreed with her political beliefs, but he had never abandoned her because of them, even when they were the reason he had fled his home.

Lei-mey had lost the support of her family, but she had accomplished more than Saracasi had ever even come close to doing.

Lei-mey gave her a considering look. "Why were you in Olan?"

Saracasi should have known this question would come when she had asked hers. There was no particular reason not to tell the truth.

It was not like Lei-mey would turn her into the AIS. She didn't like talking about it, though, as it had ruined not only her life but Maarkean's as well.

"While at university I got involved with some groups. They made me aware that the Alliance government wasn't as wonderful as I had always thought. We thought we could change things if we could only get people to listen.

"We decided to stage a protest over something idiotic. Some of the other students went a little overboard with their enthusiasm, and the AIS moved in. The protest turned into a riot. There was a lot of property damage, and at some point, a few AIS officers were swarmed and beaten. I wasn't with that group, and I left as soon as things turned violent.

"The government declared that the leaders were traitors and were to be rounded up and executed. Unfortunately, I was caught rather prominently on a video feed of the initial stages of the riot.

"Plus, I had posted some rather harsh statements on the planetary Net. My name got added to the list of suspects. Before I was arrested, Maarkean got me off of Braz. We've been drifting around the sector ever since."

Lei-mey stood there for a moment. Saracasi wasn't sure what the other woman was thinking. Ronids were so hard to read. Compared to Lei-mey's story, hers was rather pathetic.

"Your brother, he supported your cause?"

"Not exactly," Saracasi answered. "He was an officer in the Alliance Navy. Still was in the Reserves until we left Braz. Let's just say he saw things a little differently."

"Then why would he take you away from being arrested? Why would he now break you out of prison?"

Saracasi shrugged. "Who knows why he does what he does? Family is important to him, but he strongly believes in the principles the Alliance is based on, even if he doesn't see that the Alliance doesn't always follow those principles."

"Curious," Lei-mey answered quietly. "Thank you for your time. I'll let you get back to work."

Lei-mey turned and went to speak with some of the others on the bridge. Saracasi wasn't sure what to make of the other woman's interest in her and her brother. *Natural curiosity, most likely*, she decided, and turned her attention back to the environmental computer.

To be fair, it had been a while, but Zeric didn't think he had ever had sex that good. Ceta had been good before, but never that good. It must be the gratitude for saving her sister. That wasn't likely to ever be repeated, but he'd remember it for a while.

He had gone down to the makeshift infirmary to look up on Lohcja and Pasha. While down there, Ceta had called him over to the bed of a Ronid. There, he had been floored to learn the Ronid was Ceta's infamous sister, Lei-mey. He had never met Lei-mey, but the entire time he had assumed her to be Terran like Ceta. He had even pictured her as a blonde.

When Ceta introduced him as the man who had come up with the plan to save her, he had tried to downplay it. The plan had been Maarkean's, after all. Ceta had not been at any of the planning meetings and had somehow assumed it had all been Zeric. She dismissed everything he said as modesty.

During the conversation he had started to catch on to the signals she was sending him. He usually tried to avoid flings with exes, but she seemed so eager. What had been unsettling was that he was picking up some of the same signals from Lei-mey.

He realized they were indeed sisters, even if different species, when he saw that they flirted the same way. He didn't know how Lei-mey had come to live with Ceta, but he did know they couldn't be biologically related, since Terrans and Ronids could not produce offspring. But they had definitely been raised together.

The whole situation had been awkward, and he had felt lucky when Ceta had followed him out of the infirmary.

Afterwards, Zeric had given Ceta his trademark wink and then slipped out while she was still getting dressed. The closet was definitely not the place to cuddle, and he preferred to remember her naked. A glorious sight it was. Some people frowned on stripping, but in his mind, keeping something that beautiful concealed was the bigger tragedy.

Making his way toward the bridge, he passed Lei-mey coming down. Clearly, she'd been released from the infirmary. He smiled at her, and she replied with an absent, "Captain Dustlighter."

"If you must give me a title, I was a corporal."

Lei-mey stopped a few steps below him and turned to face him, her expression curious. She had obviously not given what she said a lot of thought, because she seemed to have no idea what he was referring to. It hadn't been his intent to confuse her. He just hated being thought of as an officer. "I served in the military years ago. Got out as a corporal. Never became an officer."

"My apologies. I used it merely to signify your status on this vessel," Lei-mey said guardedly.

"I prefer Zeric." With a wink like the one he left Ceta, he continued his way up the stairs. If there had been any lingering jealousies about him rushing off to be with her sister, he hoped being his charming self would defuse it.

Once up on the bridge, Zeric noted that the room was unusually loud. The people who were camped out there were talking to each other excitedly. The other former prisoners had been relatively quiet; some were clearly in shock at the sudden change of circumstances, while others thought that not talking would conserve enough oxygen to get them to Irod safely.

Zeric dismissed the chatter and went to the command station at the front of the bridge. This was one area that they had managed to keep free of people, as it contained sensitive controls. He was not normally one to worry, but with a ship so overtaxed, he wanted to check in on the systems periodically.

Bringing up status reports on the command station's displays, he read the power consumption and air consumption estimates. Neither was good, but both were well within the estimates they had made. He studied some of the data far longer than he normally would have, tuning out his surroundings to avoid distraction. There was very little to do while in hyperspace, but this was the only area, aside from the corridors, where he wasn't elbow to elbow with other people.

A cough brought his attention back to the world around him. Gu'od and Gamaly had managed to get up right beside him without his noticing.

Smiling, Zeric clapped his friend on the shoulder. "You're looking better. A good night's sleep did you good."

Gu'od smiled in return, but rubbed his shoulder. He was clearly still sore from the treatment he had received. Gamaly was practically clinging to him. Zeric considered telling them about that storage closet he had found, but decided not to. Gu'od could probably use a few more days rest before Gamaly got him alone, and the storage closet wasn't exactly comfortable.

Gu'od said, his antennae moving as he spoke, "I hate to say it, but I had more free space in the prison. But even with less space, having Gamaly there beside me made it the most comfortable sleep I've ever had."

Zeric wasn't a fan of their mushy talk, but he smiled politely in response. "We're en route to Irod, an unofficial colony, though that wasn't our original destination. Just another few days, and we can be free of this crowd. We'll have this whole ship to ourselves."

Frowning, Gamaly gave him a stare. This was the second woman to have given him a dark look in the last few minutes. Unlike with Lei-mey, he had no idea what he had done to deserve this one.

"So we're just going to dump these people on an undeveloped world and then abandon them, taking their only ship?" Gamaly asked.

Zeric sighed. He hated it when people assumed the worst about him. Especially when they were right. "Of course not. If this colony isn't there like it's supposed to be, we'll go find them some help first. Then we'll take our ship. I did steal it after all."

Even as he finished speaking, he knew his tone had been defensive. Gamaly had a way of zeroing in on his worse qualities. She was always right, but that only made it worse.

"Where were we supposed to go originally?" Gu'od asked. He was well versed in his role as mediator between Zeric and his wife.

"Kol. A small mining colony. Maarkean knew of some complex hidden in the desert where everyone could hide out for a while," Zeric answered. "But from what I've read in the survey report, Irod is a much nicer place. Much higher moisture content than Kol, and I doubt the colony is in the middle of a desert, so double that."

"What about that ship that was helping us?" Gamaly asked. "We didn't decide where to go until after we'd entered hyperspace. Aren't they expecting us on Kol?"

That thought had been nagging at the back of Zeric's mind for a while now. He didn't like the idea of leaving Maarkean and Lahkaba behind, but they had jumped before he was even aware their hyperdrive was fixed. Plus, Saracasi had been the one to make the decision.

If Maarkean's sister was willing to leave, then he'd probably be happy she escaped. They had done enough in scattering the fighters and taking some of the hits. The corvette had still been a few minutes away, and if they'd been smart, their hyperdrive would have been ready for them to go as well.

"We can't even be sure they made it away from Sulas," Zeric said, trying not to sound defensive. "But, if they did, they would be heading toward Kol. They had no idea we had any trouble, and we couldn't talk to them. Their communications were down ever since we left the prison."

"Then we will have to take Saracasi to Kol," Gamaly said decisively. Zeric cringed. On the surface, it seemed like a simple idea. Assuming there was a colony on Irod, they would be perfectly within their rights to take the freighter and leave them to their own problems. And going to Kol before they headed anywhere else wasn't unreasonable. But he wasn't sure what was going to happen with Maarkean when they no longer had a mutual interest. Though, bringing Saracasi to him might keep things civil. "Let's just get to Irod and hope there are people there that are friendly to us and not the Alliance. We can worry about what happens after that, after that."

Gamaly appeared to be content with that answer, and she went back to focusing her attention on squeezing Gu'od.

Saracasi spent most of the remaining trip in engineering. Chavatwor and La'ari were always discussing different ways they might try extending the environmental systems if they started to give out. The pair also talked about decisions they would have made differently in the design of the ship and various upgrades they thought would enhance performance. Overall, they were dismayed at the lack of foresight on a lot of small details, but they were impressed by the basic layout and stability of the ship.

The conversations went over Saracasi's head sometimes. She understood all of the basics, but sometimes the details were beyond her, especially at the speeds they would talk. She felt stupid asking questions at first, but Chavatwor was always more than happy to give her a comprehensive answer. Even La'ari seemed to learn a lot from some of his longer lectures.

Her favorite topic was conversions that could be done to the ship. They talked about how they could convert the ship to entirely different uses with the smallest number of large scale changes. Passenger ship was the first discussion, out of immediacy. Other ideas included a pocket battleship and scientific survey ship. Saracasi's favorite was one she thought her brother would like: a light carrier. Chavatwor seemed convinced the large cargo bays would be easy to convert to a hangar deck.

When she wasn't talking with the two engineers, Saracasi went down to the infirmary to visit Asirzi. Most of the time, she found her friend asleep. Dr. Istru did not have a lot of pain medication, but sedatives went a long way when the body's natural inclination was toward sleep. Saracasi would sit with her anyway.

On one occasion shortly before their scheduled arrival at Irod, she found her friend awake. Asirzi gave her a faint smile as she approached. She also pulled her blanket up all the way to her chin like she had every other time Saracasi had come when she was awake. The crumbled sheet managed to hide her missing breast.

"You'll be happy to know we are almost to our destination," Saracasi said, trying to infuse her words with as much optimism as possible. Despite Faide's belief, there was only a slim chance there would be anyone on Irod when they arrived. Their medical supplies were limited, and many people, Asirzi included, were in desperate need of some strong antibiotics and surgical procedures.

"I hear Irod is just covered with bright sandy beaches and luxury resorts," Asirzi said with mock confidence. "You should probably invest in a timeshare now before everyone else can. Space will fill up fast."

"Sure," Saracasi said, taking the seat beside Asirzi, "I'll transfer the credits immediately. I'm pretty worried about the entire planet filling up."

The two women exchanged meaningless banter for several minutes. Saracasi enjoyed talking to Asirzi. For a short time, she forgot her other worries. They never talked about Asirzi's condition, which made Saracasi think she was helping Asirzi forget as well.

After some time, Asirzi asked a more serious question. "I hear you were talking with Lei-mey Darshawn."

Saracasi was curious why Asirzi would know about that. "She just wanted to know about Maarkean. How do you know Lei-mey?"

"Most of us 'aliens' on Sulas have heard of Lei-mey. She has staged numerous protests and succeeded in getting several reform candidates elected to the Sulas legislature. Those of us who were inside Olan only got our news when new people were brought in, but that was enough," Asirzi explained. "I never even knew she was in Olan until we escaped. I guess the lockdown kept the word from spreading. But it has certainly made its way through the ship."

With a pointed look at Saracasi, Asirzi continued, "Is something bothering you?"

Embarrassed, Saracasi considered what to say. She had come to realize that she was worried about Maarkean, and it must have started to show through to her expression. She had tried to assume he made it away from Sulas perfectly fine, but the truth was that she had ordered them to escape to hyperspace and leave him behind.

At the time it had seemed so clear cut – save seven hundred people or put them at risk to help one person. It hadn't been a genuine choice, in her mind. That was part of why she felt guilty. She should have agonized over the decision to leave her brother behind. Zeric had done the exact opposite:

he had put everyone on the ship at risk to save her brother, someone he hardly knew.

She tried to rationalize it away, thinking that Zeric hadn't really had a choice. But that didn't help much, because her first reaction to what Zeric had done had been to think he was crazy.

On top of all of that, she also thought she was a coward. What she had certainly done was flee and save herself. Had she been on the *Cutty Sark* instead of the freighter, would she have made the same decision?

"I'm just worried about my brother." That, she felt, was close enough to the truth.

Asirzi gave her a comforting smile. "I would be too. But Chavatwor seems confident he made it out of there safely."

That filled Saracasi with some comfort. She had come to respect Chavatwor during her time in Olan, and he was highly knowledgeable about ships. But he hadn't even been on the bridge to see the situation.

Saracasi changed the topic. She stayed and talked with Asirzi for a while longer, until Zeric announced to the ship that they were about to come out of hyperspace.

Standing on the bridge at the command station, Zeric watched the timer tick down on the hyperspace jump. Next to it was a timer showing the approximate time until they all suffocated. Originally there had been almost a day's difference between those two numbers. Only a few hours ago, one of the CO_2 scrubbers had completely failed, and now there was only a few hours difference.

When Chavatwor had told him about the failure, Zeric had decided not to share the news with anyone else. The Kowwok had made it clear that there was nothing they could do to repair it without spare parts that they didn't have.

Since they were so close to Irod, and hopeful salvation, there was no point in alarming anyone else.

The two kids from earlier, Isaxo and Ceno, were operating the helm and one of the operations stations. Chavatwor was monitoring things in engineering with La'ari, and Saracasi had just arrived to man the engineering station on the bridge. He had asked Chungum, Jasmaine, Gu'od and Gamaly to be at the mining laser controls, just in case.

Standing beside him were Faide and Lei-mey. The two had taken on a sort of dual leadership role among the refugees. They were the ones who had decided to refer to them as refugees, rather than escaped prisoners, if they met anyone down on the moon. Zeric agreed it sounded better without being untrue, but he saw no reason to fool themselves that it would work. For one thing, too many of them were still in prison jumpsuits.

On cue, the timer reached zero and the swirl of hyperspace was replaced by two worlds. Directly before them was Irod's dark shape, and behind it was the massive colored ball of the gas giant it orbited. It was a relief to have made it.

According to the survey report in the database, Irod was a world cast in perpetual twilight. The moon matched the orbit of another larger moon, Durod, which was farther out from the gas giant, Zod – Faide had supplied the names. During the time the two moons spent on the sun side of Zod, much of the star's light was blocked by the larger moon. For only about a week and a half out of every six-week orbit did the moon have direct sunlight, rather than just light reflected from Zod.

None of that particularly concerned Zeric at the moment. The moon had breathable air. Of course, every new world carried with it a chance of unknown allergens and infections, but even if there wasn't a colony down there capable of delivering inoculations, they had no choice but to land.

"Well, we're here," Zeric said simply.

Everyone turned to look at him as if expecting more, and he stared back. No one spoke for a moment. Zeric got the sense that Lei-mey and Faide had been expecting something profound, either from him or themselves. His simple declaration had ruined that opportunity.

"So, Faide," Zeric said, trying to move things along, "where's this colony of yours?"

The Notha bowed his head in embarrassment. "I do not have a set of coordinates. It was so long ago. But should not an active colony be easy to locate from orbit if it is the only thing non-native on the planet?"

"Assuming it's a usual colony with fusion reactors, communication towers and buildings. Your friends sounded like a get-back-to-nature group."

To Zeric's surprise, Faide laughed. "Pacifism and conservationism often go together, that is true, but they are not directly tied. I assure you my friends were quite enamored with the comforts of civilization."

It was Zeric's turn to shrug. "Let's hope so. Okay, Isaxo, scan the planet for any signs of power or communication. Ceno, put us into a high fast orbit so we can get maximum view of the surface. If we don't find anything, there's a good chance the colony is just on the other side."

It felt stupid saying the obvious, but everyone responded to it. The crowd at the back of the bridge watched eagerly as they got closer and the moon filled more of the view. Ceno put them into a stable orbit and then turned the ship so they could see the surface.

Zeric had overheard that some people were looking forward to seeing their new home. A good portion of the prison population, especially those who had been inside for the longest, was ready to settle down wherever they ended up. Another segment appeared to view this as merely a safe stop on their way back to Sulas or wherever they had originated. For everyone, though, Irod was viewed as salvation.

Zeric personally didn't care one way or the other where any of them ended up. He did have the pessimistic view that, once they landed, all of them might be stuck there for a long, long time. Chavatwor had made it clear that with the failure of the CO_2 scrubber, the ship might not be going anywhere without substantial repairs, even with a small crew.

After forty-five minutes and orbiting about halfway around the moon, Isaxo called out excitedly, "I've got something. I'm reading communication signals. Faint, local surface-to-surface stuff but definitely not natural."

Zeric smiled. This was excellent news; settling permanently on an unknown moon that got little sunlight held very little appeal for him. Where there were comm signals, there were people. And where there were people, he sincerely hoped, there were spare parts.

"Okay, open a signal down to them and request permission to land. Let's not startle them."

Several more moments went by where the only sound was Isaxo speaking into his headset. He repeated his call down to the planet multiple times and finally turned back toward Zeric. "I'm not getting any response. There is no way to tell if they are receiving me. They may not have any surface to orbit comm stations, no one could be monitoring, or they are ignoring us."

Giving a sideways look at Faide, Zeric said, "Guess we'll have to startle them after all. Is there anything that looks like a starport or landing strip?"

"Yes," Isaxo replied, "there is a small open area on one side of the settlement. It looks to be paved over and is just big enough for us to land on."

Smiling confidently, Zeric turn to Ceno. The Camari was looking at him expectantly. "How are you and landings?"

"I can get us down," Ceno said confidently.

"Of that I have no doubt. Gravity will make sure of that."

Despite what he thought was a clever joke, Ceno didn't smile. Or maybe it was possible Camari lips weren't capable of smiling. The only Camari he'd known well had never smiled at him, but she also hadn't liked him very much. Either way, Zeric moved ahead. "All right, put us down."

Turning to Faide, Zeric said quietly, "Let's hope your friends are still pacifists."

CHAPTER TEN

Three days spent worrying, and now that they had arrived, Maarkean started worrying anew. He had known they would reach Kol first, and he knew the freighter would be at least three days, possibly four or five, behind them. Yet here they were, in the orbit of Kol, and worry filled him.

When the freighter had jumped into hyperspace back at Sulas, it had been a great relief. The fire from the freighter's mining equipment had relieved some of the pressure that had been on them from the fighters. It had even saved them from several missiles, but they had been fighting a losing battle. A few more minutes, and the corvette would have arrived, putting a quick end to the fight.

It had been an uncomfortably narrow escape from there. Once the freighter jumped, all six fighters turned on the *Cutty Sark*. Fortunately, Lahkaba had plotted a course for them; it was just a matter of surviving long enough to get the right bearing and engage the hyperdrive. Even then, it had been the closest jump he had ever made.

After that, it had been an uneventful journey. Maarkean had used most of the advance he had gotten from Josserand to refuel and restock the ship while on Sulas. For once, food and fuel were not a concern. A quick course change in deep space to throw off pursuit, and they had arrived at Kol.

"Doesn't look very friendly," Lahkaba said as he stared down at the planet they were approaching.

"No, it doesn't," Maarkean agreed.

The planet of Kol was like most habitable worlds, covered with varying climates and regions. However, it was dominated by one feature that tainted any description of the place. The oceans were much smaller than on a typical world, and there was one giant continent surrounded by several smaller island continents. The main continent, which covered half the planet, had a massive desert spanning its entire length.

The coastal regions and the smaller continents had relatively temperate climates. On one of Maarkean's stays on the world, he had visited one of the resorts and had found the beaches quite lovely. Yet despite the more pleasant nature of those regions, most of the planet's population lived within the massive desert. Contained within the desert were vast supplies of valuable resources that were the main reason anyone would want to live on this world.

"So tell me again why we're going to an abandoned outpost in the middle of that desert instead of those nice-looking tropical islands?"

"Because that is where no one will find us. The only Alliance presence on the entire planet is in a town on one of those beautiful tropical islands. They rarely visit the active mining towns in the desert, much less the inactive ones."

Maarkean started maneuvering the ship into her descent toward the surface. It was nice not having to try to avoid detection. There were no planet-wide tracking stations monitoring the skies of Kol. Each settlement had its own detection gear that could have been networked to provide a planetary grid.

However, each was owned by a different mining company, and they were not inclined to share data. They were also not inclined to make it easier for the few Alliance officials to track the illegal smuggling ships they all used. It was quite profitable to use smugglers to avoid having the expense of shipping all of their mined ore back through central Alliance worlds. As long as he didn't approach any settlement, they would ignore him.

"You say the planet is a nest bed of smuggling?"

"Yes," Maarkean responded.

"Why doesn't the Alliance send out ships to keep it in check?"

Maarkean replied with a disgusted tone, "Economics. They still receive enough profit from the cargo the companies do send back and pay taxes on. If they sent a permanent ship, that would cost money and would not likely net much more in the way of duties. They would need to send a task force to cover an entire planet, which is a significant cost. Plus, if they had a stronger military presence, they would be forced to deal with the rampant piracy, which would cost more."

"I heard that Kol faced a serious pirate problem," Lahkaba asked, clearly concerned.

Smiling at the Kowwok as they hit the atmosphere, Maarkean replied, "Oh, yeah. Mineral rich planet with little Alliance supervision. Lots of profit to be made by pirates."

"I'm revising my assessment of this plan," Lahkaba growled softly. "We're planning to take hundreds of recently freed and helpless political prisoners to an outpost in the middle of an inhospitable desert on a planet crawling with pirates and smugglers. Sounds like a great plan."

"You forgot the giant people-eating lizards that live in the deserts."

If Lahkaba's white fur could become whiter, Maarkean would have sworn it did. He didn't know much about Kowwoks, but one thing he had heard was that they had an instinctual fear of being eaten by lizards. Their world was home to a particularly nasty variety that had been one of the chief predators of their biological ancestors. Some believed this fear was the reason the lizard-like Dotrans had managed to subjugate the Kowwoks for so long.

Lahkaba gave him a hard stare, and Maarkean broke out into a laugh. He had come to like the Kowwok. Three days enclosed together on a small ship had afforded them the opportunity to get to know each other somewhat. Without the threat of imminent death, and no one else depending on them, they had both been able to relax.

"You're joking," Lahkaba said angrily. "About the lizards. Ha, ha. Very funny."

Trying hard to breathe properly again, Maarkean addressed his friend as calmly as he could manage. "No, actually. But don't worry, they aren't seen in this region much. They tend to stick to the northern regions, where their natural prey can find more food."

Is Lahkaba a friend? Maarkean wondered. Facing the Alliance fighters together had allowed a bond to form between them. At first he found it odd, since the last time he had felt that bond had been in a war fighting people like Lahkaba. He understood when it had developed with Zeric; he was a Terran and they both were former military.

Deciding there was no point in pursuing that line of thought, Maarkean focused on their descent. They were only a few minutes from the outpost; he started to recognize some of the terrain. Not much had changed in the last few years.

"Why is this place abandoned?" Lahkaba asked.

"It was a mining colony. They strip mined the area and extracted all of the easy resources. Then they left. That was a hundred years ago. There are colonies like this all over the desert."

Through the forward window, a collection of buildings came into view. There was one main building, a massive warehouse and four smaller structures surrounding a small natural oasis that served as a courtyard. All of the buildings were made out of sandstone that matched the surrounding terrain. The buildings all had balconies that were now covered in sand.

"Welcome to Bravo HQ," Maarkean said. "And don't ask about the name; the company that built this place called it that."

"Well," Lahkaba said, "it is definitely isolated. And up there on that hill, it's well protected from ground level."

"It's not on a hill. It's actually not much above sea level. Those canyons used to be hills though."

Beyond the warehouse stretched a large expanse of flat, dry, cracked ground that stretched for several kilometers. Surrounding this entire area were several-kilometer-deep canyons. Each crater was once a hill or mountain and was now stripped of all valuable resources. Some vegetation had started to regrow in the craters, but it was sparse.

"That warehouse should be large enough to hide the freighter; they used it for their mining equipment and the ore they extracted. It's fitting to store a mining freighter here," Maarkean said with an amused smile. "Each of those smaller buildings can house about fifty people in a barracks-style set-up. The main building served as their headquarters, but it can be converted into living space.

"Believe it or not, water will not be a problem. There is a substantial reservoir underneath; probably why the company set up headquarters here. As part of each building, they built a greenhouse using that water. Smugglers have used this place as a stay over, and several of those gardens are still producing food. Probably not enough, but it's a start."

Lahkaba looked impressed, which was a nice change from his earlier skepticism. Maarkean had stayed here with Saracasi on more than one occasion. A group they had flown with that ran goods off Kol had been based here. Until they had been wiped out by pirates, it had been a profitable time.

"What do we do if one of those groups shows up looking to hang out here?"

"They won't," Maarkean said confidently as he took the ship in for a landing beyond the warehouse. "We smugglers generally avoid each other. Hurts business if there are too many people around. If anyone swings by, they'll see our ship from the air and go to a different location."

"What about if the pirates come?"

"Then I get to see if you are as good with a pistol as you are with a turret," Maarkean said. "Kidding. I may have exaggerated the piracy problem just a bit, earlier." The Kowwok gave him a look that might have been a glower, and Maarkean grinned. "I wouldn't worry too much about it. While there are no permanent Alliance ships in orbit, the task force out of Ailleroc does make periodic visits. And the base has a few fighters that make some patrols. Not enough to prevent piracy, but enough to keep it from getting out of hand."

"You were not the only person to suggest that it was much worse than that," Lahkaba said, and then continued as if choosing his words carefully. "The few Kolians I've met suggested piracy was rampant and the Alliance was only concerned with preventing smuggling."

"Trust me. If it weren't for the Alliance presence, the situation here would be much worse. Not many people like the Alliance taxes and trade restrictions, but they provide necessary protection," Maarkean answered.

He always felt people that complained about Alliance taxation and then demanded more protection were hypocrites. Naval ships couldn't be built or operated for free. Although, he had to admit to himself, he could sympathize with the people of Kol.

The trade rules and taxes were out of proportion to the amount of protection provided to them. Piracy was a known problem, but the Alliance did not do enough to combat it.

The rest of the ride down to the surface was done in silence. Maarkean put the *Cutty Sark* down on the hard-packed ground a short distance away from the large warehouse. After a quick systems check, he and Lahkaba powered down the ship and stepped out onto the surface of Kol. The air was quite a bit hotter than it had been on the ship, but it had almost no humidity.

As they made their way around the warehouse and toward the other buildings, sand and dust swirled around them. The dark brown duster Maarkean liked to wear had been purchased because of his time here. It served its purpose well by keeping much of the sand off his clothes. He felt sorry for Lahkaba, who followed the Kowwok custom of not wearing much clothing. His fur would be full of sand and dirt.

The pair performed a quick survey of the buildings to ensure there was no one else already using the place. There was no obvious sign that anyone had been here since Maarkean's last visit over a year ago. After the search, Maarkean took Lahkaba to one of the greenhouses.

The plants in the greenhouse were either dead or overgrown. Most of the vegetables had suffered from not being tended to, but a few had taken the opportunity to expand into their dead neighbors' space. The watering system was still functioning, which was why everything wasn't dead.

"Well, we look to be alone," Lahkaba said. "At least for the time being. I guess now we wait. How long do you estimate it will be before the freighter arrives?"

Maarkean shrugged as he examined one of the vines. "The *Cutty Sark* has a hyperdrive that is about twice as fast as the freighter. If they took some damage, they might have to go slower. No sooner than three days. Maybe as many as five or six."

"Well, guess I get to see if I'm any good at gardening," Lahkaba said with little enthusiasm.

Zeric wanted to keep the prisoners, or, rather, refugees, from leaving the ship and swarming the colony. However, their admiration, respect and gratitude for him were up against their desire for space, fresh air and freedom. For a collection of prisoners, those were pretty strong motivators. He wasn't sure how successful he would be.

Once the freighter touched down on solid ground, Zeric ordered Saracasi to seal the cargo bay doors until he got down there. The Braz woman frowned at him, clearly not liking the idea of sealing anyone inside the ship. But she did it, and Zeric headed down to the cargo bay, followed by Faide and Lei-mey.

They rode the elevator down in silence. Zeric was unsure how things were going to play out. Faide claimed to know the people of this colony, but sixteen years was a long time. Even if he had known the original founders, they could be dead or no longer friendly to Faide, or even to outsiders in general. Anything was possible on an isolated colony.

In the crowded cargo bay, Zeric was relieved to find Gu'od, Gamaly and Lohcja waiting for him. The Ronid had one arm in a sling but was holding a pistol in his other hand. The injury only served to enhance the fearsomeness of his tough, spiked green carapace.

"We will not need any weapons," Faide said, his voice revealing some annoyance.

"I hope you're right," Zeric said, "but people who want to be left alone don't always take kindly to strangers showing up. And you yourself said they weren't pacifists."

With a nod to Gu'od and Gamaly, Zeric moved through the crowd of refugees. Most of them had changed into civilian attire, though there were quite a few among them still dressed in prison jumpsuits, Gu'od and Gamaly included. At least there wouldn't be seven hundred people in prison jumpsuits.

Once at the door, Zeric turned back to the crowd. "Okay, everyone, I'm going to lower the cargo bay door. I know how much you all want to get out into the open air. But we don't know how accommodating the people in this colony are going to be. Let us go out and greet them first, before you come out. The doors will be open, though, so we'll all get some nice, fresh air."

The crowd expressed some nervous agitation as Zeric spoke, but the mention of fresh air helped alleviate it a little, he thought. He just hoped they didn't all stampede him as soon as the door opened. That would be a fitting way to go.

He signaled Saracasi to unlock the door and then activated the mechanism. The massive cargo bay door groaned as it started to lower. With the first crack, a rush of cool, fresh air flowed in. Zeric closed his eyes and let the welcome breeze wash over him. The ship's entire water supply had been used as drinking water for the passengers, and Zeric hadn't been able to shower in several days.

As the door continued its arc downward, Zeric started to get a better view of the moon of Irod. The sky was a dim reddish color as the system's star peeked light out at them from behind the massive dark giant world of Zod. Locally, it was close to the moon's noon, but it looked like just a little after dawn would look on most worlds.

The freighter took up most of the concrete tarmac that they had landed on; beyond its edge was rough, natural grass. The field extended for about a kilometer before it terminated at a river in one direction and the edges of the colony in another. It took him a moment to adjust to the dimmer light, but he soon noticed a collection of vehicles approaching them from the colony.

Even without tracking systems, the colonists had responded quickly, Zeric thought. That could mean they were used to strange freighters arriving; just because the Alliance navigational database only had a century-old survey report for the moon didn't mean others couldn't find it.

It could also mean they were ready to repel outsiders.

Zeric led Faide and Lei-mey down the ramp and toward the oncoming vehicles. Gu'od, Gamaly and Lohcja fanned out from them, taking up positions on the edges of the ramp. The crowd on the ship did surge forward, but, to his relief, they stopped only a few meters beyond the ramp.

The three vehicles came to a stop a few meters away from Zeric and the others. Several figures climbed out of two of them, all holding rifles of various sorts. They weren't wearing any uniforms, so Zeric assumed they were a militia, or, possibly, hired thugs.

In the center vehicle, three figures got out: a Liw'kel, a Camari and a Notha. The Notha, with tan fur and casual business attire, stepped forward. He had a suspicious expression on his face.

"You seem to have a fairly large crew, for a freighter. I'm afraid our colony does not have a lot to trade," the Notha said.

As he approached, he looked each of them over quickly. He stopped and gave Faide a thorough examination.

"Faide?" the Notha said after a moment, his tone hesitant.

Beside Zeric, Faide's tail started twitching excitedly. "Hello, Revas."

"It is you!" Revas exclaimed and rushed forward. The two Notha embraced in a friendly hug. "I gave up on you ever joining us here a long time ago. It's good to know you hadn't forgotten about us."

"No, I just got a little delayed," Faide answered. Zeric thought that was quite the understatement.

"Revas, this is Lei-mey Darshawn and Zeric Dustlighter," Faide said. "We came here with some refugees seeking a safe harbor from the Alliance."

Revas looked past the three of them, his bushy eyebrows raised quizzically. "I see. How many have you brought?"

"About seven hundred," Faide answered.

"That's quite a few. Almost two percent of our population. We have plenty of space, of course, but I'm not sure we have enough spare housing or supplies to take in that many."

"All we ask is to be able to stay on Irod for a time," Faide answered. "Our freighter has had life support failure, so we cannot go anywhere else. We have many injured, but the rest will be willing to build their own structures and help plant more fields for food."

Zeric didn't remember any of the refugees agreeing to any of those things, but he didn't think it was an unreasonable statement. He certainly didn't plan on staying here and becoming a farmer, but if his choice was that or suffocation, he could do it. For a while, at least.

"We can work out the logistics later," Revas said, after a slight pause. "Let us see to your injured first."

Saracasi helped with moving some of the injured refugees to the colony's small hospital. The building wasn't much bigger than the common area onboard the freighter, but it did have a surgical suite and was well stocked with medical supplies. Dr. Istru immediately prioritized the surgeries and began working with the local doctors. Asirzi was taken in with the first group to receive treatment, along with Pasha, one of their rescuers.

Once the injured were taken care of, most of the refugees were taken to the colony's school. It was the only building big enough to house them all. Saracasi managed to separate herself from that group and accompanied Chavatwor around to some of the shops in the colony.

The colony had no formal starport besides the landing tarmac. There was a small building that held a deuterium storage tank, and there was an extraction facility beside the river. That filled Saracasi with some confidence – knowing they wouldn't get stranded on the planet for lack of fuel.

The closest thing to a starship repair shop they found was a small industrial parts store that sold spare parts for ground transports and industrial vehicles. They did not expect to find much of what they needed to repair the life support system, but she thought Chavatwor might be able to machine some parts, assuming there were the necessary tools.

With all the excitement that had filled the colony that morning, they had to wait a while for the store owner to return. The man was a friendly Camari who sympathized with them when Chavatwor explained the trouble with the life support system. It was clear, though, that the man did not understand most of what Chavatwor asked.

Interrupting the long explanation of how they could make the repairs, Saracasi said, "Where do you get your supplies? I take it you do not have ships of your own, so who brings your industrial parts in?"

"Oh, there are a few friendly traders that come by every few months. We place orders with them when they come and trade them some of our harvest and what comes out of the mine," the shopkeeper answered.

Saracasi's heart sank. With no spaceworthy ships, the colony was dependant on a group of merchants. That meant it could be months before one arrived and then months more before they returned with replacement parts, assuming they could afford them.

As if reading her mind, the merchant said quickly, "But one of them is due in the next few weeks. Captain Novastar is good about coming regularly."

"Captain Novastar is a trader?" Saracasi asked.

"Yes, of a sort," the merchant said cryptically.

Saracasi said, "Thanks for your help."

As she left the shop, Chavatwor followed her. "What was that about? It's good that there is a trader coming, right?"

"He's not a trader," Saracasi replied as they walked. "He'll be a smuggler. We won't be getting off this world without something substantial to give him."

They walked in silence for several minutes. Saracasi considered her options. She could wait and hope this Novastar would give them a ride or deliver a message. There wasn't much she could offer him in trade, and she knew he would demand more than she had.

Staying here was an option she considered. She liked most of the people she had met, and it would give her the chance to get to know Asirzi better. Life here might not be too bad, though she had no idea how she would make a life for herself.

She had no skills that would be of any use on a rural agricultural world. The main reason not to stay was that Maarkean would never know what happened to her. She did not want to do that to him.

There was only one real option remaining to her. "How bad was the life support system?"

"Pretty bad. It's still functional, and we can refill the oxygen tanks here. But the CO_2 filters are down to one unit. And there are no replacements," Chavatwor answered glumly.

"But it's working?" Saracasi asked. She had been under the impression that the entire system had failed. This sparked new hope.

"Technically. You couldn't provide air for more than a handful of people for a couple days though."

"That's all I'll need. We need to find Zeric."

When Lei-mey and Faide invited him to a meeting with the colony's mayor, Zeric thought it odd. Curious, he decided to attend. It started out logically, with the pair of them discussing whether the refugees were welcome and how best to integrate those who wished to stay into the colony, and what options existed for those who wanted to return home.

When the topic of leaving came up, Zeric assumed that was the reason he was brought in. He shared with everyone the sorry state of the life support system on the freighter, and that it would not be able to move a sizable group anywhere. They accepted his word and turned to housing. Zeric assumed his part was done and stopped listening. He hated meetings.

It came as a surprise some time later when he found everyone staring at him. His earlier assumption about not playing any further part in the discussion had obviously been wrong. He tried to recall what they had been talking about, but realized he had completely tuned them out.

"I'm sorry, could you repeat that?"

Lei-mey gave him a dark expression, but Faide answered, "We were asking what your assessment of the colony's defenses were. How likely are we to face Alliance retaliation?"

It was an unusual question and Zeric sat up in his chair. "Have they ever bothered this colony before?"

Revas Shim shook his head, so Zeric continued, "Then you're fine. We jumped to meaningless coordinates first and then here from there. The Alliance corvette that was tracking us on Sulas, if it decided to follow, would be heading in the complete opposite direction."

"Couldn't they have tracked us to our stopping point and then from there to here?" Lei-mey asked with evident concern.

"I'm no expert, but I do know you can't track anything in hyperspace. Once we jumped, the Alliance could only guess based on our course. They either would follow our original heading to somewhere we're not, or would assume we did what we did, but have no idea where we dropped out of hyperspace, so no way to guess where we went next."

"So we should have nothing to worry about from the Alliance?" Lei-mey prodded.

"Correct," Zeric said with finality. He knew that it wasn't completely true, but it was close enough.

"See, Mayor, your people are safe," Lei-mey said forcefully.

Zeric was taken aback by her tone. Revas Shim looked annoyed at her, and Zeric sympathized. The mayor had taken them in and offered medical assistance. Zeric didn't see any reason for Lei-mey to treat him like that. He wished he'd paid attention to what they had been talking about to end up at odds.

"For now, we are safe," Revas Shim said, sounding annoyed. "But if your people want to start leaving, we cannot guarantee we'll stay that way. Back and forth transport between here and Sulas will lead the Alliance straight here."

"Maybe. But the Alliance has no authority here. This moon is not an Alliance world," Lei-mey insisted.

"And you think that matters?" Revas countered.

Zeric realized he had missed a whole argument between the pair. Faide stepped in and tried to keep the two parties civil, but Zeric picked up that Lei-mey had ideas about creating a transit network from Irod to Sulas for other refugees. *What* other refugees, Zeric was not sure.

After a few moments, Lei-mey said something that shocked Zeric. She asked Revas Shim where they could set up a camp to start training volunteers to defend the colony. Suddenly the question about his assessment of their defenses made more sense.

If Lei-mey wanted to build an army, was she expecting him to be a part of it?

Thinking fast, Zeric said, "Um, Faide, I thought you said these people were pacifists? They don't want an army trained here."

Faide nodded, and Revas answered, "Isolationists would be a better description, but you are not far off. Most of us that came here did not want to be involved in the war that was occurring. Some for pacifist reasons, others just to stay alive. And we definitely have no interest in having an army."

"Can you speak for all of your people, Mayor? You said yourself they are not all pacifists," Lei-mey pushed. "It is a big moon; we don't have to do it here in town."

Zeric jumped in. "Maybe building an army here isn't such a good idea. These nice people have been kind enough to take you in. Besides, shouldn't you focus on more immediate things, like food and shelter?" He tried to stress 'you' instead of 'we.'

Lei-mey considered him for a moment and then nodded. "You are right. I apologize, Mayor Shim. You have been more than generous to us so far, and I should not be so quick to dismiss your wishes."

Revas Shim smiled. "It is quite all right. I can understand your desire to fight back after being imprisoned. Now let us return to the subject of housing."

The conversation returned to mundane matters, and Zeric once again stopped listening. This time, instead of letting his mind wander, he tried to figure out how to get himself out of this mess. He doubted Lei-mey would put off her plans for long, despite what she said to the mayor.

After the meeting ended, Zeric left with Lei-mey. He had not managed to come up with a solution. The meeting had not returned to the subject of the Alliance or an army. But as soon as they were away from Faide and Revas, Lei-mey brought it up again.

"This is a big moon," she began. "We don't have to remain close to the colony."

Deciding the direct approach was best, Zeric said, "Look, Lei-mey, I think you have the wrong impression. I don't want to become involved in whatever you're planning. I didn't break you out of jail because I believe in your politics. I did it to get my friends free."

Lei-mey gave him a thorough look that made Zeric feel like she was looking into his soul. After a moment, she spoke.

"I know. If it were up to me, I wouldn't want you involved. I knew from the moment we met that you were not one of us. Your willingness to immediately jump in bed with my sister proved that. I have my doubts about this Maarkean as well, though there is no way to know without meeting him."

"Then why are we having this conversation?" Zeric asked, confused.

"Because, regardless of your intentions, you're a hero now," Lei-mey said, clearly frustrated by the truth of what she said. "My friends have already shared the story with everyone freed from Olan. Pasha, Lohcja, Ceta, Meyka, all agree that this was only possible because of you and Maarkean.

"That story can be allowed to spread once we allow people to return home. The only one who might become a bigger hero is Jairyd, and I fear that is because he is likely dead."

Lei-mey's voice betrayed the most emotion Zeric had seen from her when she mentioned Jairyd. He regretted leaving the man behind, but it was unlikely that he had still been alive. They would probably never know for sure, unless the Alliance revealed what happened.

"So you see, I may not like you, but I can use you," Lei-mey continued. "You'll be the perfect example of what people can accomplish."

Zeric looked at Lei-mey with a sense of shock. He had never considered the consequences of their raid on the prison.

Death or success had been the only two outcomes he had expected. He did not like where Lei-mey was going.

"I thought you weren't a terrorist," Zeric asked. "Your friends all made it clear you were just a politician."

"I am not a terrorist, nor will I ever become one," Lei-mey said bitterly. "But there is a lot of grey area between the two. I was all about trying to find a political solution to the problems Sulas faced under Alliance rule. You've opened the door to something more."

"Believe that if you want. I don't want to be a part of it," Zeric said. "I work to get paid. This was a one-time gig to save my friends. I don't think there's a lot of money in what you're proposing."

Lei-mey gave him a dark look that almost made him regret what he'd said. He wasn't as cold-hearted a mercenary as he sounded.

But joining a rebellion led by Lei-mey did not appear to be a way to ensure a long life. As a thief, he had to take risks, but he was very careful about which ones he took.

"Very well. I could have made you into a hero across the colonies. You could have helped me save millions from oppression." Turning away, Lei-mey stalked off.

Zeric felt sure she was not done with this conversation. She struck him as the type of person who normally got her way in the end, and unfortunately, he wasn't unsympathetic to her cause. Getting off the moon soon would be his best defense.

"Saracasi, good, there you are," Zeric said as he approached her.

Saracasi turned suddenly from where she had been about to board the freighter. Her ponytail caught on her shoulder, and she flicked it off so it once again hung down her back. Zeric was approaching her, moving quickly, with Gu'od and Gamaly following behind.

"How soon can you make this thing ready to fly?" Zeric asked.

His question mirrored what she had wanted to discuss with him. The urgency in his voice concerned her, though. Even though she wanted to go meet Maarkean, she was in no rush to get back aboard the freighter.

"That depends on what you plan to do with it," Saracasi replied. "The engines are fully functional, so it will fly right now."

"Okay," Zeric said, a bit of annoyance in his voice, "how soon before it can take three people to the nearest civilized planet?"

Gamaly jabbed Zeric in his ribs. He gave the Liw'kel a dirty look before turning back to Saracasi and saying, "I mean, take four people to Kol?"

The announcement of their intentions to go to Kol filled Saracasi with excitement. It seemed Gamaly, at least, was on her side in getting her back to Maarkean.

"Couple hours," she said after thinking for a moment. "We need to refill the oxygen tanks, see if the colony can spare some deuterium, and then vent the ship thoroughly, get as much of the accumulated CO2 cleared as we can."

"Okay, let's get started," Zeric said, passing her and boarding the freighter.

Once the work began, Saracasi excused herself and headed into the colony. Zeric had insisted on leaving immediately, but Saracasi couldn't leave without looking in on Asirzi. She politely invited Gamaly to come with her, but the woman declined with a knowing smile.

Arriving at the small hospital, Saracasi looked around for a receptionist. She found none, but a few moments of looking turned up an exhausted Noti Istru. The Ronid doctor was sitting in a small cafeteria with a cold cup of coffee in front of him. Saracasi was hesitant to bother him, but he was the first person she had found who wasn't actively helping a patient.

When she approached, Noti looked up from the table and gave her a weak smile with his mandibles. "What can I do for you, Ms. Ocaitchi?"

"I wanted to see how Asirzi was doing," Saracasi asked, surprised by her nervousness. "The Liw'kel with the blaster shot and multiple lacerations?"

"Remarkably well. We were finally able to stop the internal bleeding, so her eventual recovery is almost certain. Though there is still a chance we might have to amputate her arm. The equipment is pretty rudimentary here, so we won't be able to do a clone regrowth."

The news that her friend was doing better overshadowed the news about her arm. "Can I see her?"

"Unfortunately not," Noti said. "She is still recovering from her surgery, and we have her sedated. She'll be out for quite a while."

Saracasi was filled with regret. She hated the idea of leaving without at least saying goodbye, but Zeric insisted on departing today. There was always the chance that Maarkean would bring them back here to drop off the member of this rebel group that was with him.

"Could you give her a message, then?" Saracasi asked hesitantly. "Let her know I stopped by to say goodbye. We're leaving to go meet my brother on Kol. I wanted to... wish her well."

The words sounded weak and pointless in her head, but it was all she was comfortable saying through an intermediary. Noti smiled and nodded. "Of course. I will give her the message. When do you think you will be back?"

Saracasi shrugged. "I don't know. It's a question if the freighter will even make it all the way to Kol."

"Sounds dangerous. Is it wise to go?" Noti asked, concerned.

"Maybe not. But my brother risked everything to get me out. I can't leave him on Kol wondering what happened to me."

Noti smiled. "I understand. When you get there, and emphasis on the when, thank him for me. It is nice to be free of that place and able to practice medicine again. Though, you can also tell him, the next time he wants to break into a prison, try to keep the number of lacerations and blaster wounds down."

"I'll tell him," Saracasi said with a small laugh. "Thank you, Doctor."

Noti nodded at her and appeared to immediately go back to staring at his cold cup. Saracasi assumed he was sleeping. It had been almost a day since they had arrived, and she doubted he had had any actual sleep since then. She knew he had also gotten too little during the trip here.

As she was leaving the hospital, she was stopped by another Ronid, this one with a thicker green carapace. She recognized him as Lohcja, one of the group which had broken them out. His arm was still in a sling, but he looked much better than he had the last few days. "Lohcja, right?" she asked.

"Yeah, and you're Saracasi, Maarkean's sister."

She nodded, and he continued, "I overheard you talking to the doctor. You say you're heading to Kol to meet Maarkean?"

"Yes. He had no idea we had to change our plans. He'll be waiting there. Unfortunately, the ship's life support system is pretty strained. It's going to be an iffy trip."

Lohcja nodded. "I want to come with you. My friend Lahkaba was flying with your brother."

"The ship can't support very many people," Saracasi replied. "I don't know if we can take any more."

Zeric had been pretty insistent that only the four of them left. She had wondered why at the time, but it hadn't really mattered to her. Now she wondered how serious he was about it. Lohcja appeared gravely concerned for his friend.

Deciding to pass the buck, she said, "You can come with me to the ship. It's Zeric's call, though."

"Fair enough," Lohcja said.

The pair of them walked through the dark colony. The moon's rotation was within the reasonable range, with a day taking thirty hours. However, because of their current orbital position, the gas giant Zod blocked part of the sun even in daytime. There was still enough light to call it 'day,' but Saracasi thought of it as more of an awfully long dusk.

Lohcja didn't speak during the walk back to the ship. Saracasi realized she had no idea why he had helped break them out. She understood Zeric and Maarkean's motives, but she only vaguely understood the others. Making a raid to retrieve a leader of a political group was a risky endeavor.

"I never thanked you for coming to break us all out," Saracasi said.

"No thanks necessary," Lohcja said uncomfortably.

"How did you come to join this group?" she asked, trying to get something out of him.

"I'm not really part of any group. Let's just say that Lahkaba got involved, and as his friend, I followed him."

"Lahkaba is the one with Maarkean, right? He was part of Lei-mey's movement?" Saracasi asked, curious.

Lohcja hesitated and shrugged awkwardly. "Not exactly. Lahkaba was part of the political movement that supported the Kreogh Sector Congress. When the delegates returned, the Alliance put warrants out on all of them, even though their identities were supposed to be secret. Everyone associated with them was labeled traitors and terrorists. Maarkean and Zeric stumbled upon a group of us trying to hide some of them. Lei-mey was not so lucky."

"So there were other delegates in that group?"

Evasively, Lohcja answered, "That's not really for me to say."

Saracasi decided not to press the man any more. When they reached the ship, Saracasi found Zeric talking with Chavatwor in the cargo bay. As they approached, she overheard Chavatwor saying, "I still think this is foolish."

"Any more foolish than what we've already done?" Zeric asked with a coy smile.

Chavatwor shrugged. "I guess not. Maybe by the time you return, we can get the parts we need to fully repair her."

"Maybe," Zeric replied noncommittally. "But don't go spending good money on parts. Wouldn't want you to waste your money if we just end up lost in space."

Chavatwor shrugged and turned to Saracasi. "It has been nice working with you. Let your brother know if he is ever in need of repairs or upgrades to his ship, he can look me up. I would be happy to provide what help I can."

"I'll do that," Saracasi said and on impulse, gave the Kowwok a hug, startling him. The soft fur on his shoulder tickled her nose, but she suppressed the urge to sneeze. Hugs were an important thing to share among Kowwoks.

With more emotion than she expected, he hugged her back, nodded to Zeric and Lohcja and then left the cargo bay as well. She would miss him, she realized. Despite their meeting being under less than ideal terms, she had grown attached to more than just Asirzi.

Once Chavatwor left, Zeric turned to Lohcja. "Come to say goodbye? I hope your arm recovers okay."

"Actually, I was hoping to go with you," Lohcja said. "You did this to rescue your friends. Mine is now on Kol, and I'd like to make sure he's okay."

It looked to Saracasi as if Zeric was about to say no. To her surprise, he nodded. With a quick look at the colony, Zeric led them to the elevator.

CHAPTER ELEVEN

Recent events were putting a bad face to space travel. The last three journeys Zeric had made had either ended poorly or nearly killed him. He wasn't sure that, should he survive this, he would be willing to take any more journeys. Retiring back on Irod might have been the smarter move.

With only five people breathing the air onboard the freighter, the chance of catastrophic failure of the life support systems was much less than on their first trip. However, they were spending twice the amount of time aboard, so, to Zeric's mind, things balanced out to an equal chance of death.

They had increased their odds by filling the ship with as much oxygen as possible and sealing off every section they could. As the CO_2 levels rose, they would move to a new section uncontaminated with the gas.

Despite having the entire ship to themselves, this resulted in quarters as tight as they had been during the first journey. This afforded him the chance to get to know his new traveling companions. Lohcja seemed to be a pretty simple person, not in a stupid way, but in an uncomplicated way.

For whatever reason, he had followed his friend Lahkaba into this mess and was now sticking it out. Until recently, Zeric would have found that foolhardy, but his recent actions had shown he would do the same. He decided it was a trait to admire in the Ronid.

Lohcja and Gu'od got along very well. Lohcja was a collector of ancient weapons, and Gu'od's status as a Ni'jar master fascinated him. Ancient fighting techniques that the Ni'jar practiced were on par with ancient weapons. Gu'od offered to train him once Lohcja's arm was healed and they had more oxygen to burn, but he made his customary stipulation that the Ni'jar ways were more a philosophy than a fighting technique. Lohcja seemed eager, but Zeric doubted the Ronid would take to the meditations any more than he had.

Saracasi was a different person than he had expected. Maarkean had never revealed why his sister had been arrested. Zeric had let his imagination run away with him as he had considered the options. Since Maarkean had never claimed that she hadn't legitimately been jailed, he'd expected to see something sinister about her. Instead, she came across as more idealistic and intellectual than cutthroat.

The journey was less than ideal, but they managed to reach Kol with enough air to breathe. When they emerged from hyperspace, Zeric's first view of the planet showed him a massive brown continent.

From orbit, it was clear that it was dominated by a desert. Saracasi explained that their destination was a small abandoned settlement in the middle of that desert. That did not appeal to Zeric after he spotted several archipelagos full of tropical islands.

He was wary when they encountered no resistance as they descended through the atmosphere. They were tagged by sensors on several occasions, but there were no communications. It appeared they were being tracked, but no intense scans or transponder queries were conducted.

That was a relief to him; without a more detailed scan, no one would be able to identify them as anything more than an object on a controlled reentry.

Once they arrived at the desert outpost, the condition of the base surprised him. It was not a squalid hovel or cave in the middle of nowhere, but real buildings. Maybe this place wouldn't be the hell the desert suggested it would be.

When they got close enough to see the *Cutty Sark* parked outside the largest building, Zeric noticed Saracasi brighten. Up until now, they hadn't known whether Maarkean and Lahkaba had managed to escape. Zeric hadn't been worried. He knew that if they could get away in a big lumbering freighter, a pilot as good as Maarkean in a ship like the *Cutty Sark* could manage it.

Zeric set down as gently as he could manage, but he kept the ship powered up. The strip-mined area might not be able to hold the freighter's weight, and he didn't want to collapse into a sinkhole.

After they had remained stable where they were for several minutes, he began shutting down systems. The others did not wait on him; they proceeded immediately toward the elevator to the cargo bay.

While he powered the ship down, he started to consider what would happen next. He had gotten along pretty well with Maarkean during the prison break. Guilt over trying to steal the man's ship had even crossed his mind.

But they had only been allies of convenience. Now that their mutual goals were achieved, he wasn't sure what would happen. The only thing he felt sure of was that, had he arrived here without Saracasi, Maarkean would have killed him.

Beyond that, he couldn't be completely confident the man wouldn't do it anyway.

Zeric headed down to join the others. As he exited the ship, he was hit by a strong wave of heat. The desert appeared to be living up to its reputation. The air was dry and searing, but it was fresh and plentiful. Compared to the stale and chilly ship, he appreciated the difference. He knew that appreciation wouldn't last long.

From a distance, he saw the others gathered together. He was happy to see a joyful reunion between Maarkean and Saracasi. He didn't have any siblings of his own, but the more he thought about it, the more he realized Gu'od and Gamaly were sort of like family.

The sight of them alive back at the prison had been a great comfort to him, and he could understand how Maarkean and Saracasi must feel now.

As he approached, he overheard Saracasi making formal introductions of everyone to Maarkean. Gu'od and Gamaly expressed their sincere appreciation to Maarkean and Lahkaba for their rescue, which seemed to embarrass both of them.

Zeric realized that this was the first thanks they were getting. He and the others had been overwhelmed with it during their time traveling to Irod.

"Looks like we survived your crazy plan after all," Zeric said in greeting.

The words drew Maarkean's attention to him. There was a tense moment where Zeric wasn't sure how Maarkean would respond to him. It seemed Maarkean wasn't sure, either. For that moment, there was silence from the others as the two considered each other. Fortunately, the moment passed quickly. Maarkean smiled and extended his hand to Zeric.

"Not for lack of trying, though. I was genuinely concerned we all wouldn't make it," Maarkean said as they shook hands.

To his surprise, Lahkaba reached out and took him into a bear hug. The Kowwok bore a distant resemblance to a bear, which made the hug slightly terrifying. The suddenness of the hug startled him, and he must have looked surprised.

"A hug is a customary greeting among Kowwok for friends. We have been in battle together, fighting a righteous cause. We are now friends," the Kowwok said with complete seriousness.

"With a grip like that, I'm glad we're not enemies," Zeric joked.

Lahkaba chuckled and then said, "We should get you all inside. This heat can be a killer."

Given the Kowwok's fur, Zeric could sympathize. He followed the group toward the other buildings.

Once everyone was shown around the building, they were all given a chance to shower and get cleaned up. That was one of the reasons Saracasi liked this place. The settlement had a natural oasis that provided plenty of water. In limiting their movement aboard the freighter, they had limited their chances to get clean. It was wonderful to feel the week of crud wash off her.

She emerged from the shower and found clean clothes waiting for her. Maarkean had brought some of her things from the *Cutty Sark*. After spending over two weeks in the same prison jumpsuit, it was like heaven to have something new to wear.

She felt sorry for Gamaly and Gu'od, who still would not have anything else. Their clothes had been confiscated, and unlike Zeric, they had not had a chance to purchase more. Lahkaba and Lohcja had each brought a bag of their own stuff. Maarkean's stuff might fit Gu'od, but Gamaly would find Saracasi's clothes a tight fit.

Leaving the room she had used to dress, she went in search of her brother. She found him on the roof of the main building. The sun had dropped below the horizon, and the night air had already started to cool. It proved a sharp contrast to what she had felt when she had first gone inside.

Smiling at her as she approached, he said, "You look more like a person and less like yourself."

"Ha, ha," she said. "I knew you'd be up here lazing away the evening."

He shrugged. "You know me so well."

As he said, that Saracasi frowned. She thought she had known her brother very well. His behavior of late, however, had gotten more and more confusing.

"I thought I did," she said. "I thought you were incapable of seeing the injustices and hypocrisies of the Alliance. I had resigned myself to my fate. But you saved all of those people from a life of imprisonment. You saved me."

What she had meant as a compliment appeared to have the opposite effect. The look of hurt that was on his face surprised her. She hadn't meant her words to be hurtful, nor could she identify anything that could have been taken as offensive.

"You really have such a low opinion of me?" Maarkean said with a touch of sadness in his voice. "You thought I would just abandon you to be executed?"

Confused, Saracasi replied, "Yes. You made it very clear before, when we left Braz, that you took me away only because I hadn't actually been arrested yet. You said what I had done was wrong and that I deserved to be in jail."

"I never said that," Maarkean retorted, anger starting to creep into his voice.

"No, but you made it very clear that is what you thought."

"You had just participated in a riot. What was I supposed to think, you deserved some kind of medal?"

"We didn't cause the riot!" Saracasi said, raising her voice. "I've told you that. It was a peaceful protest. The AIS stormed us, and we responded. No one was supposed to get hurt, much less killed. It was the AIS trying to disperse us by force that caused that."

"This is an old argument," Maarkean said, clearly trying to moderate his tone.

Saracasi took a deep breath before continuing. They had had this conversation many times before. "Yes, it is. The point I was trying to make was I thought you had changed.

Your decision to free us I thought showed you had come to understand what I've been trying to tell you all these years."

"What you don't understand, what you've never understood, is that I don't have to agree with you in order to protect you. You're my sister. I could never let anything bad happen to you if there was anything I could do to stop it," Maarkean said quietly and then went on with more force.

"But that doesn't mean I agree with you. The charge of treason was too harsh – you don't deserve to die for what you did. But don't tell me there weren't those in your group who were trying to provoke the AIS into cracking down on you. Your friends were anti-government radicals."

"Not everyone who disagrees with Alliance policy is an anti-government radical," Saracasi said, exasperated. "Do you really think that all those people who were in prison with me deserved to be there?"

Maarkean shrugged. "I don't know. You committed a crime. Gu'od and Gamaly were ship thieves. That makes everyone I've met who had been in there actual criminals."

With a sigh, Saracasi sat down next to her brother.

"You never got to meet any of them. Had we all been able to come here, you'd have seen most of them are just people. People who were put in prison simply for disagreeing with Alliance policy, or because they aren't Braz or Terran.

"I didn't mean for it to come off as an insult. I just had never expected you to do anything against the Alliance. It's not like you."

Silence filled the void between them. Saracasi was unsure what else to say. She had not come up here to argue with Maarkean. She had come to thank him.

"Can't it just mean I love my sister? Does what I did have to mean anything more than that?"

The tone of his voice betrayed to Saracasi that there was more going on than he was willing to talk about.

She held onto hope that it meant he was starting to see cracks in the Alliance that he believed in, although he was obviously not ready to talk about it.

"No, it doesn't," Saracasi agreed. "Let's go find the others. They should be cleaned up by now."

Maarkean nodded, and they stood up and went back inside.

Sitting down at the table in the building they were using for housing, Maarkean looked over the group. Less than a month ago, his world had consisted of himself and Saracasi. Now he was sitting down to dinner with five others. The entire experience was unusual.

Despite the conversation with Saracasi, he wasn't completely unaware what his actions meant. His motivation may have been rescuing his sister, but it could never be seen by anyone else as something so simple. In truth, he wasn't even sure his motivations were that simple. Had he felt about the Alliance the same way he did years ago, he didn't think he would have been capable of the prison break.

Around the table, the conversation turned to a discussion about what to do next. Originally, he had assumed that after everyone was free, they would all go their separate ways. Saracasi and he would return to a life of smuggling. There were a few contacts on Kol he could try to find work with. The others would take their new freighter and go do whatever they did with stolen ships.

Gamaly and Saracasi appeared to have a different idea. As the group talked, the two women kept speaking as if they would all be staying together. Or at least most of them.

"The first thing we should do is to take Lahkaba and Lohcja back to their friends," Saracasi said. "I'm sure they want to get back."

To Maarkean's surprise, Lahkaba spoke up against that idea. "Actually, we've talked and we'd both rather stay with you."

"Really? Why?" Maarkean asked, perplexed.

"There really isn't anything for us back on Sulas. We're wanted criminals," Lohcja answered.

"You do know we're not into your political movement?" Zeric said. "We just worked with you guys to get our friends out."

"We know," Lahkaba said simply. "You made that clear from the beginning. But, in my opinion, you've actually done more for the cause without trying than we ever did. So given the choice between sitting in some more pointless meetings or being smugglers and snubbing Alliance authority that way, we'll be smugglers."

The Kowwok's honest answer surprised Maarkean. During their time together, they had talked a lot about how Lahkaba felt about the Alliance. Maarkean had always assumed that fringe groups hated the Alliance and everything it stood for. Unexpectedly, he had learned that Lahkaba did not hate the Alliance; he simply had a strong desire to be out from under their control and have the chance to choose his own destiny.

"All right," Maarkean said hesitantly. Finding work to satisfy the needs of two people had been hard enough. If all of them really did stick together, he didn't know what they would do. "Well, I'll be honest. We have little fuel and supplies. No work and no money. It's not a very glamorous life."

"We've got a great big freighter," Zeric said. "I bet we could find someone who would buy it from us. That'd be some easy money."

"I thought the life support system was shot?" Maarkean asked, scratching one of his cranial horns.

"Not completely," Saracasi answered. "It's on the verge of complete failure, but it will work for a short time. I wouldn't travel a long distance in it, though."

"Plus, the types of people who will buy a stolen ship are used to them coming in less-than-pristine condition. We won't get as much as we could, but we'll get more than we have," Zeric answered.

Maarkean considered it. Selling stolen merchandise had never been something he had wanted to become involved in. Smuggling had been like shipping legal cargo, just without paying custom fees – or that's what he'd told himself. In his mind, everything he had shipped had legally belonged to the seller. In truth, much of it probably hadn't. But he had never actually known for sure, nor been the one to steal it. He knew he was just rationalizing, but it made him feel better about it.

"Do you think you can find someone willing to buy an old mining freighter?" he asked.

Zeric gave him a broad smile. "On a planet that is primarily populated by mining companies? In a heartbeat."

"It's your wife's fault," Zeric said as he and Gu'od walked the dark street.

"What is?" Gu'od asked, confused.

"If she hadn't insisted on us staying with Maarkean, we'd be able to keep the profits from this sale to ourselves. It might even be enough to retire for a while on one of this planet's tropical islands."

"They did help us steal it. And we did attempt to steal their ship. It's only fair they should share in the profits," Gu'od admonished.

"No, I stole it, and then they helped me use it to get you out of prison. By every right, it's my ship," Zeric replied stubbornly.

The loss of half the money they would have made on the sale was a hard thing to take. They had survived by stealing smaller ships before. Small ships had small crews, which made for easier hijacking. Zeric had never considered stealing from an impound lot. It had been surprisingly simple. For their next heist, he might try that again.

"We have to find a buyer first," Gu'od said as they reached their destination. "Let's not worry about who gets how much just yet."

Zeric nodded and followed Gu'od into the club.

They had been in the city of Mynhold for two days now, just long enough to pick up new clothing for Gu'od and Gamaly and scout out the local black market. Despite his declaration earlier, he had been surprised that Gamaly had managed to find a lead on a buyer so quickly. Normally, it took a while to place yourself in a new location so that people would trust you enough to talk about buying illegal goods. Perhaps the limited Alliance presence made people less cautious.

The club was only moderately crowded. Zeric scanned the crowd and located the rest of their group seated in various places around the room. There was one benefit to their situation that he appreciated: with a greater number of allies, they could place some covert assistance into the club before the meeting. Before, the three of them had been forced to go into meetings like this with only one person playing the role of backup.

After getting a drink from the bar, Zeric and Gu'od took a lazy stroll through the club. They soon found the table with the men they had been told to meet. Sitting down at the table as coolly as he could manage, Zeric eyed the three Terrans dispassionately. He wished he could give off the impression of a silent threat like Gu'od could.

"Mr. Black?" Gu'od asked. Zeric knew that was not the man's real name. The less each of them knew about the other, the better it was for everyone.

"Mr. Gee," the Terran sitting in the middle said, "I understand you have a freighter you are looking to sell."

"Indeed. It's a fine ship, could use a few minor repairs, but what ship couldn't," Gu'od said. He was far better at the negotiations than Zeric was.

While Gu'od and Mr. Black haggled, Zeric scanned the room. He knew these men probably had others situated around the room just like he did. But, for a change, he actually felt fairly confident about their chances of being able to shoot their way out, should it come to that.

Zeric knew the negotiations would go on for some time. The man would demand some incredibly low price, and Gu'od would insist on an unreasonably high price. Eventually, they would meet in the middle. Then they would have to show him the ship, and he would insist the price be lowered.

A commotion near the bar caught Zeric's attention. He turned his head and saw one of the patrons talking excitedly to Maarkean. Maarkean was doing his best to look small and avoid the other man's questions. Suddenly, the man began shouting to the whole club.

"Hey, everyone, look who it is," he said happily, pointing to Maarkean. "It's that guy who broke those people out of that prison on Sulas."

Zeric's heart sank. It had been almost two weeks since the prison break, and he had not doubted that word of what had happened on Sulas would have made it to Kol by now. An event like that was unheard of in Alliance territory. The man's declaration shattered his hope that none of them had been identified. If Maarkean was known, then he might be as well.

The commotion at the bar had stopped Gu'od and Mr. Black's conversation. They watched as Maarkean tried to convince the man, and several confused onlookers, that he was mistaken. It was clear Maarkean was uncomfortable with the attention and was looking for a way out.

"What kind of freighter did you say it was again?" Mr. Black asked.

"YM-82," Gu'od answered simply.

"Wasn't that the same type of ship that was involved in that prison break on Sulas?"

"I wouldn't know," Gu'od answered.

"I think it was, boss," one of the other Terrans said.

Standing up, Mr. Black quickly said, "I'm afraid we won't be able to come to any kind of agreement. Good luck, gentlemen."

The three men swiftly left the club via the back door. Zeric and Gu'od were left alone at the table. More people had gathered around Maarkean. Their hopes of a low-profile sale had just evaporated.

The group around Maarkean appeared to have split into two camps. Some, like the man who had identified him, were calling Maarkean a hero, while the others were calling him a terrorist.

Maarkean stopped trying to talk his way out of the situation and stood up from the bar. As he started for the door, two men, a Braz and a Terran, blocked his way to the door, flexing their hands.

"I'm afraid you're going to have to sit back down until the AIS gets here," one of them said.

"There's been some kind of mistake," Maarkean said calmly.

"Maybe," the Terran said. "We'll let the AIS officers sort that out. We don't abide terrorists around here."

Maarkean was now surrounded by a small group of tough-looking people. The few people who had been supporting him disappeared into the background at the sight of the two new men. Zeric did not like how things were going. He exchanged looks with Gu'od, trying to decide what to do.

"Closest AIS officers are a few hours away," Zeric said quietly.

"I doubt this crowd will wait a few hours," Gu'od said as he looked around. "Local authorities might be called in, but that might even be too late."

"Guess we better move fast, then."

Standing up, Zeric gave a nod toward Lahkaba and Lohcja, who were hanging back on the sides, and strode out toward the cluster in the middle of the bar.

He noticed Gamaly holding Saracasi back. Having her run into the middle of the crowd wouldn't do any good, though he was about to do much the same thing.

"Is there a problem here, gentlemen?" Zeric asked, trying to use his most charming smile.

"It's none of yours," one of the men who had first stopped Maarkean said.

"I couldn't help but notice you inserting yourself into the business of this poor man," Zeric said.

"Listen, buddy," the man said, turning toward Zeric. As he did so, his eyes grew wide. "It's the other one! Dustlighter."

The crowd momentarily got quiet as all of their eyes turned from Maarkean toward Zeric. His shoulders drooped as he realized he was known. It had been highly likely that Maarkean would be identified after using his ship in the attack. Zeric had hoped it would take the AIS longer to ID him, if they ever could.

"I think we'll be going now," Maarkean said.

The collective attention of the bar shifted off of Zeric and back onto Maarkean. Zeric smiled when he saw the man's SK-9 held up less than a meter from the head of the Braz who had stopped him. Wasting no more time, Zeric quickly drew his own pistol.

Zeric shook his head slightly at Lahkaba and Lohcja, whom he saw reaching for their weapons. He saw no reason to involve any of the others if he could help it. Lahkaba drew his hand out of his jacket without a weapon, but he still continued moving forward.

"Ladies, gentlemen, please," Lahkaba said, getting everyone's attention, "there is no need for guns. I'm sure we can work this out peacefully."

Stepping forward between the two groups, Lahkaba held up his hands to show he was unarmed. He gave Zeric and Maarkean a direct look, making it clear he was speaking to them as much as the others.

With regret, Zeric lowered his weapon. It wasn't the first time Lahkaba had convinced him to put a weapon down, but he'd never been surrounded before.

"I think what we have here is a case of mistaken identity," Lahkaba said, speaking loudly enough for the entire room to hear. "If these were the dangerous terrorists the news talks about, would they have lowered their weapons?"

Though not unanimously, many in the crowd agreed. Lahkaba continued, "You have nothing to fear from these men. Do any of us really want an AIS team coming here and questioning us all? If these men were really terrorists, or freedom fighters, if you prefer, surely we would all be taken away for questioning. Wouldn't it just be better if we let them leave peacefully, proving to us all that they aren't terrorists?"

The crowd appeared mixed on how to reply to Lahkaba. Enough of them were swayed that Zeric thought they had a good chance of reaching the door.

With a look toward Maarkean, they both started making their way toward the door. He was sure to keep his weapon down but ready.

The two men who had originally stopped Maarkean started arguing with Lahkaba that they shouldn't let them leave. Fortunately for the two of them, the men appeared content to argue their point rather than actively try to stop them from leaving. As Zeric and Maarkean slipped out the door, the argument continued, allowing them to get away without pursuit.

"What if we tried another city?" Lohcja suggested. "Maybe keep Maarkean and Zeric away from the meet?"

"No, word will have already spread throughout the planet," Gu'od answered. "If no one in the bar did, I wouldn't be surprised if those men we were meeting have already alerted the Alliance authorities. They're a Terran-run company, and being associated with a traitor wouldn't be good for them."

Maarkean knew Gu'od did not mean anything negative when he said 'traitor,' but the word stung him nevertheless. It was not untrue, he knew. He had betrayed his government and the oath he had sworn.

After the incident at the club, the rest of the group had slipped out unnoticed. Lahkaba had stayed the longest, but when the men had tired of their debate, he had been able to leave. They had all made their way back to the *Cutty Sark*.

Once free, they had accessed the planetary network and the reason for Maarkean's and Zeric's recent fame. It turned out that, within days of Maarkean's and Lahkaba's arrival on the planet, a cargo ship had arrived from Sulas carrying the story of the prison incident. The story spread across the planet. When an Alliance courier craft had arrived with the official news story, it was already known the world over.

Despite the negative spin of the news story and the mostly hostile reception they had received in the bar, Maarkean was surprised by the number of relatively positive articles that had appeared on the network. They all seemed to be by fringe elements and radicals, but it was more than he expected. Kol was not the most loyal planet.

"We're probably not going to have any luck here," Zeric said. "Most people operate a little outside the law, but no one is going to risk their company by buying the freighter that defied the Alliance."

Zeric's wording was straight from most of the news stories. Official reports cast it a different way, but some of the private articles described them in grand heroic terms. Part of Maarkean appreciated the flattery, but he believed the official reports. They glossed over the type of prisoners that had been freed, but they were honest in their assessment of him as a traitor.

"We'll have to go someplace buyers won't care about where the ship came from. We should go to the *Black Market*," Zeric continued.

Maarkean had been hoping no one would make that suggestion. Flatly, he replied, "We can't go there."

Lahkaba asked, "I didn't think that was actually a place. Weren't we technically just trying to sell the ship on the black market?"

"The *Black Market* is a ship," Saracasi answered. "It's an old Alliance battle carrier that was stolen and converted into a roaming home to criminals and thieves. All kinds of illegal activity occur there. The only problem is that the freighter is too big to dock."

"That place is real?" Lohcja asked incredulously. "I thought that was just a legend."

Ignoring Lohcja, Zeric replied to Saracasi, "Yeah, but we can take the *Cutty Sark* and make a deal. Then we can meet them somewhere else with the freighter."

"I said we can't go back to the *Black Market*," Maarkean said forcefully. Everyone stopped talking and turned toward him. "We were hired to make a delivery to Sulas, and we failed. If we go back there, Joss is going to kill us."

"He won't kill us," Saracasi said dismissively.

Maarkean fought back an aggravated response. She had always been ignorant of the threat the man posed. There was nothing Maarkean would put past Josserand. He wasn't a psychopathic killer, but Maarkean had no doubt that when he decided it was necessary, someone ended up dead.

"Maybe not right away. But we didn't deliver the goods. We now owe him twenty thousand. Assuming he doesn't tack on any interest."

"Twenty thousand?" Zeric said incredulously. "We should easily be able to get one hundred for the freighter. Your cut will cover your debt, no problem."

Maarkean looked at Zeric. "You don't pay a man like Josserand back with money."

"So how do you pay him back?" Zeric asked.

"Well, for one thing he's always had his eye on Casi," Maarkean said. "I'm sure he'd be happy to cover some of the debt for a night with you."

Saracasi squirmed a little, and Gamaly put an arm around her and said, "We won't let that happen. It's not just the two of you now."

"Of course that won't happen," Maarkean said, exasperated. "Because we're not going to give him the chance. If we stay away, there is a chance he will decide it's not worth coming after us. If we walk into his base of operations, he'll definitely want to be repaid."

Turning to Zeric, he continued, "And as for you, if he finds out you tried to steal his cargo, I can't say for sure what he'll do to you."

"He'll never know. We were very discreet when we snuck ourselves into your cargo. You didn't notice."

Throwing up his hands, Maarkean admitted defeat. "It's your funeral. If you want to risk it, that's fine with me. But remember, I warned all of you. This is a bad idea."

CHAPTER TWELVE

"So that's the *Black Market*?" Lohcja asked, gazing out the cockpit window.

Lohcja and Lahkaba were crowded onto the flight deck with Maarkean and Saracasi. They had been curious to see the legendary ship. The two were straining to get a good look without getting in the way. They were doing neither particularly well.

Maarkean wasn't sure what was so exciting about it. From the exterior, the ship was the same as any other Victory-class Alliance battle carrier. Still, he had to admit to himself that he had been impressed the first time he had seen one. But that had been after serving on the older, smaller carriers. Impressed was a far cry from overawed.

"That's it," Maarkean said with frustration, as Lohcja was once again between him and a control. "You've had your look. Now get out of the way."

Lohcja and Lahkaba were two he still couldn't figure out. At times they appeared to be hardened warriors. Lahkaba had previous combat experience during the war and had kept his cool during the previous battle. From the stories he heard, Lohcja, who had not had any war experience, had performed admirably and had even pressed on despite the wound to his arm. The Ronid claimed his family had once been part of the warrior caste, which made him an exceptional natural fighter.

Yet many things appeared new to them. Despite being much the same age as Maarkean, they clearly had not seen much beyond Sulas. Whatever their lives had been before, he couldn't imagine it had been overly criminal.

Talking excitedly, the two left the flight deck, seemingly oblivious to Maarkean's frustration. He was glad someone was having a good time. The coming meeting was not something he was looking forward to.

He was still considering just staying onboard the *Cutty Sark* while Zeric and his group went off to make their deals. There was a chance that he would be able to wait out the entire visit onboard. But Josserand would learn of his presence on the ship as soon as he docked, if he didn't know already. If Maarkean didn't go willingly, things would be a lot worse for him in the long run.

Saracasi received the clearance for docking, and Maarkean brought them into the larger ship, the dark vastness of space being quickly replaced by bright lights and the bustle of activity. The bay was only half full, which he viewed as fortunate. The fewer people around, the less the chance of any of them being recognized.

Allowing the tractor beam systems to set them down in the designated spot, Maarkean powered down the ship's engines. Keeping the ship powered up to allow for a quick escape was highly appealing, but ultimately impossible. One of the Fox's rules was for all ships to remain powered down until they were departing. That was mostly for safety reasons, but it was also to keep anyone from doing anything they might want to quickly get away from.

"All right," Maarkean said as they finished the shutdown sequence. "You stay here. Keep an eye on the newbies."

"They won't like staying on the ship," Saracasi said.

Smiling, Maarkean faced Saracasi as he backed out of the door. "Why would they? You never do."

The dark look she gave him could cut have through steel. He broadened his smile and left her on the flight deck. Despite the Fox's rules, the *Black Market* was not a safe place.

But she never enjoyed being told to stay on the ship, and she never did stay put, despite his attempts.

Passing through the common area of the crew deck, Maarkean found Gu'od and Gamaly stripping off their weapons and placing them on the table. When he reached them, he drew his pistol and placed it on the table, too. Going into a nest of thugs while unarmed was not comforting, but at least no one else would be armed either.

During the journey, he had gotten some pointers on hand-to-hand combat from Gu'od. Maarkean didn't know much about the Ni'jar, but he had always assumed they were pacifists. Gu'od had explained that it was more complicated than that, while beating back Maarkean's every attack with ease.

The weapon ban made him wish Gu'od could go with him. Unfortunately, Gamaly also needed to meet a contact on the *Black Market*, and Maarkean couldn't begrudge Gu'od his decision to go with her. Zeric had offered to accompany him, but Maarkean knew that would just lead to more trouble.

"I'll be back in an hour or so," Maarkean said as he prepared to follow Gu'od and Gamaly down the stairs to the cargo deck. "Hopefully, they'll be back then, too, and we won't have to spend too much time here. The rest of you stay put."

Maarkean went down as quickly as possible to avoid arguing. He assumed Zeric could take care of himself, and he wasn't actually worried about Saracasi's ability to handle herself, despite his attempts to keep her onboard. But if any of them left, they might take Lahkaba and Lohcja, who didn't know the rules of the ship. Anything could happen. As the captain of the ship that brought them here, anything they did was his responsibility.

He also didn't want to have to wait for them to return. When he finished this meeting, he wanted to be gone.

As they exited the ship, Gu'od gave him a nod and disappeared into the throng of people. The hangar was less crowded than it normally was, but it was still filled with people from every species Maarkean had heard of. Proceeding in the opposite direction from the two Liw'kel, he left the hangar deck.

The corridors through the carrier were less crowded than the hangar. Many visitors stayed near their ships, which, when combined with the loading and maintenance crews, kept the hangar in a constant hum of activity. The passage corridors were empty by comparison.

Heading through the ship, Maarkean wasn't sure where to find Josserand. Their usual meeting place was in the Ready Room, but those encounters had always been prearranged. Josserand had always found Maarkean and made the first contact. He was hoping his attempt to do it this time might buy him some good will.

When he reached the Ready Room, he found Josserand's usual table empty. With no other ideas, Maarkean took a seat at that table. A couple of the other patrons gave him a look, clearly concerned about his seating choice. One appeared about to come over to him, but must have decided to mind his own business.

If everyone in the bar knew not to sit at the table, that suggested Josserand stayed close. Word would reach him before too long, if it hadn't already. Maarkean decided to try to enjoy himself and flagged down a waitress. Ship rations were becoming unappealing.

It was not long after his food arrived that the ambient noise level in the bar suddenly dropped. Maarkean did not have to look up to know Josserand's two bodyguards were making their way through the room toward his table. He decided to try to play it cool and continued to eat.

Ignoring the bodyguards, he finished off his soup. The two thugs towered over him while Maarkean wiped his mouth and put his napkin over the bowl. It was incredibly difficult to manage without showing the fear that filled his stomach. The last few bites had been awfully hard to get down.

"Your boss ready to see me?" he asked, making every effort to keep his nerves out of his voice. He wasn't going to let these two thugs intimidate him – or, rather, he wasn't going to let them know he was intimidated.

One of the bodyguards stepped away from the table, and Josserand approached. "I hope you enjoyed the soup."

Leaning back as casually as he could manage, Maarkean replied, "I've had better."

"You should try the broccoli cheese next time," Josserand said as he sat down across from Maarkean.

"I'll remember that."

"Well, then, now that we have the pleasantries out of the way, how did your delivery go?" Josserand asked with fake curiosity.

"Not well," Maarkean replied. He knew Josserand was aware he hadn't made the delivery. How much more the man knew, he wasn't sure. He decided it was best to say as little as possible. "Ran into some trouble with the Alliance. Couldn't make the drop. I'm here to square up with you."

"How noble of you," Josserand said with a sinister smile. "Most people in your position would try to find a rock somewhere and attempt to disappear under it."

"We had a deal. I didn't hold up my end."

"I see. Admitting your failure is quite a gesture. Bringing me the people who attempted to steal my cargo was an even better gesture."

Maarkean's heart dropped. Josserand knew more than he had pretended from the start. If he knew that Zeric and the others were onboard, they might already be in danger.

Josserand went on, "That you have accepted your failure before telling me that you've brought me the cause speaks to your character. I may forgive some of your debt for that."

The idea of letting Josserand have Zeric, Gu'od and Gamaly briefly flashed through his mind. But he had already decided, when they met face to face on Kol, that he no longer had any desire to see Zeric pay. Too much had happened for vengeance to have any appeal.

Maarkean said, "I didn't bring anyone here for you. The issue is between you and me. The others don't concern you."

"They don't?" Josserand said with a flat, cold stare. "Three miscreants try to steal my cargo, and you're telling me I can't teach them a lesson?"

"That's right," Maarkean said. His answer lacked confidence and sounded weak. He pressed on anyway. "What happened with them is between me and them. They attempted to steal my ship. Your cargo was under my care, so your issue should only be with me."

"I see," Josserand said. "You wish to assume their debt on top of your own?"

Maarkean saw the trap but knew it was too late. If he backed down now, something would surely happen to the others. Josserand had him in a corner, and the man knew it.

"Yes," Maarkean replied, trying not to grit his teeth.

"That is a mighty large debt. It may take several years to work off," Josserand said with a smile.

"As long as you pay me enough to keep my ship fueled and stocked, I'll make any deliveries you want," Maarkean said.

"That is a mighty generous offer," Josserand said coldly. "Unfortunately, you are no longer any good to me as a smuggler."

Exasperated, Maarkean argued, "Had I not had any interference, I would have made it past that Alliance patrol without a problem. I can still deliver goods."

"Oh, you misunderstand me. I'm not questioning your skills. I have no doubt those are just as good as they have always been. I simply refer to your newfound status as a celebrity."

Maarkean cursed his luck. Their failure on Kol had been foreseeable, since the freighter would be well known after its part in the prison break. But since Maarkean was already in the habit of keeping the *Cutty Sark* away from Alliance patrols, he hadn't foreseen any fallout for his part as long as he wasn't caught. He knew the Alliance would execute him as a traitor, but he hadn't thought the criminal underworld would treat him any differently.

"What does that have to do with anything? Just don't send me to Sulas, and I'll have no problem," Maarkean countered.

"You really don't understand, do you?" Josserand replied. "You defied the Alliance. As a former officer, you should understand what that means. They're going to be hunting you."

The truth of Josserand's words sank in. He had known getting identified during the operation was a possibility, especially since he was flying his own ship. But he had dismissed the implications. His actions would be viewed as an attack on Alliance authority. As a former officer, his actions made him a subversive and a terrorist. He wasn't just a minor criminal.

"And if the extra Alliance attention wasn't bad enough," Josserand continued, "none of my clients are going to want to take deliveries from you. If they're caught, they won't simply be arrested for buying illegally imported goods. Every good Alliance citizen can sympathize with someone trying to avoid paying taxes. But working with a traitor, that's just wrong. That makes them a traitor, too."

Josserand was oversimplifying things, but Maarkean didn't doubt the truth of his words. Just a month ago, he would have thought the same thing. Directly attacking the government was an unforgiveable, traitorous act. Many thought that protesting the government in any way outside of an election was akin to being a traitor. Until it had been his sister who was ostracized and threatened with arrest for merely protesting, he had been part of that group.

"What do you want me to do?" Maarkean asked dejectedly. He knew he wasn't going to like the answer.

With a smile that made Maarkean's skin crawl, Josserand answered, "Since you are no longer in the delivery business, you'll have to go into the acquisition business."

"You want me to be a thief?" Maarkean asked.

"'Thief' has such negative connotations," Josserand said. "You'll see to the redistribution of wealth. Your success with that freighter showed how good you are at it."

"That was luck," Maarkean answered. "I'm not any good as a thief. I'm sure you have people much better at it and with more experience."

"If we were talking general thievery, you would be correct. But for what I have in mind, you are an expert."

Confused, Maarkean asked, "What do you mean?"

"You are the only revolutionary to have successfully snubbed the Alliance. Who better to steal from them?"

Disturbed by the suggestion, Maarkean replied, "You want to use my reputation to cover up your crimes?"

"Not my crimes. Your crimes. You're a criminal and a traitor, and you're just going to keep on doing what you do," Josserand said dismissively.

"Well, I won't do it," Maarkean said defiantly. "You're just going to have to break my legs, or whatever it is you do."

With a cold smile that turned Maarkean's stomach, Josserand leaned in closer. "Oh, I won't break your legs. Your sister's... maybe. And don't even think about pretending to agree and then running off. I know about your little hiding place on Kol and the 'secret' colony of Irod. There is no place in this galaxy you can hide from me."

The magnitude of the shit storm he had gotten himself into hit Maarkean all at once.

"This was a bad idea," Saracasi said.

The four of them were seated at a large booth in one of the *Black Market*'s restaurants. With large windows on all sides of the room, the Infinity restaurant was one of the most open places on the ship. According to Zeric, it also had some of the best food.

Saracasi couldn't help but recognize all of the engineering problems with the room. She assumed it was added after the ship was stolen, as she couldn't see a military ship having such a vulnerable location. Each window was a weak point in the hull, and this room had dozens. She wondered what it had been before.

"Oh, relax. Do you always do what your brother says to do?" Zeric said dismissively.

"No. But that is how I ended up with an arrest warrant of my very own," she replied sarcastically.

Lahkaba and Lohcja had been eager to see more of the legendary *Black Market* and Zeric had agreed to show them around. They had started by touring the marketplace; it had once been the ship's Marine training area, but it had been converted into a series of booth markets. Goods from all over the galaxy could be purchased there. Some were considerably cheaper than you could get legally; some were considerably more expensive, but came without the background check.

After the market, they had taken a quick tour through some of the seedier parts of the ship. They had watched one of the cage matches, and Zeric had made a nice sum on a bet. Then Zeric had almost brought them into a strip club. He had changed his mind right before going in and had taken them up to Infinity instead. Saracasi wondered if he had changed his mind because she was with them. She had almost told him she might enjoy the show as much as them, but decided against it. On a ship like this, you never knew what you might see, and once seen, some things couldn't be unseen.

"We haven't had a nice meal in forever," Lohcja said.

"Yeah, you were in prison and then on the run. Don't you want a nice meal?" Lahkaba added.

Giving them both a dark look, Saracasi said, "We had a nice meal in Mynhold. And do I have to remind you that I cooked last night? What was wrong with that?"

The table was suddenly silent, and the three men looked anywhere but at her. Saracasi knew her talents didn't lie with cooking. When it had been her turn to cook, she should have stuck with something that was simple and came from a box that had instructions. But the meal Lohcja had made a few nights before had been wonderful, and she had had delusions she could do something similar.

Ignoring the three, she continued, "Maark should be done by now. He won't know where to find us, and he seemed anxious to get away from here."

"All the more reason to come now," Zeric countered. "Give Lah and Lohcja a chance to sample what this ship has to offer."

Saracasi gave up when the waiter arrived. She did like the food here, and Zeric had offered to pay with his winnings. They took turns ordering and then slipped back into idle chatter.

The restaurant was only half full at the moment. With so many ships arriving from many different planets, the *Black Market* didn't really have a night or day.

While they were waiting for their meals, she overheard a voice that sounded like Gu'od's. "See, I told you we'd find them here."

Turning in her seat, she saw Maarkean, Gu'od and Gamaly approaching them. The look on Maarkean's face made her regret having come here. Her brother was clearly angry, and by the look on his face, he might not wait until they were in private to tell her exactly what he was thinking.

To her surprise and relief, Maarkean sat down at the booth without a word. Gu'od and Gamaly slid in, and Gamaly spoke first.

"No luck on finding a buyer for the freighter. It seems there's a pretty active search by the Alliance for that ship. They've declared all of us escaped terrorists. We should feel lucky they haven't offered a reward for our capture."

"Yet," Gu'od added. "They probably will at some point. We don't want to be here when they do. Most people aren't friendly to the Alliance, but no one here will think twice about turning us over to them."

"They also don't want to do anything to draw that kind of attention to themselves. A mining freighter isn't a small investment, and it isn't something you generally use for illegal operations. If it wasn't so high profile, it might be useful for illegal shipping. But word is that the Alliance is stopping all YM brand ships," Gamaly finished

The news is dire, but not unexpected, Saracasi thought. The Alliance would stop at nothing to quash any challenge to its authority.

Political prisoners being freed in a high-profile escape wasn't something they would back down from. The battle had occurred over a well-populated continent and in a well-trafficked area of space.

The events were never going to be kept quiet. She wondered why this seemed to surprise everyone.

"So there goes our income," Zeric said. "No tropical retirement today."

With a wry smile, he turned to Gu'od. "I made some money betting on the cage matches today. You could always enter. Take care of our financial worries."

Gu'od gave Zeric a hard stare in reply, but he said nothing. Having seen Gu'od fight, Saracasi was sure the man would win against any opponent he met in the cage, but from the little she knew of him, she doubted the idea held any appeal for him. Or that Gamaly would ever allow it.

Almost inaudibly, Maarkean said, "I know of another option."

Everyone turned toward her brother.

"We raid Alliance bases and storage facilities."

The suggestion he made surprised Saracasi. His action in breaking her out of jail had been unbelievable, but her life had been at stake. This was something she had never expected to hear him even consider, much less suggest.

"What do we do with whatever we collect?" Lahkaba asked as if the idea of raiding Alliance bases was inconsequential.

"In exchange for a cut to cover my debt, my contact here has agreed to help us fence them."

"If you want to do some raiding, commercial stuff is a lot easier to get than Alliance goods," Zeric said matter-of-factly.

"No," Maarkean snapped. "Just Alliance facilities. We're not common thieves. The Alliance has labeled us as traitors, so we might as well go with it. But we're not going to steal from people."

Lohcja shrugged in response, but Lahkaba looked eager. "I like it. We can't go back to Sulas, but we still can hit back at the Alliance."

Watching her brother, Saracasi got the sense there was something he was not saying. She exchanged a look with

Gu'od, who seemed to be the only other person at the table who noticed it. While the others discussed how to make this idea work, she tried to figure out why her brother had suggested it.

CHAPTER THIRTEEN

"Your technique is regressing," Gu'od said.

Looking up at the muscled Liw'kel from lying on his back on the floor of the cargo deck, Maarkean thought the view was becoming too familiar. The pair had been sparring, an activity they had gotten into the habit of doing every day. He was learning a lot from the Ni'jar master, but more painfully than he liked.

Taking Gu'od's hand, Maarkean got back to his feet. They were the only ones left in the cargo bay. Lahkaba and Lohcja usually joined them, but they had already left. Maarkean stumbled over to a water bottle and splashed some of it over his face.

"What do you mean?" he asked through deep breaths.

"I mean, in the weeks we have been training together, you have shown marked improvement in your hand-to-hand skills," Gu'od said. "But in the last few sessions, your technique has degraded back closer to where you were when we first met."

Maarkean considered the Liw'kel's words. It wasn't clear if there was a compliment or an insult among them. He was sure he had been getting better. His physical fitness had certainly improved.

"I thought I did pretty well. I was able to stay on my feet longer today than before. I certainly gave Lohcja a challenge," Maarkean said, trying to sound confident.

Gu'od shook his head. "Your skills have definitely improved. But your technique has not. Have you been practicing the meditation techniques I showed you?"

"Sort of," Maarkean lied. He had tried them. As they got closer to their destination, it got harder and harder to focus on anything else besides the guilt and nervousness he felt. Sitting quietly in his quarters trying to focus on nothing resulted in him thinking of anything but nothing.

"A Ni'jar is not a master of martial arts because of superior skill," Gu'od said. "The martial arts are an extension, more a byproduct, of our superior focus. The Ni'jar observe and study: life, the world around them and, most importantly, themselves. They act only when necessary."

"That I still don't really understand," Maarkean said, trying to turn the conversation away from his failures. "You say they observe life and act when necessary. But all Ni'jar I've ever heard of live in secluded monasteries cut off from the rest of the galaxy. I thought they were pacifists or isolationists."

"We are not pacifists," Gu'od said, allowing himself to be redirected. "We are patient activists. There is no central tenant of the Ni'jar, no black-and-white right and wrong. Our only quest is balance within life. Most focus on balance within themselves. That breeds a certain amount of isolationism.

"Some, not many, but some, go out into the world like myself," Gu'od continued. "I am more unusual than most Ni'jar, but I am not completely unheard of. My focus is Gamaly, and as such, here I am.

"You do not know what your focus is. You move through life with no direction, no focus, no balance," Gu'od said, bringing the conversation back around to Maarkean.

"No, I don't," Maarkean answered stubbornly. "My focus is survival and the protection of my sister."

Shaking his head, Gu'od looked disappointed. "Survival is not enough for you. It works for some, but not you. Saracasi is a grown woman now, ready to find her focus. She would be better served by you finding yourself so that she can do the same. Until you start to study yourself, you will not be able to understand the world around you."

Maarkean thought about what the Liw'kel was trying to tell him. He considered the words, but he didn't agree. Gu'od had Gamaly. Maarkean had lost his focus when he had also lost his parents and his wife. Ever since then, Saracasi had been his only focus. After fleeing Braz, survival had been the top of their list. With recent events, survival had become an even more important and more elusive target.

He was about to argue his point with Gu'od when a chime rang through the ship. It was the five-minute warning before they reached their destination and dropped out of hyperspace. His frustration at his failure in fighting and his counterpoints to Gu'od went out of his head. They were almost there.

Giving the Liw'kel one last look, Maarkean headed for the stairs. Gu'od followed him silently. That was one thing Maarkean liked about him. The man had some crazy notions, but he wasn't argumentative. He supposed it stemmed from Ni'jar teachings that Gu'od only spoke when it was necessary.

Maarkean took the time to stop in his quarters to wash his face and change out of his exercise clothes. A fresh set of clothes would have to do in place of a shower. After a quick spray of deodorizer – cramped quarters on a ship were hell when someone stank – he went to the flight deck.

Seated at the operations station, Saracasi was going through a systems check. Zeric was in the pilot's chair, helping her, and Lahkaba had taken what he had come to call his customary position, at the weapons console. There was very little room on the flight deck, but Gu'od, Lohcja and Gamaly had crammed themselves in the back.

Squeezing past them, Maarkean exchanged places with Zeric without a word. That was one nice thing about Zeric. He had tried to steal the ship before, but now he took pains to show that he respected Maarkean's place onboard as captain. It was an unexpected, but welcome, trait.

"Coming out of hyperspace in three, two, one," Saracasi said.

With her final word, the twisted colors vanished and were replaced by blackness. It took a moment to pick out anything in the void before them. Slowly, details started to emerge. They had come out of hyperspace dangerously close to the night side of the planet Dantyne. With no light from the system's star, the only things they could see were the lights from a few scattered colonies.

Dantyne had originally been a Notha colony world. During the prelude to the war with the Dotrans, the Alliance had scooped it up. The distant and militarily weak Notha homeworld had been unable to protest. It was nowhere near as populous as Sulas, and the majority of the citizens were Notha, not Braz or Terran.

"No indications that we've been scanned," Saracasi said with evident relief.

There were two main risks when making a covert entry to a world. They had gotten past the first one when they had exited from hyperspace safely, in the right spot. The other, more mundane, effort – not being seen – was directly tied to the first. The closer to the planet you emerged, the better your odds were of not being detected, but the higher your chance was of miscalculating and emerging from hyperspace inside the planet. Tall mountains on poorly-mapped worlds were always a hazard.

"I'm taking us down," Maarkean said.

As Maarkean took the ship into the atmosphere, it still amazed him how much easier it was to sneak into a place at night. Despite all of the electronic sensors and varying sleep schedules due to people operating on all kinds of time zones, darkness still played a role. All military bases kept GST no matter what the rotation of the planet they were on. Yet, even though it was the middle of the GST day, it would invariably be called the night shift down on the planet.

"Start looking for a place for us to set down," Maarkean told Saracasi. "We need to be far enough away from the settlement to not attract attention, but close enough that we can get there in a few hours' walk."

Saracasi nodded and began checking the terrain maps they had taken from orbit. The protection of darkness was easily defeated if anyone was actively trying, so they needed to set down quickly. With some computer enhancement, their orbital pictures would give them a lot of detail about the area, which included finding them landing sites and getting a layout for the Alliance depot.

"Found a spot. A clearing among some trees. Ground looks stable enough."

Maarkean nodded and took them to the coordinates Saracasi gave him. Getting the ship into the clearing only required crushing a few small trees. When they touched dirt, he began the shutdown process. They had made it this far; it would not do for their energy signature to be picked up by a random patrol.

Turning in his seat, he regretted that they did not have any Nothas among them. It would have made what they were going to do next less conspicuous. The planet was hardly Notha only, but a mix of aliens would be noticed. Unfortunately, they had little choice.

"All right," Maarkean began, "it should be a couple hours' walk to the base and to the city. No communication. We can't have our comm IDs registered on this planet."

Lack of communication made everything more difficult, but if they connected their comm devices to the planetary network, they could be tracked, and it would send a red flag to the Alliance base. Even if they used the unlinked comm feature, their signals could be tracked and would be unencrypted. Maarkean promised himself they would get other comm gear if they were going to continue operations like this.

"We'll meet back here in twelve hours," Maarkean said.

"Yeah, and try not to get caught," Zeric quipped.

Maarkean followed the group off the flight deck and then down into the cargo bay. With his arm still not at a hundred percent, Lohcja had volunteered to remain behind to guard the ship. Plus, a Ronid would stand out more than any of the others. The group heading toward the settlement wanted to remain as unmemorable as possible.

Maarkean pulled his duster on and checked his pistol's charge one more time. Zeric handed him a canteen of water, and then they both tagged their current position on their computers by reading the GPS signal from the colony's satellites. Without a word, he nodded to the others and then headed into the dark with Zeric.

The hike to the settlement went faster than Saracasi had expected. Since their escape from prison and the exhaustion she'd felt running back and forth across the freighter, she had devoted time every day to running. With the cargo bay on the *Cutty Sark* empty, there had been room for a short circuit. She liked to think it was helping.

When they reached the outskirts of the settlement, they waited at the forest's edge until daybreak. They didn't want to attract attention to themselves by walking around in the wee hours of the morning. As the light grew, she started to make out more details about the settlement.

The images she had seen from their orbital survey had shown the place to be relatively small. There was a wall running around the entire settlement with a crossroads just prior to the thoroughfare into town. They had decided to approach from the polar south to throw others off, since the ship was to the west.

As they walked the road toward the settlement, Saracasi began to notice the world around them. During the walk here, everything had been only dimly lit by the planet's two moons and their flashlights. Now, with the sun up, she could see the plant life in full color. The open field that stretched from the edge of the tree line toward the city was a brilliant shade of purple.

Gamaly stopped and picked one of the wildflowers that gave the field its color. She smiled and held it up to Saracasi's screfa, saying, "It matches."

Saracasi gave her a polite smile in return. Gamaly would not know what an insult she had committed. For a Braz, comparing the color of their screfa to a flower was the same as declaring their clan as weak as a flower. In Braz history, blood feuds had raged between clans for years for insults like that.

The group continued their walk into the settlement. As they approached the gates along the roadway, a cart pulled by a team of large animals emerged. The creatures had pale orange skin, large floppy ears and an expression that made them look kind of cute. They were almost as wide as Saracasi was tall. With two of them side by side, the group was forced to step off the roadway to allow the cart to pass.

The driver of the cart was an unusual sight. Dressed in jean coveralls and guiding the animals, he looked like an image out of the past. Yet on the cart behind him was a large piece of electronic equipment, presumably some sort of farm implement.

They continued into the city. The place was still quiet, but there were a few signs of the city coming to life. A couple of the shops had signs turned to "Closed" but lights on inside, and they passed a bakery that had a few patrons coming and going. The smells from inside instantly had Saracasi's mouth watering.

"I suppose that is as good a place as any to start asking around," Gamaly said innocently, looking at the bakery.

"Yes, there are people there to talk to. It's perfect," Lahkaba said absently and began walking over there.

Saracasi saw no reason to fight it and followed. Gu'od shook his head but came with the rest of them. Once inside, they were greeted with stronger smells. The shop's glass counter was filled with pastries and baked goods of all types. The shop appeared to cater to a mixed clientele, as there were foods from a variety of cultures. Her eyes lit up at the sight of a jilberry tart. It had been her favorite as a child.

They waited in the short line and each ordered something. Saracasi paid for the jilberry tart and took a moment to breathe in the aroma while the others ordered and paid. Gu'od was last in line, but he did not order anything. Instead, he questioned the worker behind the counter.

"I was wondering if you might be able to help us. We're new to town," he began, sticking with their cover story of not identifying themselves as off-worlders unless necessary. "We're looking for some transportation."

"You can try the stables over on the other side of the town," the Notha girl said politely.

Gu'od smiled back. "We were looking for something faster and with a bit more carrying capacity than an animal could handle."

The girl said incredulously, "You want a truck?"

"Yes," Gu'od answered simply.

To Saracasi's surprise, a look of disgust crossed the girl's face. What was even more surprising was the sudden silence that filled the small bakery. The rest of the occupants, mostly Notha, collectively turned toward Gu'od. The change in atmosphere was not lost on him, and he surveyed the room cautiously.

"Did I say something wrong?" he asked as innocently as he could.

One of the Notha, older than the others and with streaks of grey in his fur, stood up from his table. Saracasi saw Lahkaba put his hand on the pistol at his hip. They were all armed, unlike the other bakery clients. Saracasi had been opposed to that when they had left the ship, but now she was glad they were.

The Notha moved over to Gu'od, his tail flicking behind him with evident anticipation as he walked. "You say you aren't from around here. Whereabouts are you from?"

Gu'od looked around the room cautiously, but his face was calm. Saracasi realized he must have sensed that pretending to be from another town might not work because he answered, "We arrived on the planet recently."

"No starport here," the Notha asked. "How did you get here?"

Evasively, Gu'od replied, "We walked."

A mock look of surprise crossed the Notha's face. "Closest starport is Scipost City. That's over two hundred kilometers. After walking that, no wonder you're looking for transport."

Gu'od didn't respond, and the Notha continued, "Perhaps you don't know about the boycott?"

"No," Gu'od answered truthfully.

The Notha raised an eyebrow suspiciously at Gu'od and cast a look at Saracasi. "Everyone on this planet, or at least all but the traitors, has boycotted buying any motorized transport. Our benevolent Alliance overlords have seen fit to declare that only vehicles purchased from Alliance companies may be bought and sold here. In protest, we've all gone back to simpler transport. The local lomba and uka are excellent beasts of burden."

Looking darkly at Saracasi, the Notha concluded, "So you'll find no vehicles here for rent or purchase. And you'll find no one here willing to buy, either."

Saracasi did not like the way the rest of the patrons were looking at her. She should have realized that on a planet with a non-Alliance majority, Braz and Terrans might be looked at suspiciously. Apparently, the people of this town were not happy Alliance subjects.

"I was unaware," Gu'od said diplomatically. "As I said, we just arrived."

"Since you obviously didn't walk all the way here from Scipost, that only leaves one option of where you came from. You wouldn't have arrived on the ship that landed out in the woods in the middle of the night, would you?" the Notha said coldly. "We don't much like smugglers here. We won't buy any vehicles until the embargo is lifted. Not even illegally imported ones. We told the last group of you smuggler scum the same thing."

So much for a covert landing, Saracasi thought. They had been much closer to the city than the Alliance base. She fervently hoped Maarkean and Zeric weren't walking into the waiting arms of Alliance personnel. And that Lohcja wouldn't find a platoon of troops swarming the ship.

"I assure you," Gu'od said calmly, "we are not here to sell you anything. We did arrive on that ship; we were experiencing engine trouble and couldn't make it to the starport. We were hoping to get transport to a larger city to buy spare parts."

"Is that right," the Notha said. "Then I suppose you won't mind my coming and taking a look. I was a decent mechanic before moving here. It would be nice to work on something more complicated than farm equipment again."

"That is appreciated but won't be necessary," Gu'od said. "We have an extremely competent mechanic. We just need a replacement part."

"What do you need? We might have something here in town that's suitable enough to get you airborne again."

Looking a little lost, Gu'od gestured toward Saracasi. "I'm not sure exactly. But Casi here is our engineer."

Saracasi's heart sank. She knew she was a terrible liar, but apparently Gu'od didn't. "Um, our primary reactor pump is shot. No fuel flowing to the reactor."

The Notha smiled. "Well, then, you're in luck. We can make a simple bypass for you with the secondary feeder shunt."

Crap, Saracasi thought. She knew she should have thought of that. Pressure and lying did not go well for her. A bypass was a simple fix any novice could have devised. She tried to think of a reason that wouldn't work, but kept coming up with responses that would make her sound like even more of an idiot.

"I suppose we can also call over to the nearby Alliance outpost," the Notha said with a bit of a threat in his voice. "I'm sure they would be happy to help you."

Apparently the locals' distaste for the Alliance was less than their distaste for strangers they suspected were smugglers. Saracasi looked to Gu'od, hoping he had a response. If the Alliance was alerted now, they would be on the ship before they could get back there, and long before Maarkean and Zeric could get back. The best scenario would be if Lohcja could fly off-world by himself and come back for them. But she didn't even know if Lohcja could fly.

"All right!" Lahkaba exclaimed. They were the Kowwok's first words since ordering a pastry. Every head in the place turned toward him.

"We're not smugglers, and we didn't have engine trouble," Lahkaba said. His next words made Saracasi's jaw drop. "We're working with Maarkean Ocaitchi's Resistance. Surely you've heard about the events on Sulas?"

The shocked looks on Gamaly's and Gu'od's faces must have mirrored her own. Saracasi's tongue tied as she struggled to find the right curse to throw at Lahkaba. She had no idea what the man was thinking, revealing her brother's name like that, much less calling them part of his 'resistance.' When the Alliance was inevitably contacted, they wouldn't swarm the ship, they'd fire on it first.

Shock was not limited to her group. The rest of the bakery patrons were staring at Lahkaba as well. Undeterred by any of their stares, he continued, "We've come here to strike back at the Alliance. We're going to deny them vehicles just like they're denying you vehicles. We failed to understand the extent of your boycott. We were only hoping to find ourselves transport to and from the nearby base to aid in our escape."

Surveying the room, Saracasi tried to gauge the best way for them to escape. She was no tactical expert, but she thought their odds were good.

None of the other patrons appeared armed. Gu'od was probably capable of taking out half of them unarmed. A quick dash would get them to the door. From there, she had no idea. She was sure that Gu'od and Gamaly were making the same calculations.

"We have heard of the events on Sulas. And that name sounds familiar," the Notha said slowly, though his tail stiffened, suggesting he was anticipating a confrontation.

"Maarkean Ocaitchi was the leader of the group that broke those people out," another patron said.

"There were lots of Nothas imprisoned there, I heard," yet another patron said.

Unexpectedly, the atmosphere in the room made a complete change. The suspicion and animosity were replaced by a sense of welcoming. The change took Saracasi by almost as much surprise as Lahkaba's statement had.

"While, as a Notha, I may appreciate what you did there," the gruff Notha said, "you have admitted to being criminals. You are on the Alliance's most wanted listed. As sheriff, I have no choice but to arrest you."

Saracasi looked back at Gu'od, watching for a signal. Her hand moved toward her sidearm. The thought of being taken back to prison wasn't one she relished.

It wasn't especially crowded in the bakery, but any firefight, even on stun, might result in injuries; she was willing to take that chance.

To her surprise, Gu'od held up his hands and nodded to the Notha. "Very well. If you feel you must, we have no argument with you and have no desire to harm anyone here. We will come with you peacefully."

The Notha looked about as shocked as Saracasi felt, but he recovered faster. "I appreciate that. All right, come with me. You can finish your pastries on the way since you're coming peacefully. I will have to ask for your weapons, though."

"Of course," Gu'od said. He drew his pistol and placed it on the counter.

Maybe this was part of his plan, Saracasi thought. Gu'od was more dangerous without a weapon than with. Avoiding a firefight would fit his style.

Deciding to play along, she placed her pistol on the counter as well, after Lahkaba and Gamaly did the same. She just hoped her trust in Gu'od wasn't misplaced.

Several hours later, Saracasi was sure that her trust in Gu'od was completely misplaced. She paced back and forth across the small cell, fuming.

Gu'od made the mistake of catching her eye, and Saracasi took it as an opportunity to speak her mind. "Well, this was a brilliant plan," she said, knowing she sounded unnecessarily confrontational.

"It will all work out. We just have to trust in the balance of the universe. Not all problems are solved by confronting them head on," Gu'od replied calmly.

The Ni'jar philosophy Gu'od recited grated on her already frayed nerves. Her brother said similar things, saying she was too quick to take action

"You can't blame Gu'od for this," Gamaly said defensively.

Gamaly had more trust in Gu'od than she did. It only made sense; the pair was married. To Saracasi, though, at the moment, it just appeared to be blind stupidity.

"I can't? He was the one who just surrendered for all of us. Who should I blame?"

"How about Lahkaba?" Gamaly demanded.

Next to her, Lahkaba looked anxious at getting pulled into the middle of their dispute. To Saracasi's mind, he should have. Gu'od may have surrendered without a fight, but it was Lahkaba who had gotten them into this particular mess. If he had just kept his mouth closed, they would have been run out of town as suspected smugglers, but they wouldn't have been arrested – not merely on the suspicion of smuggling.

But she was to angry and didn't feel like backing down from Gamaly, even though she knew it was a pointless argument. "You're just trying to deflect blame away from your perfect husband. He couldn't have possibly done anything wrong here," Saracasi said, her voice childishly sarcastic.

"When he did nothing wrong, you bet I am. You'd rather we gunned down a crowd of innocent people? Maybe you were more involved in that riot than you claim?" Gamaly snapped back coldly.

Saracasi's eyes flashed with renewed anger. "Why would you care? You're just a low-life thief. You're only defending him because he's stooping so low as to stay with you."

Sadness crossed Gamaly's face, and Saracasi realized she had gone too far. It had been a long time since she had argued with anyone besides her brother, and arguments with siblings didn't have the same boundaries as they did with other people.

An apology hung on the edge of her lips but didn't come out. Part of her didn't want to apologize until Gamaly did.

Silence replaced the cold intensity between the two women. Eventually, they went back to ignoring each other, and Saracasi went back to pacing.

Her annoyance abated as time passed, until she felt more ashamed than angry. She tried to ignore it and consider the larger predicament. It would still be several hours before Maarkean and Zeric headed back to the ship. They weren't even due to have started back yet themselves. They would have to remain here for at least another day and would have to rely on Maarkean and Zeric to save them from prison. Again.

The door down the hallway opened, interrupting Saracasi's pacing. Now in his crisp, grey uniform, the sheriff who had brought them here came in escorting another Notha. Shorter than the sheriff and much younger, the second Notha looked vaguely familiar to Saracasi. The pattern of his fur – brown with white patches – struck her as something she had seen before, but she could not place it.

Walking up to the cell, the sheriff unlocked it, and the other Notha stepped inside. Looking uncertain, the sheriff said, "You sure you don't want me to stay?"

"Yes, thank you, Sheriff. You were the one who said they came with you peacefully. I have no reason to suspect I am in any danger."

"Very well. I'll be right outside," the sheriff said and then turned and headed back out of the room.

The four of them stared at the new Notha for a moment in silence. The open door to their cell offered Saracasi a tempting chance at freedom. There was just one Notha, the sheriff and an unknown number of deputies between her and that freedom. She squashed that thought; if Gu'od hadn't been willing to fight their way out when they were armed, he would be unlikely to do it now.

Finally, Lahkaba broke the silence. "It's good to see you again, Owrik."

Surprise broke across Saracasi's face. "You know him?"

Reluctantly, Lahkaba nodded, and Owrik spoke. "We were representatives together in the first Kreogh Sector Congress."

The surprise she had felt at the two knowing each other was overshadowed by this news. Up until now, she had been under the impression that Lei-mey had been the only representative to the Congress in their group. She wondered what else they didn't know about that group.

As if sensing the questions, Lahkaba reluctantly said, "Lei-mey and I were among Sulas' representatives to the Kreogh Sector Congress that met earlier this year. Once we returned to Sulas, the Alliance governor of Sulas declared all of us rebels and traitors. The other three representatives were Terrans and Braz, so they were relatively safe and able to remain out of prison. As 'aliens,' Lei-mey and I were subject to arrest. Meyka was a friend of Lei-mey's and offered us the safety of her friend Pasha's home. I decided to keep my part secret when we met Maarkean and Zeric."

Saracasi wanted to ask more questions, but she suppressed them for the moment. She was sure Maarkean would have a whole block of them himself. Oddly, she felt no annoyance at Lahkaba's omission, but she did feel a greater respect for the man. Those representatives had put themselves in danger, even if their identities had been kept mostly secret.

"You certainly have moved up in the world," Owrik said with a half smile that gave way to a more serious tone. "This was exactly why Dantyne did not side with you on the more aggressive stance."

"Afraid of a little prison time?" Lahkaba asked acidly. There was clearly some history here Saracasi did not understand.

"Yes," Owrik said honestly. "But we didn't quite understand what it was you were facing on Sulas. Our disagreements here on Dantyne are mostly economic in nature. Terrans and Braz are a minority here, and in our day-to-day lives, we are pretty much left alone. We have no prisons here like Olan."

After a moment's pause in which his tail went limp and his ears drooped in what looked like shame, Owrik continued, "But after the Congress was dismissed, two of my siblings, who were on Sulas, were thrown in there. I can only assume it was because of my participation in the Congress, but from what I hear, it could be just because they were Notha."

Suddenly, Saracasi recognized where she had seen the color pattern on Owrik. "La'ari and Isaxo."

Surprised, Owrik turned to her. "Yes, you know them?"

She nodded. "Yes, they helped us during the escape. Isaxo is a pretty good pilot, and La'ari knows her way around an engine room."

"La'ari was on Sulas studying starship design at Revard University. Isaxo was visiting," Owrik said. "What became of them? I have had no news. This is the first sign I've had that they are still alive."

"They are well," Saracasi said. "When we left Sulas, we went to a secret location. Unfortunately, it has limited space travel, so they wouldn't have been able to get many messages out. But they were both instrumental in our escape and were doing well when last I saw them, about a month ago."

Looking relieved, Owrik nodded. "You do not know the weight you have lifted from me. And the debt I owe. Are you Maarkean? I had heard he was Braz, but I was under the impression that he... was a he."

Saracasi laughed. She supposed it would be as hard for other species to tell Braz genders and name genders apart as it was for her to do with them. "No, I am his sister, though."

"You were in the prison as well," Owrik said. "So all Braz were not immune from imprisonment there. I only wish I had the courage your brother did when it came to the safety of my siblings."

Taking the initiative, Lahkaba stepped forward. "You were light-years away and unable to help them before. But now you can. Get us out of here. I know you didn't want to escalate matters. If you want, we'll leave the planet... just get us out."

Owrik considered Lahkaba. "Despite what I may feel toward you and what you all have done, you are technically criminals. If I see to your release, we would risk retaliation."

Saracasi's heart dropped. Things had been going well. An influential Notha, who knew Lahkaba, and whose siblings they had rescued, had come to see them. It had seemed too good to be true. Now she knew it was.

"Come on, Owrik," Lahkaba said, his voice rising. "Your fellow delegates may have wanted to keep things calm and not do anything drastic. But you wanted to agree with us. I know you did. And you still do."

Owrik appeared ready to argue with Lahkaba, but his shaggy shoulders dropped and he nodded. "There is no point in arguing with you here. I was a representative for my people before. But now I am just a private citizen. Yes, I think we need to do something more direct against the Alliance's stranglehold on us. Petitions, even united ones, will get us nowhere. I personally applaud what Maarkean did in attacking the prison.

"It is a contentious issue here. Many people are quite appalled at the violence and death that the attack caused. They feel it was the wrong thing to do. But there are just as many of us who feel it was a necessary first step to waking the population up to the evils of the Alliance. So yes, I agree with you, and I wish I did not have to see you locked up. I wish you could be out there making more statements like that."

With more eloquence and passion than Saracasi thought possible, Lahkaba put his arm on Owrik's shoulder and spoke. "So help us. The freeing of Olan was a wake-up call for people like you. The time to take action is now. Maarkean Ocaitchi and Zeric Dustlighter are out there right now, planning further action against the Alliance's oppression. But they need our help. They need *your* help."

Despite Lahkaba's words, Owrik shook his head and appeared to be about to say no. But to Saracasi's relief, he didn't speak right away. He seemed to lose himself in thought. Then he suddenly started nodding his head enthusiastically.

"You're right. If I allow you to remain in here, I will just be condoning the people who put my brother and sister into prison for the crime of being Notha. I cannot abide that. Come with me, we're leaving."

It took her a second to realize that Owrik was serious. He stepped back from the open prison door and gestured for them to follow him. She exchanged a look with Gamaly and Gu'od, their earlier animosity forgotten in the wake of the surprising turn of events.

A quiet voice in her head pointed out that this might end up proving Gu'od right.

Lahkaba was the first to follow Owrik, and Saracasi needed no more encouragement. They proceeded down the short corridor of holding cells and entered the building's main room. There, they found the local sheriff and two deputies.

"Sheriff," Owrik began, "these people are official representatives from the Kreogh Sector Congress. They are here under the protection of the Dantyne Parliament."

"Mr. Mahon," the sheriff began, "they are wanted by the Alliance. There is a sector-wide arrest warrant out for them."

"Have they broken any Dantyne law?" Owrik asked.

"No, not that I am aware," the sheriff admitted.

"Then under my authority as a member of Parliament, you are to ignore that arrest order," Owrik demanded. The young Notha's tail flicked subtly, giving the impression that he wasn't someone to be messed with.

The sheriff exchanged a look with his two deputies, and Saracasi wasn't sure which side they would come down on. She didn't know anything about Dantyne law, but Alliance law made it clear that what Owrik was doing was illegal. He had no authority to dismiss an Alliance arrest warrant.

The sheriff must have decided differently, or simply not cared, because after a moment he nodded and stepped aside. "Sorry for the inconvenience, folks."

Saracasi smiled at the sheriff and started to thank him. She stopped when Gamaly tried to do the same thing. The two women exchanged a look and then smiled.

Owrik then led them outside the sheriff's office. Her second time in jail had ended better than the first.

CHAPTER FOURTEEN

"That was not a shortcut," Maarkean complained.

Zeric let out a sigh. "It would have been if you hadn't gotten stuck."

"You mean if the path you told me to take hadn't turned out to be a mud pit half a meter deep?" Maarkean retorted.

It had looked safe enough, Zeric thought. How was he supposed to know this planet had a plant that looked like normal grass that grew on top of loose mud? When Maarkean had stepped into it, his leg had sunk half its length into the mud and become firmly stuck. The suction was too great for Maarkean to pull himself out with his other leg. It had taken Zeric nearly an hour to figure out a way of pulling him out that didn't result in him getting trapped as well.

The rest of the trip back from the Alliance outpost had been made in silence. Zeric had always thought naval officers, especially pilots, were too full of themselves. Maarkean's annoyance at a little mud amused him. Served the man right, he thought.

Their scouting expedition had gone better than Zeric would have thought possible. They had approached cautiously at first, taking up position on a hill a few kilometers away. They had used binoculars to do a visual survey, and what they had seen had been like a gift, as Lah would say, from the Great One.

The outpost was essentially a storage depot. In one corner was a hangar and landing pad, but all of the bays had been closed. There was also a long vehicle garage and a building that looked like a warehouse. The only other buildings were a few small storage sheds, a barracks and a command building with an air traffic control tower.

The entire compound was surrounded by a high wall with sensor towers at each corner. There were also weapon emplacements at a few points around the perimeter. Zeric had identified anti-air and anti-ground weapons. But they had all been unmanned. From the look of things, the only manned guard posts appeared to be at the entrance, and they had only seen two guards on duty at any time.

In the four hours they had taken turns watching the compound from the hill, they had seen no perimeter patrols and only a handful of people moving about the base. The barracks was large enough to hold an entire battalion of soldiers, but during an afternoon physical training session, only a group of ten had participated. The only other large group had been playing a ball game on a court near the barracks.

Zeric had estimated that there was probably only a single platoon in the entire compound. Like any good military unit, they probably followed Galactic Standard Time and had four watches of five hours, one squad on watch with one other squad doing housekeeping assignments while the other two rested.

Maarkean had been skeptical of such a low number. With a base as big as it was, he had insisted that there had to be more troops. With a single platoon, there was no one to support or fly the aircraft, and a dozen other jobs would be left unfilled. Zeric had countered by pointing out that those jobs were, in fact, being left unfilled. There had been no vehicle activity and no one going on patrols, and most of the defense positions were unmanned. A squad of ten could man the primary positions.

As they approached the clearing where they had left the ship, Zeric heard suspicious noises and raised his fist in a signal. He was a little surprised when Maarkean stopped instantly and squatted down without a word. Apparently the flyboy wasn't as useless on the ground as he had thought.

Creeping forward, Zeric tried to get a better view. Through a break in the brush, he could see the ship, but he also caught sight of several unusual animals. They resembled Terran ostriches, but were larger and had fewer feathers. Their beaks looked like they could do some damage if they wanted to.

Easing back a few yards, he moved to where Maarkean waited. He told him in a quiet whisper what he had seen.

Maarkean appeared unconcerned at first. "Wild herd probably."

"They were wearing some kind of saddle. They weren't wild," Zeric replied. He realized he should have mentioned that before.

"No signs of people?" Maarkean asked, drawing his pistol. He frowned when he found dried mud on the barrel.

"Aside from the domesticated animals, no," Zeric said sarcastically.

"Casi and the others should have beaten us back by a wide margin," Maarkean said as he rubbed the caked mud off his pistol. "Maybe they brought the animals. You said they were saddled."

"They went to get transportation. Why would they get those things?"

"Cheaper?" Maarkean posited.

"We'll never know sitting here. I'll swing around to the right. You stay here. If you hear gunfire, come save my ass," Zeric said with a wink.

As he moved away, he saw Maarkean shake his head. It wasn't a great plan, Zeric admitted. But with just the two of them and no communication gear, their choices were limited. The creatures had blocked his view; he had been unable to tell if the ramp was up or down.

Moving cautiously, Zeric made his way around the clearing. He hoped the creatures were not carnivorous and partial to the scent of Terran. The fact that they were saddled reassured him somewhat. Very few meat-eating animals made good rides.

Once he thought he had gone far enough around, Zeric crept up to the edge of the brush again. From here, he could see that the ship's boarding ramp was lowered. There were also some people sitting on it. Taking a closer look, he breathed a sigh of relief when he recognized Gamaly. The pistol worn at her side reassured him she wasn't a prisoner.

Trudging out of the brush, he called loudly, hoping Maarkean would hear him, "Gamaly, what's with the herd?"

His sudden shout startled the creatures, and they all started making a honking noise and shifting nervously. The noise covered up any reply Gamaly gave. Several other people emerged from the ship at the commotion. Most Zeric recognized, but there were two unknown Nothas among them.

Emerging from around the herd, Maarkean made a sloshing sound with one muddy boot as he approached the ship. When he caught sight of the Nothas, he looked exceedingly displeased. Preemptively, Saracasi went out to meet him. As Zeric got closer, the sound of shouting was heard in pieces over the sounds of the honking animals.

When he reached the ship, Gu'od stepped out to meet him, saying, "Maark does not look happy."

"I understand why. Bringing some strangers here doesn't seem to be the smartest move," Zeric said to his friend.

"Maybe not," Gu'od admitted. "But they knew about our landing out here, even if they didn't know exactly where. They offered to help us."

Zeric raised an eyebrow. "Just out of the blue like that. 'Hey strangers, you want any help breaking into a military compound?'"

Casting a sideways look toward Lahkaba, Gu'od replied, "Not exactly. They were ready to string us up as smugglers until Lahkaba told them why we were here and who we were."

"They knew the story?" Zeric asked, annoyed. "Dantyne's at the edge of the sector. As slow as communication is, I was hoping we had beaten the news."

Gu'od shrugged. "It's only a week's travel from Sulas to here. It's been over a month. I'm sure there have been a few trade ships between the two worlds."

"All right, next planet we visit has to be even further out on the fringes of civilization," Zeric said.

Zeric turned to watch Maarkean and Saracasi continuing to argue. There was nothing like a sibling argument, especially when one of them was almost like a parent. He was glad the creatures were still making so much noise.

"So what's with the creatures?" Zeric asked.

"Uka," Gu'od said. "They're one of the indigenous species used by the colonists. It seems they've boycotted Alliance-imported vehicles. So they ride these things everywhere."

Zeric looked disgusted. "So this is what you brought for transport? Might as well walk. Doesn't look like they'll be able to help us carry anything away from the outpost."

"No, not these," Gu'od said. "But these are just to get us to Arslan's farm. He makes a weekly delivery of local produce to the base."

"Ah," Zeric said, catching on. "You're thinking of a little covert insertion."

"Right," Gu'od said. "We slip in like we did on the *Cutty Sark*. Break into the arms depot and vehicle shed, blow up some vehicles, and then steal one to make our escape."

"Blow up some vehicles?" Zeric asked.

"Yeah, seems that's what Lahkaba told them we were here to do. As a way of siding with their boycott, we're going to destroy some Alliance vehicles."

"Lovely," Zeric quipped.

"Can you believe what they did?" Maarkean asked some time later.

Zeric was so focused on trying to keep himself balanced on the uka that he didn't notice Maarkean's comment at first. Two-legged creatures were not an ideal shape to ride atop. The much shorter Nothas had a lower center of gravity that seemed to suit the creatures, plus their tails could help keep them balanced. The rest of them were struggling to remain on the creatures' backs.

That didn't stop Maarkean from fuming. Once the group had climbed aboard the uka and left the ship, he had pulled back beside Zeric. Zeric wasn't sure how the man could talk and ride at the same time.

Zeric finally processed Maarkean's comment and replied, "They found us a way into the base."

He felt better when he saw that Maarkean was struggling to maintain his balance before speaking. "That may be, but they could have just as easily gotten themselves thrown in prison again. One jail break per lifetime is about all I can handle."

"I won't argue that what Lahkaba did was stupid, but it worked. I don't see any reason to overthink it," Zeric said dismissively.

"You Terrans are always so quick to rush into things," Maarkean said coldly.

"And you Braz are always overthinking everything. Once the course has been set, it's time to act, not think," Zeric said, annoyed. To be fair, he thought Maarkean was a bit different than most Braz. The man was very careful about planning, but he hadn't seemed prone to second-guessing things.

A thought occurred to him. "Is it that we're rushing into a plan with strangers, or that it wasn't your idea? I seem to recall a plan of yours that involved much the same thing not too long ago."

Maarkean was quiet, and Zeric wasn't sure if it was his comment or the difficulty of staying upright on the uka that kept him from replying. Zeric mentally shrugged and focused his attention on riding. He would be glad when they arrived. The next leg of their journey would be completed while shoved into a crate and covered in vegetables. It should be much more pleasant.

Being crammed into a vegetable crate gave Maarkean some time to think. Zeric had been right, in that what Lahkaba had done had been no stupider than what he had done in approaching the group on Sulas. However, Maarkean's actions had been necessary; lives had been at stake. This was not. All they were trying to do was steal some Alliance equipment.

For some reason, everyone else had bought into the political aspect of the mission as if it were his idea. They all thought they were doing this to continue the fight against Alliance dominance. He was sure Saracasi doubted his reasons, and Gu'od did not appear easily fooled, but they were still approaching the mission from that angle. No one else was viewing this as a simple snatch and grab.

Despite the threat Josserand posed, Maarkean started to rethink his agreement to work for the man. It was true that the man had connections on most worlds in the sector. And it was true that a bounty would likely be placed on his head if he didn't carry through with his side of the deal. But that might actually be the safer of the two choices.

Josserand wanted him to steal stuff from the Alliance under the guise of a traitor. His actions on Sulas had given him that reputation. If he just disappeared now, that would eventually be forgotten. He would forever be wanted by the Alliance and would still face the death penalty if caught, but the public would soon forget.

Continuing to perform stunts such as this would only lead to more and more people thinking he was actually trying to fight the Alliance. The incident in the town here had proven that. They had been ready to arrest his crew as smugglers until Lahkaba had mentioned his name. People he had never met were buying into this revolutionary bullshit.

His actions on Sulas had already cost the lives of an unknown number of prisoners and guards, probably including Jairyd. Now an innocent farmer was risking his life and livelihood to sneak them into an Alliance outpost.

Guilt wracked him. Was he trading the lives of others to protect himself? He didn't think so. Had Josserand just threatened *him*, he probably wouldn't be doing this. The man had threatened Saracasi, Zeric, Gu'od and Gamaly. The fact was that those three were becoming friends. In exchange for protecting them from a crime lord, his actions were putting innocent – if misguided – people at risk. Not to mention that any Alliance personnel who were innocently going about their normal jobs at the wrong time might be hurt or killed.

Aside from having time to think, being in the crate gave Maarkean a new appreciation for what Zeric and others had gone through in their attempt to steal the *Cutty Sark*. They had been in the cargo hold for a few days before they had emerged. He couldn't imagine spending that long in a space this cramped.

Granted, they had been in airtight containers and not covered in dirty, stinky vegetables. They had also had suits that allowed them to relieve themselves, food, lights, and some entertainment material. It certainly hadn't been luxury, but it had not included the stench of lomba.

The cart came to a stop, and Maarkean heard the first noise that wasn't cart wheels or lomba grunts. Voices could be heard, but they were muffled, and he couldn't make out the exact words. They didn't sound angry or confrontational, at least.

After a moment, the cart began moving again, and Maarkean felt his breathing resume. They must have made it past the front gate. That was a good start. The next step would be the most risky.

The cart stopped again, and Maarkean heard more voices. He felt the cart shift as the tailgate was lowered and someone climbed aboard. The voices became clearer and he overheard talk about moving the crates. This was where things could go sour. There had been no way to cover up the fact that the crates with people in them would be heavier than they should be. They had filled the other crates with some extra dead weight, so theirs didn't stand out from the rest, but they would still weigh more than vegetables should.

Despite his concern and even a complaint from one of the soldiers who was carrying his crate, no one seemed suspicious about the weight difference. Even still, Maarkean held his breath and had his finger on his pistol until his crate was set down. For several more minutes, he overheard the sounds of men moving heavy objects.

Then, one of the potential flaws in the plan came to light. He felt the shudder and heard the *thunk* of a crate being placed on top of his. There would be no way for him to get out. Then he heard the sound of the building's door closing.

Maarkean didn't consider himself claustrophobic, but the idea of being trapped in here started to play tricks on his mind. In the dim light, the crate felt like it was shrinking even further. Breathing became difficult, as if the weight of the vegetables on top of him were crushing him.

Trying to remain calm, he focused on breathing. His attempt to relax was almost immediately foiled when he took in a deep breath and got a chunk of dirty carrot greens in his mouth. Panic started to set in when he was unable to shift his arms enough to get it out.

With a serious effort, Maarkean forced down the panic and turned his head so he could work the greens out with his tongue. Then, with his mouth clear, he took another deep breath and calmed himself. There were only seven crates total. At least one of his teammates would surely have a way out. It would be difficult for one person to move a crate, but not impossible. And he could always shoot the side out with his pistol if need be.

Minutes of silence went by, and Maarkean finally started to relax. All they had to do was wait until nightfall while hoping that no one needed anything from these crates before then, get out of the crates, get to the armory without being seen and then escape. It would be simple, he told himself. With daylight only lasting eight hours at this time of year, they only had another three to wait before dark.

Those three hours passed agonizingly slowly for Maarkean, especially as thoughts about being trapped stubbornly resurfaced for him to beat back over and over. No one came into the storage shed during that time, for which he was grateful. Still, he admitted to himself, he might have traded being discovered and having to fight their way out for less time in this crate.

When the time came, Maarkean was counting down the seconds on his watch. Against all hopes, he had to test out his theory. Shifting around so he could get his arms through the vegetables, he pushed hard on the lid of the crate. Nothing happened.

Maarkean fought back panic all over again. It was completely different when you were actually fighting to get out and couldn't.

Several minutes went by, and Maarkean was relieved when he heard sounds of movement. He hadn't heard the door reopen, so the odds were good that one of the other team members had gotten out. He waited patiently for what seemed like hours, and then he finally heard familiar voices.

"Where's Maarkean?"

"Must be in one of those bottom crates."

Feeling better already, Maarkean knocked his pistol against the side of the crate. "Over here."

"Hold on. We'll have you out in a few," came the answer in what sounded like Gamaly's voice.

Maarkean waited while there were sounds of someone heaving and sliding the crate above him. When the lid for his crate opened, he felt immense relief. He thanked his team.

As he climbed out, he did his best not to knock any of the vegetables out with him. He picked up any that had dropped to the ground before closing the lid again. Once he was clear, they lifted the other crate back on top of his. They wanted to cover their tracks to prevent any suspicion from falling onto Arslan.

Once the room was back the way it was before they had gotten out of the crates – as far as they could determine – the hard part could begin.

Zeric slowly eased the door of the storage shed open. Maarkean and Gamaly had their weapons ready and Gu'od positioned himself near the door. Once the gap was big enough, Gu'od poked his head out.

"Clear," he said and then slipped outside.

Maarkean followed next. There was a light above the shed's door, but beyond that, there was a large expanse of darkness to the next building. He dashed through the light and to the right side of the shed as quickly as he could. Almost colliding with Gu'od in the darkness, he stopped himself and crouched down to wait for the other two.

Once everyone was outside, Maarkean tried to orient himself. In the darkness and from the ground, it was hard to translate what he had seen from the hill the day before. The hill they had been on was not visible in the dark, and there were two large buildings visible from the shed. One was the armory and one was the barracks, but they looked the same to him.

He had debated bringing Lohcja with them on this mission for his superior night vision, but the Ronid had the least combat experience, except for Saracasi. Zeric and Lahkaba were both former military, Gamaly was an excellent shot with a rifle, and Gu'od's skills were without question. In the end, they had decided four was a large enough group and any more would prove a hindrance. Maarkean had chosen the people he thought would handle themselves the best.

Fortunately for Maarkean, Zeric had a better sense of direction on the ground. He led them off toward the building to the shed's right. They tried to keep low and move quickly. Everything so far indicated very lax security, but it would only take one random soldier to notice something unusual in the darkness. Maarkean started to feel the rush of excitement he remembered from fighter combat.

Once they reached the relative safety of the shadow of the armory building, Zeric stopped them. He gestured for everyone to stay where they were and started edging toward the corner of the building. He peered around the corner, then pulled back and gestured at them. It was hard to see in the dark, but Maarkean assumed the gesture was to come forward, since Zeric himself was not moving.

He crept up behind Zeric and could see him more clearly. With his hands, Zeric indicated there were two guards a couple meters around the corner. Maarkean held his pistol up to suggest taking them out with quick stun blasts. Gu'od shook his head, laying a hand on Maarkean's weapon.

Maarkean was caught unaware when Gu'od launched himself around the corner. There were a couple of quiet noises that sounded like grunts and then something hitting the ground. Before he was even sure what had happened,

Gu'od appeared from around the corner again and beckoned everyone forward.

The two unconscious guards on the ground did not surprise Maarkean at this point. Gu'od rummaged through their pockets. After a few moments of searching, the Liw'kel stood up with an ID card and held it up to the armory door. There was a click, and the door slid open. Maarkean and Gamaly each grabbed one of the unconscious soldiers and dragged them inside.

Once everyone was inside, Zeric sealed the door and activated the lights. With no windows in the structure, it was safe to move around with the lights on, although it would kill their night vision.

When he saw what was inside, he was glad they weren't fumbling around in here in the dark. The long building was filled with row upon row of weapons and equipment. Crates of missiles, racks of rifles and boxes of grenades were sitting in every corner of the building. Maarkean was awestruck by the sheer amount of destructive power that was sitting here guarded by only two soldiers.

"Too bad we're limited to what we can carry," Gamaly said, her antennae waving excitedly. "This could supply a small army."

"Nah," Zeric said, "this is just the equipment for a battalion. This base appears to be a pre-positioned equipment depot. All the equipment a unit would need, just without the soldiers. If need be, the Alliance can get the soldiers here on a fast transport without worrying about transporting the equipment."

"What should we take?" Maarkean asked, deferring to Zeric's judgment of ground ordinance.

Zeric took a few moments to survey the room. While he did that, Gamaly helped herself to an assault rifle and bandolier of grenades. Gu'od contented himself with a more powerful pistol than he had and a combat knife. Maarkean considered grabbing something himself, but he much preferred his SK-9 to any of the weapons available. He did grab a pair of sensor goggles. It was top-of-the-line gear that incorporated light enhancement, infrared, ultraviolet, sonic and electromagnetic pulse modes. The goggles also provided a rangefinder and wind speed measurements in a built-in heads-up display (HUD), but within moments of putting on the goggles, he disabled those options. For a sniper, they would be incredibly beneficial, but they proved to be distracting to him.

Zeric had finished his survey by the time Maarkean was done playing with the goggles. The man was smiling like a little boy with a room full of toys. "Good news," he said. "I found a loading bay door in the back. If we can get a vehicle over here from the garage, we can load it up."

Maarkean frowned at Zeric's suggestion. While being able to load a vehicle up would dramatically increase their haul, it would exponentially increase the risk of discovery. The plan called for a stealthy insertion and then a quick snatch and grab. Loading a transport vehicle with crates of weapons hadn't been in the works.

As if sensing his objections, Zeric spoke first. "We can load up what we can carry, slip over to the garage, place the explosives on the vehicles we aren't going to take and then come back over here. If at any point it looks like we might be discovered, we trigger the explosives and get out quickly."

It wasn't an unreasonable plan, Maarkean had to admit. They would have to pass right by the armory again anyway to get out of the base, and the other manned guard posts had no line of sight to that side of the armory.

Maarkean conceded, "All right, grab what you can, and let's go. Gamaly, focus on explosives so we have something to use on the vehicles."

While everyone took their packs off their backs and started filling them with anything that would fit, Maarkean looked around for communication equipment. He was tired of not being able to communicate with his team members because of the unencrypted commercial gear they had. He found a rack of comm units and stuffed his bag with several.

Once he'd loaded his bag, Maarkean walked over to the two still-unconscious guards. He drew his pistol and checked the setting. Out of the corner of his eye, he vaguely registered that Gu'od had stopped his looting and was watching him, his whole body tense. He fired two stun bolts into the guards, and saw Gu'od relax.

Did he actually think I was going to kill defenseless soldiers? Maarkean wondered as he walked away.

That Gu'od might think him capable of that disturbed him. What was he becoming that those around him, those he considered friends, thought that about him?

For his part, he was reassured that Gu'od had looked relieved at the stun bolts. Before, he had been concerned that the others might not have any concern with killing Alliance soldiers. They were the enemy, after all.

Once everyone was loaded down with as much as they could fit in their bags, Zeric led them out the front door. While the loading dock door would be safe from view of the barracks, it would be clearly visible to the guards at the hangar. Until they got past them, opening it would just give them away.

Once outside, the darkness was greater than before with the deterioration of his night vision. Maarkean activated his new goggles, and the world around him lit up. Switching through the settings, he did a quick infrared check to see if there was anybody else out in the night. Nothing stood out, so he switched back to night vision.

Zeric had acquired a pair of the goggles, too, and took point again. Without some modifications, the goggles would not fit on Gamaly's or Gu'od's heads. Maarkean brought up the rear so that the two temporarily blinded team members were in the middle.

Reaching the garage was going to prove more difficult than reaching the armory had been. There was an empty, well-lit concrete expanse between the two buildings. That provided them with no cover, and Maarkean could clearly make out the two guards standing near the garage.

Zeric halted them at the corner of the armory before the concrete expanse. He surveyed the area and then turned to whisper to the group, "If I use Gamaly's new assault rifle on sniper mode, I can probably take both guards out before they can call for help."

Given Gu'od's look earlier, Maarkean stressed, "Stun setting only unless we have no choice. Besides, if you miss, we're done for. Even if you don't, your shots could be heard. Too dangerous."

"I won't miss," Zeric protested. Then he conceded, "But you're right. And I can't do it on stun from this range."

"We go around," Gu'od said. "It will take longer, but if we can sneak close enough, I can take them out silently again."

Maarkean nodded agreement. "Zeric, Gamaly, stay here. If we're discovered, take them out from a distance and then run like hell to join us."

Zeric nodded, and then he and Gamaly settled themselves into sniping positions. Maarkean, being the only one who could see clearly in the dark, led the way. Sticking to the grassy edge of the concrete field, outside the light, he led them across to the side of the garage opposite where Zeric and Gamaly remained.

The position the guards were occupying lay almost in the dead center of the northern wall. There were fewer lights coming from the south side, however. Maarkean led them across the north face, and then down the eastern side so that they came completely around the large building. They moved as quickly as they could while staying stealthy, but he hoped Zeric wouldn't get impatient.

Once around the building, Gu'od took over the point position. He edged along the building toward the edge of the lights. Maarkean followed behind him and deactivated the goggles. The lights around the guards provided more than enough illumination.

There was a gap of about a dozen meters between where the light started and where the guards were standing. Neither of the guards made any show of looking in their direction, but it would only take a small shift. The two were talking quietly and glancing occasionally around the well-lit tarmac.

Maarkean hoped Gu'od could cover the distance to them before either turned in their direction. It was a relatively short distance, but as fit as he was, Gu'od was not a star athlete, and it would take him several seconds to traverse. Readying himself, Maarkean took aim at the guard the furthest away. Gu'od would be able to reach the first one even if they were spotted; it was the second one that would have time to act.

With a quick pat on his shoulder, Maarkean let Gu'od know he was ready. Launching himself from a crouch, Gu'od dashed across the open area toward the guards. As Maarkean feared, the sudden movement and sound of Gu'od running drew their attention. There was a shout from one of the guards before Gu'od reached his first target. Not taking any chances, Maarkean fired on the second.

The two guards dropped almost simultaneously. Maarkean tensed, expecting alarms to go off and search lights to fill the area. Gu'od remained where he was, over the guards, ready to move. Several seconds went by, and nothing happened.

Gu'od bent to remove the ID cards from the guards while Maarkean continued to scan the area. He heard the sound of movement in the darkness and turned to look across the tarmac. The sight of Zeric and Gamaly approaching relieved his nerves.

The door to the garage swung open, and Maarkean moved to join Gu'od. They grabbed the two guards and pulled them inside while the other two caught up. Not waiting, Maarkean put a stun bolt into the guard Gu'od had attacked. That made four guards who would be out for several hours at least.

Once everyone was inside, Gu'od flipped on the lights. The garage lit up, and Maarkean was again awestruck by firepower. The garage stretched out a hundred meters in either direction and was filled with vehicles. He identified at least a dozen battle tanks, multiple shielded personnel carriers, and a plethora of other vehicle types.

"I don't think I brought enough explosives," Gamaly lamented.

"Let's focus on the SPCs and other personal transports. The tanks don't make good pursuit vehicles," Zeric said, taking some of the explosives from Gamaly's pack. "Also, spread them out to every other vehicle, and see if you can find the fuel tanks."

They each took a section of the garage and placed explosives. They tied each set to a single remote detonator to allow for simultaneous detonation. It was not long before they had run out of explosives.

When Zeric finished his set, he went to power up one of the SPCs. Maarkean joined him, saying, "Wouldn't one of the trucks provide more storage space for our ill-gotten goods?"

"Yes," Zeric said. "But I know I would rather run in a shielded vehicle than a fragile truck, wouldn't you? Plus, I think this thing will fit in the *Cutty Sark* cargo bay. Make a nice profit on it alone."

Maarkean wasn't as confident it would fit as Zeric was, but he did like having shields. They weren't perfect protection, and there were plenty of weapons that they were ineffective against, but they were still better than nothing.

The SPC would also be armored, which would help where the shields didn't. Cargo trucks wouldn't have armor or shields.

"All right," Maarkean said as the group gathered at the vehicle Zeric had selected. "Get over to the armory and load as much as you can. I'll join you in a few moments."

Zeric gave him a questioning look. "What are you going to do?"

"Close the garage behind you to contain the explosion," Maarkean replied.

Zeric nodded and pushed the other two toward the SPC. They hefted the two unconscious guards onboard with them. Once they were onboard, Maarkean shut off the lights and opened the garage's massive door. Zeric at the controls, the SPC lifted off the ground about a meter, and then eased slowly ahead and across the concrete field toward the armory.

Pacing the short corridor between the flight deck and the crew lounge was starting to get old. The cramped space provided little ability for Saracasi to change direction and nothing interesting to look at. She considered moving down to the cargo deck or outside the ship, but then she wouldn't be near the comm station if word came in.

She had tried sitting, napping, reading and working in the engine room. All had been marginally successful until night fell. Once the sun went down, the only thing she could think about was the fact that the others were now beginning the operation. Their chances of being discovered, shot and killed were going up and up.

Lahkaba and Lohcja were calmly playing a game in the crew lounge. She did not know how they managed it. They had been left behind as well, and they had been the most eager to see this raid through.

Every time she walked into the crew lounge, Lohcja looked up, his mandibles spread wide like he wanted to say something. But, every time, he glanced at Lahkaba and went back to the game. Saracasi wasn't sure if she appreciated being left alone or wished one of them would say something.

Aside from worrying about Maarkean and the others, Saracasi's mind drifted to thoughts of Asirzi. It tore at her that she had not had a chance to say a real goodbye to her friend. At the time, she had not thought it would be goodbye. She had been expecting to return to Irod to deliver Lahkaba and Lohcja. Their decision not to rejoin their friends had surprised her. Now she didn't know if she would ever see Asirzi again.

That would be unfortunate, but she tried to tell herself it was no big deal. She had only known the woman for a few days, and while she thought that there had been something growing between them, it wasn't really more than an infatuation. Maybe someday it could have been more, but she would never know now. Now she had more pressing worries to contend with than lost loves.

Tiring of the pacing, she stopped in the crew lounge and watched the two of them play. It was Siege, a strategy game for two that she and Maarkean had played a lot. He had beaten her almost every time at first, but she had gotten the hang of the game after a time. Recently their matches had reached a point where they were evenly matched, and as he said, they'd "finally become fun."

She watched the game for several turns. Both Lohcja and Lahkaba missed several opportunities to cause serious harm to the other. Neither were stellar players, but Lahkaba appeared to have the upper hand. It was hard not commenting on their moves, but she knew how annoying that was.

The pacing had been annoying her, but standing in silence became even more irritating. Saracasi broke the silence with an exasperated sigh. "How can you both just sit there?

We're stuck here on the ship while our friends are risking their lives."

Lohcja shrugged as he moved a piece. "Trust me, I agree with you. But there's not much I can do at the moment. I'd like to be out there with them, but I'm not."

With a sigh, Saracasi took a seat on one of the couches across from the other two. She decided to try to focus on something else. "Lahkaba, why did you get involved in all this? Lohcja said before that he did it to help you?"

Lohcja moved a piece on the board, and Saracasi cringed. It was a move that looked good, but could cost him the game.

Lahkaba cast a curious look at his friend before replying, "I've been friends with Lohcja most of our lives. When I was chosen as a representative, my wife left me. He came into hiding with me because he was worried about me."

The strength of Lahkaba and Lohcja's friendship confounded Saracasi, especially compared to Lahkaba's apparently weaker marriage. She wasn't sure she had ever had a friend she would do that for. Risking her life and livelihood for a cause she believed in – or risking her life to save a friend from death – was one thing. But just to give them support?

"As to how I became involved in all this, that's not an easy question to answer. Let's just say I believe in the goals of the Sector Congress and feel the Alliance has abused its power," Lahkaba continued.

"What exactly is the Kreogh Sector Congress?" Saracasi asked. "I try to keep up with current events, and I've heard of it, but the details were all contradictory."

"The Congress was a meeting held by representatives from all seven Alliance colonies in the sector. The colonies in Trepon and Loisa sectors were invited, but they never replied, though they are smaller and more isolated than we are," Lahkaba answered.

"Anyway, complaints to the Alliance about some of the rules and mandates they had put into place were going unheard, and it was hoped a united front from all the colonies would have more weight. Because this sort of meeting was only quasi-legal, the names of the representatives chosen by each planet were kept secret. Though, apparently, not secret enough."

"What happened at the meeting?" Saracasi asked. She had heard about the Congress being called, but that had been months ago, and she had heard nothing about it since. While she tried to stay informed, it wasn't always possible when traveling in space.

Lahkaba shrugged. "There was a lot of debate about how best to approach the Alliance. I, along with Lei-mey and the other Sulas delegates, were disappointed with the result. We were hoping for a strong united stand by the colonies, but what they came up with was a compromise petition. Lei-mey called it worthless. I wouldn't go quite that far."

"But you said you did send something to the Alliance, right? Some united document?" Saracasi asked.

Nodding, Lahkaba said, "Yes. A document was sent that outlined our grievances and was signed by all the colonies. It's a three month journey to Braz, so the message didn't get there but a few weeks ago. It could be some time before there is any response. At least, formal response. The response by Sulas' Alliance governor was to call for the arrest of all participants. That's why I went into hiding."

"Will the Congress meet again?"

"There were plans to meet after the Alliance sent their reply," Lahkaba said and then looked at the game board. "Damn. How did that happen?'

Lohcja had made a move that cornered several of Lahkaba's pieces. The conversation dropped off as the two renewed their focus on the game. Lahkaba put up a valiant struggle, but was unable to recover from his earlier mistake.

Saracasi lost herself in watching the game for a while. It was a surprise when the comm alarm sounded.

Dashing toward the flight deck, Saracasi activated the comm and heard Maarkean's voice saying, "*Cutty Sark*, come in, *Cutty Sark*."

It surprised her that Maarkean was so openly using the ship's name over the open comm channel.

"We read you, strike team," she answered.

"We're coming in. Meet us at rendezvous point Bravo."

"Acknowledged. ETA?"

"Five minutes."

Quickly moving to the pilot seat, Saracasi fired up the engines. They had designated a few locations for alternative meeting points in case they couldn't make it to where the ship was parked. Bravo was closer to the Alliance base, right on a road running through an open field.

Saracasi started to shout back to the other two, but she caught herself when she saw they were both standing right behind her. She chided herself for not realizing they would have followed her. Instead of filling them in, she told them to power up the turret.

Lifting the ship up off the ground and above the tree line, she fired the engines and headed toward the rendezvous point. She was not nearly as good a pilot as Maarkean, or even Zeric, but she could manage to get from point A to point B. She just had to fly higher than the other two would have.

It was a trip of a matter of moments, but as she took the ship back down, she saw a bulky armored vehicle floating down the road at high speed. Lahkaba identified it as an Alliance SPC. Lohcja, who had taken the operations station, said he saw no other vehicles on the ship's sensors. Saracasi wasn't sure if this was their pickup, or if they had missed them and this was the pursuit.

Her question was answered when Maarkean called over the comm again. "*Cutty Sark*, we see you. Set down along the road and we'll bring our vehicle right onboard. We're going to want to make a quick departure."

Looking down at the vehicle, Saracasi wasn't sure if it would fit inside the cargo bay. There was hardly anything down there, but the SPC was pretty bulky. Without taking the time to do detailed measurements, there was only one way to find out. She took the ship down and oriented it forward along the road.

Lohcja got up from the operations station and ran down to the cargo bay to open the door. After a few moments, a shudder went through the ship and she could hear the teeth-grinding sound of metal scraping against metal. At least Maarkean couldn't be mad at her for scraping his ship. It had been his idea.

Several minutes later, Saracasi and Lahkaba were joined on the flight deck by Maarkean. He came in hurriedly, and Saracasi wasted no time in giving up the pilot seat and moving to operations. Maarkean took the controls and immediately lifted the ship off the ground again.

"Where are we going?" Lahkaba asked.

"Away from here," Maarkean said curtly.

Surprised, Saracasi said, "We promised to meet Owrik again afterward to let him know how the operation went."

Hardly paying attention to them, Maarkean fired the engines and the ship gained altitude. "He'll find out how it went soon enough. But if we don't leave here in a very visible way, those soldiers might decide to search the nearby settlements."

"You think they'll retaliate against the locals?" Saracasi asked incredulously. "They didn't do anything."

"Didn't they?" Maarkean asked sharply. "They let known fugitives go, and they helped smuggle those same fugitives into a secure facility."

Saracasi considered her brother's words. The risk to the colonists had not occurred to her. They had not raised a weapon against the Alliance forces. There should be no way that their involvement could be traced. But the harder she thought about it, the more she realized she was wrong.

There had been many people in the bakery who had seen their arrest. Word would have spread. It would just be a matter of time before that word reached an Alliance officer. Then questions would be asked, and the sheriff would be unable to produce his prisoners. He would either say he let them go or that Owrik ordered him to let them go. Blame would fall either on the sheriff or Owrik.

It also would not be hard for the Alliance to figure out how the group had gotten onto the base. Only one non-military person had been let onto the base that day, as far as she knew. Why had none of these things occurred to her before? She prided herself on being able to see and anticipate events.

The thought struck her that she had considered these things but ignored them. Help had been so unexpected, especially after their near brush with a return to prison. Had she been so blinded by her desire to carry this mission off that she had failed to consider the consequences?

As she pondered this, Maarkean flew the ship in a trajectory that was clearly visible to the base's sensors. This worried Saracasi until she realized Maarkean was doing it intentionally. He had said they needed to make a visible exit.

CHAPTER FIFTEEN

The escape from Dantyne proved uneventful, and once they were in hyperspace, everyone got the chance for some much needed sleep. But after spending a day in a crate of vegetables, Maarkean was more interested in getting a shower first. When he got up the next morning, he found Lahkaba in the crew lounge. No one else had risen yet.

After some innocuous pleasantries, Maarkean made himself some breakfast. While he poured himself a bowl of cereal, he considered Lahkaba. There had been no chance to speak to the Kowwok since the revelation about his position as a Sulas representative. This news had left Maarkean feeling worried and slightly betrayed. He had thought that a trust had developed between himself and the Kowwok.

On the other hand, he had suspected there was more to Lahkaba than he had known. It had never been clear why he would be involved with the others. Sitting down at the table with Lahkaba, Maarkean considered how to broach the subject. There must have been a reason he had not said anything before.

While Maarkean considered, Lahkaba said, "I appreciate that you haven't asked about me being a representative to the Kreogh Sector Congress."

"I assumed you had your reasons for wanting to keep it to yourself," Maarkean said, trying to hide his relief that he hadn't asked yet.

Lahkaba began, "I was chosen as a representative because I had been in the Dotran military. Sulas wanted to send a signal to the other colonies that they were prepared to take serious action. The other colonies were not ready, and so we ended up just sending a list of grievances to the Alliance. You can't even call them demands, because the Congress wasn't prepared to do anything.

"Some colonies, like Dantyne, have their own boycotts going, but no one would even agree to joint boycotts across the colonies. Sulas wanted a united front in opposing all Alliance orders and laws until the trade restrictions and the prison camps were closed. But no other world has the prison camps that Sulas does, so no one else was willing to fight for those. I don't think they even understood them."

Maarkean began ignoring his breakfast as Lahkaba talked. The Kowwok appeared to be unloading himself. "Then you and Zeric showed up. For some reason, you believed the news stories about Lei-mey being a terrorist, yet had come seeking us out. At first, I believed Jairyd that it was some kind of set-up. But you were right, had you been Alliance, we would have just been arrested, and if you had wanted to gain our trust, you would have pretended to be opposed to Alliance rule."

Lahkaba leaned forward and looked directly at Maarkean. The intensity of the gaze was a little unsettling, but Maarkean didn't look away. Why Lahkaba was telling him all of this now was still unclear, but he suspected they were coming to that.

"You came to us with a simple request; you wanted to get your sister out of prison. A prison you thought she was in for no good reason. You asked for our help because you knew we had someone in there we wanted out, too. And you didn't just want to get those two out, you wanted to get everyone out."

Maarkean cringed inwardly. While he agreed that it was good all of those innocent people were free now, he knew a lot of not-so-innocent people had been freed as well. It had really only been convenient to their escape plan to get everyone out.

Lahkaba went on, "Now, I know getting everyone else out just happened to be the best plan. But regardless, you show up from nowhere and accomplish something representatives from seven worlds couldn't accomplish. I never wanted to reveal who I was because you did what we couldn't. And you weren't even trying. I was embarrassed."

The admission at the end surprised Maarkean more than anything else Lahkaba had said. He had never thought about the events on Sulas like that. Granted, he had been unaware of much of the background Lahkaba just revealed. He didn't think he had done anything special. Saving his sister had been his goal, and he had accomplished that. Staging a prison break was not a revolutionary idea.

Not sure what to say, Maarkean said nothing. Past experience had taught him silence was sometimes the best thing to say. He didn't always follow that advice, but this time he really didn't know how to respond.

Lahkaba continued, looking a little ashamed. "I decided not to go back to the others on Irod because I honestly thought I would do more good coming with you. And we have. Sure, we only stole and destroyed some Alliance property. And maybe it's just because you owe a criminal money. But it's more than I could do hiding on a forgotten moon."

Maarkean still wasn't sure how to respond. None of the events Lahkaba praised had been intentional on his part, and the Kowwok seemed to be aware of Maarkean's true intentions for everything that had happened, yet he still seemed to respect Maarkean.

Since Lahkaba had inferred most of his intentions, Maarkean decided honesty wouldn't hurt at this point. "I never wanted to get involved in any of this. You're right; my entire motivation on Sulas was to free Saracasi. My entire motivation for the operation on Dantyne was money and staying on the good side of a bad man. I guess I'm flattered that you thought coming with me would help your cause more than anything else, but I'm not sure that it can."

Lahkaba looked up at Maarkean with a concerned look on his face, and Maarkean continued, "You may feel like you're actually doing something right now, but all we accomplished was stealing stuff. Your Kreogh Sector Congress is the best way to get what you want. Appealing to the government reasonably and without violence is the best way to go. Sticking with me will just make you a common criminal."

Not wanting to continue the conversation any further, Maarkean picked up his half-eaten breakfast and moved back into the kitchen. Lahkaba remained quiet as he emptied his bowl. He almost thought he would make it out of the lounge without another word being said, but Lahkaba spoke when he got to the corridor.

"I think you're wrong," Lahkaba said, fixing a powerful look on Maarkean. "I don't think our message to the Alliance government is going to do anything. They've never been keen to listen to the colonies' formal governments, and they know we're not willing to stand up to them, because the Alliance Navy is just too powerful. But your actions say otherwise. They show the people of this sector that the Alliance is not invulnerable. Once they see that, they'll be willing to stand up with a stronger voice. Then, the government might listen to us."

Maarkean looked at the conviction in Lahkaba's eyes. He was seeing the fire of a true believer. *Oh, crap*, was the only thought that came to his mind.

The journey back to the *Black Market* took far longer than Zeric thought it would. When they reached the coordinates that the ship had last been, they found only empty space. The ship had moved on to a new hiding spot. This was not an uncommon experience, especially since the ship had been stationary for a few months.

Tracking down a contact with the new coordinates took several weeks. Anytime the *Black Market* moved, it took a while for the new location to spread throughout the ship's agents. The first one they visited, on Kol, didn't have the new location. With funds running low, they were also forced to pawn off some of their stolen Alliance equipment. After that sale, they couldn't afford to remain on Kol.

Then they had a four-day journey to Mirthod to use Zeric's contact, who, fortunately, had the new coordinates. But, to Zeric's disappointment, the location was over a week's journey by hyperspace, even at the *Cutty Sark*'s high speed. When they finally arrived at the *Black Market*, they had been traveling for almost six weeks.

It was a miserable journey, in Zeric's mind. Being crammed onto a small ship for that long had been driving him stir crazy. The ship was designed for a maximum capacity of eight with shared quarters. With seven of them, Saracasi was the only one with a room to herself. Gu'od and Gamaly shared, and Lahkaba and Lohcja shared. Zeric ended up bunked with Maarkean, since he didn't appear to like the idea of Zeric sharing a room with his sister. He wasn't quite sure what the problem was there. He'd figured out a while ago that Saracasi had no interest in men, so there was no hope of anything fun happening.

With the SPC taking up the vast majority of the cargo bay, they all had very little room to move around. Where before the empty bay had served as a place to exercise and play games, they were now confined to the upper deck. The crew lounge was comfortable, but it got crowded fast. Maarkean had a fair selection of movies and books. Unfortunately, Zeric had seen all of the movies that he liked, and the stuff he had not seen involved Braz humor, a lot of which he just didn't get.

Despite the cramped space, Maarkean, Lahkaba, Lohcja and Gu'od continued to practice Ni'jar techniques. His friend's abilities had always impressed him, but the concentration required was not for him. Maarkean and Lahkaba were getting pretty good, but he suspected Lohcja was more like him.

Gamaly and Saracasi continued to bond, he noticed. It was an ability that amazed him sometimes. Regardless of species, women could form friendships. They always had something to talk about, despite being cramped onboard with everyone else and nothing new occurring.

The biggest thing there had been to talk about was the news they had heard on Kol. There had been a major crackdown by the Alliance forces on Sulas. Apparently, after the Olan prison break, Governor Howell had instituted some harsh measures against the alien population. This had resulted in a backlash by the population like nothing that had occurred before.

Responding to the unrest, the Alliance had dispatched troops to the city of Chuthor, the city where Zeric had found Lahkaba and the others, and seized a collection of weapons that had been stored there. The stories weren't clear whose weapons they were. The Alliance claimed they belonged to rebel groups who were preparing to overthrow the government; they declared martial law across the planet. The cities of Ba'aar and Chuthor were under total military control.

What had surprised him was the amount of sympathy for the people of Sulas. First on Kol and then on Mirthod, there were a lot of people talking openly about the events on Sulas and speaking negatively about the Alliance's response. News was always several days old when it reached any other colony, yet the talk had been even more active on Mirthod than it had been on Kol, despite having reached Mirthod sooner.

The news upset him some, as he had to admit to himself that his actions might in some way be responsible. Saracasi and Lohcja were angry. The weirdest reactions were from Lahkaba and Maarkean. Lahkaba kept giving Maarkean pointed, and Zeric would say smug, looks. Maarkean just looked ill.

Once they reached the *Black Market*, Zeric was happy to step out onto the ship's hangar deck. By comparison to the *Cutty Sark*, he felt like he was standing in a wide open field, despite the large number of ships and people moving about.

As Zeric stood, taking in the relatively open space, Maarkean walked past him in his long brown duster. Smiling at his friend, Zeric said, "Where are you off to?"

"Meet my contact so we can get this stuff off the ship," Maarkean replied as he walked away.

Zeric did not understand why Maarkean always insisted on going alone to these meetings. Whenever Gu'od, Gamaly or Zeric had a meeting with someone, they all served as backup for the others, even when they were supposed to come alone. It was just common sense to him.

As if reading his mind, Gamaly and Gu'od came down the ramp not far behind Maarkean. Zeric eyed them curiously. "You guys going someplace, too?"

Gamaly nodded. "We're going to follow Maark."

"He'll go ballistic if he finds out," Zeric replied.

"Maybe. After some debate with Maarkean, Saracasi agreed to stay behind. But I never made such an agreement. So we're going to go in her place," Gamaly said in a tone that brooked no argument.

Zeric just nodded in response and followed the two Liw'kel through the crowded hangar deck. Following Maarkean through the corridors of the ship proved pretty easy. It helped that the location was on the same deck as the hangar. Had Maarkean boarded any of the ship's transport lifts, it would have been much harder to track him without being seen.

They followed Maarkean into a club called the Ready Room, which was moderately crowded. Exchanging nods with the others, they spread out through the room. Zeric took up a place at the bar where he was close enough to see but not hear Maarkean, who was sitting at a table in one corner alone.

While they waited for something to happen, Zeric examined the room. The place was filled with a lot of rough-looking individuals, but so was every other place on the ship. He understood why Maarkean might be comfortable coming here. There were old photos of pilots, flight helmets, squadron emblems and other Alliance pilot paraphernalia decorating the room. It must be comforting to the old pilot.

After some time, Maarkean was joined by a group. A well-dressed Terran took a seat across from Maarkean while the others stood nearby. Zeric wasn't able to get a look at the man's face, but he seemed familiar. He looked around the room for Gu'od and Gamaly.

To his surprise, Gamaly was striding purposefully toward Maarkean's table. Zeric didn't think there was any way he could intercept her without causing a commotion. What was she thinking? Their goal was to remain unseen and only be there in case something bad happened. Gamaly interrupting the meeting would count as something bad happening.

Deciding their cover was already blown, Zeric rushed to join Gamaly. Gu'od must have decided the same thing, and they reached her just as she got to one of the thugs standing guard. The tall, green-scaled Dotran gave the three of them a menacing look.

"Stand aside," Gamaly said quietly. So far, Maarkean and his contact had not taken notice of them. When the thug didn't move, Gu'od reached out and grabbed a pressure point, dropping the thug to his knees. Gamaly stepped over the wincing Dotran and strode right up to the table.

"Hello, Renard," she said with a dark smile.

Suddenly, Zeric recognized the Terran. He had seen the man before when Gamaly had gone to negotiate jobs and ship sales for them. He was the one who had hired them to hijack a number of ships, including the *Cutty Sark*.

When Gamaly approached, Maarkean looked confused. Then he looked positively furious. To Zeric's relief, his fury was focused on Renard rather than Gamaly. He was suddenly aware he had never really seen Maarkean mad before.

"Renard," Maarkean said with a low growl, "how did you and Gamaly here meet?"

It was clear from his tone that Maarkean had figured out the connection. To Zeric's astonishment, Renard remained calm and cold. He spoke in a straightforward manner as if he were talking about nothing more unusual than the weather.

"Mrs. Dos'redna and her companions here have worked for me on occasion. They acquired ships for me that I desired."

"Ever hire them to 'acquire' a Swift class courier ship?"

With a dark smile, Josserand said, "Now that you mention it, I believe I have. A few months back, actually. About the time you yourself were hijacked. What a coincidence. I believe I tried to buy yours, but you refused."

Casting a glance over at Gu'od still holding one of the bodyguards on the ground, Renard took a drink and then said, "I'd keep him down there as long as you can. Once you let him go, he will kill you."

"If there's going to be anyone dying tonight, it's going to be you," Maarkean said coldly.

"Oh, I don't think so," Josserand replied. "See, you have assaulted one of my men. That is against the Fox's rules. You can also consider our working relationship over. But your debt is not canceled."

"My debt?" Maarkean said, leaning forward over the table. "I owe you nothing. I was never supposed to deliver anything. You hired these guys to steal my ship, and the cargo was only your way of getting them onboard. The way I see it, you owe me."

Before Renard could respond, a group of people stormed into the club and headed toward their group. It didn't take

Zeric long to notice they were armed. He considered his options, but had no weapons available to him. He exchanged a look with Gu'od, who reluctantly released the Dotran guard.

One of the new arrivals spoke. "All of you need to come with us."

The look on his face and the way he held his pistol told Zeric they had little choice.

Maarkean was beginning to think that someone being arrested had become a requirement for any place they visited. The first time, it had required a prison break. The second time, they had been lucky. The third time, he was thinking, would result in a trip out an airlock.

The seven of them were in the ship's brig in two different cells. Maarkean saw that the room had hardly been modified. Every other room on the ship that was not vital to ship operations had been converted to some kind of business, storage room or meeting room.

He knew he shouldn't be surprised that Josserand had been playing both sides. The man was perfectly capable of it. Most everyone on this ship was. He had more anger directed at himself than Josserand. How else had the others infiltrated Josserand's cargo? He had considered the possibility once, but it had been irrelevant at the time. Since then, it had never come up again, and he had forgotten all about it.

Maarkean looked over at Gu'od and Gamaly. The pair was sitting on the lone bench. Gamaly was leaning up against Gu'od with her eyes closed while he slowly stroked her back. It was almost touching. They had ended up behind bars every time so far. Maarkean felt sorry for them.

After what seemed like a long time but had probably not been more than an hour, a video monitor across from the two cells activated. Displayed on them was the image of a bipedal furred creature. It bore a loose resemblance to a

Notha, though its fur was orange instead of the various brown shades of most Nothas.

Examining the creature displayed on the monitor, Maarkean tried to identify it. He had never seen a species like that before. It was possible the creature was a dyed and cosmetically modified Notha. The most likely explanation was that it was merely a computer overlay masking the real person.

"I guess he meant 'the Fox' literally," Zeric whispered beside him.

Maarkean cast a curious expression toward him, and Zeric explained, "A fox is an animal from Terra. Kind of like dogs, but not."

Maarkean had seen dogs before. They were a common companion among Terrans. Several other species had also adopted them, though Notha were often offended by it. He'd never understood that. Terrans weren't offended when other species kept monkeys as pets, and they were genetic cousins. Notha and dogs had no genetic relationship, only some common physical characteristics.

"I understand that you have violated the peace I've declared aboard my ship," the creature on the monitor said. There was no discernible accent, which made Maarkean sure the whole thing was artificially rendered to disguise the owner.

"My lord," Josserand began with a bow, "my bodyguard was accosted by the Liw'kel at the direction of his captain, Maarkean Ocaitchi. There was a business disagreement between us, and he chose to decide the matter violently."

Maarkean wasn't sure he wanted to address a digital image as 'my lord.' He decided to skip the formalities. "That was merely a safety measure to keep your thug from doing the same thing. My friends here came to confront you about the fact that you hired me to deliver cargo, and you hired them to slip aboard in that cargo to steal my ship."

The Fox did not appear to take any notice of the use or lack of use of a title. He directed his next question toward Josserand. "Is this true?"

Josserand answered semi-honestly. "Technically, my lord. I did allow these individuals to use my cargo to hide in. I had no idea what they were planning, however. I certainly had no desire to have one of my deliveries hijacked. They betrayed me just as much as they betrayed Captain Ocaitchi."

To Maarkean's surprise, the Fox said, "You have already been warned about activities like this before. What people do off this ship is not normally my concern. But for business to prosper, everyone must feel comfortable coming here and not have to worry about being pirated from within. Josserand Renard, you are hereby banned from the *Black Market*. All of your property onboard is forfeit. None of your associates are permitted to stay. You will remain incarcerated until the next jump, at which time you will be transported to a populated world, never to return."

A smile spread across Maarkean's lips. Things were looking up. Without them having to make much of an argument, the Fox had sided with them. They might make it out of here in one piece.

He regretted the thought as soon as it occurred to him. The Fox turned toward their cell again. "Gu'od Dos'redna, for assaulting another visitor to this ship, you are forever banned. You must leave immediately. Major Maarkean Ocaitchi of the ship *Cutty Sark*, as the one who brought Mr. Dos'redna aboard, you are also liable.

"Normally, this would result in a warning since he has been here before. However, because of your recent rise to fame as the most wanted man in the Alliance, you will also be banned. Likewise, this ban will extend to your sister and to you as well, Corporal Dustlighter. My visitors have no wish to have that kind of Alliance attention drawn to them.

"It is also likely that a reward for your capture will soon be issued. That would likely result in many people competing to take you in, which would disturb the peaceful business onboard."

Maarkean's heart sank. The *Black Market* was home to a lot of disreputable people, but it was also the safest place in the galaxy for them. The Fox kept things in line onboard, and its place in deep space kept the Alliance from finding them. It was also the best place to find a buyer for the stuff they had stolen on Dantyne, now that Josserand was out of the picture.

"However, Gamaly Dos'redna, Lahkaba and Lohcja Cargon will be permitted to return, if they do so on their own," the Fox continued. "Now, as a citizen of this sector, I applaud your actions. You will not be welcome here again, but there is a visitor to this ship you may want to meet. I will have this individual shown to your ship before you depart."

Of all the things he had expected to hear, that had not been one of them. Maarkean was still puzzling over the comment when the monitor went out. A second later, the cell door slid open, and the two guards beckoned for them to depart. Gamaly, Zeric and Gu'od bolted out of the cell without a moment's hesitation.

Maarkean followed last. Who was the Fox sending to him and why? He had gone to Dantyne because he had felt he had no choice. Now he was being sent toward someone else who might want him to do more of the same.

As Maarkean walked toward the brig exit, Josserand spoke to him. "You have won this round, Ocaitchi. But don't for a minute think I'm finished. This will only be a setback for me. I assure you, we'll meet again."

Maarkean's first inclination was to say something harsh, but he suppressed it. There was nothing Josserand could do to him now, and if he gave into his desire, he might not actually make it off the ship. It was difficult, but he managed to make it out of the room without responding.

On the walk back toward the hangar deck, Maarkean thought over what had occurred. They were still essentially out of funds. They had a cargo hold full of Alliance gear they couldn't sell.

Their only prospect was this mystery person the Fox was sending them. He was sure he wasn't going to like what he was going to hear from this person, but it seemed he had little choice but to listen.

Catching up with the others, Zeric turned to him. "That was some luck we got back there. Getting kicked off the ship isn't the worst thing that could have happened."

"No, it isn't," Maarkean agreed.

"And we may even have more work waiting for us," Gamaly said cheerfully.

"Maybe," Maarkean said noncommittally.

The rest of the way, the other three speculated about what the Fox had meant and who was going to meet with them.

Maarkean silently debated whether they should take off before this person showed up. That way, he couldn't get sucked into anything else.

When they reached the ship, Maarkean noticed a small knot of people standing at the bottom of the ramp. Saracasi, Lohcja and Lahkaba were standing on the ramp slightly above the others. The group consisted of a Terran, a Braz, a Liw'kel and a Notha.

The Notha, who was tall for his species, with light brown fur, turned toward them, and Zeric said, surprised, "Isaxo?"

Maarkean recognized the name but could not recall from where. He took a harder look at the others the Notha was with. The Terran was a tall man with dark skin and a shaved head.

He was definitely the eldest amongst the group, about Maarkean's age. His clothes were well maintained and of a higher caliber than those of most people on the *Black Market*.

The Liw'kel female was the oddest Liw'kel he had ever seen. Her face was a light shade of red and uncommonly beautiful, aside from a small scar across her left cheek.

She wore a collection of random armor pieces that covered most of the rest of her body and hid any feminine features.

She had a sling strung across her back that could have held any number of large weapons, several slots for knives on her belt, a bandolier with grenade-size pouches and the holster for a carbine slung to her hip.

Even though she wasn't actually armed, she was by far the scariest Liw'kel Maarkean had ever seen.

The Braz was a young male wearing a dark blue ship's jumpsuit. He had two pistol holsters on his hips and two more holsters strung across his back.

The casual way he rested his hands where the weapons should have been suggested he was used to having them. The green screfa on the boy's cheek identified him as clan Lis. Maarkean suppressed a sigh. He only knew one other from the Lis clan, and he hoped this boy was not as annoying.

As they got closer, the Notha, Isaxo, smiled at them. "Zeric, good to see you again."

"What are you doing here?" Zeric asked incredulously.

"Looking for you," Isaxo said with a grin. "Lei-mey is going to be very happy."

So much for not getting sucked back in, Maarkean thought.

Cramming all eleven people into the crew lounge on-board the *Cutty Sark* was difficult. Maarkean had insisted on moving off the busy hangar, and Saracasi admitted to herself it was much easier to hear without all the noise. Once everyone was settled, Isaxo began by introducing his companion; the Terran was known as Solyss Novastar, the Liw'kel was Asheerah Aru and the Braz was Kard Ulis.

Zeric made the formal introductions of everyone else. When Maarkean and Zeric were introduced, Novastar gave them a respectful bow. "Captain Solyss Novastar at your service, sirs. Your actions on Sulas have inspired me."

Maarkean looked uncomfortable at the proclamation, but he gave Novastar a half smile and nodded back to him. Zeric looked pleased with himself and a little surprised to be included. Up until now, most people they had encountered had heard of Maarkean from the news reports and warnings the Alliance had put out. Saracasi had no idea why Zeric would be happy to be recognized in the same way.

"After you left Irod, it wasn't but a few days before Captain Novastar arrived with a shipment of supplies," Isaxo began. "His ship, the *Chimopori*, didn't have a lot of room for passengers, but Lei-mey convinced him to take a few of us back to Sulas."

"And with only a promise of payment once we arrived," Novastar said with a smile. "An immensely persuasive woman."

"Lei-mey selected a couple of us who were from colonies other than Sulas to go with her. At the time I didn't understand why she wouldn't take people home instead, but I didn't argue," Isaxo continued. "Once on Sulas, she asked each of us to travel back to our homes and speak to our local governments about what had happened to us on Sulas.

"Captain Novastar volunteered to fly me to Dantyne. Apparently, when we got there, we had just missed you. When I met with my brother, Owrik, he told me what you had done to the Alliance base. I only wish I could have been there to help."

Lei-mey sent people out to every colony world? Saracasi thought. When she had heard the news about the crackdowns on Sulas, she had been half convinced that Lei-mey had gotten back to Sulas and carried out her plan to stage a rebellion and been overwhelmed by the Alliance. The news that she was sending people to all of the other colonies suggested something else.

"Owrik brought me before the Dantyne Parliament, and I told them what had happened to me and La'ari. Most of them were outraged by that, but a lot of them were also outraged by what you had done to the Alliance base. They seemed afraid the Alliance would open a prison like Olan," Isaxo said. Uncertainly, he went on, "I don't understand why they objected to that. You were showing the Alliance they can't push us around anymore."

It became obvious as Isaxo talked that he was mostly speaking to Maarkean and Zeric. None of the others appeared to be bothered by this fact except for Maarkean. The next comment from Novastar made her brother look even more uncomfortable, as it directed everyone's attention to him.

"I've never considered myself much for politics, though I'll admit the trade restrictions the Alliance has in place have provided me with a fair bit of profit bypassing them. But after hearing what Isaxo endured just because he was a Notha and then learning about how this injustice motivated you to turn on the Alliance, I came to realize I was just as responsible for what happened to him by not doing anything about it. We Novastars have always been at the forefront of a fight against oppression, dating all the way back to the Kravic Occupation."

Maarkean looked embarrassed. This didn't surprise Saracasi; he had never much liked being the center of attention. Ever since Sulas, he had drawn more and more attention toward him, though. She wondered if that had occurred to him before now.

"After we met with the parliament, I decided to come and seek you out. We got lucky when we got a message saying we could find you here," Novastar continued. "When he heard what my plans were, Isaxo asked to come along. He'd proved himself to be a pretty capable pilot – better than myself, in truth – so I took him along. So here we are. Ready to help you on your next mission."

Looking at her brother, Saracasi decided this had not been something Maarkean had anticipated. She sighed inwardly. Despite all his talk about needing to think carefully before you acted, he obviously had not thought this one all the way through. Though she decided she couldn't use it against him the next time he chided her for rash action.

"I'm afraid our next action won't be very exciting," Lahkaba said and then turned toward Maarkean. "While you all were out, I caught up on the news feeds. The Kreogh Sector Congress has been recalled."

This news piqued Saracasi's interest. If the Congress was being recalled, then one of two things had occurred: either the Alliance had responded to their earlier message, or people like Isaxo who Lei-mey had sent out had had an impact on the leaders of their colonies.

"Where are they meeting?" Maarkean asked.

"Enro," Lahkaba answered. "City of Perth. The news article is intentionally vague as far as when and where they will be meeting, for security reasons. But the Enro delegation offered the city for the next meeting. I don't know when, exactly, but I should get there."

"Then that's where we're going," Maarkean said definitively. Then, turning toward Novastar, he said, "I'm afraid this probably won't be the fight you were looking for. This meeting could take a while."

Novastar shrugged. "We're not out for adventure. We have decided to follow you to make a stand. The Congress is one way to do that. We will continue with our original purpose for coming here and meet you there later."

Maarkean looked perplexed, but he nodded. "Very well. All right, well, let's go before they kick us off."

Chapter Sixteen

The journey to Enro took less than a week, but Maarkean had to watch their fuel status closely. Their reserves were falling dangerously low. He worried they might not be able to go anywhere after Enro if they couldn't refuel. If anything happened that prevented an on-time landing, they might get stranded on the planet.

Before arriving, Maarkean sought out Lahkaba to discuss an idea he had about the Alliance equipment they had on-board. The SPC in the hangar bay did not make it fuel efficient to break out of a planet's gravity well. With their funds depleted, the SPC was also their only potential source of income.

He found Lahkaba and Saracasi talking while Saracasi ran a diagnostic in the engine room. When he entered, she was asking, "Do you think the Congress will take a stronger stand this time?"

"Possibly," Lahkaba said. "The fact that we are meeting now suggests something has changed. The other colonies may be willing to listen to our proposal for a complete hold on Alliance taxes until the government gives each colony equal representation in Congress, or at least closes down all of the prisons."

"Do you think that will be enough?" Saracasi asked.

"It will have to be. We could close down the prisons with force, but that will probably lead to military retaliation like it has on Sulas. I doubt the other colonies will be willing to risk that."

"Wasn't that the reason you came with us in the first place? To do things like what we did on Sulas and Dantyne?" Maarkean asked from the entryway.

Startled by his sudden appearance, Lahkaba and Saracasi turned toward him.

Lahkaba said, "It *was*. Since the news from Sulas and the occupation of Ba'aar and Chuthor, I've had to rethink it. I still think attacking Olan was more than justified. But, at the same time, we put a lot of innocent people at risk. That was never my intention."

Maarkean considered Lahkaba's words. It had certainly not been his intention when he had conceived of the idea. In truth, he had never even considered that as a possible consequence.

Their death, capture or becoming wanted as criminals had been the only possibilities he had considered.

"On the other hand," Maarkean replied thoughtfully, "our actions have affected a lot of people positively as well. There are more people in those two cities than were in the prison, to be sure, but the occupation will hardly amount to more than an inconvenience. Those in the prison were being imprisoned unjustly. In the grand balance, doesn't that make it worthwhile?"

"True," Lahkaba said simply. He paused, considering what Maarkean had said.

Maarkean was dismayed when he realized he had said that last thought out loud. He hadn't really wanted to defend what they had done.

Despite what he had just said, he still thought what they had done was wrong. They had killed innocent Alliance officers. There was no forgiving that.

But were the officers innocent? That thought had never occurred to him before. If it was wrong to imprison all of those people without cause, were the people who kept them confined just innocent bystanders? On one hand, he thought they had to be.

They were just following orders. But he also knew it was the responsibility of every officer to uphold the principles of the Alliance. Just following orders was not an excuse for obeying an unlawful order.

Maarkean looked over at his sister. Saracasi was giving him a terribly odd look. It felt like she was staring at an unusual growth coming out of his cranial horns. He returned the stare, and she smiled at him.

The smile reminded him of a parent smiling proudly when their child accomplished something. It felt very unusual, because their relationship usually went the other way.

"Regardless," Lahkaba finally said, "I doubt anyone else will see it that way. I think there is just as likely a chance that those who were opposed to stronger action will be even more opposed to it now."

Maarkean decided to get to the point of this conversation. "You think they will feel more comfortable with an SPC and some grenades to help them?"

Lahkaba cocked his head and looked at him questioningly. "You want to give them what we took from the Alliance?"

Shaking his head, Maarkean tried to dissuade the Kowwok of that notion immediately.

"No, but I would like to sell it to them. We're pretty much out of money. If we can't sell this stuff on Enro, we might not be able to leave."

With an uncertain shrug, Lahkaba said, "Maybe. If they are willing to take stronger action, buying military hardware might be a way of sending a message that we won't be intimidated."

"I'm sure your powers of persuasion can bring them around," Maarkean said with a smile.

After he said it, he realized he wasn't sure if he was talking about Lahkaba convincing the Congress to buy the SPC or to take a tougher stance against the Alliance. That he could have meant either one bothered him.

Arrival on Enro saw Maarkean's warnings about fuel reserves come dangerously close to coming true. When they touched down outside the city of Perth – the starport would have charged a docking fee they could not afford – they barely had enough fuel to make a safe touchdown.

While Maarkean, Zeric and Lahkaba went into the city to find out about the Congress, Saracasi was forced to remain behind and set up the ship's emergency solar arrays.

The solar arrays would never draw enough power to operate the engines, but in space they were designed to provide enough backup power to keep life support running.

With the intense cloudiness that Perth was under at the time, Saracasi wasn't sure the panels would be able to draw enough power to even keep the lights on. While the temperature was quite cold, it was above freezing, so running the ship's heating systems was not essential.

By the time she had the arrays online, Maarkean and Zeric had returned. Saracasi had been disappointed about not getting to accompany them, because she had wanted to see the Congress in action. Her resentment was decreased somewhat when she learned that everyone except Congress members was being excluded from the meeting. The rule was intended to keep reporters and potential Alliance spies out of the proceedings.

The next several days proved to lack any real excitement. Lahkaba returned late the first night to inform them that he had been given rooms in a local hotel by the Sulas delegation. When they all questioned him about what had happened, he told them he was not allowed to discuss anything that went on in the Congress. He looked reluctant to say that, and

Saracasi suspected his inability to confide in them was half the reason he had taken the rooms in the city.

Since he was not allowed to share anything about the Congress, she tried to quiz him about what had become of the people on Irod. Lei-mey would certainly be among the delegates, and she would know the latest. Lahkaba had only been able to tell her that some of them had returned to their homes and some were still there. That was not enough to answer her questions about what had become of Chavatwor, Faide and Asirzi.

The downtime gave Saracasi a chance to make some long-needed repairs to the *Cutty Sark*. Much of the battle damage she had taken in the escape from Sulas had yet to be completely repaired. Maarkean and Lahkaba had patched up the worst damage, mainly getting the transmitter working again, while they had waited on Kol. But neither of them was a real engineer, and the work had been amateur, at best.

Lacking new supplies, Saracasi was forced to make most of the repairs in a similar patchwork way. She complained vehemently to Maarkean about the shoddy state of the ship and the likelihood of complete failure. Secretly, she enjoyed the challenge of trying to figure out how to get things working again. Still, she fantasized about what she would do if she ever had access to unlimited supplies and parts.

Lohcja proved to be the one who enjoyed their being stranded on Enro the most. The planet was primarily populated by Ronids, and he spent most of his time in the city visiting with his own kind. Zeric's enthusiasm for being near a city with no one hunting them or shooting them had been tempered when he had learned it was a Ronid planet.

Maarkean and Gu'od continued their training now that they had a lot of open space to work in. The pair would go on long runs into the surrounding woods and return hours later covered in sweat, bruises and cuts. At first, the bruises and cuts were all on Maarkean, but as time went on, some would occasionally appear on Gu'od. Whenever that happened,

Gamaly would frown, but she would go out to meet them with bandages and disinfectant.

After almost a week on Enro, their routine was interrupted by the arrival of three ships that set down in the field near them. Saracasi identified them all as small transports similar in size and capability to the *Cutty Sark*. All three had also seen better days.

When the ships landed, Saracasi was working on the dorsal hull. She quickly made her way down and joined the rest of the group, which gathered at the boarding ramp. She was surprised to find Lahkaba there, as she hadn't noticed him approach while she worked. Everyone but her was armed, and Zeric kept glancing back at the SPC still in the cargo bay as if he was considering bringing it out.

A single individual from each ship headed toward them while most of the rest of the ships' crews headed in a cluster toward the city. Gamaly said, "At least they don't appear hostile. Not if they are sending most of their people away."

"Could be a ruse," Zeric said, still holding a rifle at the ready.

As the small group approached the *Cutty Sark*, they were able to make out faces. The dark Terran in the lead she recognized as Solyss Novastar, whom they had met on the *Black Market*. The Liw'kel she did not know. The Braz with them had a green screfa and a jovial expression on his face. When she recognized him, she knew her brother wouldn't be thrilled.

"Frac," Maarkean said, letting out the Braz's name in such a way as to make it sound like a curse. Fracsid Relis was a fellow smuggler they had encountered on a number of occasions. The man claimed he could get anything for anyone anywhere, if the price was right.

In Maarkean's opinion, the price was always too high, and he was always annoyed by what he called the immature antics of the man. Saracasi found him amusing, but she had never had to work directly with him.

Maarkean looked distressed at the sight of them. Saracasi wasn't sure if it was just because of Fracsid or something else. In the excitement of the news about the Kreogh Sector Congress, she had almost forgotten the strange meeting with Novastar on the *Black Market*.

She had not talked to Maarkean about that, but she suspected the idea of some more people wanting to follow him on a grand quest to snub Alliance authority did not sit well with him.

When the group got within earshot, Maarkean called out, "Captain Novastar, I didn't expect to see you so soon."

When they were close enough, Novastar stretched out his hand with a wide smile. "Our business did not take long. It is not quite the numbers I was hoping for, but it's a start, right?"

Saracasi wasn't the only one who didn't understand what the man was referring to, because Zeric asked, "A start for what?"

"Major Ocaitchi's squadron, of course," Novastar answered as if it were obvious. He then turned toward the two others. "This is Fracsid Relis of the *Unending Justice*; my crewman Kard is his cousin. And Eri'dos Ar'cher of the *Durandal II*."

Fracsid had a big grin on his face as he looked at Maarkean. Saracasi was not sure if he enjoyed tormenting Maarkean or was completely unaware he annoyed him.

Neither of those would surprise her, but she suspected the latter. The man was amusing and could usually carry through with his promise to get what he claimed, but he was not especially perceptive.

The other smuggler, Eri'dos Ar'cher, looked to be a completely different sort. The look he gave each of them was cold and calculating. Unlike Fracsid, who wore a pistol on his hip,

Eri'dos had no visible weapons. Her first impression of the Liw'kel, however, suggested that he had knives or small blasters concealed somewhere on him.

Ar'cher just nodded at Maarkean, but Fracsid continued to grin and said, "Long time, no see, Maark. How's the ship holding together, Casi?"

To avoid Maarkean saying anything unseemly, Saracasi answered quickly, "She's good. Better than the *Justice*, I'm sure. I never took you for anyone interested in politics, Frac. What are you doing here?"

"I'm not," he said. "But I've heard the stories about Maark's exploits, and it sounds exciting."

Maarkean frowned at that, and before Saracasi could say anything else, he unleashed a tirade. "Excitement? You're here for excitement? Do you think this is fun? Turning against your government and causing the death of her servicemen and women, a group of people you were once a part of, is not fun. If you want some excitement, do a poor job next time you try to sneak past Alliance security patrols. Then you can have all the excitement you want while they chase you down. At least then, when they catch you, you'll only be thrown into prison instead of being executed for being a terrorist."

The grin on Fracsid's face disappeared, and everyone looked at Maarkean in astonishment. He continued, holding everyone's attention with his rant, "This isn't a game, and this isn't fun. It's not a grand adventure, and I'm not some damn hero. I'm not some kind of revolutionary leader, either. I saved my sister from a life in prison. That's it. Now I'm on the run, with no money, no work and a warrant hanging over my head. If this is the life for you, then, by all means, jump right in.

"I actually believe Novastar has good intentions with this squadron he's trying to form. But we'd just be pirates in all but name. That raid on Dantyne was a mistake and the wrong thing to do. Doing more things like it will only harm the chances this Congress has of succeeding. Associating with us is only going to make the rest of you into traitors too."

Saracasi had never seen her brother speak so passionately. The others looked just as surprised as she was. She found him hard to read, but if she had to guess, she would say Lahkaba did not look particularly happy. The rant had not been directed at him, so she was unsure why.

"Are you done?" Lahkaba asked sharply.

Maarkean nodded.

Lahkaba said, "You may be right about Dantyne. We probably did come close to crossing a line there. But I don't think we crossed it. We may have gone there just to steal stuff, but we ended up doing more than that. No one was killed, and we were able to inspire the people of Dantyne to stand up against the Alliance's harsh rules. Their delegation is now one of the most outspoken for a stronger response, when before, they were quite against it.

"We formed a Congress to try to speak as a united front. But we could hardly agree on what to send in what was basically just a letter of grievances. It wasn't until you stood up and acted at Olan that things changed. Before, people would complain in private, and only a very few would complain in public. Now everyone's talking openly in public. The voice of the people got so loud the Alliance declared martial law on Sulas."

Lahkaba paused and rubbed his forehead before continuing. "But none of that matters anymore. A packet ship arrived in orbit this morning. That's why I came out here. The Alliance government has responded to our message."

A sense of dread filled Saracasi. It was clear by Lahkaba's manner that the news was not good. She had been hopeful that the message, even if Lahkaba had considered it weak, would have gotten the Alliance to listen to the people out here. The fact that it had been weak had made her more hopeful it would be listened to. Weak was, most likely, more peaceful.

Lahkaba continued, "The Alliance government has declared that all members of the so-called Kreogh Sector Congress are to be arrested as agitators and insurgents. It has also declared that all planetary governing bodies are hereby disbanded and all power of government now rests solely in the hands of the Alliance appointed governors.

"One of the Enro delegates has already received a tip that Colonel Cage is dispatching troops to Perth to arrest the Enro Parliament. There are three Alliance bases on this planet; they won't take long to arrive. I'm sure if they knew we were here, they would arrest us, too.

"It's ironic, though," Lahkaba said with a sigh. "The time stamp on the message from the packet ship was less than three weeks after the prison break on Sulas. The fastest packet ship would take two months to reach the Alliance capital. So when they decided on these actions, there was no way they could have known about that. They declared us traitors and disbanded our governments, and all we did was send a letter."

When Lahkaba stopped speaking, the whole group remained silent. Saracasi felt sorry for her friend. She knew he had felt as hopeful for the Congress' success as she did.

She also felt sorry for Novastar and his bunch. They had come here hoping to join Maarkean's fight, only to be told there was no fight.

She also worried about what would happen next. Without fuel, they would be stranded here when the troops arrived in the city.

Being on the outskirts, they might avoid notice, but it was unlikely that their position out there wasn't known. Once the troops arrested the delegates, they would come to get those who had attacked or escaped from Olan.

"What's the Congress going to do now?" she asked. There was a small chance they might have come up with a plan.

"We're disbanding," Lahkaba said sadly. "We're all returning home. With the legislatures disbanded, we no longer have any authority, and none of us want to be arrested."

That squashed Saracasi's last hope. They had only the hope of begging or stealing fuel and escaping before troops arrived. It was not the glorious end to their time as rebels she had secretly imagined. But it was the end Maarkean had said they would face.

"But we don't have to give up. We can keep up the fight you started on Sulas," Lahkaba continued. "Now we have more ships, and we can gather even more support. They called us rebels. Let's go be rebels."

"No," Maarkean said quietly. Saracasi almost didn't hear him, and it wasn't until he continued that she was even really sure he had spoken.

"No. Call the Congress back. They aren't running. The Alliance has no right to disband the legally elected leaders of any planet. They've gone too far this time. We're not going to allow that to happen."

Saracasi blinked in surprise. The calm determination in Maarkean's voice rattled her, but also gripped her. She found that she wasn't the only one grabbed by his words.

"But what can we do? There are highly trained Alliance troops on their way. The Congress can't stop them."

"We can if we fight," Zeric said. "They won't be expecting any resistance. We can scare them off pretty easily. It will probably just be troop transports. They wouldn't see a need for an escort."

Maarkean turned to Novastar. "Looks like I'm going to need your squadron after all."

Novastar nodded respectfully, Relis smiled like a boy with a new toy and Ar'cher's expression remained the same as it had through the entire conversation. They all pulled out their comm devices and began calling their crews back.

Turning back to Lahkaba, Maarkean said, "We're going to keep the Enroian Parliament in place. And you need to get Congress to authorize this."

Confused, Lahkaba said, "What do you mean?"

"We're not going to be criminals anymore. I don't think the Alliance should be able to do what they are about to do. But if the representatives aren't going to make a stand against it, I'm not going to, either."

Pointing to Novastar and the other smuggler captains, he said, "None of us are. Either they do something, or we do nothing."

Lahkaba looked uncertain. Saracasi wasn't sure if he objected to Maarkean's plan, but he was clearly less enthusiastic than he had been a moment before.

The smuggler captains all seemed eager and ready to put their lives and ships on the line at his order, and they had just met Maarkean, though admittedly they were here in the first place because they wanted to follow him.

Hesitantly, Lahkaba said, "I agree with you that we can probably repel these first troops. But convincing the Congress of that in such a short time will be difficult. Gathering them together again might itself be impossible."

"Then you better get moving," Maarkean said flatly.

Spontaneously, Lahkaba gave him a salute and then dashed to the vehicle he had used to get out here. Lohcja followed him while Maarkean turned to talk quietly with Zeric. Gu'od and Gamaly remained standing impassively in the background as if they weren't sure what to do next.

Saracasi was impressed with her brother's change of attitude. She was definitely seeing the command presence his old Navy buddies had told her about.

When he had given her guidance or orders in the past, it had always been in the tone of a parent or a brother. This had a definite difference in attitude.

Driving the SPC toward the city, Zeric wasn't sure how he ended up involved in this plan. Sure, he admitted, he had been the one to declare that they should fight.

Maarkean was right that the Alliance had overstepped its authority by a wide margin with this act. And yes, even the SPC had been his idea to help Lahkaba bolster the confidence of the delegates. But that didn't mean he had to drive it.

Sitting beside him, Maarkean had his eyes closed and was calmly breathing. Probably doing those meditations Gu'od was always talking about. Zeric wasn't sure if it was due to those meditations, but Maarkean suddenly seemed more focused and confident. He was like the man Zeric had worked with back on Sulas.

After they had escaped from Sulas and met up on Kol, Maarkean had been different. At first, he had assumed it was because the man had relaxed after freeing his sister. But Zeric thought it was more than that. The raid on Dantyne had been completely different than on Sulas. Zeric wouldn't go so far as to say it, but Maarkean had almost been whiny and wishy-washy.

Zeric, Gu'od and Gamaly had decided to stay with Maarkean for a variety of reasons. Gamaly had come to be friends with Saracasi, and Zeric had realized he was becoming friends with Maarkean. He had also come to respect the man's abilities and trust him in combat.

The months since the prison break on Sulas had seen Zeric start to rethink his opinions. They had bounced around from several places with only half-formed plans. He couldn't truly blame Maarkean for that. Everywhere they went, their reputations preceded them. Being at the top of the Alliance most-wanted list and regarded as folk heroes made a life of crime difficult.

Regardless of that, Maarkean's behavior had made Zeric question his decision. Following him had gotten them all stranded on a planet with a cargo full of Alliance gear they couldn't sell. The operation on Sulas had gone pretty well, but everything since then – not so much.

The Maarkean of the last thirty minutes was markedly different. He had completely taken charge of the situation, and Zeric found himself happily following along, just like he had on Sulas.

Though, just because he was happy Maarkean was back to his old self didn't mean Zeric agreed with the plan. Attacking the Alliance ships made sense. It would delay their arrival with almost no risk to either themselves or the troops. But that time should be used to get everyone out of the city. As far as he knew, the Enroians had no militia to call up. The Alliance troops would just return with escorts.

Zeric also didn't understand the need to get the Congress to agree to it. That seemed like a waste of time. He understood the notion of gaining legitimacy in their actions if the Congress backed them up. But he didn't think it was needed. No one had authorized them to attack Olan. And defending these people was the right thing to do, with or without their orders to do so.

The countryside they drove over gave way to the outskirts of the city of Perth. Unlike on Dantyne, the road they followed had not been paved, though it changed once the city structures began. Zeric liked that about the planet. Hovering vehicles didn't need paved roads and left the planet more natural.

Several people came out of buildings as Zeric drove the SPC down the street. There was a lot of confusion and staring at the vehicle. It was probably an uncommon sight, especially alone. Alliance vehicles would always move in small squads whenever they did patrols.

Following the map coordinates Lahkaba had provided, Zeric took them to the hotel that was hosting the Congress. Zeric found it funny that something called the Kreogh Sector Congress was being held in a hotel convention hall. The name gave it the impression of something much more grand. But with seven planets each sending five delegates, that was only thirty-five people; that didn't require much room.

He brought the vehicle to a gentle stop directly in front of the hotel. The valets stood around awkwardly, clearly unsure what they were supposed to do. Zeric expected at least one of them had a faint hope he'd get to park the SPC.

Once the vehicle came to rest on the ground, Zeric turned toward Maarkean. "Well, now what?"

Maarkean opened his eyes. "It's too bad neither of us has our old dress uniforms."

Zeric blinked in confusion. "Why?"

"We'd look much more impressive."

Zeric said, "I much prefer my Razors cap to a stiff military hat. And all those buttons are so pointless. Besides, you'd look horrible in Alliance green. Clash horribly with your screfa."

"It did. Maybe something more neutral? BDU's?

"I'd be okay with that. Camo patterns work in any setting. Wars, weddings, political conventions."

Maarkean smiled. "Think we've stalled enough?"

"No," Zeric said truthfully. "But we might as well go inside. It gets pretty stuffy in here with the engine off."

Maarkean squeezed out of his seat and opened the exterior hatch. They had left the troop compartment filled with the crates of weapons they had stolen. If things went the way Maarkean intended, they would put them to some use. Zeric regretted that they might not make any money off them.

Zeric climbed out of the vehicle and joined up with Maarkean at the entry door to the hotel. He winked at the valets. "No need to park it, we won't be long."

The pair headed into the building side by side. Zeric thought they cut an impressive image even without the military dress uniforms. Maarkean's duster billowing behind him and Zeric's cap certainly didn't give off the same impression, but with their pistols at their sides, a rifle slung on his back, and their determined stride, he thought they looked damned menacing. Everyone quickly turned their attention to the two of them as they entered.

The lobby was opulent, with several exotic plants and bright lights that contrasted with the cloudy dark outside. There were some wildly colorful and distorted paintings that made Zeric a little nauseous to look at. He assumed they looked quite nice to the compound eyes of a Ronid.

Their confident stride into the hotel lobby was mitigated somewhat when they both realized they had no idea where they were going. A secret gathering that had just been declared illegal would not have a big sign directing any random passerby to where they were meeting. Zeric turned toward the check-in desk and put a big smile on his face for the Ronid female behind the counter. At least, he thought she was female – he wasn't good at telling gender on some species.

"Hi, I was hoping you could tell me where the Kreogh Sector Congress is meeting?"

The receptionist blinked at him and said hesitantly, "I'm afraid I don't know what you're talking about."

"Come now, I know you do," Zeric said. "See, very shortly a team of Alliance troops are going to storm through those doors and ask the very same question. And they won't be doing it nicely. That is, unless I can find them first."

Looking from Zeric to the crowd that was watching them and then back again, the receptionist considered her choices.

She lowered her voice and almost whispered to Zeric, "To your right, down the hall, third room on the left."

With a wink, Zeric thanked her and walked over to rejoin Maarkean. He took a slight lead, guiding them where the receptionist had indicated. The eyes of everyone in the lobby followed them until they were out of sight. Zeric imagined that, after they left, the silence was broken by confused chatter.

When they came to the door, Zeric looked at Maarkean. "Think we should just go in or knock?"

"Let's slip in, but not make a scene," Maarkean answered.

Zeric shrugged. He liked making a scene, but he gently opened the room's door and the two of them slipped into the room. What he saw was not at all what he had expected.

In his mind, he had pictured the delegates sitting around in an orderly circle, listening while one person stood up and gave a boring speech. That's what the Alliance Congress always looked like when it was shown on the news. Stuffy people standing around looking bored while one droned on about something.

What he saw instead was akin to pandemonium. The room itself was set up in a pretty orderly way, with eight tables arrayed in a circle. However, the delegates themselves were all in various states of sitting, standing and pacing. Everyone seemed to be talking at once – most of them shouting.

Zeric examined the eight groups. The number surprised him, as he had been under the impression there would be only be seven: one for each of the seven Alliance colonies in the sector. He picked out the Cardine table, made up exclusively of Camari; the Enro table, with four Ronids and a Liw'kel; Dantyne, where he recognized Owrik with several other Notha; two tables with a mix of species he assumed represented Kol and Mirthod; Ailleroc, he assumed, was the one with only Terrans. He saw Lahkaba and Lei-mey sitting for Sulas. He was pleased to see Pasha Nolan sitting with them, looking much better than he had the last time they'd met.

At the last table, Zeric recognized Faide Darkthorne, Meyka and the mayor of Lost Hope, Revas Shim, plus two others he didn't know. Irod must be a new eighth delegation. He wondered what they were doing here, and why Meyka wasn't with the Sulas delegation.

Zeric and Maarkean stood in the back of the room, unnoticed by anyone, for several minutes. Finally, a lone Liw'kel man who stood in the center of the tables banged a gavel on his desk several times. He shouted over everyone that he would have order, and the room quieted down.

The Liw'kel looked over the group until they were all seated, and then he spoke in a more level tone. "The motion before us by Delegate Lahkaba from Sulas is that we should oppose the order by the Alliance government to disband and should give aid to the Enroian Parliament which, as we all know, is already under threat of arrest."

One of the Terrans stood up. "It is the consensus of the delegates from Ailleroc that we obey this order to disband and return to our own planets. Further opposition will only lead to our arrests as well."

Several others from different tables shouted out disparaging comments, and the Liw'kel banged his gavel again. The Terran sat down, and Lei-mey stood up. "I've spent some time in an Alliance prison already. I have no wish to repeat it. But turning and running won't keep us from prison; it will, at best, delay it. We have a squadron of ships standing by for Mr. Lahkaba's word to prevent the troops from reaching us. Onboard one of those ships is the brother of Mr. Mahon from Dantyne. He is ready to fight for the people of Enro. Why are not the rest of you?"

For a moment, shouting started to rise up again, but Lei-mey continued, "Maybe it is because most of you have not had to face having yourselves or your family imprisoned for no legal reason until now. I have and Mr. Mahon's brother has. But none of you need go through that. We have with us now the men who freed those of us imprisoned on Sulas. And, with your blessing, they will keep all of us from facing that."

The entire group shifted when Lei-mey gestured toward Zeric and Maarkean. Zeric was impressed by Lei-mey's ability to grab the crowd. Everyone else was surprised to see them, but Lei-mey looked perfectly calm. Zeric assumed her composure was because the Sulas table was the only one with a clear line of sight to them standing at the door.

"Major Ocaitchi, Corporal Dustlighter, what is the status of your forces?" Lei-mey asked as if she was old friends with them. This was despite the fact that Zeric hadn't left her under the best of circumstances, and she had never met Maarkean.

Maarkean started to speak, but it came out too quiet to hear. He paused and cleared his throat and then said loudly, "We have three armed ships standing by. Alliance ships from local bases are making their approach to the city, but we have them on our sensors. We are ready to engage at your order."

For an unpracticed performance, it was impressive. Zeric liked the bit Maarkean had added about the ships already being in their sights. They actually hadn't talked to Novastar and his group for quite a while. The words had the intended result, though.

Once again, the room erupted in shouting. Many people were shouting at the Ailleroc and Cardine delegations. Zeric guessed they were the biggest holdouts. Ailleroc's opposition made some sense to him; the planet had a very large Terran population and still had the greatest freedom over all the other colonies.

One voice stood out over the rest. It belonged to an elderly Ronid from Enro, who introduced himself as Halin Corte, Prime Minister of Enro. He stood, and the others quieted down. "If this delegation will not answer in the time we have left, then we will be forced to defend ourselves. My parliament has already met. We will not disband. Major Ocaitchi, if I use the power I've been granted to form a militia, will you lead it? We have no one experienced in the art of war in the government to call upon."

Maarkean replied, "Mr. Prime Minister, if the people of Enro wish to defend their right to democratic government, then I would be happy to join you. However, I can only do so if this body supports that decision."

Maarkean had everyone's attention. Zeric was glad it wasn't him. He hated speeches and thought he was terrible at talking to a group.

It was clear that they were expecting Maarkean to say more. He went on, "If everyone doesn't come together, then I can only help you to hold off these arrests. In six months or less, the Alliance will send the full force of their military down on you. I will not help bring about that level of destruction. But if every planet represented here stands together, then it's a fight worth having, because then there's a chance we can win."

Corte appeared disappointed, but he nodded. "I understand your decision, Major. I therefore, formally call for the Congress to mutually support all governments represented here in any effort to resist the Alliance's order for them to disband."

Shouting broke out as soon as Corte finished speaking. Zeric hadn't expected it to work, but a part of him had hoped that a few words calling for unity would be enough. Maarkean continued to stand beside Zeric as the delegates shouted at each other. After a moment, the Liw'kel who appeared to be serving as the arbitrator of the group got everyone's attention again.

"A motion has been made. Does anyone second?"

Lei-mey stood up. "Sulas seconds the motion."

"The motion has been seconded. We will now vote on the motion," the arbiter said. "Sulas, how do you vote?"

"Sulas votes aye," Lei-mey said defiantly, looking at the rest of the tables.

"Mirthod?"

The delegates from Mirthod were speaking furiously to each other. Zeric would have thought such a diverse group would strongly oppose the Alliance. He did not know much about the place, but their trade in exotic animals was heavily regulated.

"Mirthod abstains until we can confer with our senate," one of the delegates finally said.

"Kol?"

The delegates there were similar to Mirthod. Both were planets with small, diverse populations. With Mirthod abstaining, Zeric was sure Kol would do the same. He knew how important even the limited Alliance patrols were to fending off their piracy issues.

One of their delegates stood up. "Kol votes aye."

"Irod?"

Without much discussion among his fellow representatives, Faide stood up. "Irod votes aye."

"Enro?"

"Aye," Corte said, but without shouts of support from the rest of his delegates.

"Dantyne?"

The Nothas were speaking rapidly in their native tongue, which Zeric could not understand. Owrik was clearly the most passionate of the group, and after a few moments, the rest appeared to nod their agreement to him. Standing, Owrik declared Dantyne's support.

Zeric turned to look to the last two tables. Cardine and Ailleroc were the two he would have pegged as against this move. By his count, they already had five of eight votes, so he wasn't concerned with what they voted. But there was still a heavy air of anticipation from everyone.

"Cardine concurs with our fellows from Mirthod. We must consult with our parliament."

"Ailleroc?"

One of the Terrans from Ailleroc stood and answered the same as Cardine. At that, everyone in the room appeared to relax, including Maarkean. Zeric didn't understand why their vote had mattered. Wasn't abstaining the same as voting no?

"The motion carries with five votes, three abstentions, and zero no's," the arbiter said.

A cheer went up from the Enroian and Sulas tables. The other tables clapped but with less enthusiasm than the others. Once the excitement had died down, Prime Minister Corte turned toward Maarkean and Zeric again.

"Major, Corporal, with the full support of the Kreogh Sector Congress, Enro has decided to resist the order to disband our parliament. Will you accept my offer to lead our defenses?"

Maarkean gave a slight bow to Corte and answered for both of them. "We will. With your permission, we will see to dealing with the troops already on their way."

With a nod of consent from the prime minister, Maarkean drew the secure comm device he had taken from the Alliance equipment and activated the speaker function. "*Chimopori*, this is Ocaitchi, come in."

There was slight bit of static, and then Novastar's voice could be heard over the speaker. "This is *Chimopori*, we read you."

The room quieted down as they all tried to overhear the conversation.

"We have just been conscripted into the Enro defense militia. You are hereby authorized to engage the Alliance troopships. Attempt to warn them, and shoot to disable. Take lethal action only if necessary, but keep those ships from landing in the city. Report when you have been successful."

"Acknowledged. Non-lethal force if possible."

The comm line closed, and Maarkean turned the speaker feature off. Zeric saw Faide give them both a respectful bow of his head, and beside him, Meyka looked relieved. The rest of the delegates ranged from concerned to angry to ecstatic.

Zeric leaned over to Maarkean and whispered, "Now we get to wait."

CHAPTER SEVENTEEN

"Way to put me on the spot back there," Zeric said. Maarkean wasn't sure if his friend was joking or was mad.

The two of them were sitting in a briefing room at the Perth police headquarters. The police chief was currently meeting with the prime minister, and they were waiting on her and several others to join them. They were supposed to be analyzing the city's maps to develop a battle plan.

In response, Maarkean said, "Sorry, but you know more about ground combat than I do."

"Which isn't much," Zeric said despondently.

After the vote by the Congress to support the Enroians, Maarkean had contacted Novastar. The three ships in the private squadron had engaged and warned off the Alliance troop transports that had come from the nearest base. Unfortunately, they had needed some persuading, and one of the transports had been shot down. That had left little hope that things would not escalate.

Prime Minister Corte had then asked the obvious question: What next? Maarkean knew the Alliance would make a strong response, but he realized he wasn't really sure what to expect. That was when he had turned to Zeric. Zeric claimed to have been blindsided, but his idea to enlist the planet's police force and begin planning for a siege had been a good one.

"There is an entire planet full of people out there. Shouldn't there be one person with more combat experience than us?" Zeric said, breaking Maarkean's thought.

"Hmm?" Maarkean said as he tried to recall what Zeric had just said. "Oh, maybe not. Enro fell without much of a fight during the Colonial War. They didn't militarize after the Kravic Invasion like we did, so their military isn't very big. Ronid tried to keep itself out of the larger conflict and ceded Enro to the Alliance pretty quickly. There haven't been any major conflicts since. It's doubtful there are many Ronids who have seen much fighting, aside from a few random individuals like Lohcja."

They returned to studying the maps of the city. Their first evaluation had been disheartening. Perth was an open city with broad avenues that would provide plenty of room for Alliance military vehicles to move through. There was no city wall, and all of the land around the city was well traversed and cultivated, pushing the planet's native wildlife well away from the population center.

What Maarkean found almost criminal was that there were no anti-air or anti-orbital defenses. The city was basically defenseless from an orbital attack. Energy weapons tended to disperse quickly in an atmosphere, so only specially designed assault ships had the firepower. He could forgive the lack of a city shield. But no defensive batteries meant the city was open to any kind of air attack.

Things did not look optimistic. Maarkean would have reconsidered the option to evacuate the city, but their action earlier made that impossible. The Alliance troops had been challenged and made to turn back. There was no way they could evacuate the entire city's population on the available transport.

Acting rashly and without considering the consequences was starting to become a habit of his. Just like he had always tried to tell Saracasi, when you reacted without thinking it through, it got you into trouble. Now he was most definitely in trouble, stuck defending a city that was indefensible because he had let his emotions guide him and, in the process, had endangered the entire population.

Maarkean and Zeric's silence was interrupted by the room's door banging open and admitting a small horde of people. The city's police chief, Lannah Kamalas, came in first, followed by Lahkaba, the prime minister, Halin Corte, Leimey, Owrik, and Captains Novastar, Ar'cher and Relis. They were followed by several other members of the Congress and several members of Kamalas' police staff.

"I'm told I am to report to you about overseeing the city defenses," Chief Kamalas said by way of greeting.

Maarkean had grown accustomed to Lohcja's spiked carapace and dangerous-looking mandibles. By comparison, Kamalas' carapace was a smooth, deep blue and her mandibles were much smaller, giving her mouth a far less threatening appearance. He realized that there was something more to Lohcja's claim to being descended from the warrior caste than just pedigree.

Maarkean stood up and tried to figure out an appropriate response. Turf wars had been one thing he had hated while in the military, but he seemed to have found himself in the middle of a big one. As an outsider, he now found himself in command of the planetary defense. He imagined how he would feel if he were in Kamalas' place.

He decided to take a lesson from all the way back from his officer training. When in command, be in command and don't give anyone a chance to question your authority. "That's right. How many police forces do you have available?"

"About two hundred and fifty," Kamalas answered.

She looked ready to say something else, but Maarkean never gave her a chance. "Do you have any special units?"

"Yes, twenty special response units. Though we rarely need them."

"We'll need them today," Maarkean replied and turned toward the map, pressing forward. "Based on your knowledge of the city, where is the best place to secure civilians' safety?"

"Well," Kamalas said, thinking. Her initial confrontational posture was slipping. "The hospital has a reinforced structure and a large basement. It's designed as an emergency storm shelter. Every few years, we get bad hurricanes."

"Hurricanes?" Zeric asked as Kamalas pointed the hospital out on the map. "I assume that means you have a planetary weather satellite network?"

The prime minister nodded. "Yes, thirty-six orbital satellites provide us with planetary weather information, communication and navigational data."

"We need someone who has control of the satellites," Zeric said. "We can use them for real-time intelligence on the Alliance bases."

"Good idea. That'll give us some idea when the troops are coming," Maarkean said as Kamalas dispatched one of her aides to see to that. Maarkean continued, "Prime Minister, have you gotten a count on volunteers?"

Shaking his head, Corte said, "About two hundred have gathered outside City Hall so far. But it is still early. I am hopeful more will appear."

"Are they armed?"

"About half of them," Corte replied.

Looking toward Kamalas, Maarkean asked, "How many spare weapons do you have?"

"Spare?" Kamalas answered. "Well, every officer has their side arm. And we have about one hundred rifles and a small collection of specialty equipment. Not enough to equip an army."

"It will have to be," Maarkean said.

Zeric asked, "I assume they are stun-only weapons?"

"The pistols are, of course," Kamalas answered. "We're a police force, not a military. The rifles do have lethal settings, though."

"Well, that's something," Zeric said. "Have your officers distribute their pistols to civilians; that way they can't accidently kill anyone because they don't know which way to point a gun. Then equip your officers with the rifles and the weapons we'll supply."

If Kamalas had looked annoyed at taking orders from Maarkean, she looked even more so taking them from Zeric. He had been introduced to her as Corporal Dustlighter. A non-commissioned officer (NCO) as his second in command might not sit well with a police chief, Maarkean thought. He might need to do something about that.

While Zeric was talking with Kamalas, Maarkean took a look around. The rest of the crowd had moved in closer to them, filling the small room. Maarkean hated crowds, especially when he was the center of their attention.

The aide that Kamalas had sent out returned to the room and, after whispering to her, went to the display table in the room's center. The holographic map of the city was replaced by a display of the entire planet of Enro. Three bright symbols appeared on three of the continents.

"These are the locations of the Alliance bases," the officer said. "We've redirected the cameras from the satellites to observe the areas around them."

The holographic image of the planet shifted back to a view of the planet's surface. Maarkean could make out the layout of an Alliance base on a large plain. A long train of vehicles could be seen heading away from the base.

"This is the base on the continent of Joisu, the one furthest away from us." The aide switched the view. "The base on Usoji."

The image looked much the same as the first one. He switched it one more time to show a base that was very similar, but didn't have a stream of vehicles leaving it. "And the one here on Siuso."

"That's good, right?" the prime minister asked. "They don't seem to be coming here."

"No, Mr. Prime Minister," Maarkean said. "They are most definitely coming here. That's why the base closest to us hasn't deployed their forces yet. They are waiting for all their troops to assemble."

"Why are they taking ground vehicles?" Lei-mey asked.

Zeric turned toward her. "They won't have enough air transports for all of their troops. They're likely dispatching the SPCs first and will follow when they get closer to the engagement with the transports."

"It will take at least two days to get from Joisu to here," Kamalas said. "Can't your ships attack them en route?"

Maarkean shook his head. "I wouldn't. We only have lightly armed transports. We were able to fight off their troop transports before because it was a pretty even fight. Since the first job of the transport pilots is the safety of the troops they carry, in a fair fight they usually back off and wait for fighter support.

"The S in SPC stands for shield, and it's a pretty good one. They are also armed, not as well as a tank, but still at least equivalent to our ships. We have four transport ships, and they're moving in convoys of about ten. The odds are in their favor. And that's not including the fighter support they would launch as soon as we approached."

The room was silent after Maarkean's grim assessment, which gave him a moment to think. He wished he knew exactly how many troops he would be dealing with, but battalion strengths could vary quite widely. There were at least sixteen SPCs worth of troops coming their way, plus whatever was at the closest base.

"Zeric," Maarkean asked, "what's your assessment of their strength? How many troops and SPCs might they have?"

Zeric frowned as he examined the satellite images. Maarkean knew he didn't like being put on the spot, but Zeric knew far more about troop deployments than he did, and despite his earlier protests about not knowing what he was doing, Maarkean thought he managed to come off sounding like an experienced professional.

"Well, if they really do only have a single battalion on Enro, it is likely a large one," Zeric began. "Typical battalions are three to six companies. Most of those are combat infantry units with at least one support company – typically a mixed transport and headquarters unit.

"Out here with no support closer than a few weeks, it is likely closer to a small brigade than a typical company. I'd assume four to five infantry companies, a full headquarters company, two logistics companies and a squadron of fighter/bombers."

Zeric leaned in and looked closer at the image. "Each logistics company would have about sixteen to eighteen SPCs and four to five air transports. Total, that would allow them to transport five infantry companies, about six hundred troops, plus all the support personnel."

Six hundred infantry troops plus another couple hundred support troops. That meant they would be facing close to one thousand trained soldiers. Currently, they only had four transport ships and fewer than five hundred armed people. Half of those were civilians, and the other half were police. Most of their people would be using stun weapons, and the Alliance would not.

A thought occurred to Maarkean as the bad news sunk in. "With ten SPCs coming from each base, that's a little under five hundred troops. Plus whatever they send in the air transports. Let's say they send half of those; that's another fifty or so. So we're looking at 550 infantry troops, plus about 150 operating the vehicles. Out of about one thousand total?"

"Sounds about right," Zeric said.

"That's so many," one of the congressional delegates said, probably louder than he had intended.

The mood in the room seemed to shift to a more negative tone than it had had at the start. However, as everyone else became more despondent, Maarkean grew more confident. A plan was forming in his head. It would be risky, but it was better than the alternative.

"Okay, here's the plan," Maarkean said, trying to infuse as much confidence into his voice as he could. "The Alliance obviously knows the prime minister is here in Perth. They dispatched troops immediately after receiving the message, but came here instead of Enro's capital. We need to make sure their attention stays here."

Shifting the map back to a layout of Perth, Maarkean centered it on the hotel. "Let's let them think the entire Kreogh Sector Congress will still be here at the Perth hotel. Mr. Prime Minister, keep making announcements from there and get any willing delegates to do the same. Make sure the Alliance knows that the Congress supports Enro's defense and that you won't move."

The prime minister nodded, but Kamalas snorted, "That building isn't secure. Lots of entrances, lots of windows. Not a very good building to hold in a siege."

"Better than having a firefight outside a hospital," Maarkean responded. "We'll still evacuate civilians and any delegates who want to get out of harm's way to the hospital, which is on the other side of the city. Zeric, what lanes of approach do you think they will use?"

Zeric examined the map for a moment and then pointed to three avenues leading into the city. "I'd come in along these three lanes. They are the widest and straightest. They'll also likely send ground troops through a couple other entry ways to try to come around any defenses we set up."

"Okay, let's talk defenses," Maarkean said, beginning the next of many more long discussions.

The next two days passed in a blur for Zeric. He was placed in charge of preparing the ground defenses. Moving around the city constantly, monitoring preparations and answering questions, he got to know the city pretty well. All of the traveling around made him glad they weren't doing this on Dantyne, where he would have had to ride an animal instead of a motorized vehicle.

Resources and equipment for establishing the defenses were limited, but that forced him to get creative. The police department had a few barriers available, but they were designed to impede people and normal vehicles, not vehicles with guns. For most of the entry routes, they had begun setting up makeshift barriers with whatever they could find. These barriers were crude and would do little more to stop the Alliance than the police barricades.

The windfall came when Zeric drove past a construction site. Sitting abandoned in one corner, where the fleeing construction workers had left them, were two trucks loaded with steel girders. With the trucks resting on the ground, the cargo was high enough that an SPC's hover system couldn't climb over, and the trucks were long enough to stretch across most of the roadway.

Using the trucks, Zeric felt reasonably confident about obstructing two of their routes. The Alliance would eventually be able to get through or go around, but it would give them time. He set the other main avenue with the majority of the police's interdiction mines.

Designed to disable vehicles with an electromagnetic pulse, or EMP, they were used to stop fleeing criminals.

Alliance military craft were hardened to resist such devices, but Zeric was hopeful that enough of them might do the trick.

Zeric's biggest worry was manpower. The well of volunteers had slowed to a trickle, and most did not have their own weapons. In total, they had fewer than two thousand people. Almost a hundred of the best trained were being used for Maarkean's special operation.

Of the rest, only some of them were armed, and half of those only had stun weapons. If they were not able to stop the SPCs, those stun weapons would be completely useless. They had more people than the Alliance, but each soldier probably counted the same as four or five untrained civilians.

On the morning of the third day, Zeric woke from his four hours of sleep and staggered over to where food was being distributed. Out of the tens of thousands in the city, not many civilians had been willing to fight, but many were willing to help. He had had lots of extra hands for setting up the barricades, and the hospital was full of volunteers ready to help any injured. Food was coming from some of the best restaurants in the city.

As Zeric got into line, his stomach rumbled, reminding him he had not had a chance to eat the night before. The smells coming down the line were like heaven, and he licked his lips in anticipation. In hindsight, he should have known that was a sign he wouldn't get a chance to eat anything.

His comm beeped, and he reluctantly activated it and answered gruffly. "Yes?"

"Lieutenant Dustlighter?" asked the timid voice of the aide who had been assigned to him.

That had been the other thing he had had to contend with. Maarkean had decided it wouldn't do for a corporal to be running the defenses, so he had convinced the prime minister to issue Zeric an officer's commission in the Enro defense militia, which, up until three days ago, hadn't existed. The annoying thing to Zeric was that Maarkean had refused the prime minister's offer to make him a general. Zeric thought it was rather hypocritical to force an officer rank on him, but refuse a generalship.

Zeric had never wanted to be an officer. After his basic service, he had trained as an NCO, and left the service as a corporal. He was good at leading troops into battle, but he didn't think he had the skills to devise strategy and handle administrative work. Give him a gun, tell him who to kill, and he'd do a good job.

Unfortunately, he had been doing exactly what officers did the last few days. Working out defensive plans, organizing the volunteers and the police into teams, settling disputes, and allocating resources had consumed him. To be sure, he was also tasked with doing a lot of NCO jobs, since there was no one else with any experience.

"What is it, Kumus?" Zeric asked, trying to keep himself from snapping. The boy was one of the few Terran volunteers. Kumus Stryker and his brother Kelvine had volunteered together in the first wave. They were part of a small collection of teenagers who had decided Zeric was someone to idolize. Kelvine, almost 18, had been put on the front line in one of the defensive positions, while Kumus, barely 15, had been given a safer place as Zeric's aide.

"Our scouts have reported that the Alliance forces are deploying from their base. We estimate three hours until they are in position," Kumus answered nervously. "Major Ocaitchi has ordered all forces to report to their designated positions."

Well, so much for breakfast, Zeric thought. To Kumus, he replied, "Thank you. Keep me informed of the latest changes."

With a heavy sigh, Zeric looked at the weary people in line for breakfast. It extended well behind him now, and he was only about halfway through it. Those closest to him looked almost ill. They had undoubtedly heard part of the conversation.

Stepping out of line, Zeric climbed up onto a nearby table. The eyes of everyone turned toward him, and the low roar that had been dozens of individual conversations slowly faded. An air of nervous energy slowly built in the room as everyone waited for Zeric to say something.

"The Alliance is on their way," Zeric said simply. He didn't shout, but his voice carried over the silent crowd. "Get to your assigned positions and get ready."

For a moment, everyone remained where they were, frozen in a kind of surprised terror. That did not bode well for things to come, Zeric thought. He decided to try a trick from one of his old drill instructors. He yelled, "You heard me! Move, people! Move!"

The crowd broke apart like shattering glass, and everyone started scurrying away in a rush.

Driving to the starport from the hotel gave Maarkean ample time to think about what was coming. In truth, it was the first time he had had nothing to do but think. The last few days had kept him busier than he could ever remember being. Now, with nothing to do but pilot a vehicle through empty streets, his mind started to wander.

Doubt was the biggest thing on his mind. It was guaranteed that a lot of innocent people were going to die today. Those people would most likely be those who had decided to follow him in this foolhardy rebellion.

Even if they succeeded and weren't thoroughly wiped out, it would be because they killed a good number of soldiers – soldiers who only thought they were defending their government; soldiers who were little more than boys and girls who didn't know any better.

He had doubt about the validity of his plan. Doubt about his ability to carry off his part in it. Doubt about everyone else's abilities. He even began to doubt whether his assessment of the Alliance was correct, and they wouldn't just bomb the entire city to ash.

All of these things played out in his head as he drove. Every conceivable outcome, each one worse than the last, ran through his mind. Yet despite all of his doubts and despite all of the chances for him and hundreds of others to meet a gruesome death, the one thing he didn't doubt was that they were doing the right thing.

Reaching the starport, Maarkean drove straight to the tarmac where the *Cutty Sark, Chimopori, Unending Justice, Durandal II,* and a handful of police interceptors and transports were waiting. The captains of the other ships waited, gathered at the base of the *Cutty Sark*'s boarding ramp. Some were pacing, some were standing stoically still, but it was clear all of them were nervous.

Maarkean parked his vehicle away from the ships and walked over to the assembled group. As he approached, they stopped what they were doing and formed a semi-circle around him. Maarkean looked over each of them.

It was still unclear to him what they were all doing here. The police pilots had been ordered here and were defending their home city. He understood that. Novastar had spent significant time with Lei-mey and Isaxo, delivering messages about the horrors the Alliance had committed, and he supposed that had influenced the man. Maybe Relis felt some clan loyalty to his cousin, Kard, who flew with Novastar, though clan loyalty did not mean much these days. But Ar'cher was clearly a true-blood smuggler, and there was no profit in what they were about to do.

"This is your last chance to back out," Maarkean began. "Once we're airborne, people's lives will be dependent on you. No one will think any worse of you if you back out now. But back out later, and I'll kill you myself."

The captains all held his gaze, and there was a decided lack of nervous shifting. For whatever reasons, the people in this group were firmly committed to their cause. Maarkean appreciated the commitment. He just hoped that it didn't get them all killed.

"All right, let's get into the air before the Alliance decides to launch a fighter wave to attack us while we're on the ground. Remember to use the encrypted comms, and let's try to avoid any needless heroics."

Turning toward the boarding ramp, Maarkean started to head up, intending that last comment as a dismissal, but Relis saluted him. It was a sloppy salute, to be sure, but in an inexperienced rather than disrespectful way. Novastar followed quickly after, as did the police pilots.

Ar'cher, however, gave the group a disgruntled grumble, nodded to Maarkean and walked toward his ship.

Maarkean knew how Ar'cher felt. They weren't in any military, though technically he had been appointed into Enro's defense force. He was unsure if he wanted to quash this saluting business or support it. He decided it would be disrespectful not to return the salute, and he snapped off the best he could manage.

When the rest of them dispersed, he made his way aboard the *Cutty Sark* and closed the ramp behind him. The cargo bay was once again almost completely empty, but he knew it would not stay that way for long. He dashed up the stairs, sprinted down the corridor and stepped onto the flight deck.

Saracasi was going through the pre-flight routine with Owrik. Maarkean was unsure why she had picked the young Notha delegate from Dantyne to help them out. Owrik appeared to be familiar with starship operations, as far as Maarkean could tell, so he could find no fault there. He did wish she had found someone who was a good gunner, though. Not that Saracasi was bad; he just didn't want her to have to shoulder that responsibility.

"How we doing?" Maarkean asked, catching the others' attention.

"All warmed up, fully fueled for a change and ready for lift off," Saracasi said, moving away from the pilot seat toward the weapon controls.

Maarkean slipped in behind her and adjusted the seat back to his preferences. He trusted Saracasi but couldn't break the old habits and ran through a brief check of systems himself. Once he was satisfied everything was in the green, he turned to Owrik.

"Signal the squadron; see if they are ready."

Owrik nodded, a little nervously for Maarkean's preference, and spoke into the comm. "This is *Cutty Sark*. Report status."

Despite everything else Maarkean had to worry about, he had debated whether or not to give the ships fighter designations. The transports were not exactly fighters, but it would have felt more familiar going into battle. In the end, though, he had forgotten about it.

"*Chimopori*, ready to go," Novastar said from his ship.

"*Unending Justice*, standing by," Relis' operations officer said.

"*Durandal*, we're good," Ar'cher's crew answered.

The police pilots checked in, in order, and then Owrik turned to Maarkean. "Squadron reports ready."

"Well," Maarkean said almost to himself, "here we go."

Chapter Eighteen

Saracasi watched as the ground outside the forward viewport shifted as the ship rotated. It was very unsettling to watch the planetary surface turn until it looked like it was above you and the sky was below you. Maarkean made the turn gradually enough so that the artificial gravity could adjust its direction and strength against the changing pull of the planet's own gravity. The end result was feeling like you were sitting on the flight deck as usual while the planet of Enro was now upside down.

Her time over the last few days had been spent getting the ships ready for combat. The *Cutty Sark* had been given access to fuel and spare parts on the Enro government's dime, and she had taken full advantage of that. Time had been the limiting factor, and she had only been able to replace the most important parts, but that had included a faulty capacitor in one of the shield generators.

The maintenance crews from the starport had also been at their disposal, which had been a great help. Despite that, the crews from the other smuggler's ships had all come to her first. Isaxo had apparently spread the word that she knew what she was doing, and they were more comfortable with a fellow smuggler tinkering around than a government engineer.

During those days, she had not had a lot of free time, but she had managed to find a moment to speak to Faide. When she had learned that Irod was now part of the Congress, she had been eager for news. Faide had been able to relieve her worry about Chavatwor and Asirzi. Her friend had fully recovered from her injuries, and Chavatwor was making a name for himself tinkering with Lost Hope's residents' farm equipment and power supplies. He even promised to pass on a message to either of them when he returned home. If any of them returned home.

"Thirty seconds," Owrik said from the operations station.

Pulling her attention away from the confusing scene outside, Saracasi focused on the targeting computer. Even though they had rotated upside down, the turret controls faced aft, giving her no view of the outside world. The only thing she had to face now was being shot at by Alliance troops and shooting back at them. That was enough to contend with without worrying about the world having flipped upside down.

They were flying in a circle around the city of Perth in flights of two transports and a police interceptor. Their goal was to do as much damage as possible to the SPCs before they made it into the city.

Saracasi had practiced on the ship's weapon before. When they had left Braz, Maarkean had insisted that she be able to perform every function necessary to operate the ship. This was despite the fact that he left all of the engineering work to her, though she admitted he did know enough to get by.

Though she knew how to operate the weapon and had even managed to successfully shoot some space debris in practice runs, she had never fired at a live target before. She would have preferred that Owrik operate the weapon while she ran ops, but even though Owrik was quite familiar with ship operations, he had never fired a weapon. Since Maarkean needed to fly, that left her on the gun.

Saracasi's heart was pounding rapidly, and she was sure it would explode out of her chest. Her hands were slick with sweat, and she wanted to wipe them off on her clothes. But Owrik had said thirty seconds and that must have been five minutes ago. She couldn't afford to take her hands off the controls. Their pass over the Alliance convoy would last only a handful of seconds.

The wait stretched on, and Saracasi's leg began to shake nervously. She tried to hold it still, but when she did, the other one began. Her legs shaking suddenly reminded her of when she had taken her graduate school entrance exam. She had been more nervous than she had ever been before. Now it seemed like a stupid thing to be nervous about, and it made her laugh.

"Something funny back there?" Maarkean asked.

Realizing that she had actually laughed out loud, Saracasi regained control over herself. "No, no, everything's good."

She could almost feel Maarkean give her a questioning look and raise an eyebrow at her, although she was sure he never looked away from where they were going. Refocusing her attention on the weapon controls, she checked all the systems again. Then she took a few slow, deep breaths to calm herself.

"Ten seconds," Owrik called out. "Unlock safeties."

Ten seconds? Saracasi thought. As she disengaged the weapon's safety, she felt more confident. Those last twenty seconds had seemed like an eternity. Maybe she would have more time to lock on and fire on the Alliance ships than she'd thought.

"Alliance convoy on sensors!" Owrik shouted. "Police interceptor firing EMP on lead SPC!"

The Alliance SPCs appeared on her targeting scopes, and Saracasi froze for half a second. All other thoughts went from her mind except that now she had to shoot at real live people. She was now going to try to kill people who were what her brother used to be: serving their government and protecting their people by being in the military.

"Fire!"

Maarkean's shout broke through her thoughts, and Saracasi squeezed the trigger. Her first few shots blew holes in the dirt around the SPC before she remembered to lock her target. As they flew over the convoy, she rotated the turret to stay fixed on the SPC and kept firing.

In the time she thought it would have taken her to blink, they were suddenly out of range of the convoy, and she stopped firing the weapon. She looked at her sensor display, but the convoy was now lost on the ground. Saracasi had no idea if she had hit the SPC or if they had managed to destroy it.

"One SPC took minimal damage. We only sustained a few minor hits to our shields," Owrik said.

"They'll be better ready for an attack next time," Maarkean said flatly. "We'll need to be, too. Signal the *Chimopori* and make sure that we're all focusing on the same target."

Owrik relayed the message, and Saracasi took advantage of the momentary lull to wipe her hands on her pants. Shifting in her seat, she tried to get herself into a better position. Taking another few deep breaths, she tried to keep herself from worrying about her mistake on that first run. If things continued like that, this would all be a good waste of time.

"Coming up on the second convoy," Owrik said.

The SPCs in the second convoy suddenly appeared on her screen, and Saracasi locked onto the lead vehicle without hesitation. She unleashed blaster shots as fast as the turret would allow. She also noticed blasts coming in from the *Chimopori*. As they flew over the convoy, she was startled when the SPC suddenly exploded.

"That's one down!" Owrik said excitedly. "Moderate damage to our shields with some minor hull damage. There were definitely more of them firing at us that time."

"Twenty-nine to go," Maarkean said soberly.

As Maarkean took them toward the third convoy group, Saracasi tried not to think about the fact that she had just killed almost twenty people. It was a sobering thought that she wanted to suppress. Distraction could get her or her friends killed.

A warning from Owrik brought her attention back. "I'm reading a dozen enemy fighters coming in from above."

"Signal the other ships; we're leading them to our trap. Saracasi, shift to air targets," Maarkean ordered.

The ship rotated, and the sky was once again above them. Maarkean altered the heading of the ship away from the city.

Early in the mission planning, Zeric had decided that their single SPC would be no use in the defense of the city. While its shield would provide protection and its gun would add firepower, it would be a giant target. Going up against thirty other SPCs, it would mainly serve to draw fire.

After Zeric's assessment, Maarkean had decided on a better use for the SPC. Taking it and the small supply of anti-air weapons they had taken from Dantyne, Lahkaba and Pasha Nolan had gone outside the city and set up a hidden position on a hill overlooking the area. Covered up with local brush, the SPC and volunteers with shoulder-launched SAMs – surface to air missiles – waited as an ambush.

Saracasi switched the targeting computer from ground mode to regular mode. She began scanning for the incoming fighters, but they were still outside the range of the targeting system.

That did not last long, however; before she expected them, the fighters suddenly appeared on her screen. Then the dozen fighters multiplied by two, almost immediately growing to twenty-four targets on her screen.

Half of them began approaching at double their previous speed. It took the computer a second to recognize the new targets as incoming missiles.

Ignoring the sudden shouts of warning from Maarkean and Owrik, Saracasi immediately began laying down a defensive firing pattern toward the missiles. Fortunately for her, the incoming missiles appeared evenly distributed among the other ships – only two were heading toward them. She watched as the missiles rapidly advanced toward them despite her unrelenting fire.

As the missiles approached, she continued to fire and was finally rewarded with one of the missiles exploding. Her elation was short lived as the second missile continued to come.

Just when she thought she might be able to hit it, the missile suddenly vanished from her firing arc as the *Cutty Sark* swung in a sharp maneuver. She watched the missile begin to make a change to follow them, but it was moving too fast to turn before impacting the ground. Watching the missile detonate into the ground, Saracasi stopped holding her breath and gulped in several lungfuls of air.

Her heart was still pounding louder than anything else on the flight deck, but it was more comforting than distracting now. At least she still had a heart to beat.

"Both police interceptors were hit, and the *Chimopori* is reporting damage," Owrik said. "*Durandal* and *Justice* are fine and have formed up on us."

"How close behind us are those fighters?" Maarkean asked.

"Almost within weapon range and closing."

"Time to destination?"

"They'll be on us before we get there," Owrik replied.

Saracasi was only half listening. She was still trying to get over their close brush with death. Her mind kept coming back to a newly passionate belief that they needed to get more advanced targeting software so the turret could better serve as a missile defense.

Then Owrik's last statement sank in, and she recognized that their brush with death was not quite over.

Turning her attention back to the console, Saracasi rotated the turret toward the ship's aft section. She watched as the Alliance fighters' range to them rapidly decreased. It was not long before they were in the effective range for the turret. Selecting the lead fighter, she began blasting away at it.

The sky behind them was filled with flying blaster bolts as the other three transports in their group and the twelve fighters fired. She felt the impact as some shots hit them, but there were no warning alarms, so she ignored them. Focusing on one fighter, she tried to ignore the others in order to better bracket that one.

Saracasi scored a few glancing hits against the fighter, but was unable to do serious damage through its shields. As she continued to try to get a target lock, the fighter suddenly exploded. When several more fighters went up in flames and smoke, she realized that they had finally reached their destination.

With the fighters busy engaging the transports in the air, they had not noticed the additional targeting scanners that had suddenly appeared – or they had noticed too late. A handful of missiles and the SPC's cannon had been a surprise, taking down four of the fighters in short order.

While taking out a third of the fighters in a single volley was a big advantage, they were still fighting two-to-one odds.

Saracasi searched for another target. This time, instead of one of the fighters pursuing the *Cutty Sark*, she selected the fighter that the *Chimopori* next to them was targeting.

The combined fire from two turrets firing from two different angles was able to overwhelm the pilot, and they dropped another fighter.

Now we just need to get seven more before they get us, Saracasi thought.

When Zeric reached the forward command post, he was dismayed to find Lei-mey there. One of the reasons he had decided to take a position so close to the front lines, aside from wanting to be part of the action, was to avoid any of the politicians. Enro's prime minister had been very supportive, but also very curious. The delegates hadn't been any better.

The command post was on a balcony of one of the city's taller buildings. It afforded him a clear view down the street that he would be overseeing. Ignoring Lei-mey, he went straight to the edge of the balcony and put on the combat goggles he had taken from Dantyne. He activated the binocular function and zoomed out to where he could see the Alliance vehicles just coming into view.

"Won't be long now," he said out loud. "Kumus, signal the other command posts that we have the Alliance vehicles in sight."

Kumus, working the comm, relayed the message. Zeric was relieved that, for a change, communication was not something they would be lacking. Along with the dozen encrypted comms they had taken from Dantyne, the Perth police force was well equipped with communication equipment. They had been able to distribute encrypted devices to every command post, ship and forward team.

Surveying the street, Zeric checked the defensive positions. His position was the one that didn't have a truck loaded with steel girders blocking the street. They did have an array of barriers set up just past a curve in the street. This would keep the Alliance forces from being able to fire on it from a long way out and would serve as a perfect bottleneck point. Most of their heavy weaponry was stationed around there.

All of the side streets from the edge of the city to the barriers had been blocked off as best they could. Most of them were too narrow for the SPCs to maneuver down while their shields were active. Zeric hoped they would only have to worry about troops moving down them.

"The transports report they have engaged the Alliance fighters. Bravo and Charlie positions report that Alliance vehicles have been spotted as well."

Nodding to Kumus, Zeric wished Maarkean luck. He then looked over the two civilians who had been assigned to protect this position. He'd failed to convince the police chief not to waste anyone on guarding him; instead, he had succeeded in only getting two inexperienced people. At least he would not be wasting the time of anyone who knew how to fight.

Finally, Zeric turned toward Lei-mey. He was impressed that she still had not said anything. 'Quiet' and 'patient' were not qualities he would have pegged her with.

"Why aren't you back at the hotel?" he asked.

Lei-mey gave him a dark look before saying, "I volunteered to help fight. Not hide in a hotel."

"You're part of the Congress. You shouldn't be on the front lines. And trust me," Zeric said as seriously as he could manage, "guarding the hotel will mean you'll see some fighting."

"Not if we do our job out here," Lei-mey countered. "Lahkaba, Pasha and several others are on the front lines, and they are members."

"Lahkaba and Pasha have been in fights. I've seen them capable of holding their own. You haven't. If I were you, I wouldn't be so eager to see that change," Zeric said, getting angry. He hated politicians. "And that doesn't explain what you're doing here, out of all the places you could have gone."

"I thought what you did on Sulas was a one-time thing?" Lei-mey said quietly enough that the others nearby couldn't hear.

"It was."

"So why are you here?"

Zeric stared back. He was glad that she kept her voice low. He didn't have a good answer to that question, and it wouldn't do for the morale of the others to see him fumble the answer.

"Let's just say I see the value in this fight."

"I don't know what game you're playing," Lei-mey replied quietly but roughly. "I'm willing to let you lead this battle and be a symbol to people. For now, you're useful. But you made it clear to me you don't believe in what we're fighting for. There has to be some other motive. If I determine that those goals are going to harm us, I'll make sure you regret it."

Zeric wasn't sure how to respond. He had made himself out to be an uncaring mercenary to her before, when she had wanted him to join her fight on Sulas. It appeared she had taken that to heart.

Before he could respond, Kumus announced, "Charlie position reports Alliance forces have entered the city."

Turning away from Lei-mey, Zeric peered over the balcony and took another look at the vehicles approaching his street. The first vehicle had just crossed from the unpaved grass around the city's edge to the beginning of the paved street. He ordered Kumus to relay that and then to order their defensive teams to get ready, but hold their fire.

Zeric tracked the SPCs as they floated down the street. It did not take them long before they were almost to the curve in the street. Soon the fighting would begin, and Zeric could be done with this intolerable waiting. Sitting and waiting for the enemy to come to him was not his favorite thing.

"Tell the EMP teams to trigger their mines on my signal," Zeric ordered. Their position had the majority of the mines, since they didn't have a truck of steel. It was a long shot, but with luck, they'd do something.

As the first three SPCs came around the bend, they trained their guns on the barriers in their way. Blaster fire filled the air, and the street was suddenly filled with a cloud of debris as the first barriers were pummeled by the cannons. The first barriers had no one defending them, and the SPCs continued to advance without resistance.

When Zeric saw the vehicles make it past the first barriers and begin targeting the second layer, he turned to Kumus. "Activate the EMPs."

Zeric heard the popping sound of electricity in the air, but saw nothing. Invisible to the eye, the electromagnetic pulses were released; the three lead SPCs suddenly stopped firing and sank to the ground.

"Open fire," Zeric ordered, and Kumus relayed the message.

From all around the street and from behind the second barrier layer, blaster fire shot out, converging onto the three stopped SPCs. Instead of the usual glow of energy shields appearing as the blaster bolts hit, they all made contact with the vehicles' outer armor layers. Each defensive post had access to only a single heavy weapon, so the damage of each shot was relatively minor.

Watching, Zeric counted down the seconds. It had been a miracle that the EMPs had managed to work, but he had no illusions that the SPCs would be down permanently. Unless they could do sufficient damage to them before they could reset, the vehicles would be moving again in moments.

After several seconds of sustained fire, the right and left vehicles came to life and lifted back up off the ground. The lead vehicle failed to reactivate. The shields of the other two SPCs winked back to life, but Zeric was rewarded with the sight of the right vehicle's shields failing again almost immediately.

The defensive positions continued to fire on the unshielded SPC. It started to back down the street and managed to get off a few shots from its cannon before it crashed back to the ground. The final SPC started to move forward again, but found itself without enough room to move between the nearest building and the former lead SPC, which was now motionless.

"Keep the heavy gun on the active SPC," Zeric ordered through Kumus. "Have all other positions cease fire and prepare to target troops."

Their entire plan hung on the next few minutes. The two disabled SPCs were acting as additional barricades for the street. It was only wide enough for two vehicles to move side by side, and the lead vehicle was sitting in the center of the street, which did not leave enough room on either side. If the remaining SPCs could find a way around or over the disabled vehicles, though, there would not be anything else to stop them.

The heavy blaster continued to pepper the SPC, and Zeric saw some shots slipping through the weakened shield. The SPC turned its blaster turret and began returning fire. After a brief exchange, both positions stopped firing.

Zeric scanned the street but was unable to see the heavy weapon's position from his vantage point. Swinging back to the SPC, he was disturbed to see that the vehicle's weapon still appeared to be functional. After a closer inspection, however, his mood lifted as he saw that the vehicle was no longer hovering off the ground.

"Getting no response from our heavy weapon position," Kumus said quietly. It was clear the kid was disturbed by this, but Zeric had no time to comfort him.

"Won't be the last position to go quiet," he said. "Let all positions know the road is now blocked. Prepare for troop assault. Keep an eye on any side street movement."

Surveying the area from his position on the balcony, Zeric watched as three more vehicles came to a stop behind the disabled SPCs. In unison, all six vehicles lowered their rear ramps, and Alliance soldiers started pouring out. From positions all around them, blaster fire started raining down onto the troops, but it was intercepted by the SPCs shields.

Sticking close to the SPCs, the troops started spreading out. Most of them made their way forward and took cover around the disabled vehicles. Groups of at least squad strength started moving toward some of the side streets that were blockaded. Zeric watched as the soldiers moved quickly to the barricades and then quickly away.

"Let the roaming defense teams know that troops are about to come down two of the side streets," Zeric told Kumus. Even as he spoke, two explosions could be heard, and Zeric watched the side streets fill with clouds of dust.

He supposed things were going well. They had managed to stop the SPCs, and even though the troops were still advancing, they were on foot, which would slow them down. Zeric scanned down the street to find out what happened to the last three SPCs that had not stopped.

While he was looking, Zeric was suddenly pulled to the ground. He looked to see Lei-mey on top of him, but before he could say anything, the roof of the building behind him exploded. A wave of heat and then a concussion of air hit him, followed by a shower of shrapnel.

Dazed, Zeric stared into the vast cloud of dust that was billowing up. Confusion filled him, and he wondered where the dust had come from and what he was doing on the ground. Wasn't there something important he was supposed to be doing right now?

After a second, Zeric's senses returned to him, and he realized the building they were in had just been attacked. He had known this would be a possibility, but he had been hopeful the Alliance would avoid causing unnecessary damage to the city. If they were shooting at buildings now, things could go very badly for them.

Trying to sit up, Zeric felt a dead weight half across his own body, and remembered Lei-mey pulling him to the ground. He still couldn't see anything in the dust. He called her name and realized he could not hear his own voice. He'd been deafened.

Running his hands over the weight across his torso, he identified the clammy carapace of a Ronid. He checked for major wounds. All of the limbs appeared to be attached, but his hands did come away covered in blood.

The dust cloud started to blow away with the wind, and Zeric was able to make out Lei-mey in the haze. Her back was covered in small holes from shrapnel, but she still appeared to be breathing. Shaking her, he was relieved to get a response, if just a groggy shift of the head.

Deciding that Lei-mey would live, at least for the next few minutes, Zeric struggled to shift her off of him, and then stood up. There was debris everywhere. Going slowly, Zeric made his way toward where he had last seen Kumus. He found the boy's communication equipment smashed under a piece of ceiling and feared the worst.

Another minute of searching turned up the boy lying covered in chunks of debris a short distance away. Fortunately, all of it appeared to be light material, and Zeric was able to pull it all off of him. Kumus was covered with cuts, including a nasty one on his forehead, but was also still breathing, and he began to regain consciousness as Zeric pulled debris off of him.

Zeric helped Kumus sit up, and then started looking for the other two who had been with them. Even though it was a small balcony, he only managed to find one of them. The unfortunate Ronid had been impaled by a piece of steel and was no longer breathing. He found no sign of the other one.

He looked around and saw that Lei-mey was up, though on her knees. He experimented with shouting and found that he could almost make out his own voice. He added exaggerated gestures as he attempted to communicate with Kumus and Lei-mey. They both looked at him blankly. In frustration, Zeric grabbed each of them by the arm and pulled them toward the back of the room.

Making their way through the rubble that had once been the floor above them was slow going, but Zeric got them to the door that led into the building's central hallway. Once through, there was less dust, and Zeric led them toward the building's emergency exit. As the three of them ran down the stairs, Zeric hoped they could get out before whoever fired on them decided to do it again.

Maarkean watched as the last four Alliance fighters disengaged and flew away at full speed. It had been a costly engagement. Two police interceptors shot down, the *Justice* down for repairs, the *Chimopori* barely able to fly, the expenditure of all of the SAMs, their SPC destroyed and the *Durandal* and *Cutty Sark* weren't in pristine condition, either. But they had shot down or forced down eight fighters and damaged two of the others. The skies over Perth were empty.

Wearily, he turned the ship off of a pursuit course and back toward their ambush site. The engagement had been short, but the stress of combat made him feel like he hadn't slept for days. He truly hadn't gotten much sleep the last few days, and as the high started to wear off, he felt it tenfold.

"Nice work, both of you," Maarkean said to the other two on the flight deck with him. He had been impressed with the way Owrik had kept his head during the fight. The young Notha had kept track of all of the ships and the condition of the *Cutty Sark*. There had been mistakes, but nothing critical, and he had managed to recover. That was an important trait that most couldn't learn. Experience would reduce the mistakes.

He'd known Saracasi would keep her cool. They had been in tough situations before, and she had not panicked. It was her future that concerned him. Everyone reacted differently to having killed someone. Some of his friends from the Dotran war had broken down years later. He didn't want that fate for his sister.

Only time would tell. He had known pilots and soldiers who hadn't been able to come to terms with what they had done. For now, Saracasi and Owrik both were stable and appeared able to handle more. That, unfortunately, was all he could worry about at the moment. The day was far from over. This would not be their last engagement.

Setting the ship down at the base of the hill where the smoldering wreckage of the SPC sat, Maarkean focused on their immediate problems. Their intention had been to go next to capture the nearest Alliance base, but first he had to evaluate their condition.

The other three transports set down beside them. None looked in great condition, but the *Justice* was clearly the worst off. Smoke drifted off damaged spots on the ship's hull and was also billowing out of the open boarding ramp. Maarkean's first impulse was to rush over and offer assistance, but he was relieved when he saw all three of Fracsid's crew already standing a short distance away from the ship.

Unstrapping himself from the pilot's seat, Maarkean told Saracasi and Owrik to stretch but to remain on the ship. Moving quickly, he made his way through the ship and out of the cargo bay. As he exited, he saw several ground transports riding over to their impromptu landing site.

While the transports approached, Maarkean walked the short distance over to where Fracsid and his crew were waiting. He was joined by Novastar and Ar'cher. Fracsid had always annoyed him, but the man had offered his help with no request for payment. And now his ship was burning.

"How is she?" Maarkean asked with genuine concern. The crew had survived, but a ship was more than just a means of transport. To most pilots, the ship was just as much a member of the crew as anyone of flesh and blood.

Fracsid had a distant expression that was in stark contrast to his usual happy-go-lucky attitude. With a cough, he said, "Engines are a wreck. I managed to get us down on thrusters, but just barely. We're gotten the actual fires out, but there are a lot of things still smoldering."

"You saved Ar'cher's ass with that maneuver, though," Novastar said.

Ar'cher looked uncomfortable; his antennae twitched and he half smiled. "Uh, thanks for that."

"Don't worry, Frac," Maarkean said, trying to sound reassuring. "We'll get her running as good as new. Unfortunately, that will have to wait for another day. See to your crew."

Turning toward the others, Maarkean said, "We'll have to either cram everyone into two ships or go in without air cover."

"Either way isn't good," Novastar said. "*Chimopori* is damaged, so she's no good as air cover. But it's also doubly risky if she has to carry half of the troops. And Ar'cher's ship can't fit the other half, so you'll have to carry them and leave air cover to him."

"You also have three more guns to fit in," Fracsid said, interjecting himself back into the conversation. Maarkean had intended to let the man and his crew recover instead of diving right back into combat. He eyed Fracsid and the other two and decided it was their call.

"Right," Maarkean answered. "All right, we'll load all three ships. One down won't be as bad. None of us are really in any condition to fly cover anyway. We'll all fly in and stay down until we're dead or we win."

The other captains nodded, and then they all turned to watch as the transports began arriving. Lahkaba, Pasha, Gamaly and Gu'od, forty Ronid special forces and about a hundred others emerged from the vehicles and walked over to join them. The senior Ronid officer, Kueff Kahl-Amarr, gave Maarkean a salute, which he returned without thinking about it.

"Slight change of plans. We have one transport down, so we're going in without air support. Once we're on the ground, we won't be taking off again. We're all going in. Get to your ships."

To Maarkean's surprise, the group let out a cheer. Their enthusiasm for their mission heartened him just as much as the thought that he was about to lead them all to their deaths gnawed at him.

Creeping through a war-torn city escorting a kid with no experience and a politician hell-bent on proving she could fight was not Zeric's idea of good tactics. The front lines were holding, as far as he knew, but they were far from rigid. Three SPCs had backed up and could have found a way around the barricades, and there were too many side streets in the city to cover them all. There could be Alliance troops anywhere.

When they had first left the building, he had intended on heading back toward the hotel, but Lei-mey had insisted that they were fine and that Zeric was needed on the front lines. He had argued that they were not fine and that Kumus' head wound was still bleeding, but the boy had tried to show he was tough by insisting it didn't hurt. In the end, Zeric had relented because he did think his place was on the front. He could do nothing from the hotel but wait.

As they made their way through the city, moving as quickly and stealthily as they were able, Zeric listened to the sounds of battle. The ringing of blaster fire and the reverberations of explosions echoed through the air and the ground. Alliance troops were not pulling any punches, it seemed. Aside from aerial bombardment, they were using everything they had.

Zeric was relieved that Lei-mey and Kumus were remaining quiet. Talking would only raise their chances of discovery and annoy him. He felt bad for the boy, injured when he was supposed to be safe in a command post, although there was never any safe place in a war zone.

Approaching the main defense line, Zeric slowed. The barricades could be seen up ahead, and the sounds of blaster fire were getting louder the closer they got. Sneaking up on his own troops would not be a good idea. Even if half of them were wielding stun weapons, most weren't trained and would likely fire if startled.

Something caught Zeric's attention out of the corner of his eye. He immediately halted their advance behind a mobile food stand that had been left in the street. He turned to look down one of the side streets, but he didn't see anything. He was about to dismiss it as his imagination when something on the street moved. It was too big to be an animal.

Looking closer, Zeric spotted what was either a collection of junk or an Alliance soldier's helmet. From the position of the suspected soldier, he had a good line of sight on the troops defending the barricade. If there was one, there would be more.

Cursing to himself, Zeric considered his options. He was caught between the two groups with no experienced troops, aside from himself. Kumus had lost his weapon when the ceiling had collapsed. With all of the weapon fire, he was too far away from his troops to get their attention by shouting. If they continued to the barricades, they would likely be among those taken out in the opening volley.

"Why did we stop?" Lei-mey asked in a harsh whisper.

"Trouble," Zeric answered simply. "We're about to walk into an ambush."

"Then we need to do something," Lei-mey said.

"I'm thinking," Zeric said.

He considered turning around and heading away from the fight. It wouldn't be the most glorious or honorable thing for a leader to do. But it would be his best chance to survive and keep Lei-mey and Kumus alive.

"Ah, hell," Zeric mumbled.

Standing up slightly around the stand, Zeric started firing indiscriminately down the side street where he had seen the figure. His suspicions proved to be true when blaster fire was returned from the street toward him. Suddenly blaster fire erupted from all around them, and Zeric realized there were several other soldiers sneaking around.

Diving back behind the food stand, Zeric pushed himself and the other two as close to the ground as he could manage. Glancing up, he was relieved to see that several of the defenders had turned from the barricade and were firing at the soldiers to their rear. After a moment, the rain of blaster bolts aimed at them shifted and was directed at those at the barricade.

"Stay down," Zeric growled.

Crawling forward, Zeric watched the exchange of fire for a moment. He tracked where the blasts were coming from and eventually identified an Alliance soldier who was in his line of sight. Taking careful aim, he tried to slow his breathing as he waited for the soldier to move to where he could get a shot off.

The soldier shifted slightly, and Zeric fired. He was rewarded with the sight of the soldier dropping. Zeric immediately rolled sideways, hoping to avoid any retaliation fire. Coming to a stop a few meters away, he surveyed the scene.

Blaster fire around him had stopped, and there was a momentary lull in the noise of battle. Standing up, he took the opportunity to shout, "Watch the lines! Prepare for an assault!"

As if in response to his shout, a renewed barrage began from the other side of the barricade. The Alliance troops redoubled their assault. Zeric's first shot had caused the ambushing troops to attack early, and the forward troops hadn't been ready to make their assault. The delay in their attacks had been small, but it was enough that they could not strike simultaneously.

Zeric was starting to feel a sense of relief that the ambush had been stopped when the blaster bolt hit him.

CHAPTER NINETEEN

"Coming into weapons range in ten seconds," Owrik declared.

Maarkean could feel himself tensing. They were moving over the ground at high speeds. In a matter of seconds, if they were being monitored via satellite, weapon fire would start cascading up at them. If they weren't, the weapon fire would still come, just a short time later.

The ten seconds passed, then more. Maarkean suppressed any sense of relief. They were merely past the first obstacle, which allowed them to face far greater obstacles. He readied himself for the next set of tricky maneuvers.

Owrik shouted that their target was on sensors at the same time as Maarkean saw it rise up on the horizon. He gave their flight path a slight upward angle and prepared for rapid deceleration. Seconds later, the barrage began.

The air around the *Cutty Sark* was suddenly filled with blaster shots and concussion shells. They had made it this far without being spotted. The remaining distance would be dangerous but short. It was better than he could have hoped.

"Shields weakening. We're taking hull damage," Owrik declared.

"Almost there. Just a few more seconds," Maarkean half growled through gritted teeth. He hated flying through anti-aircraft fire.

The ship rocked from a nearby concussion wave that threatened to throw him off course. Maarkean narrowly avoided flying directly into a stream of blaster fire. Slipping the ship back on track, he rapidly increased their ascent angle and flew up over the walls of the Alliance base. Just as soon as the ship went up, he fired the retro thrusters and angled her back down again.

Coming up quickly, the ground filled the viewport. Maarkean continued firing the retro thrusters, slowing their descent. Deploying the landing struts, they made contact with the ground. With a rougher landing than he liked to make, the ship came to a stop.

It was time to make their assault.

Maarkean quickly unstrapped himself from the pilot's seat and drew his pistol as he exited the flight deck, shouting an order for the bay door to be opened. Dashing through the crew quarters and down the stairs, he reached the cargo bay just as his men began streaming out of the open cargo door. There were twenty police specialty forces clad in riot gear, which offered them protection from shrapnel but minimal resistance to blaster bolts, and thirty volunteers less well equipped. In the rear, directly before Maarkean, with no protective gear, were Gu'od and Gamaly.

The two Liw'kel turned to Maarkean as he came down the stairs. Both wore determined expressions and were holding their rifles ready. He moved to stand beside them and watched the cargo bay empty out. After a moment, only the three of them remained, plus a Terran named Seesz Owwoke and a Dotran named Atoshi Dren.

"How long should we wait?" Gamaly asked.

"Until the sounds of blaster fire get further away," Gu'od answered.

The police units were tasked with securing the base's defensive emplacements. Their group would follow after that wave and head for the base's command and communications center. The *Chimopori* and *Durandal* had, hopefully, placed their forces down in other areas of the base in order to secure the armory and vehicle bay.

In silence, the group of them listened to the sound of blaster fire coming from outside the ship. Maarkean didn't hear the sound of footsteps approaching until Saracasi and Owrik were right behind him. Both were holding weapons.

"I told you two, you're staying with the ship," he growled.

Saracasi gave him the determined stare that only she could. "That was when we had air cover. You said it yourself: we're all going in."

Maarkean fixed a glare on his sister. She could be profoundly irritating sometimes, especially when she was defying him. The last thing he wanted to do right now was fight with his sister in front of everyone while others were out there dying. She knew it, too.

"All right," Maarkean conceded. "But you do what I, Gu'od or Gamaly say immediately, without question. If I tell you to run, you run. No questions, no hesitation."

Saracasi and Owrik nodded their consent. With luck, most of the fighting would occur elsewhere, and the communications center would be lightly manned, but Maarkean worried they had used up all their luck making it inside the base in one piece. The Alliance forces had not been monitoring the area around their base like they should have been.

"Sounds like things are quieting down," Gu'od said.

Maarkean nodded. "Let's go."

Gu'od headed out first. As he left, he exchanged a message of love with Gamaly with his antennae. Maarkean, having picked up some of the antennae language, was embarrassed that he could understand their meaning, as it was obviously meant to be private between them. As Gu'od exited the ship, Gamaly watched him go with a worried expression.

Seesz and Atoshi went next, followed by Maarkean and Saracasi, leaving Owrik and Gamaly to bring up the rear. Sounds of warfare could be heard in the distance, but none here. The Alliance must have believed the transport empty now, or else they were more undermanned than Maarkean had hoped for. Either way, it was a good sign.

Moving as quickly as they could while maintaining some stealth, they dashed from cover to cover. After a short time, they came across unconscious Alliance soldiers who had run afoul of Gu'od. The soldiers were still alive, but it was the first sign they had seen that there was fighting occurring.

Approaching the command center, they saw their first active soldiers. Outside the door to the building, two soldiers were hastily stacking sandbags while two others kept a watchful eye. Maarkean's hope of finding an undefended post evaporated.

They caught up to Gu'od at the corner of the next closest building.

"Frontal attack will be risky," Gu'od said when everyone reached him.

"Have you scouted around?" Maarkean asked.

"There is another door on the other side of the building. Looks like a service entrance. There is also an emergency exit halfway between. No guards on either of them, but they are sealed tight," Gu'od replied. "It will require explosives to get through the doors – they look pretty sturdy."

"They'll be reinforced and bomb proof," Seesz said. "Any explosives we have on hand will just draw attention."

Maarkean wasn't sure what the man's background was. He had been one of the few Terran volunteers, and when Maarkean had asked, Seesz had just said he was a load lifter operator at the starport. But he had checked out as a good shot with a rifle and appeared to know his stuff.

"It's never good attacking a fortified position," Maarkean said quietly.

"Then maybe we should attack soon, before they finish fortifying," Saracasi suggested. "We have the numbers advantage."

Casting a sharp look at his sister, Maarkean considered their options. If they didn't secure the command post, the operation here would be for nothing. Of all of the possible obstacles they could face, four soldiers was the best one. He also knew that there might be more inside.

If they attacked, they would be going up against trained soldiers with inexperienced civilians. They would be attacking a fortified position without overwhelming numerical superiority. Their only advantages were surprise and the hope that the best soldiers had been sent to Perth.

An attack could get all of them killed. He was loath to lead his sister into a suicide mission, although he had to admit that this entire adventure was a suicide mission. The moment those first Alliance transports had been warned away, he had committed himself, Saracasi and everyone in Perth to a suicide mission.

"Seesz and Gamaly are our two best shots," Maarkean began. "Gamaly, take Saracasi and Atoshi around to the other side of this building. You have five minutes to get there. In exactly five minutes, you and Seesz will each take out the soldiers standing guard. Once you do, the rest of us will make a charge and try to overwhelm them."

Looking hard at Seesz and Gamaly, he said, "Success lies with the two of you getting kills on your first shots. If we can take those two out, we'll have a chance."

Gamaly returned Maarkean's look with a determined expression that said he shouldn't doubt her. Seesz looked nervous, but determined. Deciding that was the best he would get, Maarkean looked at his watch, and the others did the same.

"Five minutes... starts... *now*."

With a final glance at Gu'od, Gamaly led her team in a run along the edge of the building away from the command center. Maarkean watched them go and tried not to think about all the ways things could go wrong. Despite his best efforts, the possibilities just swirled in his head.

While they waited, Gu'od squatted down against the wall and closed his eyes in meditation. Despite the danger his wife was in, the man appeared perfectly calm and at peace. Maarkean wished he could master that. He tried to emulate Gu'od and took several long slow breaths. The desire to know how much time was left and the worry that they would be discovered kept gnawing at him.

Maarkean's effort to meditate was cut short by the sound of blaster fire. It was much closer than any of the sounds they had been hearing in the background. Wondering if he had missed the time, he looked at his watch and saw that only three minutes had passed.

Owrik, who had been peering around the corner of the building, turned back to the rest of them. "There are three Alliance soldiers running toward the command center. They are firing behind them, and they are also being shot at."

Standing back up, Maarkean glanced around the corner, quickly confirming Owrik's report. The three soldiers were almost to their half-finished defenses. Work had stopped on the sandbag walls and the soldiers were retrieving their weapons. He didn't know who was pursuing the soldiers, but their plan had definitely become outdated.

Not waiting, Maarkean started firing on the soldiers behind the barricades. The walls were not very high, and two of the soldiers were standing up, looking for their weapons. As soon as he started firing, his shots were joined by more from the rest of his team.

Caught in crossfire, two of the soldiers who had been running for the building were brought down. Deciding to seize the advantage, Maarkean charged out from around the corner and continued firing. He recognized the look of panic on one of the soldiers' faces as he fumbled with his weapon.

To his amazement, Maarkean reached the sandbag barrier without being shot. Drawing on some of the lessons he had managed to learn from Gu'od, Maarkean leapt over the barrier and delivered simultaneous blows to two of the soldiers, knocking them from their feet.

Another soldier brought his gun up, and Maarkean was sure he was done for. Then the boy convulsed and dropped from a stun bolt.

Looking in the direction the stun bolt had come from, Maarkean saw Gamaly leading her team toward him.

It was a moment before he realized that the firing had stopped and that he was the only one left standing in the doorway to the command center. Everything had happened so fast, he was not sure how he was still alive.

While the others advanced, Maarkean examined the soldiers at his feet. He was relieved that most of them appeared to be stunned, not dead.

He found the highest-ranking one, a lance corporal, and searched the woman for an identification card. Finding one in her jacket pocket, he tried the building's door with it. To his immense relief, the door clicked open.

Maarkean grabbed the door and held it slightly open until the rest of the team reached him. He almost asked Gamaly what had happened but decided it didn't matter right now.

Gesturing for everyone to get ready, he pulled open the door all the way. Gu'od and Seesz charged in first, followed by everyone else. Holding the door, Maarkean went in last.

The first room inside the building was merely an entrance foyer. There was a directory for offices and a few nice-looking plants.

Maarkean expected to meet more resistance, but had no idea how much. It was a good sign that there hadn't been a squad of troops just inside the door.

Watching carefully for anyone trying to sneak up on them, Maarkean followed the group down the right hallway.

They moved quickly. Everything seemed quiet. That's why it was such a surprise when Maarkean heard the sound of blaster fire ahead and saw Gu'od fall to the ground.

"I'm fine," Zeric growled, once they made it to their fall-back position at the hotel. "Get back to the line."

The young Ronid who was helping him walk looked unsure what to do. He looked from Zeric to Lei-mey. It irritated Zeric that the man waited for Lei-mey to nod before releasing Zeric and heading back toward the sound of weapon fire.

Left to walk on his own, Zeric immediately regretted his decision. The blaster shot he had taken had seriously messed up his leg.

Without a word, Lei-mey slipped in and took the soldier's place. Zeric appreciated the assistance, but he was sure she would make him pay for it later. Happily, Kumus would soon be back from getting his head wound patched; he could take her place.

With Lei-mey's help, Zeric climbed the barricades that had been assembled in front of the hotel's entrance. Peering over the top of them, he examined the scene before him. A couple dozen meters away was another line of barricades manned with everyone left in the city who could still fight. Beyond them were the vast majority of the Alliance forces that had stormed the city.

After Zeric had been shot, possibly by friendly fire, the Alliance's push to break through the barricade had continued relentlessly. Barely holding onto consciousness, he had ordered them to fall back and to detonate the barricade.

As the survivors raced away from their defensive position, Zeric had watched as their emergency explosives had failed to detonate, leaving the way clear for the Alliance to follow. The EMP mines must have disabled the triggers at his position.

It had been a tough fight back to the hotel, and along the way Zeric had heard two loud explosions. That meant that the other positions' explosives hadn't failed, but also that they had been overrun.

Back at the hotel, he learned that the best count had a third of their forces dead or captured during the retreat back to the hotel. Fighting through the pain while a medic hastily wrapped up his leg, Zeric directed the defense of the hotel. There was little information available to him that was not bad.

After a short time, a Ronid runner came up to him. "Sir, rear positions report that Alliance forces are holding position across the street from the hotel. They are no longer advancing."

Glancing back across the defenses before him, Zeric saw that the troops were doing the same thing in the front. Why were they stopping? All of his efforts to stop them so far had been swatted away. He had no doubt that the Alliance forces had suffered casualties, but he had no illusions that their losses had been anywhere near as great as his own.

Optimistically, Lei-mey said, "Maybe they aren't able to break through our defenses."

Frowning, Zeric said, "We're weaker here than we were on the streets. Just more concentrated. But so are they."

"Maybe we hurt them more than we think?"

"Possibly," Zeric said absentmindedly. "More likely, they're holding back until they can get their SPCs through the streets, or their fighters can be rearmed for a bombing run."

Shocked, Lei-mey said, "They couldn't possibly be planning to level the entire area from the air, could they?"

"Well, if they're as hurt as you hope they are, bombing us would be the safest plan. If they're only as hurt as I suspect they are, it would still be the safest plan. Even if they aren't planning on bombing us, the SPCs' cannons can level the hotel pretty good," Zeric said.

Easing back from the barricade, he looked around and realized that the runner and a few others were standing around him and Lei-mey. He immediately regretted what he had said and mentally kicked himself. Fatalistic talk was dangerous for any fighting group. Words like those coming from a leader could kill morale.

Zeric tried to find a way to recover from what he had just said, but nothing was coming to him. This was why he had never wanted to be an officer. Shooting the enemy was easy. Morale was hard.

Shrugging, Zeric said, "We'll just have to win before they can do that."

Easing down from the barricade, Zeric eyed the others and thought that they appeared satisfied with his response. Not that he had any idea how to go about doing it, though. In his mind, things were pretty hopeless.

Lei-mey slipped in and helped Zeric move toward a table that had been set up with a map of the city. The Alliance had jammed their connection to the satellites, so he had to rely on static maps and visual sightings of troops. Their comm gear was also being jammed.

"If only we knew how Maarkean was doing," Zeric said as he looked down at the map. The one of the city had just been replaced by one covering the block where the hotel was. Markers were being set up representing all of the Alliance forces. The markers indicated that the Alliance had twice as many forces now as when they had arrived, but since there weren't that many troops on the planet, the spotters must have been exaggerating out of panic. It was an ironic consolation that they weren't actually facing almost two thousand troops.

Zeric stared at the map, trying to find some option that didn't result in all of their deaths. Surrender would accomplish that. It seemed that it might be their only option. With his leg injury, slipping out and trying to escape by himself wasn't even a choice anymore.

"Sir."

Turning, Zeric saw Kumus standing beside him. He had not even noticed that the boy had returned. A thick bandage was wrapped around his head, partially covering his left eye. It took Zeric a second to realize the boy was holding a comm device out to him.

"What is it?"

"Colonel Cage is calling, sir. He wants to speak to whoever is in charge," Kumus said grimly.

Zeric looked from Kumus to the comm device and back to Kumus. "Don't give it to me. Go and get the prime minister."

"He's on his way, sir. But the colonel is sounding impatient."

"Good, let him wait," Zeric said grumpily.

The last thing Zeric wanted was to have to negotiate with the Alliance commander. He knew how hopeless their position was, and so did Cage. If they talked, Zeric doubted he would be able to bluster enough to pretend it was any different. Then he wouldn't even be in a good position to negotiate anything for them.

Several minutes went by while they waited for the prime minister. The waiting played into both sides' hands. It gave the Alliance longer to get their SPCs through the city, and it gave Zeric longer to stay alive. He hoped no one ever found the prime minister.

While waiting, Zeric was almost glad his leg was injured. He hated it when people paced when they were nervous. Instead, he contented himself with tossing around a piece of concrete from the barricade that had fallen into his pocket.

After what seemed like forever – probably a matter of seconds – the prime minister appeared. Zeric told him what was going on, and Kumus handed over the comm device. The prime minister looked as nervous as Zeric felt.

"This is Prime Minister Corte."

Kumus must have switched the comm to speaker, because Zeric heard the response clearly. "Prime Minister, this is Colonel Cage. I must say, I did not expect you to turn rebel."

"Colonel, you received the statement from my office ordering you not to leave your base."

"I did. But, as you know, you have been relieved of your office and no longer hold any authority. I was, however, content to leave some of your government in place until the new governor arrived. But now you have made that impossible."

The expression on Corte's face did not match the tone of his voice. "Colonel, you are a reasonable man. The order to remove my legitimately elected government from power is an illegal order. You must know that."

"We can debate that at another time, Mr. Prime Minister. Right now, I am putting down an insurrection."

"What you call an insurrection, I call the people defending their right to democracy. A right supposedly guaranteed by the Alliance Charter."

Zeric wished he knew more about Colonel Cage. He thought he sensed some conflict coming from the colonel. Any good officer would find himself conflicted in Cage's position: caught between principles and orders. But Zeric knew many soldiers and officers who would have had no conflict. They believed in their government and following orders above all else.

"Prime Minister, give up this rebellion. Order your people to lay down their arms. We will take these Kreogh Sector Congress members into custody. Then we will discuss what is to be done about all of your people who raised arms against the Alliance. They will have to be punished for this act of treason, but if you surrender peacefully now, we can discuss what that punishment might entail.

"If you do not, I will be forced to storm your position. My SPCs are making their way through the city now. To ensure the safety of my troops, I will be forced to bombard your positions before moving in. The death toll will be higher than either of us wants to see."

Prime Minister Corte lowered the comm device and cast a look at Zeric and Lei-mey. Despite the Ronid features, Zeric could see the conflict on his face. The vast majority of the people defending the hotel were locals. As their leader, he was responsible for their safety.

If it had been Zeric in that situation, he didn't know what he would have done. He didn't like the sound of surrender, but his natural inclination was to try to stay alive.

While Corte continued to ponder his decision, the colonel spoke again. "Mr. Prime Minister, what is it going to be? Will you surrender, or will there be more bloodshed?"

Another voice came in over the comm after Cage. "This is Major Maarkean Ocaitchi, commander of the Enro Defense Forces. Colonel Cage, you are hereby ordered to surrender your forces."

Zeric could hear the amusement in Cage's reply. "Major Ocaitchi, I will not talk with officers who betray their uniform. Please put the prime minister back on. Let's not hear any more bluster."

"Colonel, I am not calling from Perth, but from your command center. We have taken control of your base."

"Nice bluff, Major."

Maarkean was replaced by another voice. "Sir, this is Lieutenant Graham. The enemy has overrun our position, and the base is in their control."

A wide smile spread over Zeric's face. Maarkean's mission had been a long shot.

"Colonel," Maarkean went on, "you have limited supplies and, now, no chance for more. All your fighters are now in our hands. As we speak, they are being repaired, refueled and rearmed. Their targets will be your other two bases.

Should you fail to surrender your forces, they will level those bases."

There was silence for several minutes. Zeric pictured Cage trying to verify the information he was receiving. He hoped Maarkean wasn't bluffing. There were still two bases out there.

When no response came, Maarkean spoke again. "Colonel, reinforcements are weeks or months away. You have injured troops and no supplies. The entire planet's population will oppose you. If you make your last action a massacre, there will be no place you can hide to escape justice."

Silence continued, and Zeric started to think Cage might be preparing to assault the hotel. He leaned over and whispered to Kumus, "Tell everyone to prepare for an assault."

The boy nodded and then raced off to the other command positions. Zeric hobbled over to the barricade. He pulled himself up and looked out at the troops surrounding them. There was no immediate indication that they were about to attack. Not much had changed since he had looked earlier.

"Very well." The voice of Colonel Cage came through the comm again, startling Zeric. "We surrender."

An eerie silence enveloped Zeric, and he lost track of everything around him for a moment. He must have hit his head or something, he thought. This must be an illusion. There was no way the Alliance would have just surrendered.

Slowly, so as not to end the illusion too quickly, Zeric turned to look at Lei-mey and Corte. He wished he could read Ronids better, but he would bet good money that their current expression was pure shock.

Fortunately, Maarkean was able to react to the news better than Zeric or the two politicians could, because Zeric heard his voice come over the comm again. "Thank you, Colonel. I assure you, your troops will be treated well."

"I expect nothing less from a former Alliance officer, Major. I will order my troops to lay down their arms," Colonel Cage said, and then clicked off the conversation.

Zeric turned back to look out at the surrounding troops. Nothing happened immediately, but then he realized he had not informed the troops that the Alliance would be surrendering. If they stepped out and were shot, everything would collapse.

He grabbed the comm and quickly announced, "All troops, hold fire. The Alliance has surrendered. Team leaders, take Alliance forces into custody."

As his words filtered out across the defenders, Zeric could track its progress by the sounds of cheering. With some difficulty, he restrained himself from feeling the same excitement – until he saw the first Alliance soldier step from behind cover, holding his arms up in surrender.

With a spontaneous surge of joy, Zeric let out an excited yelp. He loved winning.

Maarkean heard Zeric saying over the comm, with disbelief mixed with cheerful enthusiasm, "They're complying with the order to stand down."

Maarkean let out a breath, feeling a tremendous weight fall from his shoulders. He had no idea how tense he had been for the last several minutes. When Cage had said he surrendered, Maarkean kept expecting some kind of trick or double-cross. It had felt like several long minutes while he waited for Zeric's confirmation.

"Please give my congratulations to Prime Minister Corte," Maarkean said in reply, genuine pleasure coming out for the first time in a while. "His people fought well."

With a thud, he dropped the comm mike and allowed himself to collapse into the chair behind him. Around him in the Alliance command bunker, the members of his assault team were cheering. Sounds of greater excitement filtered in from outside the building, where the bulk of their forces were located.

Was it really over? he thought. Utter annihilation had suddenly turned into complete victory. Apparently, leading a grand battle was no different from being in a dogfight when it came to how quickly the tables could turn.

With the acceptance that the battle was over, Maarkean realized he had to face the worst part of any battle: the consequences. There would be many after this one. He had no idea how many people had died or been hurt already.

Despite his concern for everyone who had fought for him, he first went to check on his friends. Stepping out of the command center, Maarkean went down the hallway to where Gamaly knelt beside Gu'od. The male Liw'kel had more emotion on his face than Maarkean had ever seen him have. His antennae were flattened against his head, and his face was contorted in pain. But he was alive.

When Maarkean had seen Gu'od go down, he had been sure his friend was dead. In the chaos of battle, he hadn't had a moment to find out for sure. The idea he might be dead had played no small part in his drive to ensure that the battle ended well.

Giving Gamaly a reassuring squeeze on the shoulder, Maarkean said, "He'll be all right. A simple blaster bolt can't take down a Ni'jar master."

"That's what I keep telling her," Gu'od said through gritted teeth.

Gamaly gave him a small smile at that, and Maarkean left her to tend to her husband. He had already sent Saracasi to find a medic, Alliance or one of their own, to see to all of the wounded in the command bunker. Reassured that Gu'od would live, he turned to the others.

Of the rest of his team, Seesz Owwoke stood guard inside the command bunker, none the worse for wear. Atoshi Dren was their only confirmed casualty. The big Dotran had gone down shortly after Gu'od, during their charge into the command center. It felt odd to feel more grief over a dead Dotran than over Alliance soldiers.

There were many Alliance soldiers down, most of them stunned. Even though they were the enemy, he still took comfort in knowing that most of them would live. He just wished they had shown the same courtesy to his forces and used their stun settings.

Looking up from the Dotran, Maarkean saw Saracasi leading a group of people down the hallway. A Braz with a medical bag rushed past her when he saw the bodies on the ground. He started to head toward the command center, but Gamaly grabbed the man and directed him to Gu'od.

Relief flooded Maarkean as he recognized the others with Saracasi. Lahkaba, Lohcja and Solyss Novastar followed her toward him. Showing no interest in decorum, Lahkaba reached out and pulled him into a strong embrace. Even though it wasn't terribly professional, Maarkean relished the physical contact. After any battle, it felt good to know it was still possible to care.

"How are your teams?" Maarkean asked, once the Kowwok released him.

"A few injuries, no fatalities," Solyss said confidently. "Asheerah led them well."

Maarkean nodded in relief to that news. Apparently, there was more to Solyss' Liw'kel crewmember than just a scary presence. The *Chimopori* had the largest cargo hold out of the four ships, so it had carried the most troops. If there were no fatalities among them, their total losses would not be too high, though he would have to wait for reports from Ar'cher and Relis for the final tally.

"We won an important victory today," Lahkaba said somberly. "We have sent a message to the Alliance."

"Yeah, don't mess with Ronids," Lohcja quipped.

"A righteous cause will always be victorious," Solyss added.

"And no matter the odds, the people of the Kreogh Sector will stand up for their rights," Lahkaba concluded.

Maarkean nodded in reply to his friends' sentiments. He agreed with all of them, though he knew the Alliance would not interpret things the same way. To them, the message would be to bring more firepower.

Stepping away from his friends as they discussed the battle, Maarkean looked over the scene again. How much had changed for him in just a few short months. Before, he had been a slightly disillusioned, but still loyal, Alliance citizen. Now, he was fully committed to seeing their power broken.

But things had not changed only for him. In the corner of the command center, he saw Saracasi sitting by herself. She had a blank and distant expression on her face, and Maarkean felt his heart go out to her. The fight against the Alliance she had always wanted was now here. And the reality of what that meant was starting to sink in for her. As much as he wanted to, he knew there was nothing he could do to protect his sister from that now.

He could only work to make sure they won.

ACKNOWLEDGEMENTS

This book would not be a reality without the help and support of many people:

First, without the support and faith of my wife and parents I never would have taken this chance at pursuing my dream.

I owe a debt to all of my friends and family: Dad, Coleen, Dave, Erik, Charles, Yvonne, Everett, who were willing to read the early incoherent drafts.

My editor, Hilary, for her hard work in correcting my many grammatical mistakes and identifying where the story needed to improve.

And to Jason at Grey Gecko for taking a chance on an unknown author.

ABOUT THE AUTHOR

Wayne currently lives in Houston with his wife, dog and soon-to-be-born son. He remains a fan of geek culture, board games, video games, fantasy, science fiction and all around silliness.

CONNECT WITH WAYNE

Email

wayne@waynebasta.com

Blog

www.waynebasta.com